Map
of the
Heart

SUSAN WIGGS

HarperCollins*Publishers*

HarperCollins
PUBLISHERS
—— Since 1817 ——

HarperCollins*Publishers* Ltd
The News Building
1 London Bridge Street
London SE1 9GF

www.harpercollins.co.uk

A Paperback Original 2017
1

Copyright © Susan Wiggs 2017

Susan Wiggs asserts the moral right to
be identified as the author of this work

A catalogue record for this book
is available from the British Library

ISBN: 978-0-00-815132-4

Printed and bound in Great Britain by
Clays Ltd, St Ives Plc

MIX
Paper from
responsible sources
FSC™ C007454

FSC™ is a non-profit international organisation established to promote the
responsible management of the world's forests. Products carrying the FSC
label are independently certified to assure consumers that they come from
forests that are managed to meet the social, economic and ecological
needs of present and future generations, and other controlled sources.

Find out more about HarperCollins and the environment at
www.harpercollins.co.uk/green

For my husband, Jerry: For all the journeys we've made, for all the moments of inspiration, for getting lost on lost byways, for endless rambles and flights of imagination, for knowing that the greatest journey in life is the one that takes you home.

You're the best adventure I've ever had.

PART I

Bethany Bay

Thank you for all the Acts of Light which beautified
a summer now passed to its reward.

—LETTER FROM EMILY DICKINSON TO
MRS. JOHN HOWARD SWEETSER

One

❧

Of the five steps in developing film, four must take place in complete darkness. And in the darkroom, timing was everything. The difference between overexposure and underexposure sometimes came down to a matter of milliseconds.

Camille Adams liked the precision of it. She liked the idea that with the proper balance of chemicals and timing, a good result was entirely within her control.

There could be no visible light in the room, not even a red or amber safelight. *Camera obscura* was Latin for "dark room," and when Camille was young and utterly fascinated by the process, she had gone to great lengths to practice her craft. Her first darkroom had been a closet that smelled of her mom's frangipani perfume and her stepdad's fishing boots, crusted with salt from the Chesapeake. She'd used masking tape and weather stripping to fill in the gaps, keeping out any leaks of light. Even a hairline crack in the door could fog the negatives.

Found film was a particular obsession of hers, especially now that digital imagery had supplanted film photography. She loved the thrill of opening a door to the past and being the first to peek in. Often while she worked with an old roll of film or movie reel, she tried to imagine someone taking the time to get out their camera and take pictures or shoot a movie, capturing a candid moment or an elaborate pose. For Camille, working in the darkroom was the only place she could see clearly, the place where she felt most competent and in control.

Today's project was to rescue a roll of thirty-five-millimeter film found by a client she'd never met, a professor of history named Malcolm Finnemore. The film had been delivered by courier from Annapolis, and the instructions inside indicated that he required a quick turnaround. Her job was to develop the film, digitize the negatives with her micrographic scanner, convert the files into positives, and e-mail the results. The courier would be back by three to pick up the original negatives and contact sheets.

Camille had no problem with deadlines. She didn't mind the pressure. It forced her to be clearheaded, organized, in control. Life worked better that way.

All her chemicals waited in readiness—precisely calibrated, carefully measured into beakers, and set within reach. She didn't need the light to know where they were, lined up like instruments on a surgeon's tray—developer, stop bath, fixer, clearing agent—and she knew how to handle them with the delicacy of a surgeon. Once the film was developed, dried, and cured, she would inspect the results. She loved this part of her craft, being the revealer of lost and found treasures, opening forgotten time capsules with a single act of light.

There were those, and her late husband, Jace, had been among them, who regarded this as a craft or hobby. Camille knew better. One look at a print by Ansel Adams—no relation to Jace—was proof that art could happen in the darkroom. Behind each finished, epic print were dozens of attempts until Adams found just the right setting.

Camille never knew what the old film would reveal, if it hadn't been spoiled by time and the elements. Perhaps the professor had come across a film can that had been forgotten and shoved away in the Smithsonian archives or some library storage room at Annapolis.

She wanted to get this right, because the material was potentially significant. The roll she was carefully spooling onto the reel could be a major find. It might reveal portraits of people no one had ever seen before, landscapes now changed beyond recognition, a rare shot of a moment in time that no longer existed in this world.

On the other hand, it might be entirely prosaic—a family picnic, a generic street scene, awkward photos of unidentifiable strangers. Perhaps it might yield pictures of a long-gone loved one whose face his widow longed to see one more time. Camille still remembered the feeling of pain-filled joy when she'd looked at pictures of Jace after he'd died. Her final shots of him remained in the dark, still spooled in her camera. The vintage Leica had been her favorite, but she hadn't touched it since the day she'd lost him.

Working with film from complete strangers suited her better. Only last week, a different storage box had yielded a rare collection of cellulose-nitrate negatives in a precarious state. The images had been clumped together, fused by time and neglect. Over painstaking hours, she had teased apart the film, removing mold and consolidating the image layers to reveal something the camera's eye had seen nearly a century before—the only known photograph of a species of penguin that was now extinct.

Another time, she had exposed canned negatives from a portrait session with Bess Truman, one of the most camera-shy first ladies of the twentieth century. To date, the project that had gained the most attention for Camille had been a picture of a murder in commission, posthumously absolving a man who had gone to the gallows for a crime he hadn't committed. Write-ups in the national press gave her credit for solving a long-standing mystery, but Camille considered the achievement bittersweet, knowing an innocent man had hanged for a crime while the murderer had lived to a ripe old age.

Touching the digital timer, she scarcely dared to breathe as she prepared to launch the special alchemy of the darkroom.

The moment was interrupted by a ringing phone, located just outside the door. She couldn't have a phone in the darkroom, due to the keypad that lit up when it rang, so she kept the volume turned on loud to hear incoming voice mail. Ever since her father's cancer diagnosis, her pulse jumped each time the phone rang.

She waited through several rings, chiding herself for panicking. Papa's disease was in remission now, though his doctors wouldn't say how long the reprieve might last.

"This is Della McClosky of the Henlopen Medical Center, calling for Camille Adams. Your daughter Julie has been brought into the ER—"

Julie. Camille ripped open the door of the darkroom and snatched up the phone. The film can clattered to the floor. Already, fear thudded through her. "This is Camille. What's Julie doing in the ER?"

"Ma'am, your daughter has just been brought by ambulance to the ER from her surf rescue class at the Bethany Bay Surf Club."

Ice-cold terror. It took her breath away. "*What?* Is she hurt? What happened?"

"She's conscious now, sitting up and talking. Coach Swanson came with her. She got caught in a riptide and aspirated some water. The doctor is checking her out."

"I'm on my way." She lunged for the back door, scooping her keys from the hook as she leaped down the porch steps to her car. There was no thought. No planning. Just action. When you get a call that your kid is in the ER, there can be no room for thinking. Just the deepest fear imaginable, the kind that gripped like a steel band around her chest.

She hurled herself into the car, started it up, and tore down the driveway, her tires spitting an arc of crushed oyster shells in her wake. She roared around Lighthouse Point at the end of her road. The rocky shoals there had been guarded for a century by the sentinel overlooking the bay.

The car radio was on, broadcasting a surf report at the top of the hour by Crash Daniels, owner of the Surf Shack. "We are getting our first taste of summer, people. The whole Delmarva Peninsula is basking in temperatures in the mideighties. The oceanside looks rad. Bethany Bay is *totally* off the hook . . ."

She snapped off the radio. Panic about her daughter demanded total focus. Surf rescue class? What the hell was Julie doing in surf rescue? She wasn't even taking that class, an optional PE credit offered to ninth graders. Camille had forbidden it, even though Julie had begged. Far too dangerous. The tides on the ocean side of the peninsula could be deadly. There was no satisfaction in being right. Julie got caught in a riptide, the nurse had said. A surge of horror filled Camille's throat, and she felt like puking.

"Easy," she told herself. "Deep breath. The woman on the phone said Julie is conscious."

Jace had been conscious, too, moments before she had lost him forever, five years before, when they were on a romantic second-honeymoon getaway. She couldn't stop herself from thinking about that now. That was the reason she had refused to sign the permission slip to allow Julie to participate in surf rescue. She simply couldn't survive another loss.

There had been a time when Camille had led a charmed life, cheerfully oblivious to the devastation that could strike without warning. Throughout her idyllic childhood in Bethany Bay, she'd been as wild and carefree as the birds that wheeled over the watery enclave at the edge of the Atlantic. She herself had excelled at surf rescue, a rigorous and physically demanding course all high schoolers were encouraged to take. In this community, surrounded on three sides by water, safety skills were mandatory. Thanks to the popularity of the beach, with its pipeline waves rolling in, local youngsters were trained in the art of rescue using special hand-paddled boards. It was a time-honored tradition at Bethany Bay High. Each May, even when the water was still chilly from the currents of winter, the PE department offered the challenging class.

At fourteen, Camille had been clueless about the dangers of the world. She'd shot to the head of her group in surf rescue, ultimately winning the annual competition three years in a row. She remembered how joyful and confident the victory had made her feel. She still remembered reveling in the triumph of battling the waves under the sun, laughing with her friends, intoxicated by the supreme satisfaction of conquering the elements. At the end of the course, there was always a bonfire and marshmallow roast on the beach, a tradition still observed by the surf rescue trainers so the kids could bond over the shared experience. She wanted that for Julie, but her daughter was a different girl than Camille had been.

Up until five years ago, Camille had been an adrenaline junkie—surfing, kiteboarding, attempting harrowing rock and mountain climbs—anything that offered a dangerous rush. Jace had been her perfect partner, every bit as keen as she for the thrill of adventure.

Those days were long gone. Camille had been remade by tragedy, cautious when she used to be intrepid, fearful when she used to dare anything, restrained when she used to be unbridled. She viewed the world as a dangerous place fraught with hazards for those foolish enough to venture out and take a risk. She regarded everything she loved as fragile and apt to be lost as quickly as Jace had been.

Julie had processed the death of her father with the stoic innocence of a nine-year-old, quietly grieving and then accepting the fact that her world would never be the same. People had praised her resilience, and Camille had been grateful to have a reason to put her life together and go on.

Yet when Julie brought the permission packet home and announced she was taking surf rescue, Camille had flatly refused. There had been arguments. Tears. Stomping and flinging on the bed. Julie had accused Camille of trying to sabotage her life.

With a twinge of guilt, Camille knew her own fears were holding her daughter back, but she also knew they were keeping Julie out of harm's way. Yes, she wanted the same kind of fun and camaraderie for Julie that she herself had found in high school. But Julie would have to find it through tamer pursuits. Apparently she had found a way to join the surf rescue class, probably with the age-old trick of the forged permission slip.

There were few forces greater than the power of a fourteen-year-old's determination when she wanted something. A teenager would stop at nothing in order to get her way.

Camille should have been more vigilant. Instead of becoming so deeply absorbed in work, she should have kept a closer eye on her daughter. Maybe then she would have noticed what Julie was up to, sneaking off to surf rescue instead of dodgeball or study hall or some other tame substitute for the course on the beach.

When Jace was alive, he and Camille had both made sure Julie was a strong swimmer. By the age of eight, she'd learned about the way a riptide worked, and how to survive if she happened to get caught in one—tread water, stay parallel to the shore, and don't fight it. Camille could still remember Jace explaining it. The riptide would come back around in three minutes, so there was no need to panic.

These days, panicking was Camille's specialty.

Keeping her eyes on the road, Camille groped in her bag for her phone. Her hand bumped up against the usual suspects—wallet, pen, checkbook, hair clip, comb, mints. No phone. Shoot, she had forgotten it in her rush to get to the hospital.

The hospital, where her wounded daughter had been taken while Camille was holed up in her darkroom, ignoring the world. With each negative thought, she pressed her foot harder on the accelerator, until she realized she was going fifty in a thirty-mile-per-hour zone. She refused to ease up. If she got pulled over, she'd simply ask the police for an escort.

The word *please* echoed over and over in her head. She begged for this to not be happening. Please. Please not this. Please not Julie.

Fourteen, smart, funny, quirky, she was Camille's whole world. If something happened to her, the world would end. *I* would simply end, thought Camille with rock-solid certainty. I would cease to exist. My life would be kaput. *Over. Sans espoir,* as Papa would say.

The coast road bisected the flatlands embraced parenthetically between the teeming mystery of the Chesapeake Bay, and the endless, vast expanse of the Atlantic. Fringed by sand dunes filled with native bird rookeries, the bay curved inward, framing the crashing Atlantic and forming one of the best surf beaches on the eastern seaboard. It was there, on this stunningly beautiful sugar-sand beach that drew tourists every year, that Julie's accident had occurred.

Camille accelerated yet again, on the home stretch. Five minutes

later, she careened into the parking lot of the medical center. The
place held both distant and recent memories for her. She leaped from
the car, hitting the ground at a run.

"Julie Adams," she said to the woman at the reception desk. "She
was brought in from surf rescue."

The receptionist consulted her screen. "Curtain area seven," she
said. "Around to the right."

Camille knew where that was. She ran past the memorial wall—the
Dr. Jace Adams Memorial Wall, which never failed to pierce her heart
with remembrances.

She missed Julie's father every single day, but never more sharply
than when she was scared. Other women could turn to their husbands when disaster struck, but not Camille. She could turn only to
the sweetest of memories. In the blink of an eye, she had found and
lost the love of her life. Jace would remain forever in the shadows of
her memory, too distant to comfort her when she was terrified.

Which was pretty much all the time.

She hastened over to the curtain area, desperate to see her daughter.
She caught a glimpse of curly dark hair, a delicate hand lying limp.
"Julie," she said, rushing to the side of the wheeled bed.

The others present parted to let her near. It was a singular nightmare
to see her daughter hooked up to monitors, with medical personnel
surrounding her. Julie was sitting up, a C-spine collar around her neck,
several printed bands on her wrist, an IV in her arm, and an annoyed
expression on her face. "Mom," she said. "I'm okay."

That was all Camille needed to hear—her daughter's voice, saying
those words. Her insides melted as relief unfurled her nerves.

"Sweetheart, how do you feel? Tell me everything." Camille de-
voured Julie with her eyes. Did she look paler than usual? Was she
in pain? Not really, Camille observed. She was wearing her annoyed-
teenager face.

"Like I said, I'm okay." Julie punctuated the statement with a classic
roll of the eyes.

"Mrs. Adams." A doctor in seafoam-green scrubs and a white lab coat approached her. "I'm Dr. Solvang. I've been taking care of Julie."

Like a good ER doc, Solvang went calmly and methodically through the explanation. He looked her in the eye and offered short, clear statements. "Julie reports coming off her rescue board when she was trying to knee-paddle around a buoy during a speed drill. She got caught up in an undercurrent. Julie, isn't that right?"

"Yeah," she mumbled.

"You mean a riptide?" Camille glared at the coach, who hovered nearby. Hadn't he been watching? Wasn't avoiding riptides the first lesson of surf rescue?

"Apparently, yes," said the doctor. "Coach Swanson was able to bring Julie to shore. At that point, she was unresponsive."

"Oh my God." *Unresponsive.* Camille could not abide the image in her head. "Julie . . . I don't understand. How did this happen? You weren't even supposed to be in surf rescue." She took a breath. "Which we'll talk about later."

"Coach Swanson brought her in and performed CPR, and the water she'd aspirated came up. She came around immediately and was brought here for evaluation."

"So you're saying my daughter drowned."

"I got knocked off my board, is all."

"What? Knocked off? My God—"

"I mean, I fell . . ." Julie said, her eyes darting around the curtain area.

"The contusion should heal just fine on its own," Dr. Solvang said.

"What contusion?" Camille wanted to grab the guy by his crisp white lapels and shake him. "She hit her head?" She touched Julie's chin, looking for the injury amid Julie's dark salt-encrusted curls. There was a knot at her hairline above one eye. "How did you hit your head?"

Julie's glance skated away. She lightly touched the damp, salt-encrusted hair above her temple.

"We've done a neural assessment every ten minutes," said the nurse. "Everything is normal."

"Weren't you wearing a safety cap?" Camille asked. "How did you get a contusion?"

"Mom, I don't know, okay? It all happened really fast. Do me a favor and stop freaking out."

Surliness was a new thing with Julie. Camille had started noticing it earlier in the school year. At the moment, her surliness was a hopeful sign. It meant she was feeling normal. "Now what?" Camille asked the doctor. "Are you going to admit her?"

He smiled and shook his head. "No need. The discharge papers are already being prepared."

She melted a little with relief. "I need a phone. I dashed out of the house without mine, and I need to call my mother."

Julie indicated her Bethany Bay Barracudas team bag. "You can use mine to call Gram."

Camille found it and dialed her mother.

"Hey, you," said Cherisse Vandermeer. "Did school get out early today?"

"Mom, it's me," said Camille. "Using Julie's phone."

"I thought you would be buried in your darkroom all day."

The darkroom. Camille had an "oh shit" moment, but thrust it away in favor of the more immediate matter.

"I'm at the hospital," Camille told her. "Julie was brought to the ER."

"Oh, dear heavenly days. Is she all right? What happened?"

"She's okay. She had an accident in surf rescue class. Just got here myself."

There was an audible gasp. "I'll be right over."

"I'm all right, Gram," Julie said loudly. "Mom's freaking out, though."

Now Camille heard a deep, steadying breath on the other end of the line. "I'm sure it's going to be all right. I'll see you there in ten minutes. Did they say what—"

The call dropped. Cell-phone signals were iffy this low on the peninsula.

For the first time, Camille took a moment to look around the curtain area. Principal Drake Larson had shown up. Drake—her ex-boyfriend—looked utterly professional in a checked shirt and tie, knife pleats in his pants. But the rings of sweat in his armpits indicated he was anything but calm.

Drake should have been perfect for her, but not long ago, she'd admitted—first to herself, then to Drake—that their relationship was over. He still called her, though. He kept hinting that he wanted to see her again, and she didn't want to hurt his feelings by turning him down.

She'd tried for months to find her way into loving Drake. He was a good guy, gentlemanly and kind, nice-looking, sincere. Yet despite her efforts, there was no spark, no heart-deep sense that they belonged together. With a sense of defeat, she realized she was never going to get there with him. She was ready to close that short and predictable chapter of her utterly uninteresting love life. Breaking it off with him had been an exercise in diplomacy, since he was the principal of her daughter's high school.

"So when my daughter was being dragged out to sea in a riptide, where were you?" she demanded, pinning Coach Swanson with an accusatory glare.

"I was on the beach, running drills."

"How did she hit her head? Did you see how it happened?"

He shuffled his feet. "Camille—"

"So that's a no."

"Mom," said Julie. "I already told you, it was a stupid accident."

"She didn't have my permission to be in the program," Camille said to the coach. Then she turned to Drake. "Who was in charge of verifying the permission slips?"

"Are you saying she didn't bring one in?" Drake turned to the coach.

"We have one on file," Swanson said.

Camille glanced at Julie, whose cheeks were now bright red above the cervical collar. She looked embarrassed, but Camille noticed something else in her eyes—a flicker of defiance.

"How long has this been going on?" she asked.

"This was our fourth session," said the coach. "Camille, I'm so sorry. You know Julie means the world to me."

"She *is* my world, and she nearly drowned," Camille said. Then she regarded Drake. "I'll call you about the permission slip. All I want is to get my daughter home, okay?"

"What can I do to help?" Drake asked. "Julie gave us all quite a scare."

Camille had the ugly sense that the words *tort liability* and *lawsuit* were currently haunting Drake's thoughts. "Look," she said, "I'm not mad, okay? Just scared out of my mind. Julie and I will both feel better once we get home."

Both men left after she promised to send them an update later. The discharge nurse was going down a list of precautions and procedures when Camille's mother showed up. "The X-ray shows her lungs are completely clear," the nurse said. "As a precaution, we'll want to have a follow-up to make sure she doesn't develop pneumonia."

"Pneumonia!" Camille's mother was in her fifties, but looked much younger. People were constantly saying Camille and Cherisse looked like sisters. Camille wasn't sure that was a compliment to her. Did it mean she, at thirty-six, looked fifty-something? Or did it mean her fifty-something mom looked thirty-six? "My granddaughter will not come down with pneumonia. I simply won't let it happen." Cherisse rushed to the bed and embraced Julie. "Sweetheart, I'm so glad you're all right."

"Thanks, Gram," Julie said, offering a thin, brief smile. "Don't worry. I'm ready to go home, right?" she asked the nurse.

"Absolutely." The nurse taped a cotton ball over the crook of her arm where the IV had been.

"Okay, sweetie," said Camille's mom. "Let's get you home."

They both helped unstick the circular white pads that had been connected to the monitors. Julie had been given a hospital gown to wear over her swimsuit. Her movements as she got dressed were furtive, almost ashamed, as she grabbed her street clothes from her gym

bag. Teenagers were famously modest, Camille knew that. Julie took
it to extremes. The little fairy girl who used to run around unfettered
and unclothed had turned into a surly, secretive teen. "You don't need
to wait for me," Julie announced. "I can dress myself."

Camille motioned her mother out into the waiting area.

"I'm ready to go," Julie said, coming out of the curtain area a few
minutes later. She wore an oversized "Surf Bethany" T-shirt and
a pair of jeans that had seen better days. There was a plastic bag
labeled *Patient Belongings* that contained a towel, headgear, glasses,
and a rash guard. "And just so you know, I'm not going back to
school," she added, her narrow-eyed expression daring them to con-
tradict her.

"All right," said Camille. "Do we need to stop there and get your
stuff?"

"No," Julie said quickly. "I mean, can I just go home and rest?"

"Sure, baby."

"Want me to come?" asked Camille's mother.

"That's okay, Gram. Isn't this your busy day at the shop?"

"Every day is busy at the shop. We're getting ready for First Thursday Arts Walk. But I'm never too busy for you."

"It's okay. Swear."

"Should I come in later and help?" asked Camille. She and her
mother were partners at Ooh-La-La, a bustling home-goods boutique
in the center of the village. Business was good, thanks to locals looking to indulge themselves, and well-heeled tourists from the greater
D.C. area.

"The staff can handle all the prep work. The three of us could have
a girls' night *in*. How does that sound? We can watch a chick flick and
do each other's nails."

"Gram. Really. I'm okay now." Julie edged toward the exit.

Cherisse sighed. "If you say so."

"I say so."

Camille put her arm around Julie. "I'll call you later, Mom. Say hi
to Bart from us."

"You can say it in person," said a deep male voice. Camille's step-father strode over to them. "I came as soon as I got your message."

"Julie's okay." Cherisse gave him a quick, fierce hug. "Thanks for coming."

Camille wondered what it was like to have a person to call automatically, someone who would drop everything and rush to your side.

He gathered Julie into his arms, enfolding her in a bear hug. The salt air and sea mist still clung to him. He was an old-school waterman who had a fleet of skipjack boats, plying the waters of the Chesapeake for the world's tastiest oysters. Tall, fair-haired, and good-looking, he'd been married to Cherisse for a quarter century. He was a few years younger than Camille's mom, and though Camille loved him dearly, Papa owned her heart.

After the bear hug, he held Julie at arm's length. "Now. What kind of mischief did you get yourself into?"

They walked together toward the exit. "I'm okay," Julie said yet again.

"She got caught in a riptide," Camille said.

"My granddaughter?" Bart scratched his head. "No. You know what a riptide is. You know how to avoid it. I've seen you in the water. You've been swimming like a blue marlin ever since you were a tadpole. They say kids born out here have webbed feet."

"Guess my webbed feet failed me," Julie muttered. "Thanks for coming."

In the parking lot they parted ways. As Julie got into the car, Camille watched her mother melt against Bart, surrendering all her worries into his big, generous embrace. Seeing them caused a flicker of envy deep in her heart. She was happy for her mother, who had found such a sturdy love with this good man, yet at the same time, that happiness only served to magnify her own loneliness.

"Let's go, kiddo," she said, putting the car in gear.

Julie stared silently out the window.

Camille took a deep breath, not knowing how to deal with this. "Jules, I honestly don't want to stifle you."

"And I honestly don't want to have to forge your signature on permission slips," Julie said softly. "But I wanted this really bad."

She'd been blind to her daughter's wishes, she thought with a stab of guilt. Even when Julie had pleaded with her to take surf rescue, she'd refused to hear.

"I thought it would be fun," Julie said. "I'm a good swimmer. Dad would have wanted me in surf rescue."

"He would have," Camille admitted. "But he would have been furious about you going behind my back. Listen, if you want, I can work with you on surf rescue. I was pretty good at it in my day."

"Oh, yay. Let's homeschool me so people think I'm even more of a freak."

"No one thinks you're a freak," said Camille.

Julie shot her a look. "Right."

"Okay, who thinks you're a freak?"

"Try everyone in the known world."

"Jules—"

"I just want to do the class, Mom, like everyone else. Not have you teach me. It's nice of you to offer, but that's not what I want, even though you were a champ back in your day. Gram showed me the pictures in the paper."

Camille remembered the triumphant photo from the *Bethany Bay Beacon* years ago. She had big hair, railroad-track braces, and a grin that wouldn't quit. She knew taking the course was not just about the skills. Surf rescue was such a strong tradition here, and the group experience was part of the appeal. She remembered the end of the course, sitting around a bonfire and telling stories with her friends. She remembered looking around the circle of fire glow, seeing all those familiar faces, and there was such a feeling of contentment and belonging. At that moment, she'd thought, I'll never have friends like this again. I'll never have a moment like this again.

Now she had to wonder if she was robbing her own daughter of the same kind of moment.

"*Your* mom let you do the class," Julie said. "She let you do everything. I've seen the pictures of you surfing and mountain biking and climbing. You never do any of that stuff anymore. You never do *anything* anymore."

Camille didn't reply. That had been a different life. *Before.* The Camille from *before* had grabbed life by the fistful, regarding the world as one giant thrill ride. She had thrown herself into sports, travel, adventure, the unknown—and the greatest adventure of all had been Jace. When she'd lost him, that was when *after* began. *After* meant caution and timidity, fear and distrust. It meant keeping a wall around herself and everything she cared about, not allowing anything or anyone in to upset her hard-won balance.

"So, about that permission slip," Camille said.

Julie lifted one shoulder in a shrug. "I'm sorry."

"If I wasn't so scared by the accident, I'd be furious with you right now."

"Thanks for not being furious."

"I'm going to be later, probably. My God, Julie. There's a reason I didn't want you to take the class. And I guess you found out today what that reason was—it's too dangerous. Not to mention the fact that you shouldn't be sneaking around behind my back, forging my signature—"

"I wouldn't have done it if you'd just let me take the class like a normal kid. You never let me do anything. Ever."

"Come on, Jules."

"I kept asking, and you didn't even hear me, Mom. I really wanted to do the course, same as you did when you were my age. I just want a chance to try—"

"You took that chance today, and look how that turned out."

"In case you're wondering, which you're probably not, I did great at the first three sessions. I was really good, one of the best in the class, according to Coach Swanson."

Camille felt another twinge of guilt. How could she explain to her daughter that she wasn't allowed to try something Camille had been so good at?

After a few minutes of silence, Julie said, "I want to keep going."

"What?"

"In surf rescue. I want to keep going to the class."

"Out of the question. You went behind my back—"

"And I'm sorry I did that, Mom. But now that you know, I'm asking you straight up to let me finish the class."

"After today?" Camille said, "You ought to be grounded for life."

"I *have* been grounded for life," Julie muttered. "Ever since Dad died, I've been grounded for life."

Camille pulled off the road, slamming the car into park alongside a vast, barren salt meadow. "What did you say?"

Julie tipped up her chin. "You heard. That's why you pulled over. All I'm saying is, after Dad died, you stopped letting me have a normal life because you keep thinking something awful is going to happen again. I never get to go anywhere or do anything. I haven't even been on an airplane in five years. And now all I want is to take surf rescue like everybody else does. I wanted to be good at *one thing*." Julie's chin trembled and she turned away to gaze out the window at the swaying grasses and blowing afternoon clouds.

"You're good at so many things," Camille said.

"I'm a fat loser," Julie stated. "And don't say I'm not fat because I am."

Camille felt ill. She'd been blind to what Julie wanted. Was she a terrible mother for being overprotective? Was she letting her own fears smother her daughter? By withholding her permission to take surf rescue, she'd forced Julie to go behind her back.

"I don't want to hear you talking about yourself that way," she said gently, tucking a strand of Julie's dark, curly hair behind her ear.

"That's right, you don't," Julie said. "That's why you're always busy working at the shop or in your darkroom. You stay busy all the time so you don't have to hear about my gross life."

"Jules, you don't mean that."

"Fine, whatever. I don't mean it. Can we go home?"

Camille took a deep breath, trying not to feel the places where

Julie's words had dug in. Was it true? Did she throw herself into her work so she didn't have to think about why she was still single after all these years or why she harbored a manic fear that something awful would happen to those she loved? Yikes. "Hey, sweetie, let's do each other a favor and talk about something else."

"Jeez, you always do that. You always change the subject because you don't want to talk about the fact that everybody thinks I'm a fat, ugly loser."

Camille gasped. "No one thinks that."

Another eye roll. "Right."

"Tell you what. You've been really good about wearing your head-gear and your teeth look beautiful. Let's ask the orthodontist if you can switch to nighttime only. And something else—I was going to wait until your birthday to switch your glasses for contacts, but how about you get contacts to celebrate the end of freshman year. I'll schedule an appointment—"

Julie swiveled toward her on the passenger seat. "I'm fat, okay? Getting rid of my braces and glasses is not going to change that."

"Stop it," Camille said. God, why were teenagers so hard? Had *she* been that hard? "I won't let you talk about yourself that way."

"Why not? Everybody else does."

"What do you mean, everybody else?"

Julie offered a sullen shrug. "Just . . . never mind."

Camille reached over and very gently brushed back a lock of Julie's hair. Her daughter was smack in the middle of prepubescent awk-wardness, the epitome of a late bloomer. All her friends had made it through puberty, yet Julie had just barely begun. In the past year, she'd gained weight and was so self-conscious about her body that she draped herself in baggy jeans and T-shirts.

"Maybe I do need to let go," Camille said. "But not all at once, and certainly not by putting you in harm's way."

"It's called surf *rescue* for a reason. We're learning to be safe in the water. You know this, Mom. Jeez."

Camille slowly let out her breath, put the car in drive, and pulled back out onto the road. "Doing something underhanded is not the way to win my trust."

"Fine. Tell me how to win your trust so I can take the course."

Camille kept her eyes on the road, the familiar landmarks sliding past the car windows. There was the pond where she and her friends had once hung a rope swing. On the water side was Sutton Cove—a kiteboarding destination for those willing to brave the wind and currents. After a day of kiteboarding with Jace nearly sixteen years before, she'd emerged from the sand and surf to find him down on one knee, proffering an engagement ring. So many adventures around every corner.

"We'll talk about it," she said at last.

"Meaning we won't."

"Meaning we're both going to try to do better. I'm sorry I've been so buried in work, and—" A horrid thought crash-landed into the moment.

"What?" Julie asked.

"A work thing." She glanced over at her daughter. "Don't worry about it. I'll deal." Her stomach clenched as she thought about the project she'd been working on for Professor Finnemore. The moment the ER had called, Camille had dropped everything and burst out of the darkness—thus ruining her client's rare, found film forever.

Great. The one-of-a-kind negatives, which might have offered never-before-seen images nearly half a century old, were completely destroyed.

Professor Finnemore was not going to be happy.

Two

Every time he came back to the States from his teaching post overseas, Finn made a stop at Arlington Cemetery. He walked between the endless white rows of alabaster markers etched with black lettering, nearly a half million of them, aligned with such flawless precision that they outlined the undulations of the grassy terrain. Somewhere in the distance, a set of unseen pipes was playing—one of the thirty or so funerals that took place here each week.

He paused at a headstone upon which was perched a small rubber bathtub duck. On the back of the toy, someone had written *Hi, Grandpa* in childish scrawl.

Finn paused before taking out his camera. The messages from little kids always got to him. He shut his eyes and murmured a thank-you to the soldier. Then he photographed the marker and added the memento to his bag. As a volunteer for the Military History Center, he visited Arlington whenever he was in town, recovering items that had been left on headstones. With his fellow volunteers, he helped catalog the items for a database so each remembrance, no matter how small, would be preserved.

Moving on, he made a detour to view the markers of his first bittersweet accomplishment. Working with a group of villagers in the highlands of Vietnam, he'd discovered the crash site of four U.S. soldiers who had gone missing fifty years before. The soldiers—an aircraft commander, a pilot, a door gunner, and a gunner—had been hit with enemy fire, and their chopper had crashed into a mountainside. For decades, the men had been lost. Finn had talked to their families, hearing echoes of his own family's story. With no way of knowing what had become of their loved ones, there was no place for the grief to go, no closure. It lingered like a fog, impenetrable on some days, lifting on others, but it was always present.

The remains had been interred in a group burial service with horse-drawn caissons and a white-gloved honor guard, while their families looked on, clinging together like survivors from a storm. One of the daughters had written Finn a note of gratitude, telling him that despite the revived grief, there was also a sense of relief that she was finally able to lay her father to rest.

More than a thousand veterans still remained unaccounted for, and his father, Richard Arthur Finnemore, was one of them. For years, Finn had searched for his father's likeness in the faces of panhandlers outside veterans' halls, wondering if torture had left him impaired and unable to make his way back to his family.

Finn picked up a small scrap of paper from a marker in Section 60, where the recently fallen were laid to rest. The handwritten note said, *I have to leave you here. You should be home playing with our kids and laughing with us. But this is where you'll stay. Forever. I guess in that sense, I'll never lose you.* Despite the summer heat, Finn felt a chill as he dutifully photographed the marker and added the note to his collection.

Finally, he consulted an app on his phone and located the new marker of a very old casualty—army air forces first lieutenant Robert McClintock. Finn had scoured the countryside around Aix-en-Provence, where he was living and teaching. His research had led him to the crash site of a single-seat P-38 aircraft, piloted by McClintock on a strafing mission against an enemy airfield in 1944. Combing through archives, Finn had discovered that on the day in question, poor weather conditions had impaired visibility. A scrap of news on a microfiche had reported that McClintock's aircraft had dived through the clouds and seemingly disappeared.

With a group of private citizens, Finn had worked with a recovery team, finding teeth and bone fragments, all that was left of the twenty-one-year-old airman. The Armed Forces DNA Identification Laboratory matched three sisters from Bethesda, and last year, Lieutenant McClintock had been repatriated here at Arlington. Finn had not attended the burial, but now he stood looking at the freshly etched marker. Again, there had been letters of gratitude from the family.

He appreciated the kind words, but that wasn't the reason he did what he did. He let people think he was looking for accolades and recognition in his academic work, because it was easier to explain than admitting that he was really looking for his father.

Standing amid the sea of alabaster headstones, Finn felt a breeze on his neck, redolent of fresh-cut grass and newly turned earth. Where'd you go, Dad? he wondered. We'd all love to know.

The roll of film his sister had found, with his father's initials on the small yellow can, was the best hope of finding out. The film expert, Camille Adams, was finally going to reveal his father's last images, taken somewhere in Cambodia decades before.

The thought made him lengthen his strides as he headed for his rental car. Maybe the courier charged with picking up the processed film would be back already. Finn got in and grabbed his mobile phone from the console. It indicated multiple voice mails from the courier company. As he tapped the phone to play the messages, Finn thought, Please, Camille Adams. Don't let me down.

"You don't sound happy," said Margaret Ann Finnemore, her voice coming through the speakers of the rental car.

Finn stared at the road ahead as he drove across the Chesapeake Bay Bridge, heading for the Delmarva Peninsula. Delaware-Maryland-Virginia. He had to cross state lines just to find Camille Adams.

"That's because I'm not happy," he said to his sister. "The film was supposed to be ready today, and the courier company can't even locate the woman responsible for developing it. She totally flaked out on us.

Stopped answering her phone, isn't reading text messages or checking e-mail."

"Maybe something came up," Margaret Ann suggested reasonably. In the Finnemore family, she was known as the reasonable sister.

"Yeah, she blew me off. That's what came up."

"She came so highly recommended. Billy Church—the guy at the National Archives—gave her such a strong recommendation. Didn't he say she's done work for the Smithsonian and the FBI?"

"He did. But he didn't say we'd need the FBI to find her. I should've called her references instead of just checking her website." The site for Adams Photographic Services had featured dramatic examples of photos she'd rescued or restored. It had also displayed a picture of Camille Adams, which had caught his attention. She was a beauty, with dark curly hair and faraway eyes—but apparently, no sense of responsibility.

"I'm sure there's an explanation."

"I don't need an explanation. I need to see what was on that roll of film, and I need to see it before the ceremony."

"You couldn't have sent someone else all the way out there?"

"The courier bailed after waiting around for an hour. Everybody else in the family has a job to do, so I decided to track her down my-self."

"Wouldn't it be great if there were pictures of Dad?" Margaret Ann sounded wistful. As the eldest of the Finnemore siblings, she had the most vivid memories of their father. Finn had none of his own, which was probably why each surviving photo meant so much to him. "If there are any shots of him, they'd be the last ever taken. We could add them to the display at the White House."

Finn tempered his expectations. "He shot that roll long before selfies were a thing."

"Maybe one of his fellow officers or men took a picture of him."

Finn had about a dozen things he could be doing instead of driving out to the edge of the known world, but he wanted to get his hands on those pictures. He hated the idea of letting his family down. The tightly knit clan consisted of steps and halves in every combination, and somehow it all worked. The somehow was his mom. They all revolved around her wellspring of strength and love.

Tomorrow would have been his father's seventieth birthday. On the night before Richard Arthur Finnemore had been deployed on a mission to Cambodia, he had kissed his children good night, and then made love to his wife one last time. Nine months to the day after that, Finn was born to a woman who had recently been informed that her husband was missing in action. Sergeant Major Richard Arthur Finnemore had performed an act of heroism, surrendering his position to the enemy in order to protect a group of men involved in a covert operation.

And he had never been seen again.

Tavia Finnemore had managed to put her life back together. In time, she fell in love with a guy who was completely unfazed by the fact that she had three kids. In fact, he had two of his own. They went on to have two more boys together. It was an unwieldy tribe of a family, filled with noise and chaos, pathos and laughter, and most of all, love. Yet all his life, Finn had felt the absence of his father, a man who had died before Finn had drawn his first breath of air. It was entirely possible to miss someone you'd never met. He was walking, breathing proof of that.

"We'll find out soon enough," he said, "assuming the film expert didn't abscond with the goods."

"She didn't abscond. Why on earth would she abscond with an old roll of film? And besides, who says 'abscond' anymore, except maybe my overeducated history-professor brother?"

"I hope like hell she didn't." Finn had no patience for people who didn't keep their commitments. If he found the woman—and he fully intended to, even though it meant a two-hour drive from Annapolis—he was going to have some choice words for her.

"Promise you'll call the minute you find out if she was able to salvage any of the pictures. Oh my gosh, Finn, I can't believe what's happening. A presidential Medal of Honor ceremony at the White

House. For our *dad*." Margaret Ann's excitement bubbled through his phone's speaker.

"Pretty surreal." The whole Finnemore-Stephens clan would be in attendance—the family his father had before he was reported MIA, and the family his mother had started when she married Rudy Stephens. More than four decades after the shocking telegram had reached a young woman with two little girls and a babe in arms, his mom was finally getting closure.

Then a thought occurred to him. "Shit. I'm supposed to pick up my dress uniform at the cleaners this afternoon, and here I am driving across the Chesapeake."

"If you were married again, you'd have a wife to help you out with stuff like that."

He gave a bark of laughter. "Seriously? *That's* your rationale for wanting me to remarry? You just set the women's movement back fifty years."

"Everyone needs a partner. That's all I'm saying. You were so happy when you were with Emily."

"Until I wasn't."

"Finn—"

"You're still ticked off at me for not liking the last one you set me up with."

"Angie Latella was perfect for you."

He winced, remembering the painfully awkward setup his sisters had organized. "I don't get why you and Shannon Rose—and Mom, for that matter—are on a mission to get me married off again. Because the last time turned out so well for me?"

The women in his family were endlessly preoccupied with his love life. They were convinced that his life would never be complete until he found true love, settled down, and started a family. He wasn't afraid to talk about it. He was afraid because they were probably right.

He wanted the kind of love his siblings had found. He wanted kids. Yet he had no desire to see if his luck would change the second time around. These days, he wasn't even sure he knew how love happened, and how it felt.

"It's been three years. You're ready. And Angie—"

"She was a half hour late, and she had an annoying laugh."

"That's code for she didn't have big boobs and an obsession with extreme sports."

"Come on. I'm not *that* shallow." Christ, he hoped not. His sister loved him, but when she tried to boss him around, he always pushed back.

"Then what about Carla? Now, *she* has boobs, *and* she's a world-class mountain biker."

"Daddy issues. And you're the one who told me a woman with a bad history with her father is a problem waiting to happen. Besides, I live overseas now, remember? Not interested in a long-distance gig."

"That's temporary. You'll be back in the States soon enough."

He decided now was not the time to tell her his visiting professorship in Aix-en-Provence had been extended. "Can one of your kids pick up my stuff at the cleaners? It's the one on Annapolis Road."

"I'll have Rory pick it up on her way home from work. She goes right by there."

"Thanks. Tell her there's a good bottle of wine in it for her."

"You're going to turn your niece into a wine snob like you. Remind me again when you have to go back," Margaret Ann said.

"A week from Saturday. Summer term starts on Monday."

"Teaching in Provence in summer, you lucky dog."

"Living the dream." He said this with a touch of irony. He had once believed he could find the kind of happiness his mom and other members of his family had found. But finding that would mean opening himself up to a new relationship, and he wasn't so sure he was up for that. Casual sex and no commitment made life simpler. More empty, yes. But simpler.

"What topics?" asked his sister.

"Advanced studies in historical inquiry, and it's awesome, not boring."

"And working on your next book?"

"Always." He was researching a work on World War II resistance fighters. And he was always looking for long-lost soldiers, searching out crash sites and battlefields for remains to restore to families yearning for closure.

She sighed. "Such a tough life."

"You should come for a visit and see how tough it is."

"Right. Dragging along my three reluctant teenagers and workaholic husband. I'm sure your archivist girlfriend—what's her name?"

"Vivi," Finn said. "And she's not my girlfriend. Hey, coming up on a tollbooth," he said, suddenly tired of the conversation. "Gotta go. I'll call you about the pictures, if there's anything to report." He ended the call and drove past the nonexistent tollbooth.

The bridge led him into a whole new world. Refocusing his mind on finding the AWOL film expert, he made his way across to the low, teardrop-shaped peninsula. He'd never actually explored the region, which was odd, since he'd spent so much of his life in and around Annapolis. He'd attended the U.S. Naval Academy, and after five years of service, attained his Ph.D. and became a professor there. Yet this area had always been a mystery to him.

The remote lowlands traversed a place of watery isolation, and the vibe felt entirely different from the pricey suburbs that clung to the western side of the Chesapeake. The road and town names reflected the region's varied colonial heritage—Native American, Dutch, and English: Choptank, Accomack, Swanniken, Claverack, Newcastle, Sussex.

A series of winding, ever-narrowing roads took him past courthouse towns, fishing villages, and long marshy areas alive with shorebirds. Finally, crossing a narrow neck of land dividing the ocean and the bay, he reached the township of Bethany Bay.

The colonial-era town, with its painted cottages and old-fashioned buildings, had the lived-in look of a seaside village, the landscape and structures battered by wind and weather. Nearly every house had a boat in the yard, a stack of crab pots, and a web of netting hung out for drying or repair. The main street was lined with charming shops and cafés. He passed a waterway labeled EASTERLY CANAL, and a marina filled with pleasure boats and a fishing fleet. Then he followed the beach road along a three-mile crescent clinging to the Atlantic shore.

If he hadn't been so annoyed at having to drive all the way out here, he might have appreciated the sable-colored sand and rolling surf, the smooth expanse of beach, where pipers rushed along in skinny-legged haste. A few surfers were out, bobbing on the horizon as they waited for a wave. A lone kiteboarder skimmed across the shallows under the colorful arch of his kite. A towering red-capped lighthouse punctuated the end of the beach like an exclamation point.

He was in no mood to savor the small-town charm of the remote spot. He had other things on his mind. Checking the business address on his phone, he came to a clapboard cottage about a block from the lighthouse. Gray with white trim around the small-paned windows, the cozy house had a front and back porch and a chimney on one end. It was surrounded by a picket fence and climbing roses, and a martin house on a tall pole.

He got out of the car, let himself in through the front gate, and promptly stubbed his toe on a garden stone carved with the words *J.A. Always in my heart.* Grabbing his foot, he let loose with a stream of cusswords he saved only for special occasions. Nothing said "You're having a bad day" quite like a freshly stubbed toe.

He took a moment to compose himself before approaching the house. Under the brass mailbox was a logo that matched the one on her website—a line drawing of a vintage camera, with the name of her company—Adams Photographic Services.

He saw no car in the driveway. Maybe it was in the garage, an elderly structure with a sliding door on iron rails. He walked up to the front porch and knocked sharply. The air smelled of the sea and blooming roses, and was filled with the sounds of the waves and crying gulls. Two pairs of gardening boots stood on the mat.

He rang the bell. Knocked again. Called her number for about the fourth time and got no answer. Leaning toward the door, he thought he heard a ringtone inside.

"Do not do this to me," he said to the voice mail. "It's Finn—Malcolm Finnemore. Call me as soon as you get this message."

He shoved a hand through his hair as if it would keep him from building up a head of steam. Maybe he could find a neighbor who would know how to get in touch with her.

Damn.

As she turned down the beach road toward home, Camille felt exhausted, her nerves worn thin after the ordeal in the ER. Julie was staring straight ahead, her face expressionless.

"Mom," Julie said. "You can stop checking me out. They said I'm okay."

"You're right, but that doesn't stop me from worrying. You have a contusion. You've never had a contusion."

"It's a fancy name for a bump on the head. Jeez." Julie pointed at the house. "Who's that guy?"

"What guy? Oh." Camille turned into the driveway and parked. The guy Julie was referring to stood on her front porch, a phone clapped to his ear as he paced back and forth. He was tall, with a ponytail and aviator shades. His lived-in shorts and dark T-shirt revealed a physique of tanned skin and sinewy muscles. Shoot. Was this the courier sent by Professor Finnemore?

She got out and slammed the car door, and he turned to face her, taking off the glasses. And something unexpected happened—her heart nearly jumped out of her chest, yet she had no idea why. He was a complete stranger. But she couldn't take her eyes off him. There was something about his stance and the way he held himself. He was just a guy, she thought. A stranger on her porch. There were a few glints of blond hair at his temples, framing gumball-blue eyes and a face that belonged in a Marvel Comics movie—he was that good-looking.

Well, hello, Mr. Courier Guy.

As she came up the walk, his eyes narrowed into a hostile squint. Clearly, he hadn't felt a similar jolt of attraction.

"Can I help you?" she asked, stepping onto the porch.

He put his phone away. "Camille Adams?"

"That's me."

"I'm Finn." He hesitated. His eyes were now cold and flinty. "Malcolm Finnemore."

Whoa. She took a second to regroup. This was not how she had pictured the nerdy history teacher. "Oh, uh, Professor Finnemore."

"I go by 'Finn.'"

She knew instantly the reason he was here, and why he looked so annoyed. "I missed the courier pickup," she said. "I had a personal emergency, and—"

"You couldn't have called? Sent a message?"

Julie came up behind her and mounted the porch steps, a surly expression on her face. "Hey," she said.

"My daughter, Julie," Camille said, her face turning bright red. "Julie, this is Professor Finnemore."

"Glad to meet you." Julie looked anything but glad. "Excuse me." She edged past them, pressed the door code, and went inside.

"My personal emergency," said Camille. Her stomach pounded. She had some explaining to do. "Please, come on in."

His gaze assessed her, from her unkempt hair to her grubby work garb—stained shirt, cutoffs, flip-flops. Spilled developer staining one ankle. She held the door, feeling utterly self-conscious. Not only had she ruined his film, but she was totally unprepared to meet a client. She was dressed like a slob in her darkroom clothes, hair piled into a messy bun. No makeup. Not showered.

He gave a nod, passing close to her as he stepped through the door. Oh God, she thought, he even *smelled* good-looking. Ocean air and fresh laundry. And he exuded the kind of effortless grace she observed in the wealthy "come-heres," as the locals called the summer people and power brokers from D.C. who came for the sand and sea.

They tooled around the peninsula in their foreign cars, bringing their friends from the city for sailing trips and shore dinners, or cruising with the skipjack watermen to dredge for oysters while under sail.

Camille knew the type—arrogant, entitled, treating the locals like servants. She suspected he might be one of them.

Her house wasn't ready for company either. Particularly not for a come-here whose film she'd destroyed.

Everything was just as she'd left it when the phone rang. Her morning mess was everywhere—yesterday's mail, library books, towels that had yet to be folded, her bikini hung on a doorknob to dry, sand-crusted flip-flops kicked to the side, dishes waiting to be loaded into the dishwasher. Her now-scummy coffee cup sat abandoned on the counter next to her forgotten mobile phone, its screen indicating multiple missed calls.

"So . . . can I offer you something to drink?" she asked. Lame. She was always so tongue-tied around good-looking men. It was silly. She didn't even *like* good-looking men. Probably because they made her uncomfortable. Particularly when she was about to deliver some bad news.

"Thanks, but I'm in a hurry," he said. "Wondering how the film turned out."

Of course he was.

Camille placed her keys on the hook by the door. She could hear Julie upstairs in her room, the old floorboards creaking. Julie spent so much time alone lately—or alone with her smartphone and laptop. Her punishment for forging the permission slip was going to be a severe restriction on screen time.

"I'm so sorry," she said. "I feel terrible that you had to drive all the way out here."

"The courier service said no one was here at the pickup time."

"I got called away." The sinking feeling dragged her lower and lower. "The film is ruined. And I'm sorry I didn't have my phone on me and I didn't get in touch with you."

He was very quiet. His face was stony, like a gorgeous sculpture. "You mean the film wasn't viable. It had sat in the can too long?"

Her mouth went dry. He was offering her an out, and for a split second, she considered taking the coward's route. It would be so simple—she could explain that his film had been spoiled by age and environment, and couldn't be developed. But that would be a lie. She had rescued film far older than his. Camille was not a liar. She never had been, even when it was more convenient to lie.

Excusing herself, she went down the hall, ducked into her workroom, and found the spooling canister she'd dropped when the hospital called. The film was now a dark ribbon of nothing with tractor perforations on the sides. She paused and looked down the hall, studying her angry visitor. As he stood there in profile, staring out the window at the beach in the distance, she felt that powerful beat of pure, unadulterated attraction again. It was such a singular feeling that she scarcely recognized what it was. It's nothing, she thought. Nothing but a momentary blip of feeling. A guy with looks like that could inspire even someone whose heart had been broken beyond repair.

Too bad she'd ruined his day for him. With grim fatality, she brought the long black failure back to the kitchen.

"I blew it," she said, hating the admission as she showed him the dark nothingness. "It was entirely my fault."

"Seriously?" A tic of irritation tightened his jaw as he eyed the blank film. "I don't understand. Was the film—"

"It was probably salvageable. But I accidentally let light into the darkroom at a crucial moment, and the light ruined the film." She considered a longer explanation, but didn't feel like dragging this stranger through her whole hellish day.

"Damn. Damn it to hell."

"I know," she said quietly. "I'm sorry."

He glared at the film again, and then at her. "Jesus Christ, I needed those pictures."

She nodded. "I realize that. I feel terrible."

"Shit. *Shit.* You're supposed to be an expert at this. I trusted you—"

"You did, and I'm so sorry." God, she hated letting people down. He had every right to be pissed.

"What the hell happened?" he demanded, glaring at the empty length of film. "Do you just take people's irreplaceable film and . . . what? Destroy it? Damn, I could have done that myself."

"I was working on it this morning and everything was going fine. I got a call . . ." She hesitated. She did not want to tell the angry stranger she was a negligent mom. "I dropped everything. Including your film. I feel horrible about it, and . . . and . . ."

Something in her voice, a waver of emotion she couldn't control, seemed to catch his attention. The winter-ice eyes changed. He had a slow, burning way of looking at her. As if his anger might set her on fire.

"You got a call," he prompted. "You got a fucking call."

She could barely speak past the lump in her throat, so she nodded. Something melted inside her. She'd just had the most terrifying day. A call from the ER was every mother's worst nightmare. For Camille, it revived the deep trauma of losing Jace, and now here was this furious stranger. Suddenly the strain of being a widowed single mother overwhelmed her. To go through a day like this without the love, support, and partnership of Julie's father felt like too much to bear. Julie's accident, and now this screw-up brought her long-buried grief to the surface.

To keep herself from shattering, she went into defense mode. She began to tremble as fear, stress, and then a delayed response of anger swept over her. With shaking hands, she set the film and canister in the sink, struggling to hide her emotions. It was horrifying, this reaction to the stress of the day, and she refused to let a work disaster take her apart.

She braced her hands on the edge of the sink and tried to collect herself. She glanced at her phone. Four missed calls, six new text messages, four new e-mails—all from "M Finnemore." She whirled around to face him. "I can't say it enough. I'm sorry about the negatives. I wish you hadn't wasted your time driving clear out here. And of course there's no charge for anything."

She glared at him, trying to hold fast to the anger. Instead, a hot tear slipped out. And then another. The guy stood there, seemingly frozen by anger. Then he spotted some tissues on the counter and handed her the whole box.

"Do you need to call someone?" he asked, indicating her phone. "Your husband . . . ?"

"No husband," she said through gritted teeth, swiping angrily at her cheeks.

He cut her with a laser glare, as if her lack of a husband inexplicably deepened the offense. "Thanks for nothing, lady."

Shaken by the encounter, Camille watched him through the window. What an incredible tool. He strode to his car, yanked open the door. Just for a moment, he hesitated, turning back toward the house. His anger seemed to soften into something else—regret, maybe. Could be he realized he was being a tool. Then he swiped at the back of his neck as if something had bitten him there, and climbed into the car.

Julie came down from her room. "That your client?" she asked, watching as he threw the car into reverse and peeled out.

"My client," Camille said. "My extremely disappointed client." She used a tissue to give her cheeks another swipe.

"Why disappointed?"

"I ruined his film."

"Oh. That's too bad." A pucker of concern knitted her brow. "You okay?"

"Yes." Camille took a deep breath. "God, he was pissed."

"I can tell. Is he single?"

"What? Jules."

"Just asking. I know how you feel about guys with ponytails."

Camille felt a flush creeping into her cheeks, because she had already wondered the same thing. *Is he single?* "I'm done with guys, with or without ponytails." Maybe she was reading her daughter wrong. "Do you feel bad because Drake and I parted ways?"

Julie's eyes widened. "Are you kidding? *No.* Having my mom date the school principal was the worst."

Camille studied her daughter's face. Julie was so beautiful to her— curly dark hair, bright brown eyes, a sweet saddle of freckles across her nose. Sometimes she recognized a flicker of Jace in Julie, and it made her heart melt. You're still here, she thought.

"What?" Julie rubbed her cheek. "Do I have something on my face?"

Camille smiled. "No. How's your head?" She inspected the bump. It was barely visible now, thank goodness.

"Fine. Really, Mom." She tucked her phone in her pocket. "I'm going out for a walk."

"You're supposed to be resting."

"I saw the discharge papers. They said I can resume all normal activities. I'll just go down to the lighthouse and back."

"I don't want to let you out of my sight."

"Not helpful," Julie said, a storm gathering in her eyes. "It's just a walk."

Camille hesitated. Julie spent way too much time alone in her room, staring at her phone screen. Anything that got her out of the house was a welcome distraction.

"All right." Camille didn't have the energy for a big argument. "But be—"

"I know. Careful." Julie went out the front door. "I won't be long."

Camille watched her walking down the road toward the lighthouse. In that moment, she looked so isolated and lonely in her shapeless clothes. It bothered Camille that none of Julie's friends had called or come by to make sure she was all right. Ninth graders were not noted for their compassion, but when one of their own was taken to the emergency room, she assumed at least one of them would follow up. Now that she thought about it, she hadn't seen any of Julie's friends around in a while.

Three

Julie stepped out onto the ledge of the Bethany Point Light. The lighthouse was still in use, though it was all automated now. Every few seconds, the beam at the top swung in an arc to encompass the entrance to the bay. Most folks assumed the lighthouse interior was locked up tight, but Julie knew how to climb to the top. She and her friends—back when she had friends—had found an access panel under the stairs at the base of the tower.

Once inside, it was a matter of climbing the winding brick steps to the rim that surrounded the old Fresnel lens. Most kids were too creeped out to climb the cobweb-infested steps, but Julie had persevered, using a broom to clear the way. This was her special place. She came here to be alone, to think, to dream.

As far as she knew, she was the only one who still came here. Her friends had all dumped her, moving on to hang out with the cooler kids. The popular kids. The thin kids. The kids whose moms were not dating the school principal.

With one hand on the railing behind her, Julie leaned over and studied the rocky shoals a hundred feet below. She wondered what it would be like to fall that far. Would there be time to feel scared, or would it all be over in the blink of an eye?

From her vantage point, she could see the beach where this morning's drama had occurred. In the deep sunset colors of the evening, she could pick out the eddies of the riptide, the one that had nearly carried her away to see her father.

Although it could be nothing but a fantasy, Julie held a vision in her head of where her father was now. He lived in a place that was parallel to the world she knew. It was right next door, yet invisible until she crossed the threshold, leaving the here and now behind and stepping into the new place.

There, Julie would be perfect. She would have friends rather than mean kids making fun of her. She would have boobs, not fat rolls. She would be everyone's favorite, not some chubby loser.

It worked like this in her mind, anyway. She was probably wrong, but a girl could dream. Sometimes she felt like talking to her mom about it, but she never did. Mom worried about every little thing and she'd find a way to worry about Julie's dream of paradise.

Plus she would start digging around and she might find out the real reason Julie kept getting in fights with other kids. Above all else, Julie could not allow her mother to find out what had provoked the fights. Because the only thing worse than having kids say her mother had caused her father's death was having to *tell* her mother what the kids were saying.

She heaved a lonely sigh, and then watched the colors of the water change as the sun went down behind the east-facing lighthouse. The colors were so rich, they made her heart ache. Maybe that was where her father lived, in a world so beautiful that mere mortals couldn't bear it.

She stooped and picked up a stray bird feather and held it out in front of her. It looked like the feather of an eastern shorebird, maybe a piping plover. When you grew up at the shore, you learned these things. She opened her fingers and let the feather drift downward, watching it dance on an updraft of wind, then swirl as it made its way to earth. Down, down, down.

She used to be light as a feather. When she looked at old pictures of herself—and there were hundreds, because her mom was a photographer—she was amazed at how cute she had been, like a little fairy. Not anymore. These days she was a fat blob. A fat blob nobody wanted to talk to, except to talk shit about her and tell lies about her mom.

She stooped and picked up a loose brick from the rim of the structure and sent it hurtling to earth. Then she picked up another and did the same, waiting for it to smash on the rocks below.

"Hey!"

The loud voice startled Julie so much she nearly let go of the railing. Her heart pounding, she jumped over the rail to safety.

"What the hell?" yelled the voice in a funny accent. "You almost hit me."

Oh, good God. She had nearly hit someone with a brick. Then everybody would be calling her a killer, too.

Horrified, she yanked open the door and clattered down the dark, dank-smelling stairs. Maybe she could run away before the someone saw her. Maybe if she ran really fast, the victim of her falling bricks wouldn't see her.

She pushed at the door at the base of the lighthouse and burst outside. It was nearly dark now. She sprinted over to the break in the fence, threw herself on the ground to crawl under. Before she could escape, she came face-to-face with a worn-out sneaker.

"You almost hit me," the kid repeated.

She recoiled, scrambling backward and leaping to her feet. "I didn't mean to. I didn't know you were there." She brushed off her jeans, studying him until recognition struck. "You're Tarek," she said. He had enrolled in school fairly recently, along with several of his brothers and sisters. They were a family of refugees, being sponsored by some people in town.

Tarek was in ninth grade, and he was even less popular than Julie. She took a perverse comfort in that. Some of the kids said rotten things about him, like he was a terrorist and stuff. He didn't seem bothered by the insults; maybe because he didn't understand.

Or maybe it was because the things he had seen in his homeland were a million times worse than a bunch of dumb kids teasing.

"And you are Julie Adams," he said.

"That's me. I didn't mean to drop anything on you."

"It is A-OK."

"The sign says no trespassing," she pointed out.

"And yet here you are."

"I've been coming here all my life," she said.

"Does that make you legit?"

"Makes me a native."

"Makes you a trespasser."

She shrugged. "Only if I get caught." She grabbed the chain-link fence and crawled under it, then stood up and turned back to look at him. She felt self-conscious as she brushed herself off again. He was probably staring at her giant fat butt.

He was paying no attention to her at all. He simply opened the gate and stepped outside.

"Hey," she said, "how did you get that unlocked?"

He turned and snapped the padlock in place. "Very simple. It's a four-digit combination. I guessed the combination."

"How'd you do that?"

He gestured at the lighthouse itself. Over the door were the numbers 1824—the year it was established. "Sometimes it is best to start with the obvious."

Tarek was cool. She liked him. It surprised her that she liked him, because lately she hated everyone. And everyone hated her right back.

"The first time I climbed the lighthouse, I was nine years old," she said. "One of my mom's friends told me my dad was up in heaven, so I thought if I climbed to a high place I might be close enough to see him." After she said this, she felt foolish.

He didn't seem as if he found her ridiculous. He thought for a moment, then said, "My father is also gone. He was arrested, taken away right in the middle of a class he was teaching, and we never saw him again."

"That's terrible."

He nodded.

"So your father was a teacher."

"He taught English."

They sat on a big rock, looking out at the water. The colors of twilight pooled on the surface and melded with the sky. Tarek watched a gull take flight. "I saw what happened to you in surf rescue class."

Her stomach clenched. "It was an accident."

"I don't think so. Unless you would call Vanessa Larson chasing you an accident."

"It's a free-for-all during drills," she insisted, cringing at the memory. Once Vanessa's dad started dating Julie's mom, Vanessa had turned everyone against her. At first the teasing had been subtle—digs about Julie's weight, her braces, her glasses. Then it had caught on, and before long, other kids piled on. Finally, after Julie's mom broke up with Vanessa's dad, it became an all-out campaign against Julie.

"You're a good swimmer," she said, trying to change the subject. "Where did you learn?"

He was quiet for a moment. "While on my way to Turkey. It was sink or swim."

She suspected there was a lot more to the story.

"You are a good swimmer, too," he stated. "That is how I know you didn't have an accident."

"Just drop it, okay?" She tried to divert him again. "So are you staying in Bethany Bay for the summer?" Maybe, just maybe, they would hang out.

"No. We are leaving as soon as the school year ends. We are going to Canada to see my grandparents. Their sponsor family is in Toronto."

Thus killing off her one shot at making a friend.

"What about you?" he asked.

She shrugged her shoulders. Summers used to mean endless beach days, bike riding with her friends, staying up late, bonfires and campouts. She had no idea what she'd do with herself this coming summer, other than look at the Internet and wish she had a different life.

"I have to go," Tarek said abruptly. "See you tomorrow in school, yes?"

"Sure," she said, the back of her neck prickling at the idea of school. "See you around."

She took her time walking back home. The house was lonely and empty. There was a note on the counter: *Went to pick up Billy at the ferry. We're going to First Thursday. Want to come?*

No, Julie didn't want to come to the First Thursday walkabout. She might run into the very kids she was trying to avoid. Frustrated, she yanked open the pantry door, looking for something to eat.

Her mom never had chips and cookies in the house anymore. Julie knew it was because she was fat. She didn't use to be. She poured a bowl of cereal—whole grain, sugar-free—and added plenty of sugar and milk. Then she took it up to her room and stared at her phone while she was eating, looking up kids from her school. Vanessa Larson had the most followers. She immediately attracted attention because she was not only the daughter of the school principal, she was drop-dead gorgeous and had giant boobs.

Julie decided that if she didn't have to go to school, her life wouldn't suck so much. Last year, some kid had gotten himself expelled for bringing a Colt .45 to school. Boom—he was gone in a matter of minutes.

Julie didn't have a firearm to bring to school. She wouldn't dream of it, even if she did have one. But if she could find a way to never go back to that school again she would grab on to it.

There was homework. She flipped open her binder. She looked at the top page of the binder and recoiled. Someone had drawn a carica-ture of her, making her look like a hippo in a tutu. The caption read *Hungry Hungry Julie.*

Julie ripped the page from the binder and crumpled it into a tiny hard ball.

"Screw homework," she muttered. "Screw everything."

She had to get away from school. Away from the living hell she endured every single day. She hated school. And school hated her. She had to do something.

"I blew it," Camille said to Billy Church, stopping on the porch to pick up her mail. She stepped back, holding the door open to let him in. Professor Finnemore's film lay neglected on the counter. Her head was still spinning from his visit.

"Let me guess," Billy said, his open, friendly face verging on a smile. "You fixed me a soufflé for dinner and it fell."

"I only wish it were that simple."

She poured two glasses of wine—a dry rosé that was the perfect pairing for a summer evening and the end of a rotten day.

"The negatives I was working on are ruined," she told Billy. "I'm sorry."

"It happens," he said. "I told the client not to expect a miracle."

"No. You don't understand. I blew it. The film was salvageable. But I dropped everything when the hospital called. I didn't even think of it."

"No one's going to blame you for dropping everything when you get a call to say your kid's in the ER."

She smiled. It might have been her first smile of the day. And it was already evening. "He didn't seem too interested in an explanation."

"Oh. So he was a dick."

"Pretty much, yeah. I still feel terrible," she said.

Billy picked up a handmade holder with sunglasses in it. "You've taken up arts and crafts?"

"No. The guy left that behind." She'd found it after he'd gone, and now she was trying to figure out what to do about it. Offer to mail it, probably. Which meant she'd have to get in touch with him again. Great.

Billy checked the tag on the glasses holder. "Says 'handmade by Mom.' Very cute. His mommy still makes him presents."

"Don't be mean."

"Come here, you." Billy folded her into a hug.

"Thanks," she said, her words muffled against his shoulder. "I needed this."

"You need more than a hug, my friend," said Billy.

"Are you hitting on my mother again?" Julie asked, coming into the kitchen. She put a cereal bowl and spoon into the dishwasher.

Billy stepped back, palms up and out. "Guilty as charged. She's been rejecting me ever since she turned me down for the eighth-grade dance."

"Did not," Camille said. "You were too scared to ask me."

"Because I knew you'd turn me down. And I did ask you in ninth, tenth, and eleventh grades. Guess I'm a slow learner."

"I'm sure I had my reasons." Camille caught his eye, and he winked at her. She knew what he was up to. He had a knack for lightening the mood, not just for her, but for Julie. After the rotten day they'd both had, he was a ray of sunshine. He was the best kind of friend, even when he was teasing her.

"Yes. They were Aaron Twisp, Mike Hurley, and Cat Palumbo."

"You dated a guy named Cat?" Julie asked.

"I did," said Camille. "And yes, he was that cool. He was so cool he couldn't have a normal name. He had long hair, skinny jeans, combat boots, played the bass like a rock god. Whatever happened to him, anyway?"

"Easy enough to find out." Billy took out his phone and tapped the screen. "Here's your rock god now." He showed them a picture of a pale-faced, slightly pudgy man in an ill-fitting shirt and tie. "He works in D.C. for the bread lobby. And his actual name is Caspar."

That drew a giggle from Julie.

"See?" said Billy. "*Somebody* in this family likes me."

"For what it's worth," Julie said, "I think she's crazy to reject you. You're funny, smart, and you know all the words to 'Bohemian Rhapsody.'"

"Keep going."

"You're totally Hemsworthy."

Billy frowned. "Is that a good thing?"

"As in the Hemsworth brothers. So, yeah."

He took a sip of wine. "Cool. Now, how about you today? Getting yourself swept out to sea was quite a feat."

She shrugged. "It happens."

"Well, just make sure it doesn't happen again. Except maybe to the douche bag who was rude to your mom today."

"You got it."

"Seriously, Jules, you scared the crap out of everyone." He indicated the picture of Jace and Julie on the mantel. Taken on the beach about five years before, it depicted the two of them posed with their surfboards, squinting into the sun and laughing. "That guy—I bet he'd ground you for life if he knew you got caught in a riptide and let yourself float out to sea."

"Maybe then I'd finally get to see him again," Julie stated.

Camille's blood turned to ice. "Don't ever say that, Julie. Oh my God, do you hear yourself?"

Julie's chin came up. "According to you, he's the greatest thing that ever walked the earth. But he seems so far away, like I never really knew the guy."

The comment worried Camille. How could she keep his memory alive for her daughter? Julie had been so young when she'd lost her dad.

"Well, I knew him," Billy said, going to the bar cart and taking out a bottle of Don Julio, "and even though I begged your mom to wait for me during college, do you think she listened? No. She had to go and meet Dr. Dreamboat, and boom. Nobody else had a chance."

"That's because he was the love of her life, and when she lost him, the world came to an end," Julie recited, all too familiar with the story.

Billy measured out two generous shots. "I was jealous as hell of him, but I never resented the guy, because he gave you to the world, Jules."

Camille's heart ached as it always did when the subject of her late husband came up. She'd met him when she'd gone to the ER with a dislocated shoulder from a rock-climbing mishap. A few months later, she was married to the doctor who had helped her that day. She had every expectation of a lifetime of adventure with Jace. No one had counted on the spectacular manner of his demise, or its far-reaching effects. Since the accident, she wanted nothing to do with adventure. She wanted—she needed a safe, predictable existence.

"Lecture over?" Julie asked.

"Sure, why not?" Billy said. "Who's your mom seeing these days?"

Camille was in the middle of swigging down the tequila, and she nearly choked on it. "Hey," she objected.

"Mom never talks about the guys she dates," Julie said.

"That's because she broke so many hearts," Billy said. "Mine included."

"Knock it off." Camille gave him a friendly slug. "I've dated, what—three guys? Four?—since Jace. It's not like I haven't tried. But it never works."

He shot her a wounded look. "So is there another old flame in the picture?"

"All my flames are old. It's the only kind I have. Is there such a thing as a new flame?"

"She's not seeing anybody," Julie chimed in. "She stopped seeing my school principal, thank God."

"Why thank God?"

"Because it was so awkward. It messed with my head, you know?"

"No. But I'll take your word for it. What about the dogcatcher?"

"Duane. And he's not a dogcatcher." Camille bristled. "He's an animal control officer. We only went out once. Turned out he was not as loyal as the dogs he rescues."

"And the one before that? Peter? The super-handsome one."

Another one-date wonder. "He got all weird and Catholicky on me."

"Catholicky? Is that even a word?"

"He took some of the doctrines a bit too literally." Privately, Camille believed he simply didn't like using a condom. Reason enough to show him the door.

"And what about that guy who Tindered you?"

"Mom. Please tell me you're not on Tinder," Julie begged.

"I'm not on Tinder."

"Your grandmother signed her up," Billy said.

"Your grandmother is still in trouble for pulling that stunt," Camille said.

He poured a shot of club soda for Julie, then added a squeeze of lime. "*My* mom still thinks tinder is something you take camping."

"Let's talk about something else," Camille suggested. "Tell us about your week so far. Have you whipped your department into shape at the National Archives?"

"Not even close. The budget gets slashed every time somebody in Congress cuts a fart. When it comes to funding historical treasures, it's a mummy-eat-mummy world." He slammed back his tequila shot. "I laid a nasty rumor about Rutherford B. Hayes to rest. And I sent Gerald Ford's college senior thesis and his football helmet back to Michigan, his home state."

"What was the ugly rumor about President Hayes?" asked Julie.

"That he took up with a saloon gal named Mary Chestnut. His political enemies made it up." Billy put the glasses in the sink. "What say we go to the village and grab a bite, then walk around and look at First Thursday."

"I don't really feel like it," Julie said. "But thanks."

"I should stay home with Julie," Camille said.

"Wrong answer. You should both come with me."

"No, thanks," Julie said. "I'd rather hang out here."

"You used to love First Thursday. You can see all your friends, let them know you're okay."

"Mom," Julie cut in. "I said no thank you."

Camille stepped back, stunned by her daughter's vehemence. "Ah. The queen has spoken." She turned to Billy. "We'll just hang out here."

"No," he said. "I'm taking charge. You're coming with me. And Julie can stay home and Snapchat or Instagram with her friends, or whatever it is they're all doing."

"Good plan," Julie said, sending him a grateful look.

Camille felt torn. She really, really wanted to get out for a bit. She really, really wanted a cocktail at the Skipjack Tavern. "Are you sure you're okay?"

"Positive. I'll be even more okay once you quit worrying."

"I'll never quit worrying."

"We're leaving." Billy handed Camille her bag. Then he ushered her out the door. "Let's walk to the village," he said. "The weather is fantastic."

The promise of summer filled the evening air. The lingering warmth of the day emanated from the brick sidewalks, and sunset colors glinted off the canal and the bay. The air smelled of the coming season—blooming honeysuckle, cut grass, and the rich, lively odor of bounty from the sea. The sky was beautifully clear, and the laughter and conversation that bubbled from the crowd in the village were filled with energy.

Founded by Dutch and English settlers three centuries before, Bethany Bay combined the old-world charm of both cultures. The squared-off, gabled rooflines and old colonial homes blended with the seascape surrounding the town. It was an authentic snapshot of a place that had been treated kindly by time, retaining the character of the past in its very soul.

First Thursday was a bustling event, with locals coming out to socialize, and the come-heres taking in the small-town charm. Visitors from the cities—D.C., Dover, Bethesda, even New York and north Jersey—had escaped early for the weekend. Bethany Bay was not as popular as Rehoboth and Annacock, an unfortunate name for a lovely town, but for those who made the extra effort to reach the remote spot, the rewards were many. Development was held at bay by the fact that the entire region was surrounded by a wildlife preserve, and the inner core of the village consisted of listed and registered structures.

The sound of an ensemble playing under the gazebo on the village green added a festive touch to the evening. Fairy lights surrounding the gazebo and hanging from the cherry and liquidambar trees created an irresistible atmosphere.

The seaside town was the backdrop of her childhood, a cocoon where she felt safe. A refuge. The place where she had made her life in the wake of an unspeakable tragedy.

Yet sometimes it felt like a walled fortress with her stuck inside, unable to escape.

Just for a short while, the small-town festivities took her mind off Julie. She and Billy dropped into various shops and galleries that lined the main street. The art ranged from borderline kitsch to sophisticated originals to purely magical. At the Beholder, owned by her mother's best friend, Queenie, they munched on almond toffee and checked out the latest offerings—nature scenes printed on copper or aluminum. The gallery occupied what had once been a customs house, dating back to the eighteenth century. The light-flooded hall and grand hearth created the perfect setting for displaying art.

"They're mesmerizing," Camille said to Queenie. Glancing over her shoulder, she saw Queenie's young assistant shamelessly flirting with Billy, which was no surprise. He was the kind of good-looking that made a bow tie and horn-rimmed glasses sexy, and women went nuts for him. "I'm not the only one being mesmerized."

"He's quite a catch. Your mother and I often wonder why the two of you never—"

"I'd like to meet the artist," Camille broke in.

"Of course," said Queenie. "I was hoping you'd stop by tonight. You and Gaston have something in common."

"Gaston. He's French?"

"From Saint-Malo. You're going to love him." Taking Camille by the hand, she towed her through the milling crowd to a slender, sandy-haired guy in a striped T-shirt and thin neck scarf. "Gaston," said Queenie. "This is Camille, my best friend's daughter."

He looked up, and when he saw her, his eyes flared wide, making her glad she'd decided to shower and put on makeup before coming out tonight. "Hi," he said, extending his hand. "Very happy to meet you."

Camille could tell he was struggling with his English, so she an-

swered him in French. "Your pictures are truly beautiful," she said.
"Congratulations on this amazing show."

A smile lit his face. "You're French, too?"

"My father is. He raised me to speak his native language."

"He must be from the south," Gaston said. "Provence? I can hear
it in every word you speak."

The southern part of France had a dialect and cadence all its
own, comparable to the unique sound of people from the Chesapeake
region, a blend of accents and archaic terms.

"All right, you two. Stop being so foreign and cliquish," Queenie
said.

"We are foreign," Gaston said with a wink.

"Camille works in photography, too," Queenie said. "Did she tell
you?"

Camille could smell matchmaking a mile off. Her mom and friends
and half sisters abhorred a single woman's status the way nature abhorred a vacuum. Sometimes it seemed her mother had recruited the
whole town to find her a boyfriend. For no reason she could fathom,
her thoughts strayed to Malcolm Finnemore. The ticked-off client.
Not boyfriend material.

"Sorry," she told Gaston in French. "She always tries to throw me
together with random men."

"Not to worry," he said, also in French. "I'm an artist. Everybody
knows it's dangerous to hook up with an artist." He grinned and reverted to English. "So. You like photography."

"Yes."

"She specializes in old film and prints," Queenie said. "I keep trying to get her to do a show here at the Beholder."

One of Queenie's assistants came over. "Sorry to interrupt," she
said. "We've got a buyer for the big landscape."

Queenie went straight into action. She pressed her hand against
Gaston's elbow and steered him to the large piece that dominated
what had once been the mantel over the hearth.

Camille took the opportunity to pull Billy away from the puppy-eyed shopgirl, and they went back out into the street.

"Hey," said Billy. "She was cute."

"All twenty-year-olds are cute."

He sent her a fake-resentful look. "Since when are twenty-year-olds too young for me?"

"We're thirty-six," she reminded him.

"In that case, you should take me up on my offer to marry you. I'd make an honest woman of you."

"Where to next?" she asked, ignoring the suggestion. "Ooh-La-La?"

"Lead on," he said. "I haven't seen your mom in a while. Plus, Rhonda always serves those little crab croquettes. They taste like an angel farted in your mouth."

"No wonder I'd never marry you. You're too obnoxious."

"Let's get over there before the angel farts are gone."

The shop looked bright and twinkly and inviting, as always. Located in a vine-clad brick building that used to be a milliner's shop a century before, it had twin display windows facing the street. As always, the display was gorgeous, a blend of beach style and continental chic. Despite the kitschy shop name, Camille's mother had exquisite taste, and her half sister, Britt, had a keen eye for design.

Cherisse filled the place with supremely interesting things—unique home goods, sommelier tools, glass rolling pins, printed toile curtains, Clairefontaine writing paper and pens that felt just right in the hand. Camille had practically grown up in the boutique, listening to Edith Piaf and Serge Gainsbourg while helping her mom display a set of crystal knife rests or a collector's edition of Mille Bornes or the Dutch bike game of Stap op.

In the 1990s, the first lady was photographed in the shop, buying a fabulous set of Laguiole cutlery, and business kicked into high gear. Socialites from D.C. and even a couple of celebrities became regular customers. There were write-ups in national magazines, travel articles, and shopping blogs touting the treasures of Ooh-La-La, designating it as a must-visit destination.

Camille owed her very existence to the shop. Although she never realized it growing up, her parents had married for reasons of cold-blooded commerce. Her father, Henry, was looking for a marriage path to citizenship. Cherisse, who was fifteen years younger, needed a backer for the shop she'd always dreamed of opening. They both wanted a child, desperately. Desperately enough to believe their shared desire for a home and family was a kind of love. What they eventually had to admit—first to themselves privately, then to each other, and finally to Camille—was that no matter how much they loved their daughter, the marriage wasn't working for them.

When Camille was eight years old, they sat her down and told her just that.

Their divorce was, as the mediator termed it, freakishly civilized. After a couple of years, Camille adjusted to dividing her time between two households. A few years after the divorce, Cherisse met Bart, and that was when Camille finally learned what true love looked like. It was the light in her mother's eyes when Bart walked into a room. It was the firm touch of his hand in the small of her back. It was a million little things that simply were not there, had never been there, between her mom and dad.

She was grateful that her parents got along. Bart and her father were cordial whenever they encountered each other. But despite their efforts, the decades-old breakup of her family felt like an old wound that still ached sometimes. When she thought about Julie, she wondered which was harder, to have your family taken apart by divorce, or to lose a parent entirely.

Cherisse, at least, had thrived in her new life. She and Bart had two girls together, Britt and Hilda. Ooh-La-La annexed the building next door, turning it into its sister property, Brew-La-La, the best café in town. All through her high school years, Camille had minded the shop while her two younger half sisters played in the small garden courtyard.

These days, Camille worked behind the scenes with the book-keeper, Wendell, an insatiable surfer and skateboarder who financed his passion by keeping the books. Despite his shaggy hair and surfer duds, he was smart, intuitive, and meticulous. The sales staff consisted of Rhonda, who was also an amazing cook, and Daphne, a transplant from upstate New York with a mysterious past.

Britt was the resident merchandiser and display designer. Cherisse was in charge of "flying and buying." Two times a year, she went to Europe to find the lovely offerings that had put the shop on the map. Before losing Jace, Camille used to accompany her on buying trips, soaking in the sights of Paris and Amsterdam, London and Prague. It was a mother-daughter treasure hunt, those unforgettable days.

After Jace died, Cherisse urged Camille to come along on trips the way she used to, but Camille refused. She never flew anywhere. Just the idea of setting foot on a plane sent her into a panic. She never again climbed a mountain or rode a trail, rafted on a river, surfed a wave, or flew on a kiteboard. Other than routine commutes to D.C. for work, she didn't go anywhere. These days, she regarded the world as a dangerous place, and her job was to stay put and keep Julie safe.

She had failed miserably at that today. She vowed not to make that mistake again.

Rhonda greeted them at the shop entrance with a tray of her legendary crab croquettes.

"I'm never leaving you," Billy said, helping himself to three of them.

"Promises, promises," said Rhonda. "Come on in, you two. We're having a great night. The tourist season is about to kick into high gear."

Camille's mother was in her element, greeting visitors, treating even out-of-towners like cherished friends. Billy made a beeline for her. "Hello, gorgeous," he said, giving her a quick hug.

"Hello yourself," she said, her face lighting up. Then she noticed Camille. "Glad you came after all. How's Julie doing?"

"She shooed us both out of the house," Camille said. "She's okay, Mom. Thanks for showing up at the hospital. I was a mess."

"You were not. Or did I miss something?"

You missed me having a meltdown in front of Malcolm Finnemore, Camille thought, but she simply said, "I'm all right now."

Billy surveyed an antique table displaying a polished punch bowl in the shape of a giant octopus. "The shop looks great, as always."

"Thanks. Did you see Camille's new prints? I can't keep them in stock. I've sold four of them already tonight." She gestured at a display of the three newest prints, matted and framed on a beadboard wall.

The center image was one Camille had rendered from an old daguerreotype of Edgar Allan Poe. Printed on archival paper, the portrait had a haunting quality, as elusive and scary as his poems. Next to those prints were examples of Camille's own work. She almost never took pictures anymore, so these were from years before. She'd used a vintage large-format Hasselblad, capturing local scenes with almost hyperrealistic precision.

When Jace was still alive, Camille had been a chaperone on one of Julie's school trips to the White House. It had been one of those days when shot after shot seemed to be sprinkled with fairy dust, from the dragonfly hovering perfectly over a pond in the Kennedy Garden, to a frozen moment of two girls holding hands as they ran along the east colonnade, framed by sheer white columns.

"I love these," said a browsing tourist. "That's such a beautiful shot of the White House Rose Garden."

"Here's the artist," Billy said, nudging Camille forward.

"It's very intriguing," the woman said. "It looks as if the picture was taken at some earlier time."

"They're from six years ago. I was shooting with an antique camera that day," Camille said.

"My daughter has a great collection of old cameras," Cherisse said. "She does her own developing and printing."

"Well, it's fantastic. I'm going to get this one for a good friend who loves old photographs, too." She smiled, picking up the Rose Garden print.

Camille was flattered, and she felt a wave of pride. She wished Jace had lived to see this. "Maybe this hobby of yours will turn into something one day," he used to tell her.

". . . on the back," the woman was saying.

"Sorry," Camille said. "What was that?"

"I wondered if you could write a message on the back," she said. "To Tavia."

"No problem." The woman seemed a bit quirky, though perfectly nice. Camille found a pen and added a short greeting and her signature to the back of the mat.

"Let's go drink," Billy said after she finished. "I can watch you get hit on at the Skipjack."

"Good plan," she said, making a face. Guys didn't hit on her, and he knew it.

She and Billy made their way to the rustic tavern, a nineteenth-century brick building near the fishing pier. The crowd here was friendly and upbeat, spilling out onto the deck overlooking the water.

"Is it just me," Billy murmured, scanning the crowd, "or do we know at least half the people here?"

"The perks of growing up in a small town," she said.

"Or the drawbacks. There are at least two women here I've slept with. Should I say hi, or pretend I don't see them?"

"You should order a drink for me, and pick up the tab because I've had a rotten day." Camille stepped up to the bar. "I'll have a dark-and-stormy," she said to the bartender.

"Camille, hi," said a woman, coming up behind her.

Camille tried not to cringe visibly. She knew that voice, with its boarding-school accent and phony friendliness. "Hey, Courtney," she said.

Drake Larson's ex-wife wore a formfitting neoprene dress and a stiff smile. Years earlier, she'd been one of the come-heres, the kind that used to make Camille feel self-conscious. Camille was never as cool, as polished, as sophisticated as the kids from the city. One of the reasons she had worked so hard to excel at sports was to find a way to outshine the come-heres.

"I didn't expect to see you out tonight," Courtney said. "Vanessa told me your Julie had a terrible accident this morning."

"She's fine now," Camille said, wishing she didn't feel defensive.

"Well, that's good to know. I can't imagine leaving Vanessa after she suffered a head injury."

"How do you know she hit her head?"

Courtney looked flustered. "That's just what Vanessa heard. So, Julie's all right, then, since you're here drinking with some guy." She eyed Billy, who was paying for the drinks.

"Julie is fine, and Vanessa is welcome to give her a call," Camille said.

"I'll pass that along," Courtney said. "Vanessa's busy tonight, though. She and her friends are by the gazebo, listening to the band. Maybe you could text Julie and tell her to join in."

"Julie decided to stay home," Camille said.

"You know," Billy broke in, "just chilling out and being awesome."

"I see. Well, I suppose she's reached that awkward stage," Courtney said, taking a dainty sip of her dirty martini.

Billy regarded her pointedly. "Some people never outgrow it."

Courtney sniffed, either ignoring or missing the dig. "Kids. They change so quickly at this age, don't they? Vanessa and Julie used to be such good friends, but lately they don't seem to have much in common."

"Is that so?" Billy asked.

"Vanessa is so busy with cheerleader tryouts. Is Julie going out for cheerleading, too?"

Julie would rather have a root canal, thought Camille.

"Julie doesn't like being on the sidelines," Billy said.

"She should try cheerleading," Courtney said. "She has *such* a pretty face, and the practice is really good exercise. The drills are a great way to get in shape."

Camille could feel Billy starting to bluster. She gave him a nudge. "Our drinks are ready."

As they took their cocktails to the deck outside, Camille overheard

Courtney boasting to someone else about Vanessa's latest achievement. She knew she shouldn't let the woman's remarks get under her skin, but she couldn't help it, especially when she looked across the way at the village green and saw a group of kids dancing and having fun. Perky blond Vanessa was the life of the party. Julie didn't seem to belong anymore. And Camille had no idea how to fix it.

four

Camille walked home, feeling slightly better after the village social time and two dark-and-stormies. Julie's light was on upstairs, and Camille could see her through the window, staring at her computer screen, which seemed to be her main channel for socializing these days. Camille hoped the self-isolation was just a phase. She intended to restrict Julie's screen time, but at the moment she didn't feel up to a fight.

She let herself in and put down her things. The film was still in the sink along with the shot glasses. She tidied up, trying to shake off the residue of the day. So she'd lost a client. It happened, and now it was done, and the world had not come to an end.

Thanks for nothing. Finnemore was a jerk, she thought, blowing up at her like that. Sure, she'd let him down, but that was no reason for him to rip into her the way he had. Good-looking guys thought they could get away with being mean. She was mad at herself for being attracted to him, and for letting his temper tantrum bug her.

A car's headlights swept across the front of the house, and crushed shells crackled under its tires. She glanced at the clock—nine P.M.— and went out onto the porch, snapping on the light. Her heart flipped over. Mr. Ponytail Professor was back.

"Did you forget something?" she asked when he got out of the car.

"My manners," he said.

What the . . . ? "Pardon me?"

"Do you drink wine?" he asked.

"Copiously. Why do you ask?"

He held out a bottle of rosé, the glass beaded with sweat. "A peace offering. It's chilled."

She checked the label—a Domaine de Terrebrune from Bandol. "That's a really nice bottle."

"I got it from a little wine shop in the village."

She nodded. "Grand Crew. My father was one of their suppliers. He's retired now."

"He was in the wine business, then."

"He owned an import and distributing firm up in Rehoboth. And why are we having this conversation?"

"I came back to apologize. I got halfway across the bridge and started feeling bad for yelling at you, so I turned around and came back."

She caught herself staring at him like a smitten coed with a crush on her professor. She flushed, trying to shake off the gape-mouthed attraction. "Oh." An awkward beat passed. "Would you like to come in?" She held open the door.

"Thought you'd never ask."

In the kitchen, she grabbed some glasses and a corkscrew. What was he doing back here? "Actually, you did forget something—your sunglasses." She handed them over.

"Oh, thanks." He opened the wine and poured, and they brought their glasses to the living room and sat together on the sofa. He tilted his glass toward her. "So . . . apology accepted?"

She took a sip of the wine, savoring the cool, grapefruity flavor of it. "Apology accepted. But I still feel bad about your film."

"I know. You made a mistake. I should have been more understanding." He briefly touched her arm.

Okay, so maybe he wasn't such a jerk. She stared at her arm where he had touched it. Why was this stranger, whose one-of-a-kind film she'd ruined, taking care of her? Watching him, she tried to figure it out. "I've never screwed up a project like that," she said.

"So what happened?"

"Everything was going fine until I got a phone call from the local hospital that my daughter had been brought in by ambulance. I dropped everything and ran out the door."

"The girl I met earlier? Oh, man. Is she all right?"

"Yes. Yes, Julie's fine. She's upstairs now, online—her favorite place to be."

"So what was the emergency?"

"She was in a surf rescue class—most kids around here take it in ninth grade. She hit her head and got caught in a riptide." A fresh wave of panic engulfed Camille as she pictured what could have happened.

"Thank God she's okay."

Camille nodded, hugging her knees to her chest. "I was so scared. I held myself together until . . . well, until you showed up. Lucky you, getting here just in time for my meltdown."

"You should have said something earlier. If I'd known you rushed off because you got a call about your kid, I wouldn't have been such a tool." He offered a half smile that made her heart skip a beat.

At least he acknowledged that he'd been a tool. "Well, thanks for that, Professor Finnemore."

"Call me Finn."

She took another sip of wine, eyeing him over the rim of her glass. "You look like a Finn."

"But not a Malcolm?"

"That's right. Malcolm is totally different."

He grinned, flashing charm across the space between them. "How's that?"

"Well, buttoned down. Academic. Bow tie and brown oxfords."

He laughed aloud then. "You reduced me to a cliché, then."

"Guilty as charged."

"Want to know how I pictured you?" Without waiting for an answer, he rested his elbow on the back of the sofa and turned toward her. "Long dark hair. Big dark eyes. Total knockout in a red striped shirt." He chuckled at her expression. "I checked out your website."

Oh. Her site featured a picture of her and Billy on the "about us" link. But a knockout? Had he really said *knockout*? He was probably disappointed now, because on this particular night, she didn't look anything like the woman in that photo.

"You look just like your photo," he said.

Wait. Was he coming on to her? No. No way. She should have looked at *his* website. Did history professors have websites?

She saw something flicker across his face, an expression she couldn't read.

"Go ahead," he said. "You can look me up on your phone. You know you want to."

She flushed, but did exactly that, tapping his name on the screen. The information that populated the web page surprised her. "According to these search results, you're a graduate of the U.S. Naval Academy and a former intelligence officer. You're now a professor of history at Annapolis, renowned for tracing the provenance of lost soldiers and restoring the memories to their families. You're an expert at analyzing old photos."

"Then we have something in common. If you ever come across something mysterious in a picture, I can take a look."

She couldn't decide if his self-confidence was sexy or annoying. In the "personal" section of the page, it was noted that he had been married to "award-winning journalist Emily Cutler" for ten years, and was now divorced. She didn't read that part aloud.

"I'm renowned? You don't say." He shifted closer to her and peered at the screen.

"I don't. Wikipedia says. Is it accurate?"

"More or less." He grinned. "I don't know about the 'renowned' part. I've never done anything of renown. Maybe choosing this exceptional wine. Cheers." He touched the rim of his glass to hers and took a sip. "So your father was in the business."

"He's an expert. Grew up in the south of France."

"Then we have something else in common. I've been working in France. Teaching at Aix-Marseille University in Aix-en-Provence."

"Papa was born in that area—a town called Bellerive. It's in the Var—do you know it?"

"No, but I've driven along the river Var, and down to the coast. It's fantastic, relatively unspoiled by tourists," he said. "Vineyards, lavender, and sunshine. Do you visit often?"

"I've never been."

"Seriously? You have to go. No one's life is complete until they've gone to the south of France."

She didn't want to discuss the matter with him. "Then I'll have to make sure I live for a very long time."

"I'll drink to that." He surveyed the tall glass case across the room. "You collect cameras?"

"I do. I started taking pictures as soon as I figured out what a camera was, and then I found an old Hasselblad at a flea market that turned out to be a treasure. I taught myself photography with it. That got me interested in the old ones."

Camille could not remember the first time she'd held a camera in her hands or the first time she'd peered through an eyepiece, but the passion she felt for taking pictures felt new every day. Her passion had died with Jace, and she hadn't photographed anything since. "I figured out how to restore a camera mostly by trial and error. Lots of error. Lots of late nights bent over a magnifying work lamp, but I love it. Billy's father worked in the film industry, developing daily rushes, and when we were kids, he showed us the old techniques and equipment to process expired film."

"So are those pictures your work?" He indicated the two unusual, angular shots of the Bethany Point Light.

"One of them is. I found some old, undeveloped film in a camera, which is pretty much my favorite thing, coaxing images back to life. That shot was taken during a storm in 1924, and I found it so striking that I replicated it myself." Then she blurted out, "I don't take pictures anymore. I work in the darkroom on other people's pictures."

Her gaze flicked to the vintage Leica in its glass case by the fireplace mantel. It had sat there for five years. No one but Camille remembered the last time she'd used that camera—to take a picture of her husband, moments before he died. She had put the camera away and never touched it again. There was still film in the Leica, a partially exposed roll she had shot that day. Even now, she couldn't bring herself to develop it.

Several beats of silence passed. She didn't know why she'd admitted that to this guy. Maybe because she missed it. She used to take pictures, wandering for hours on her travels, a favorite camera thumping against her sternum. She used to disappear into the act of capturing an image, exposing its secrets, freezing a moment. That was all in the past. These days she didn't go anywhere. She'd photographed Bethany Bay so many times she was numb to its charms and beauty.

"From what I can tell, you're really talented," he said. "Why'd you stop taking pictures?"

"Busy with other things, I suppose." She couldn't decide how much to elaborate, because she didn't really know what this was—a social call? An apology? "Mostly contract work in digitizing services."

"So you work with Billy Church—he's the guy who referred me to you?"

She wondered about the way he asked the question. Was he curious about whether or not she was available? No. Guys like him didn't wonder about the status of women like her.

"We're associates," she said. "We grew up together here in Bethany Bay. There's not a lot of money in doing this, so we both have day jobs. Billy is with the National Archives, and I'm the co-owner of a shop in town."

"You have a shop?"

She nodded. "My mom started a boutique years ago, and we're partners now." She noticed that he hadn't moved his arm from the back of the sofa. "I really wish I could have helped you today," she added.

"It was a long shot."

"I specialize in long shots." She eyed him, wishing fervently that she really *did* look more like her website photo instead of a worried mom whose day had unraveled. "Did you have an idea of what might be on the film?" She assumed it was something related to his work as a history professor.

He was quiet for a few moments. She started to feel awkward again. Should she not have asked?

He took a swallow of wine. "The initials on the film roll?"

"RAF," she said, recalling the writing on the yellow-and-black barrel. "Royal Air Force?"

"Richard Arthur Finnemore. My father."

"Oh. Old family photos?" She winced. In her experience, the most poignant projects were the personal ones. People brought her their mysterious canisters of found film, desperate for one last glimpse of a departed loved one, or an almost forgotten time of life. Restoring those memories gave her a sense of mission, even though, when she showed the results to the client, it often led to tears.

Finn set down his wineglass. He pressed the tips of his fingers together. He had good hands, strong hands, not the sort of soft, manicured hands she pictured for a university professor. "We think it was the last roll he shot before he was listed as missing in action in Cambodia."

She took a moment to digest this. "Missing . . . You mean he was fighting in the Vietnam War?"

"He wasn't fighting, but he was there with a strategy and comm team when he was captured. An intelligence officer and communications specialist."

"Didn't the war end in 1973?"

"The Paris peace ended the conflict in Vietnam that year. The cease-fire did not apply to Cambodia and Laos, so the losses there didn't stop. So my father . . . he never came back. And I never met him. My mom was pregnant with me when he left."

She set down her glass and turned slightly to look at him, seeing a different man than the angry stranger who had come blustering into her life this afternoon. What a horrible irony for a soldier to reach the end of a war, only to go missing while the others went home.

Now she realized it was probably no coincidence that Finn's specialty was finding lost soldiers. Yet he'd never found his own father. "It must have been a nightmare for your family. That's so sad. Finn, I'm sorry. Even more so now that you've told me the provenance of the roll." She tried to imagine what might have been on that film—the last images Richard Finnemore had shot. "Do you have any other undeveloped film? I mean, I've given you no reason to trust me, but if there's something else, anything, I'd be happy to help."

He shook his head. "That's it. My oldest sister found it in a box of his things that's been in storage for about forty years."

"Please tell your sister—and all your family—how sorry I am."

A text message appeared on his phone screen, and he glanced at it. "Speaking of family. That's my mom telling me to get a haircut tomorrow."

She wanted to tell him to keep the ponytail. It was wildly sexy. Instead, she asked, "What's the occasion?"

"My father's going to be awarded the Medal of Honor."

"The Medal of Honor. Isn't that—doesn't it have to be awarded by the president?"

He nodded. "It's a White House ceremony."

"That's amazing. Finn, what an honor for your family. And I hate myself all over again for letting you down. I wish I could say I'll make it up to you, but those pictures are lost."

He offered a fatalistic shrug. "When the ER calls about an emergency with your kid, you get to drop everything." Then he placed his hands on his knees. "I should probably get going. Big day for my family coming up."

She walked with him to his car, making sure he had his sunglasses. "Thanks again for the wine," she said.

"I'll call you," he said, turning toward her when they reached the car.

"What?"

"You know. On the phone."

"Why?"

"So we can make a plan."

"A plan?" Camille was talking like a monosyllabic idiot.

"We could go to dinner or something. I'm around for a few more days . . ."

"You mean, like a date?"

"Not *like* a date. Just a date."

Her heart flopped over in her chest. "Probably not a good idea."

"Are you seeing someone?"

"No, but—"

"Skittish, then?"

She smiled. "Right."

"That's okay. I'm a lot nicer than I was earlier today. I'll call you." He touched her arm. Not in a sexual way. Yet just that brief, casual touch ignited something in her that felt very sexual, taking her completely by surprise.

"Finn, don't call me, okay? Don't ask me on a date. I'm . . . I wouldn't be good company."

"How about you let me be the judge of that?"

"Don't call," she said again. "Sorry again about the film. Drive carefully."

Five

Ever since Camille's parents had divorced, she'd spent each Friday night having dinner with her father, unless he was away on business. What had started as a way to keep their relationship growing had turned into a cherished tradition—family time, even when they were just a family of two. Each Friday after school, she would go to her father's house and they would make dinner.

She and her father spoke French together. Henry and Cherisse had agreed from the start that Camille should learn both languages, and she had grown up seamlessly bilingual. The rest of their weekends together were spent tending his extensive garden, going to the shore when the weather was fine, or touring the sights of Washington, D.C. Together, she and Henry had visited each one of the Smithsonians, the National Zoo, all the monuments and parks and fountains. He took her to Paris for two weeks every summer, and they stayed at a homey little *pension* on rue Bachaumont. During the week, Papa would meet with wine vendors, and Camille would explore the fascinating city with her host family.

After Julie came along, she had only added to the fun. She and her grandfather—she called him Papi, like a French kid—had a special bond. The two of them lit each other up, and always had. Thanks to Henry, Julie now spoke excellent French. He read her all the books Camille remembered reading as a child—*Babar, Astérix, Le Petit Prince, Mon Petit Lapin*—and they laughed themselves silly over the

zany French movies he brought back from his travels. He was the
father figure Julie had lost, and he reveled in the role.

There were two rules of Friday-night dinner, and the rules never
varied. First, they had to speak French and listen to Papa's music selections. And second, they had to cook together at home. No sending
out for pizza or getting a corn dog at the Tastee-Freez.

The promise of summer lingered in the evening air when Camille
and Julie arrived for their weekly visit. They found Henry in the garden, gathering greens for the salad. His straw hat and gardening clogs
might have looked funny on anyone else, but on Camille's father, they
only made him seem more French.

"Ah," he said, setting down his basket. "There you are, my love-
lies." He gave them each a hug and three kisses, one on each side and
a third for good measure in the French way. "It's such a fine evening,
I thought we would have our aperitif on the patio. We can make socca
on the grill."

"Sounds perfect." Camille set down her bag, grateful to have
reached the end of a trying week. Socca was comfort food—a simple
flatbread made of chickpea flour baked on a grill with caramelized
onions and finished with flaky salt.

"I bet you're the only guy in town who owns a socca pan," Julie
said in French, taking down the flat copper pan that hung near the
outdoor grill.

He set it over the flame. "And you are the only young lady in town
who knows what socca is. I learned to make it by watching the street
vendors in Nice when I was about your age. I need a few snips of
rosemary."

Julie went to the flourishing bed of herbs to find it.

"What can I do?" Camille asked.

"Take the salad greens inside and give them a wash. And bring the
wine when you come. There's a bottle of Apollinaris for Julie."

She picked up the basket and headed inside. The kitchen smelled
amazing—something simmering in wine. Her father had bought the
historic colonial house the year he'd married her mother. Bearing a

historical plaque, it was a classic of architecture peculiar to the shore, once known as a "big house, little house, colonnade, and kitchen." The original dwelling had begun life centuries before as a simple home—the little house. As the family and fortune grew, the colonnade and kitchen were added, and finally the big house, a two-story structure with three lovely bedrooms upstairs. There was a porch set on an east–west axis to catch breezes from the shore.

Together, Henry and Cherisse had restored the place, staying faithful to the traditional style. But after Camille came along, the family didn't grow, and most of the rooms in the house sat empty. In the wake of the divorce, Camille had spent most of her childhood with her mom, stepdad, and two half sisters, setting aside Fridays for Papa.

Her mother had declared that she had enough of drafty rooms, creaky floors, and the like, and she and Bart moved to a modern townhome near the beach. It had been an unusual childhood for Camille, shuttling between Mom and Papa, but she'd always felt loved and supported. When her half sisters came along, she never felt like the odd one out. It was her normal. And it was a good normal, right up until she had lost Jace. After that, finding normal was impossible.

So she did what was possible. She took care of Julie, spent time with friends and family, worked at the shop, and rescued other people's pictures. It wasn't the life she'd once envisioned for herself, but it was the only one that made sense to her.

She placed the greens in the sink and turned on the water. The plumbing shuddered and groaned. A house this age was a constant repair project. More than once, she'd asked him why he needed such a big place.

"It's too much house for me," he readily agreed, "but I do love old things."

Camille did, too, and she was glad he'd kept it. Sometimes, though, she worried that the upkeep was getting to be too much for him. She didn't like to think of him all alone in his historic, too-large house, tending his garden and cooking beautiful meals for friends. Though he was retired, Henry often poured samples at the Grand

Crew Tasting Room on busy summer evenings. People loved him, with his quick, expert way of pouring and his in-depth knowledge of wine.

Camille liked knowing he got out every once in a while, especially now that his cancer had gone into remission. Still, she worried about what would happen to him when he grew too old to manage the big house.

When she was young, she expected her father to meet a woman and bring her home. She used to envision what it would be like to have a stepmother, which caused her some apprehension. As she grew older, she *wanted* him to find someone, the way her mom had found Bart, wearing her new happiness like a glistening mantle.

Henry was good-looking even now, at seventy-two. He was stylish and interesting . . . and so very French. He was also a master gardener and an excellent French country cook. He was creative and sure of himself, and totally resourceful. Sometimes when they worked in the kitchen side by side, he would give her a wink and say, "I would make someone a wonderful wife, eh?"

Every few years, she would ask him the same question. "Papa, why have you never remarried?"

After Jace died, her father had asked her the same question. "Why have *you* never remarried?"

That shut her down entirely. After that conversation, she never asked her father again why he went through life alone. Because now she understood. After Jace was gone, everyone had expected her to move on, including Camille herself. It hadn't happened. Five years later, there didn't seem to be room in her heart for anything but grief. It was the one constant in her life, and she knew there was a part of her—admittedly irrational—that didn't want to let go of her grief, because that would mean losing him completely. Holding on to sadness kept him from fading away forever. She knew—on an intellectual level—that this was not the healthiest way to grieve. She'd gone to months of therapy to arrive at that realization. Yet knowing this hadn't helped her move on. She had never remarried because she'd come to believe that no love was worth the pain of loss.

After emerging from the fog of shock and grief, she had put together a life for herself and her daughter that made sense—most of the time. Except for those moments when she felt so lonely that her heart felt like a bottomless well.

Her dating life was mostly ridiculous. Her relationships had been short—mercifully short—until Drake Larson. She'd stuck with him for six months before admitting defeat.

People said she was attractive. She had her father's dark hair and eyes, and her mother's dramatic cheekbones and full lips. But when she looked in the mirror, she didn't see a beautiful woman. She saw a woman who worried constantly, who lived inside a sadness she couldn't manage to climb out of, and who regretted how daring and incautious she had once been, long ago.

Perhaps in matters of the heart, she took after her father. Perhaps she was only meant to have one shot at marriage.

She spun the greens in the colander, at the same time trying to shake off a wave of melancholy and the residue of a rotten week— Julie's accident, and ruining Professor Finnemore's film. Then she found the wine and sparkling water, and brought a tray outside.

"The garden looks wonderful this year," she said, surveying the oblong patch on the south side of the house.

"I put in two more rows of tomatoes this week," he said, pointing out the staked plants on the end. "Brandywine and Belgian Giant. One can never have enough homegrown tomatoes, eh?"

"Exactly. Yours are the best, Papa."

"Come, let's sit," he said, gesturing at a small café table on the brickwork patio. The socca was done, crunchy around the edges and fragrant with the onions and herbs. He poured a chilled rosé wine from Provence, the traditional pairing with socca, and sparkling water for Julie.

"Santé," they said together, lifting their glasses.

"Any day aboveground is a good day," her father declared.

"I've never been fond of that one," Camille said. "So grim."

"After my year in hell," he told them, "it has never been truer. Now that the treatment is done, I am determined to live my life."

His diagnosis had been a devastating blow. The ensuing chemo and radiation had been grueling, but the goal had been attained—the cancer was in remission. A year ago, when he was in the throes of his illness and treatment, Camille had wanted to move in with Julie to help him through the ordeal, but he wouldn't hear of it. He valued his privacy and independence too much.

He insisted that they keep their regular Friday schedule. Often, during that terrible time, Camille and Julie prepared a croque monsieur or an omelet with pesto and spinach while Henry lay shivering under a woolen blanket. For Julie's sake, Camille tried not to show how sick with worry or how terrified she was of losing her father. They got through it with stubborn determination, and the help of a caregiver named Lamont Jeffries. Lamont had stayed with Henry while he was ill. He'd proven to be invaluable, keeping the household and garden running, looking after Henry, and taking care of all the painful indignities of cancer treatment. He still came around every week to visit and to do a bit of housekeeping and gardening.

Henry went to shut down the grill, moving with cautious deliberation, a leftover from his disease and treatment. Before the illness, he'd been gloriously youthful—as slender and fit as a man ten years younger, his abundant hair peppered with a distinguished sprinkling of white. After the chemo, his hair had grown back a dramatic snow white. He was still as handsome as ever, though he was no longer the spry, robust man she remembered. There was something fragile about him.

"How are you feeling?" Camille asked.

"I'm well," he said with a satisfied smile. "I feel well. Have you ever studied the term 'in remission'? In French, it is the same. It means an abatement of symptoms, but also, forgiveness."

"That's good, Papi. I'm glad you feel good again," Julie said.

"I always feel best when I am with you, *choupette*," he told her, putting their glasses on the tray. "You are the most beautiful part of my week."

Julie offered the special smile she seemed to reserve just for him.

"What a fantastic evening," he said. "Julie, I miss seeing your friends. Where have they been lately? You used to bring a friend or two over."

She stared at the ground, scuffing her foot at the brickwork. "Busy, I guess."

"You must tell them to come around more often now that the summer weather is here."

Her shoulders hunched up slightly. "Sure."

"Madeline's ducklings will hatch next week," he said, gesturing at the wire enclosure in a corner of the yard. "Bring your friends around to see the babies."

"All right. Maybe. Let's go inside to dinner." She picked up the tray, and they went to the kitchen together.

"I'm pretty sure that incredible smell is bouillabaisse," Camille said.

"You are correct. The seafood from the local docks was excellent this week."

"What's the occasion?"

"Every time I sit down with my two lovely ladies is a special occasion."

Julie plunked herself down on the sofa and took out her phone.

"What do you look at, so fixated on that small screen?" he asked.

Julie shrugged without looking up. "There's a whole world in here. That's why it's called the World Wide Web."

"The world is out there," he said, gesturing at the view out the window. "I am an old man, but I do know the difference."

"I've known that world all my life and I'm bored with it."

"Put the phone away," said Camille. "Screens off during mealtime."

"I know. I know."

Camille, too, wondered what Julie studied with such absorption in that small rectangle of light. There were new apps and games all the time, and her daughter was a known techno-wizard. No wonder real life seemed boring. In the screen world, all a person had to do was watch. Participation was optional—the screen created a shield or barrier. You could observe things at a safe distance. If your world inhabited a tiny screen, you didn't have to be scared or out of control. You didn't have to deal with the real world around you.

"How can we help?" she asked her father.

"You can toss the salad and lay the table. I will show Julie how to make the rouille." The two of them made a spicy mayonnaise of olive oil, garlic, saffron, and cayenne pepper, spreading it on slices of grilled bread to float in the fish stew. Then he ladled the fragrant broth and fish onto soup plates, topping them with the bread slices.

Camille sighed with pleasure over the dinner of casual elegance. The broth was made of fresh tomatoes and olive oil, fennel, and onions, bright with saffron. "Papa, you're the best. This is delicious."

"The secret is to wash the fish in seawater," he told them. "When I first came to America, I worked at a restaurant in Cape May, and every Friday night, my job was to wash the fish. It was a good restaurant, but the wine list was pathetic."

"Is that when you decided to become a wine importer?" Julie asked.

"Yes, but it took some time. I was very young and quite ignorant. But I studied my craft and worked very hard, and founded my little enterprise."

"Did you grow up liking wine?" she asked. "Because I can't make myself like it."

"Ah. You will, eventually. You're the granddaughter of a Frenchman. You have no choice."

She grinned. "Got it."

They finished off the meal with the salad. Henry pressed the palms of his hands to the table and pushed back. "Tonight, I'm glad it's just the three of us here," he said. "There is something to discuss."

Camille's stomach clenched. Was there a dire note in his tone of voice? Was his latest checkup not a good one? "Is everything all right?"

"Yes. Stop worrying. You worry far too much. I have something to show you," he said. "I had a special delivery today."

He led the way to the front room, with its fireplace and grand bay window projecting out over the laurel hedge. It was decorated in a spare, chic style that somehow worked with the architecture of the rustic old house. Over the mantel was a painting Camille had always admired, depicting a region in the south of France called the Calanques—the towering, rocky inlets along the coast of the deep blue Mediterranean. The painter had managed to capture the deep, golden quality of light Camille had always associated with Provence, even though she'd never been there. What had Finn said? *No one's life is complete until they've gone to the south of France.* Camille had to admit that loneliness did make her life feel incomplete, but going to Provence wasn't the answer.

In the middle of the room was a large cardboard shipping crate plastered with customs forms.

"What's this?" she asked her father.

"It arrived late this afternoon from France. Madame Olivier had it shipped to me."

"Wait. What?" Camille was confused. "Who is Madame Olivier, and why is she sending you something?"

"She lives at Sauveterre—my family home in Bellerive. It's an ancient house, and a section of the roof caved in. While clearing the attic for the renovation, she came across a trunk full of my mother's old belongings, and she thought I might like to have it."

Julie's face lit up. "Your mother, Lisette?"

"Yes, that was her name. Lisette Galli Palomar." He offered a gentle smile. "I never knew her."

"It's so sad that she died when you were a baby," Julie said.

"It is. I was an orphan mere hours after I was born."

"And your father? You never talk about him," Julie said.

Camille held her breath. Long ago, Papa had told her in the vaguest of terms that his father had died before he was born, but when she'd pressed for details, he'd simply said he knew virtually nothing about the situation. He never said much at all about his early life in the small village in the south of France. He'd left at the age of eighteen to make a life for himself in America.

"I never knew him either," he told Julie. "My father was killed at the very end of the war in Europe."

"He was killed in the war, then? He was a soldier?"

"He was in fact the *maire* of the town of Bellerive."

"You never told me he was the mayor," Camille said.

"So what's in the trunk?" Julie asked.

"I have not opened it yet. I have been waiting for you."

"Oh my God, I can't believe you waited. Let's open it." Julie was all over the trunk. She and Camille tipped the cardboard crate on its side and slid the trunk out onto the floor. It was old and battered, the kind of thing people stored in the attic or basement and then forgot. "Is it locked? How does it open?"

He held out a letter in shaky handwriting. "Madame says the key was long lost. We'll have to break in like thieves."

"Cool." Julie was all over that, too.

Camille stood back, deeply intrigued. It was the same feeling she had in the darkroom the moment an image came to light. Anticipation. Discovery. A twinge of fear.

They cut the rusty lock in the center of the lid, then pried open the latches on the side. The lid was stuck, and it took the three of them and several sprays of lubricant to get it open. Finally, the lid yielded with a rusty grind of hinges.

The smell of dust and age and dried lavender filled the air. The trunk was lined with peeling paper, raining dry flakes onto the floor. There was a tray in the top section, which was filled with a collection of the ordinary and the prosaic—yellowed linens, hand-embroidered with floral sprigs and edged with lace, wrapped around a matching vanity set of a hand mirror, comb, and brush.

Julie took each item out and set it aside. "Papi, do you recognize any of this stuff?"

"No." Henry shut his eyes. "That scent—the lavender. It takes me back. My aunt Rotrude used to sprinkle the linens with lavender water as she was ironing them."

"Rotrude? That's a weird name," said Julie.

"She was my father's sister. She's the one who raised me at Sauveterre. By the end of the war, it was just the three of us—Rotrude, her daughter Petra, and myself."

Through the years, he'd given Camille only snippets of his boyhood. His aunt, he'd said, was not a pleasant person. His cousin Petra was ten years older than he was, and after he left France, they had lost touch. Both women were long gone by now.

They went through the items one by one—old clothing, books and maps, a few tools, French magazines from the 1940s, a handmade knife from Opinel. Camille studied a cloth badge of some sort. It was a torch with wings, frayed at the edges as if it had been sewn to something else. There were three ancient volumes of Sherlock Holmes stories in English.

"Did someone speak English in the house where you grew up?" Julie asked.

"No," said Henry. He opened one of the books, and there was a frontispiece that said *From the Library of Cyprian Toselli.* "I don't recognize that name," he said, and put the books aside. He pulled out a yellowed wall calendar from 1945 and studied the image at the top. It appeared to be a colorized photo. "Here is the town where I grew up. Here is Bellerive."

Camille and Julie moved in close. The top of the calendar depicted a pretty hill town that appeared medieval in character. Crowning the hill was a church rising from the middle, like the center of a flower, its roof of overlapping slate surrounding a grand steeple. The tiny streets spiraled downward to a cliff-topped shore where the river flowed into the sea. It was a typical wide-angle shot, and the hand-coloring romanticized the seascape and sky, giving it a dreamy look.

While Camille and her father gazed at the calendar image, Julie summoned up present-day images on her phone. The town appeared as charming and bucolic in the present as it had in the past, tucked amid the craggy, sun-drenched landscape of the Var. "It looks almost the same," she said. "When was the last time you went there, Papi?"

"I left the village in 1963," he said.

"And you never went back," Camille said. He'd never had much to say about his early life, offering her only the sketchiest of details. "That's . . . wow. Did you ever feel like visiting?"

"No. Sometimes I miss the countryside, the food and the pace of life. At my age, I am feeling nostalgic, perhaps."

"Check it out," Julie said, brandishing an oversized envelope. On the front someone had scrawled, *photos—Henri Palomar.* As she undid the envelope clasp, she said, "Wasn't that your name before?"

He nodded. "I prefer the American version—Henry Palmer." Then he frowned at the envelope. "That is Rotrude's handwriting."

Julie took out the photos, and her eyes lit up. "Pictures of you, Papi!"

Camille leaned forward, as fascinated as Julie. He had come to America with almost nothing, least of all pictures and memorabilia from the past. The oldest one was dated 1948. It showed a little boy with huge eyes and a mop of curly dark hair, framing a face that was oblong, with high cheekbones, an adorable nose, and unsmiling lips. He stood beside a teenage girl in a school uniform, her hair in two blond braids.

"That would be my cousin Petra," he said.

"Look how cute you were," Julie said.

"But so serious," Camille said, studying the shot. In her work, she was trained to inspect a photograph with a detective's eye. What was happening the moment the camera's aperture blinked open? Henri had a chastened look, his lips soft, his lash-fringed eyes vaguely ashamed, as if he'd just been caught doing something wrong. His shoulders were slightly hunched, his hands were in the pockets of his dungarees, and there was a small bit of space between him and the girl beside him, as if they were loath to touch each other.

"I can see a bit of Julie in this sweet little boy," Camille said. They both shared a certain vulnerable look, maybe because they had both been hurt by the world at a tender age. She scanned the background of the picture—a pitted stone wall, some straggling plants, a broken gate, and a large building. She wondered what Finn would make of it. Then she chided herself for letting her mind wander to Finn.

There were only three more photos. She wished there were more. Did no one care to take pictures of this lovely little boy?

A school photo showed a grinning Henri, a missing front tooth indicating he was probably six or seven. Then there was a picture of him in a long robe, walking in a line of similarly garbed boys and girls.

"Graduation?" Julie asked.

"Church confirmation," he said. "It was a big deal back then."

Camille noticed a shadow under one eye, and the lid was puffy. "Looks like you were in a fight."

"Does it?" He shrugged. "I don't recall." His mouth twitched slightly, and he passed a finger over the somber, wounded face of the boy in the processional. Camille wondered what memories the photo sparked.

"There's one more," said Julie, studying a picture of a heavyset boy standing in front of the same broken wall. "Is this you, Papi? It doesn't really look like you."

He glanced at the yellowed print. "Yes, that is me. I was probably about your age, or perhaps a year or two older."

In that final photo, he looked like a different child. His clothes were ill-fitting, his haircut terrible, and there was a distant look in his eyes. He appeared extremely uncomfortable—and overweight. Camille had only ever known her father to be slender and quite ridiculously handsome.

He smiled at Julie as if reading her mind. "I went through a chubby phase. This was when I was known as Bouboule."

"What's that mean?" she asked.

"Tubby. Butterball."

Julie stared at the boy in the picture. "I've heard worse." Then she picked up a thick cardboard folder bound with twine. On the front was a label that read *Lisette*. "What do you suppose is in this?" She untied the string and peeked inside. "More photos! Maybe these are pictures of your mother," she said, taking out the large collection.

The photographs depicted a small town and countryside. There were close-ups of random objects and landscapes of farms, hills, and a river to the sea, fishing boats, faces, open-air markets, stone-built sheds and huts, scenes of daily life.

Camille was struck by the quality of the pictures. Unlike the snapshots of her father, these compositions were sophisticated, the images crystal clear and expertly developed. "These are seriously good," she said. "Do you know who took them?"

He shook his head again. "I don't recall anyone taking photos. Perhaps Lisette collected them."

"They're pretty wonderful. Someone had a good eye and a good camera." The backs of the photos were unlabeled and undated. She carefully placed the photos back in the pleated folder. "I'd like to study these further."

"Of course," her father said.

They continued sorting through the contents of the trunk and came across a sketchbook of pen-and-ink drawings. The sketches were simple, but showed maturity and control, probably not the work of a child. They depicted a variety of country scenes—an old stone farmhouse, fields and pastures, stone walls and rocky meadows.

"Your artwork?" Camille asked.

"No. I don't remember these drawings. Look how old the paper is. It's practically falling apart. And here—more photographs." He took a collection from a pocket in the back of the sketchbook. They appeared to be pictures from which the drawings were rendered.

"I think these were taken by the same photographer as the ones in the Lisette folder," Camille said. "They're in the same style."

"Do you think these are pictures of a real place?" Julie asked.

"Certainly. This is Sauveterre—our farm near Bellerive. Sauveterre means 'Safe Haven' in English. It's a type of farm called a *mas*, very common in that part of the world. It was my home until I came to America."

"It's beautiful," Camille said, laying the photos in a row on the coffee table.

"A typical *mas* is a whole community unto itself, almost entirely self-sustaining. Everything the family needed was produced right there—crops, dairy, meat, grapes, olives . . . There was a winepress we used for making wine from our own grapes."

"That's so cool," Julie said. "Do you think it's still there?"

"I know that it is, though apparently the main house is in dire need of repairs. The Oliviers have occupied it on lease ever since I left."

Camille frowned. "On lease? From your cousin?"

He shook his head. "From me."

She heard the words, but they didn't seem real to her. "Wait a second. You're saying you own a farm in France."

"I have the official deeds filed away in a safe-deposit box."

She stared at the pictures. "You still own this place. Why didn't you ever tell me about it?"

"I rarely think of it. Sauveterre belongs to me in name only, because truly, the Oliviers have a ninety-nine-year lease on the place. The rent provides only a modest income, just enough to cover the taxes and upkeep. Although with the roof caving in, I suspect it'll run into some expense."

"But you *own* it." Camille was amazed.

"The property has been in the Palomar family for generations, and upon the death of my father, it was placed in trust for me until I reached the age of eighteen." He passed his hand over a detailed panorama of the *mas* in the sketchbook. "Sauveterre will be yours one day."

"Whoa," Julie said. "That's awesome—a farm in France. Papi, why didn't you want to live there? Why did you come to America? And why don't you ever go back for a visit?"

"All these questions. It is as if I suddenly matter," he added in a teasing voice.

Julie grabbed his hand. "You've always mattered. And I think you're awesome. This whole trunk thing is awesome. It's like figuring out a puzzle about you, Papi."

It was the first glimmer of enthusiasm Camille had seen from Julie in ages. And it wasn't a mere glimmer, but an actual spark. Julie seemed to love the old things, even mundane objects like a pair of sewing scissors and a cap with a feather in it, a fountain pen and inkwell crusted with old turquoise ink.

Camille spotted something tucked into the pages of one of the Sherlock Holmes books—not a bookmark but a prayer card, about the size of a playing card, depicting the head of Christ. It was a familiar image, a portrait with an incandescent glow around the face and flowing hair. She knew she'd seen it somewhere before. She turned it over, and was surprised to see a printed prayer in English, not French, and *Chicago Offset Printing Company* in tiny letters at the bottom. Next to that: *Distributed by the USO.*

On the edge of the card was a handwritten phrase, but the ink was so faded she couldn't decipher it. She put the card aside to research later.

Then something else in the trunk caught her eye. Bending down, she moved aside a folded linen doily and a pair of dusty women's shoes. Under these lay a dark-colored oblong case or box of some sort, about the size of a shoe box, its lid held in place with tarnished buckle latches. The box was not ostentatious but homely, the textured faux-leather board filled with creases of dust. On the top of the box was a symbol that tweaked her memory. A stylized letter *E* with a curlicue flourish next to a lightning bolt. Where had she seen that before?

A slight ripple of awareness skimmed over her. It was like the feeling she sometimes experienced when she was working on an old picture and realized she was on the verge of a major find.

"Papa," she said, her voice barely above a whisper as she handled the case. It felt substantial in her hands. "Do you recognize this?"

He gave a Gallic shrug. "Open it."

She set the box across her knees and passed her hand over the lid. It rattled softly. Its weight was substantial. Attached was a small brass plate with the letters *CT* pressed into it.

"Someone's initials?" she asked.

"Not that I know of," he said. And then, "Ah. That name is in the front of these books." He indicated the Sherlock Holmes set. "Cyprian Toselli. I have no idea who that might be."

"Mom, what's in the box?" Julie bounced up and down, acting like her younger self. It was refreshing to see her showing something besides attitude.

"Let's find out." She released the latches, lifted the lid, and moved a moleskin cloth aside.

"It's a camera," Julie said. "Cool. Looks really old."

Camille was amazed. "It's an Exakta. I've never seen one this old before." She picked it up, turned it over in her hands. Then she looked at her father.

He held out his hands, palms up. "Monsieur C.T.?" Then he rubbed his jaw, looking at the camera. "Or perhaps my mother was fond of taking pictures." He offered a wistful smile. "Maybe that is where you get your talent in photography." He leaned back, watching as Camille inspected the remarkable find. "My mother has always been a great mystery to me. I wish I had known her."

Camille set aside the camera and reached for his hand. "I wish you'd known her, too, Papa. I wish we all had. It's so sad."

"Way to ruin the mood, Mom," Julie said. "We were all excited about the camera."

"Right." Camille picked it up again. "We have a mystery right here. What I know about Exakta cameras is that they were made in Germany, and they're very fine instruments—the first single-lens reflex. I think this model is from the 1930s. I can tell from this socket—it's for the first built-in flash synchronization." She inspected the pristine camera. "Wow. This could be a museum piece. It's a rare find."

"Well. I must write to Madame Olivier and thank her for this box of wonders," said her father.

"*Ça alors,*" Camille said, touching the film winder with her thumb. She felt the slightest bit of resistance.

"What is it?" Julie leaned forward to see.

"I think there's film in this camera."

Six

✢

*f*inn had attended a good number of ceremonies in his lifetime. After his father had gone missing in Cambodia, his mother had become an activist for the missing, and Finn had many early memories of somber ceremonies to acknowledge those few times when the truth about some poor guy's demise came out.

Later, as his mom had advanced through the ranks of the Diplomatic Corps, ultimately attaining an ambassadorship when Finn was twelve, there had been ceremonies to commemorate, decorate, and designate, all crammed with pomp and circumstance. As he went through high school, there were more—his appointment to the Model UN, Boys State, honor society. Eagle freaking Scout.

There had been induction ceremonies when he and his two sisters had enrolled in the Naval Academy. And then the appointment ceremonies when they had finished. His change-of-command ceremony as a naval officer.

And then there had been his marriage ceremony. It was supposed to be the start of his happily-ever-after. He had nailed the happy part for a good long time. Unfortunately for him, when it came to ever after, he and Emily had different ideas.

"I'm pregnant," she had said on the day of their ten-year anniversary. She was sobbing as she told him.

And then, before his heart had a chance to soar with wonder and joy, she'd dropped a hasty bomb: "It's not yours."

"Perfect," said a woman's voice behind him, drawing Finn back from that painful memory.

He turned to see a gorgeous redhead in a tight navy dress, with a White House press pool badge clipped to her collar. Ever so briefly, she touched the tip of her tongue to her upper lip.

"How's that?" he asked, though he knew exactly how it was. "What part of this is perfect? The part where I get to meet the president because my father went missing?"

"Don't be nasty," she said. "I meant you in your dress uniform. You look absolutely perfect. I imagine you haven't worn it in a while. How are you?"

"I'm fine." He studied her for a moment. "How about you, Emily?"

"Also fine. Busy. I love it, though. No such thing as a slow news day around here."

Finn's ex-wife was an award-winning journalist. In fact, her biggest award had been the Richard Arthur Finnemore prize for war correspondence. The prize, named to commemorate Finn's father, honored each year's outstanding achievement in reporting on global conflicts. That year, they had still been married, and Finn used to tell people, "Emily won the trophy, but I walked away with the real prize." She turned out to be not such a prize after all.

He looked at her now, and felt nothing but a mild twinge of familiarity. It was strange, the way a love that had once filled a person up could simply vanish like a cloud in a breeze. Where did those feelings go? Maybe they dissolved into the ether or morphed into something useful: Wisdom. Life experience. Determination to avoid getting his heart tangled up again.

He knew that cutting himself off emotionally was probably not the best way to deal with the damage she'd done. Knowing this and actually doing something about it were two different things.

"Hold still," Emily said. "You're not quite perfect." With practiced movements, she reached up and brushed the back of his collar. "You have a fresh haircut."

"Guilty as charged. An hour ago, I had a ponytail."

She offered a wistful smile. "Our lives are so different now. How is France?"

He could go on about the sun and the food, the history, the people, the scenery. The wine. He didn't, though. "It's great," was all he said. "And congrats to you for landing this gig. I know you worked hard to get here." He was able to say this without a tinge of irony. When he first found out about the affair, Finn had been ready to rip the guy's head off. Now he was philosophical about it. Emily's affair had shown Finn exactly what her priorities were. And they'd shown him exactly what he needed to avoid if he was ever stupid enough to fall in love again.

He surveyed the East Room of the White House, where today's event would take place. Everyone in the family was here, along with friends and colleagues who had known his father, including the four survivors whose lives Richard Finnemore had saved by surrendering to the enemy. Next to the podium stood an easel with a large, framed portrait of his father, also in full dress uniform—a stranger Finn had never known.

"I can't get over how much you look like him," Emily said.

Finn studied the portrait, trying to find himself in the face of the man who had disappeared. Sometimes he saw the resemblance— something about the jawline, maybe, and definitely the eyes. I wish I'd known you, he thought, offering a brief salute. He'd searched for his father in old photo albums and a few reels of ancient Super 8 home movies. Richard always seemed to be wearing a smile. People said he was a man who loved his life, his family, and his country. All his life, Finn had tried to emulate those values. But when his marriage fell apart, he'd come to realize he wasn't going to accomplish that on his own.

A ripple went through the assembly, and everyone was directed to take a seat. Finn and his sisters were ushered to the front with his mother. She reached over and patted his knee briefly. He knew she would get emotional today. They all would.

A buzz of energy heralded the arrival of the president. Everyone rose, and then a hush settled over the audience as they took their seats. The president greeted everyone, adding a personal welcome to the families of the three men being honored today. Finn almost didn't recognize his own name when she addressed him as Lieutenant Commander Malcolm Arthur Finnemore. It had been so long since he'd answered to that name. Another life, for sure.

The president gave an eloquent summary of the heroic actions of the four honorees, all of them being honored posthumously. Her voice wavered as she spoke of the stark reality of the ceremony—that the valor they were gathered to celebrate, the courage and selflessness, stemmed from the most dreadful moments of war, claiming the ultimate sacrifice.

"On his very worst day, each one of these men managed to summon his very best. Each one embodied the essence of courage. It is not the state of being unafraid, but the rare ability to confront fear. These heroes showed guts, they showed their training, and they put it all on the line for their fellow soldiers. We are free because of these men."

Finn's mother received the Medal of Honor in a glass-front box. The expected tears came, particularly in the aftermath, when the surviving teammates from Cambodia gathered around. Some of them remembered Richard Finnemore with photographic clarity. In a moment of decision no man should have to make, Richard had snapped a final photo, dropped his gear, and surrendered, somehow distracting his captors long enough for his team to escape. One man's freedom, his life, in exchange for four others.

With a giant lump in his throat, Finn walked over to the freestanding photo display on one side of the podium. It had been created for the ceremony, a collage of smiling brave soldiers in the prime of life. Some of the pictures chronicled his father's career, from Naval Academy graduate to combat strategist and communications specialist, reporting on the conflict in Vietnam, Laos, and Cambodia.

Finn wondered what might have shown up on the film roll he'd entrusted to Camille Adams. Stark images of war-torn villages? Recon photos? Pictures of his teammates on the mission? Damn, he wished he could have seen them.

Yet he couldn't get mad at her, given the circumstances of the mishap. That was the reason he gave himself. But the real reason he couldn't get mad at her was that he'd never met anyone like her before. After a rocky start, he'd found himself relaxing with her, listening and talking in a way that felt completely right. So often with women, there was that unspoken tension—will we or won't we? Yet with Camille, the tension felt different, spun of warmth and attraction, not uncertainty.

There was a part of him that wanted to get to know her better, and that was strange, because after the ego-crushing experience with Emily, he'd turned into a player, pursuing women who weren't complicated, who didn't make emotional demands, who could be satisfied with a physical relationship. This had been working for him for a long time. But instinct told him it wouldn't work with Camille Adams.

No matter. He was heading back to work in France, and her life was here in the States, raising a teenager, running her business, doing whatever it was she did in the utterly pleasant, remote beach town where she lived.

Despite knowing their paths were not likely to cross again, he briefly toyed with the idea of contacting her once more, despite her insistence that she wasn't open to seeing him again. He was arrogant enough to think he could persuade her. Let's get a drink. Go out together. But no. What would be the point? It would likely make the inevitable parting more frustrating.

But oh, man. She sparked something in him. He wasn't sure why. She lingered in his mind, reminding him that there was more to life than hooking up and getting laid. He had never felt anything like this, not even with Emily.

Camille didn't want him to call. He shouldn't call. But when had "shouldn't" ever stopped him? Bad idea, he reminded himself. One thing Finn was good at was knowing when to walk away. When to leave well enough alone.

This was one of those times. Yes, Camille Adams was intriguing and beautiful and there were undiscovered layers he longed to explore. Since his divorce, he'd walled himself off from the kind of feelings she inspired. But her soft eyes and soft lips, the way she lit up when she talked about her daughter and her work—those things exposed vulnerable cracks in his wall. No. Finn shored up his defenses. He was not going to do a long-distance anything.

The beauteous, sad, worried photography expert would stay where he'd left her—a missed connection.

And so, when his phone vibrated against his heart to signal a message, he was blown away to see the name of the sender—Camille Adams. Camille "Don't Call Me" Adams. Camille "I'm in a Bad Place" Adams.

Camille "I Don't Even Know How Sexy I Am" Adams.

"I wonder if I did the right thing," Camille said to her mother and half sister Britt. "Maybe I shouldn't have sent him that text message about the pictures I found in Papa's old camera."

The three of them sat together at Brew-La-La. They met here every Monday morning for coffee, a business meeting, and girl talk.

Sometimes they were joined by Hilda, the younger daughter of Cherisse and Bart. Hilda was still in college, currently doing a semester abroad in Cape Town.

The shop specialized in local snacks—Kaiserschmarrn with macerated berries, breakfast croissants filled with scrapple, Taylor ham sandwiches for the visitors from Jersey. Camille always opted for a tartine with butter and strawberry freezer jam.

"Why are you wondering?" asked Britt. "Because you think he might still be upset at you for ruining his film? Or because he's hot and single?" She turned her laptop screen toward them on the table. "I mean. Look at him."

The pictures were on the *Washington Post* website, accompanying a piece about the Medal of Honor ceremony.

"I'm looking." Camille's cheeks felt warm. She thought far too much about Finn. She told herself he was the embodiment of a bad idea—too handsome, too cocky, too . . . everything. "He really looks different with short hair."

"But no less hot," said Britt.

Their mom scrolled to a shot of Finn's mother accepting the flat presentation box from the president. "He had a remarkable father, didn't he? Gave himself up to save his team and was never seen again."

"The pictures I ruined could have been a clue about what happened," Camille said.

"Stop it," her mother scolded. "It's unfortunate, but it's done. No point in beating yourself up about it."

"You're right. Still, I feel weird asking him for advice about Lisette's pictures. The film we found in that old camera at Papa's dates back to 1945. I was able to process it with no trouble at all. And yet I decimated the last roll Finn's father ever shot."

"It happens," her mother said.

"He was disappointed. That's even worse than him being mad. I hate disappointing people."

"You should go out with him and pick up the tab to say you're sorry," Britt suggested, still gazing at her screen. "He's gorgeous. Annapolis grad. Professor. What's not to like?"

"The fact that he lives thirty-five hundred miles away," Camille reminded her.

Britt sighed. "Well, there's that."

"I've decided not to date anyone for a while," Camille told them. "Drake was really good to me, but it just didn't work. It's like something in me is broken."

"Nonsense." Her mother rubbed her shoulder. "There is nothing wrong with you. Nothing broken. Breakups are always hard. Don't you dare give up hope."

"I'm not giving up hope. I'm giving up men."

"Let me see the pictures again," said her mother. "I'm just so fascinated."

Camille opened a screen on her own laptop and they looked together at the seventy-year-old photos. There were eight images in all.

They studied each one—a town, a broken bridge, the rubble of a building, a glade by a stream, a gaunt man, his face turned away from the camera, his shoulders hunched with hopelessness. The final image was the most startling of all—a stunningly beautiful woman in the late stages of pregnancy. She faced a tall cheval-glass mirror with the camera held against her distended belly.

It was a self-portrait of Lisette. She looked ethereal, like a fairy. Although the photo was in black and white, it was clear that her hair was blond.

"I have so many questions," Camille said. "Papa could only tell me so much about the shots, because they were all taken before he was born. Obviously. I thought if I showed them to Finn, he could tell me how to find out more."

"Then you should definitely show him," Britt said. "But be honest. You could contact any number of experts, and yet you thought of him."

"He's the only expert I know on postwar France," Camille protested. Flustered, she changed the subject. "Mom, did Papa ever talk about Sauveterre?"

Cherisse shook her head. "Not so much. I knew of the family property. He said there was a tenant with a long-term lease, and we never really discussed it further."

"How do you not discuss something like that with your husband?" asked Britt. "If Wylie kept something like that from me, I'd wonder what else he was hiding."·

Cherisse sighed. "Henry didn't keep it from me. He had so little to say about it. On one of our trips to France for business, I suggested a visit to Bellerive, but he looked at me like I was crazy. Said it would be a total waste of time—a tiny village in the Var. He said we'd be totally bored." She sighed again. "Your father is a singular man. Intensely private. His heart was always a mystery to me. I was young and naive enough to believe we'd grow closer as time went on, but instead we grew apart. I don't believe I ever really knew him."

"He's not a mystery," Camille said. "He's just . . . Papa." She gazed at Lisette's picture. "And he had a mother he never knew. She looks so sad. It makes *me* sad to know she never got to see her son grow up."

"It's awful that he was born an orphan," Britt said. "Did it mess with his head to be raised by his aunt?"

"He told Julie and me that his aunt Rotrude wasn't kind," Camille said. "She resented him because she was a war widow with a child of her own, and Papa—her baby nephew—was the legal owner of Sauveterre. When he turned eighteen, they could no longer afford to pay the taxes, so he leased the place out to a family called the Oliviers, and Rotrude had to move out. Papa came to America, and he never went back."

Cherisse signaled the barista for another round of coffee. "All right, ladies. Let's get down to business. Summer is right around the corner. Summer hours at the shop start next week. It's going to be our best season yet."

Camille knew her mother wasn't exaggerating. Business was thriving at Ooh-La-La, thanks to the bustle of sun-seeking tourists, well-heeled locals, and power brokers from D.C. stealing away for the weekend. The wealthy come-heres had built luxurious summer places amid the courthouse towns and fishing villages of the peninsula. Camille had grown up observing their ways. They had always seemed like a breed apart, driving their European cars along the Chesapeake Bay Bridge or the over-and-underwater highway crossing of the Hampton Roads, where aircraft carriers and nuclear submarines were nearly as common as skipjack watermen dredging for oysters while under sail.

The merchants and restaurateurs of Bethany Bay were all too happy to cater to the expensive needs of folks from Philadelphia and New York, offering sailing trips and shore dinners, fishing charters, and luxury home goods from the boutique.

"We got another mention in *Time Out*," Britt said, showing them the item on her tablet screen. "'Despite its quirky name, there is something magical about Ooh-La-La, with its irresistible fusion of French country charm, sleek modern design, and local offerings.'"

"I'd change that quirky name if I could," her mother said. "But it stuck, and we're stuck with it. I came up with Ooh-La-La back when I was a silly girl."

"You're still a silly girl," said Britt. "You'll always be a silly girl."

"Keeps me young. Okay, let's focus. We need to make sure we have the go-to items. We want people to come in to browse around, and leave with something they can't live without. The question is, what exactly is that something?"

"I think it's going to be the glug jug again," Britt said. "I know it's nothing new, but they've got all those yummy fresh colors." The pitchers, shaped like stylized swans and fish, made a distinctive gurgling sound when poured. They were last year's bestseller.

"Did we order enough?" asked Cherisse. "And I'm wondering the same about the Laguiole corkscrews and champagne sabers. Ever since that article came out about genuine Laguiole from France being so much better than the knockoffs, they've been selling fast."

"I think we're good on cutlery," Camille said. "The Lena Fretto pottery is going to be a winner, too. No one else carries that. Good job, Mom."

Having a home-goods shop was both an art and a business. On the one hand, everything had to pencil out—the cost of the item versus the retail value. That was the business part. But on the other hand, each choice was very personal. What did people want to surround themselves with? What did they want to bring into their homes and use or appreciate every day? What did they want to share with their friends? Irish linen tea towels? Baltic crystal champagne flutes? Humble Mason jars that could be converted into birdfeeders?

The right choice meant excitement and profit. It meant happy customers telling their friends about that charming shop in Bethany Bay. It meant better terms from the suppliers. It meant the Adams and Vandermeer women got to feed their families and pay their taxes.

The wrong choice—that surefire hit that turned out to be a miss— meant sidewalk sales, the clearance bin, selling at cost. They tried to avoid being led astray by reps at the gift fairs Cherisse attended, but supply and demand was not an exact science. Occasionally, they got caught with far too many questionable yard ornaments. Even now, the sale rack had last season's aebleskiver pans, absinthe spoons, asparagus tongs, and the carrot pencil sharpener they were sure no one would be able to resist.

They made some decisions about fall and winter buying, then concluded their meeting with a calendar of events for summer.

"You should do a meet-the-artist evening at the shop with Lisette's pictures," Britt suggested to Camille. "Who knows, maybe you'll meet someone."

"What part of 'no more dating' did you not understand?" asked Camille. She did like telling people about her work, the photos she printed from found film. Back when she did her own photography with vintage cameras, her prints were bestsellers. That was all in the past, though. She didn't have the heart to take pictures these days. "I'll look at my calendar and get back to you."

They left the coffee shop and crossed to the Marina Park, where Britt's husband, Wylie, was watching their two little ones, Zoe and Van.

"Mommy!" The kids spotted Britt and ran to her, both clamoring to be swooped up.

"Hey, what about us?" asked Camille's mother. "Our turn."

"Grammy! Aunt Camille!"

Camille scooped up her niece, earning a snuggle. "I love how you always speak in exclamation points. You smell like an ice cream cone," she said.

"Daddy bought us ice cream!"

"Right before lunch!" said Van.

She picked him up next. "You smell like a hamster."

"I do? Cool!"

"How'd the strategy session go?" Wylie asked.

"We're all set for summer." Britt stood up on tiptoe and gave her husband a kiss. "Thanks for watching the rug rats."

"Let's do something this weekend," Camille suggested. "If you're not busy."

Britt's mouth turned down in a moue. "We'd love to, but there's something on the calendar already. Playdates and soccer tots. Let's aim for another time, okay? I'll e-mail you."

"Sounds good."

They all walked together along the waterfront holding hands like cutout paper dolls. Cherisse sighed. "So freaking cute. I love being a grandma."

"I love being an aunt. Easier than being a mom, eh?"

"You were easy," her mother said. "How's Julie doing?"

Camille's stomach knotted. In a very short time, her sunny, funny daughter who'd never given her a bit of worry had become a problem child. "Not so easy. Spends all her time alone, doesn't want to talk about anything. She seems really down on herself. I offered to take her shopping for summer clothes, but she said she hates shopping because she hates the way she looks."

Cherisse dropped her voice. "She's gotten awfully chubby."

"Don't you think I've noticed, Mom? Don't you think *she* has?"

"I feel so bad for her. She's such a pretty girl."

"And how much do you think that helps?" Camille felt helpless, exasperated. "I've been trying to get her to stay active and eat right without giving her body-image issues. It's a sensitive subject." Mostly, she didn't say a word, but kept junk food out of the house. Drinks other than water were a thing of the past. Cookies and carbs—no longer on the menu. Camille herself had lost five pounds trying to keep sweets and treats at bay. "Julie's going through a rough time, and she's smart enough to know it. She's barely started puberty, while the other girls look like lingerie models. And even though I know it's not all about looks, Julie wants to fit in. And I want her to be confident in who she is."

"I understand," said her mother. "You're doing your best. I want her to feel good about herself, too. She's at such a tough age."

Camille nodded, her stomach tying in knots. When things weren't right with her kid, things weren't right at all. "I hope she has a better week. Honestly, she's changed so much in the last six months. Not just her weight, but her attitude. She can't stand school. Her friends don't come around anymore. Sometimes I think she can't stand me."

"She's a teenager. That's her job. How about sending her over to the shop tomorrow after school? I'll spend some time with her, and bring her to the house for dinner."

"That sounds good, Mom. Thanks." Camille *was* grateful, but that meant an empty night for her. "Every once in a while I think about what life will be like once Julie's on her own. Who'll keep me company then?"

"You don't want to know my answer," her mother reminded her. "Camille, I'm sorry things didn't work out with Drake, but—"

"I know. I know." They'd had the discussion too many times to count. Camille's independence had become a sort of isolation. "Okay, maybe I'll get a dog. Or wait, a cat. Less of a commitment."

"Maybe you could quit waiting for the perfect guy to come along and stop holing up in your darkroom," her mother suggested.

"I *like* holing up in my darkroom."

"And I like the idea of all my daughters having wonderful, fulfilling relationships." Her mother brushed Camille's hair back, the way she had ever since Camille was a little girl. "Sorry, I'll lay off. Isn't that Stan Fenwick?" Cherisse shaded her eyes and faced the picnic area. There was a family of five gathered around a table, enjoying a picnic in the sunshine. The sound of their laughter and chatter drifted on the breeze.

"It is. Gosh, look how big his kids are now." Stan was the first guy Camille had gone out with, a year after Jace's death. Stan had been great—kind and respectful, really hoping for a relationship. He'd wanted to marry her, be a father to Julie, and raise a family together. Camille had not been ready. She had not been close to ready. Now she looked at Stan, and felt a pang of envy for the vibrant life he'd found with someone else. Envy . . . but not regret.

Her phone buzzed, and she checked the screen. "Oh boy." Her chest felt suddenly tight, and then, just as suddenly, it was full of weird flutters.

"What?" asked her mother.

"Professor Finnemore wants to see me."

Seven

❧

$f$inn didn't know what to expect, based on Camille Adams's cryptic message. She wanted to see him about some photos she'd developed from film found in an old camera. The pictures had been taken in postwar France, which had immediately piqued his interest. When she got out of the taxi in front of the Georgetown restaurant, he caught his breath. Damn. She made him feel like the Big Bad Wolf.

"You're staring," she said.

"You look very nice," he said. Those legs. He was going to think about those legs all through his overnight flight to Paris. But oddly enough, it was her big, soft brown eyes that interested him even more than the legs. A feeling of unease stirred inside him. He'd grown accustomed to keeping things simple, and he already knew instinctively that Camille Adams was complicated.

"Fair enough," she said, "considering how I was dressed the first time you met me."

He didn't remember what she was wearing that day, but it was not a tight skirt and high-heeled sandals. "Thanks for meeting me here," he said.

"Well, I thought since I'm the client this time, I should come to you."

"You're not a client," he said. "I don't have clients. I'm a teacher. I have students." Oh my God, he thought. Please be my student, Camille.

"Your services aren't for hire?" The wind lifted her silky dark hair away from the curve of her neck.

He wanted to bury his nose there and inhale deeply. He wanted to— "Nope," he said. "My advice is free."

"Then you have to let me buy lunch."

"No way. Don't even think about it."

She opened her mouth to protest, and he held up a hand. "It's not a date," he said. "Okay? It's lunch, and I'm buying, end of story. Come on, Camille. Let me be just a little bit nice to you."

Her shoulders relaxed, and she smiled at him. She was even prettier when she smiled. "I would love to let you be nice to me." She looked up and down the lush, elegant street. "I've always liked this neighborhood," she added. "There's something about the atmosphere."

"Agreed. It reminds me of my favorite boulevards in Paris. When was the last time you visited Paris?"

"Not since I was in college." Her gaze shifted. "I don't travel much anymore, so . . ." She didn't finish. Instead, she seemed to mentally regroup, and looked up at him with those gorgeous, sunshiny eyes. "What made you think of Arnaud Loves Patsy?"

"It's trendy, I know, but it follows one of my favorite trends."

"What's that?"

"It's quiet. You can actually have a conversation here." And to his own amazement, he actually wanted that from her. His meddling sisters would be amazed. "So I thought it would be a good place to talk about the pictures you found. Also, it's closer to the airport than Annapolis. I'm catching a nine P.M. flight."

"Oh. Where are you going?"

"Marseille. Back to work."

She hesitated, looking at him with an expression he couldn't read. Not disappointment. Relief? "Then we should get started."

He stepped aside and gestured for her to precede him up the figured gray stone steps of the 1880s building. A pair of Louis Tiffany lamps flanked the entryway. "How's your daughter?" he asked. "Julie?" He hoped like hell he got the girl's name right.

"She's fine. Thanks for asking. You caught us both on one of our worst days."

"I still feel bad about that. I've made a career out of repatriating lost soldiers, and I'm usually better at dealing with people on their worst days."

"The film meant a lot to you. I feel bad, too." She regarded him calmly for a moment. In that moment, he realized she disarmed him, and he couldn't figure out why. Maybe—

"Professor Finnemore." The maître d' greeted him with a slight bow. "Your table is right this way."

She smiled slightly. God, he couldn't get enough of that smile. "Friend of yours?" When she saw the prime location of the table, her eyes narrowed in suspicion. "Obviously."

They were ushered to a curved, upholstered bench at an intimate table by the front bay window—an ultraprivate spot reserved for VIPs. "My mother comes here a lot," he said. "She's in the Diplomatic Corps."

"They must think she's awesome."

"Everyone thinks she's awesome."

"Including the *Washington Post*. I read the coverage of the ceremony for your father. What an incredible moment for your mother and your whole family."

"It was. Seeing the survivors—the guys on my father's reconnaissance team . . . They're all the age my dad would have been, surrounded by their kids and grandkids . . . that was something. After the ceremony, they gave my mom a collection of letters they'd written."

Camille gazed across the table at him. Okay, maybe she wasn't gazing, but he could tell he had her attention. "That must have been nice," she said. "Hard, though, for your family."

"You're right—it was both. We went back to my mom and step-dad's place afterward and got drunk and read the letters," he said. "That probably sounds disrespectful, but it was . . . well, we drank toast after toast to my father, there were tears, and we bonded."

"It's good that you spent some time with your family." She folded her hands on the table and held his gaze. "Tell me about them."

Shit. Now *he* was the one gazing. And he liked her. Not just because she was pretty, but because she was . . . interesting. Cool. She didn't fit the mold of the kind of woman he usually hooked up with. She made him want something more than a hookup. She made him want to get to know her. And even more risky—she made him want to let her know *him*.

"Let's see. Short version. When my dad went missing, Mom had three kids—my sisters Margaret Ann and Shannon Rose, and she was pregnant with me. She met my stepfather while on assignment in Belgium," he said. "Rudy had two kids by his first marriage—Joey and Roxy—and he and Mom had two more—my brothers, Devon and Rafe."

"Wow, that's quite a clan."

"Even more so now that we're all grown and have kids."

"You have kids?"

"Not me, but all the others. I'm a professional uncle." After he'd been burned by Emily, he wasn't sure he was cut out for family life. His sisters kept saying he just hadn't met the right woman yet. Sitting here now, having lunch with Camille Adams, made him wonder . . . no. *No.*

"Is your stepfather in the Diplomatic Corps, too?"

He shook his head. "Rudy is a journalist. He's been a correspondent for every major bureau you can think of. And he plays a mean slide guitar. When we lived in Frankfurt, he was in a garage band called the Trailing Spouses."

"Interesting name . . ."

"It's an official designation for the spouses of people with government posts. In the Diplomatic Corps, almost everybody has one." A waiter came to pour water from a crystal pitcher. "Anyway, that's my family in a nutshell. I'd rather hear about yours." Finn was startled, because he really did want that. He wanted to know everything about her.

"My parents divorced when I was eight, so I spent weekends with Papa and the rest of the time with my mom and stepdad, Bart. I have two half sisters. Britt is married and works with us at the shop, and Hilda's in college. Papa never remarried. When I was younger, that was fine with me, because I always thought a stepmom would be scary. Too many fairy-tale readings, I guess."

"Fairy tales are awesome. I once taught a class on the historical context of fairy tales. Stepparents get a bad rap."

"True. My stepdad, Bart, is totally great. He's an oysterman."

"And your dad's a wine expert. You guys must eat like kings."

"We do, actually. Papa and I make dinner together every Friday night. It's a tradition. And we mostly speak French together, because I wanted my daughter to speak it like a native. Actually, a native of the Languedoc, so not the usual—"

"You mean she sounds like a southerner," Finn said in Occitan, the vernacular he'd picked up on his latest teaching assignment.

Camille's eyes widened. "Okay, now you're showing off."

Yes. Yes, he was. "You should come to Aix-en-Provence." The idea of hanging out with her in France seemed incredibly appealing.

She looked down at her lap. "Like I said, I don't really travel."

"Why's that?"

She paused, then let out a sigh. "You have a plane to catch tonight."

"Long story?" He wanted to hear all her stories. Preferably while lazing in bed with her after a night of—

The waiter came back for their drink orders. She asked for a glass of sweet tea, extra lemon. "Let's take a look at the menu," she suggested, opening hers. "Oh boy. Really, you didn't have to do this."

The cuisine here was a fusion of Patsy's soul food and Arnaud's French classics. "We both have to eat. It's my last day in the States for a while. I might as well make it pleasant." He set his menu aside. "Do you have a favorite restaurant in the city?"

She shook her head. "I'm not one for foie gras and Reblochon cheese. In Bethany Bay, we're happy enough with local backfin crab and sliced cukes in ice water." A flush rose in her cheeks. "Thus revealing my townie roots."

"I chose wrong, then."

"Not at all. The shrimp and grits sounds delicious."

"And just so you know, I'm partial to townies."

"Even though you're a come-here."

"A what?"

"That's what locals call the visitors from the city."

"Who serve foie gras at their parties." Finn ordered the crab cakes and a side of fresh cucumbers. "I'll share," he said, savoring her shy smile. His pleasure wavered when he noticed a table full of D.C. power brokers across the room. Among them was a lobbyist Finn had slept with not long after his divorce—not his finest moment. He turned slightly, facing Camille.

"What?" She dabbed at her lips with a napkin. "Do I have something on my face?"

"I was just wondering about something."

"About what?"

"Why are you single?"

"I beg your pardon?"

"Most women like you are already taken."

"Women like me?" Her eyes sharpened with suspicion.

Okay, that came out wrong. "Smart, interesting, cool . . . It just occurred to me to wonder why you're single. Was your divorce recent?"

"I'm not divorced. My husband died," she said, her mouth tightening.

"What?" Shit. He wasn't expecting that. "I mean, I heard what you said . . ."

"It always creates an awkward moment," she said.

Shit shit shit. "Sorry I brought it up. I just assumed . . . Has it been . . . when did he die?" Finn realized he was babbling. There were no smooth come-ons or pat phrases for this.

She hesitated, then added, "It's been five years."

That was slightly less freaky. Five years seemed like long enough.

"Oh man. Was he in the service?" Finn flashed on the endless alabaster rows of markers at Arlington. All the guys he knew who had died young had been in the service.

"No," she said. "It was an accident."

"I'm sorry for your loss. And for what Julie will never get to know. I'm sure you've been hearing that for five years, but I do mean it, Camille." Shit, he thought again. A divorce was one thing. But a death? At a loss for words, he touched her hand. A crazy feeling went through him. He had no idea what was going through her, but she looked down at their hands, and gently moved away.

"Thank you. I guess . . . so maybe you can relate to Julie's situation. Growing up without your dad."

"Yes and no. I had a stepfather by the time I was two. My sisters, especially Margaret Ann, missed my dad horribly, but they adjusted. I hope your daughter does, too."

"She seems resilient," said Camille. "I hope so. I hope she doesn't carry sadness around with her all day every day."

"I hope you don't either," he said. "I mean, losing your husband must have been a nightmare, and I'm sorry as hell it happened to you, but he's going to be dead for a long time, and there's nothing wrong with moving on."

"That's a blunt way of putting it."

"Sorry. I get flustered over gorgeous women. And gorgeous tragic women . . . that's even more . . ."

"More what?"

"Flustering." He was sounding like a genius now.

She lightened the moment with a smile. "Did you just call me gorgeous?"

"I did. And tragic. Also smart and interesting. I could go on . . ."

"I'd rather you didn't."

"Okay." He was usually pretty good with the pickup lines, but today, everything was coming out wrong. Maybe it was because with Camille Adams, he didn't want a pickup. He wanted to pick *her*. This was a new, exhilarating feeling. Highly unexpected, but undeniable.

She dabbed with her napkin again. "Truth be told, I've always thought I'd find someone. I wanted to. After a few years, I dated a bit. Julie's still young, and I loved being a family. I wanted more kids—a bigger family for Julie. And being single started to feel lonely." She took a swig of her water. "Plus I wanted to get laid."

"You're making me wish I wasn't leaving," he said.

"That's not my point. I'm trying to explain . . . I've stepped back from dating. I gave a lot to the last relationship. We both really tried, but it wasn't right, and I realized it was never going to be right. I keep wondering if it's me . . . or him . . . or us together that simply didn't work. And I realized I simply don't care for dating. It just doesn't work for me." She drummed her fingers on the table. "So I'm taking myself off the market. Or out of the pool. Whatever."

"How can you be off the market? We only just met." What about more kids? he wondered. What about getting laid?

"Very funny," she said, clearly assuming he was joking. "Let's finish our lunch, and I'll show you what I came here for."

All righty, then. Finn decided not to push it. If he came on too strong, she'd bolt. He knew this because when a woman came on to him, *he* was the one who bolted.

He backed off and enjoyed the excellent meal, watching her while trying to appear not to. There was this raw, elemental attraction he couldn't deny, but it wasn't just that. She was entrancing, with those deep brown eyes and delicate skin, and the unconscious way she bit her lip when she was listening.

"So here's what I have," Camille said during a lull after they ate. "I'm pretty good at reading old photographs, but I could use an expert opinion." She explained the provenance of the photos. A large box of old artifacts and photographs had been delivered to her father from the village of his boyhood, most of them shrouded in mystery. "Do you know much about cameras?"

"A bit. Probably not as much as you."

She opened her bag on the bench between them and handed him

an odd-looking old camera. "It's an Exakta from the 1930s. And it had film in it."

Finn melted a little in that moment. The thing he found most sexy about any woman was passion—not just in the usual sense. That went without saying. But passion that lit her from within, when something fired her up. For Camille Adams, it was her excitement over old cameras and film. It transformed her, made her eyes sparkle and her whole being light up. She was already attractive. But when talking about her craft, she was . . . something more.

". . . eight pictures," she concluded.

He realized he'd been staring, and forced himself to listen.

"My father says they're pictures of Bellerive, the town where he was born, and a farm called Sauveterre, where he grew up. He says the beach is in an area called the Calanques, but he doesn't recognize this couple." The coastline was starkly beautiful, flanked by towering cliffs, with soft-looking pale sand in the middle. There was a wicker basket and what appeared to be a makeshift stretcher that had been dragged to the surf. A man and woman were in the water facing each other, holding hands and smiling. "My guess is, one of them couldn't walk and was brought into the water on the stretcher," she said. "What I find striking is the quality of these pictures. This is a really good camera, but the shots are very professional. We thought they might have been taken by someone named Cyprian Toselli." She indicated the initials pressed into the camera case. "There were some books with his name in them. But when I saw the final picture, it made me think someone else took these shots."

She opened another image on her tablet. It was a beautifully composed shot of a very young, pregnant woman in an old-fashioned mirror. An oval window echoed the shape of the cheval glass, the curve of her belly, and the curve of her cheekbone. The play of light and shadow added drama and mystery to the scene. "This is the final one on the roll—and the most fascinating one to me. It's a self-portrait of my father's mother. I was so surprised and moved to see it. I think it means the pictures were taken by the grandmother I never knew. It makes me feel . . . a deeper connection, I suppose."

"She's . . . Wow. She looks like you. A blond version of you."

"Well, that's flattering, since she's twenty years old in this picture. And very beautiful."

"Like I said. She looks like you. Or you look like her."

"Her name was Lisette Galli Palomar," Camille said. "I think she looks sad in the picture. Haunted."

She had the same delicate cheekbones, full lips, and fine skin as Camille. The eyes . . . yes, he thought. He could see a sadness there. "Do you know why?"

"The war had recently ended. She was a widow by then. And she died in childbirth shortly after taking this picture. Other than that, I know nothing about her. And neither does my father. But I know from experience that being widowed . . . yes, it haunts you."

He looked up from the picture into Camille's face. Studying the self-portrait of her grandmother, she seemed haunted, too.

She tapped the screen to enlarge the other images. "I'd like to understand what I'm seeing in these shots. I thought, with your knowledge of France during the war, you could help me figure out the context."

"I'm glad you got in touch." This, in fact, was *his* passion— uncovering the mysteries of the past. He studied the set again. "See this stone hut? It's called a *capitelle* or a *borie,* common in the area, usually in far-lying fields. They're used for shelter, like a shepherd's hut, or to store tools. This next one—the hut's been destroyed." He studied the poignant image—scattered rocks and debris around a ruined foundation with a pit in the middle. "That might have been caused by a bomb strike."

"I wonder why she took that picture. It's a nice composition, with the scrubby trees and some kind of stream in the background."

"Yes. And . . ." A detail of another picture caught his attention. "Hello."

"What?"

He zoomed in on a pile of rubble. "See this bridge?"

"It's been ruined, too. In the war?"

"Probably. I'm going to have to check my facts, but I'm pretty sure there was an Allied operation here in 1944."

"It was in Lisette's village? In Bellerive?"

"Like I said, I'd have to check." He summoned a map image on his phone. "The town was close to the DZ—the drop zone—of an Allied invasion called Operation Dragoon, when the area was liberated from the Germans. It was a major airborne operation, but most people have never heard of it, because it was overshadowed by D-Day, which took place a couple of months before. These pictures are quite a find."

A gentle smile played across her lips. "Some days I love my job."

The waiter came by with the dessert menu, but Camille declined, settling for another glass of sweet tea instead. She showed him a prayer card and a cloth badge. "These were in the trunk along with the camera. Any clue?"

"This is the Sallman *Head of Christ*," he said, recognizing the image on the card. "The USO printed millions of them to distribute to soldiers during the war."

"I wonder how it ended up with my French grandmother's things."

"This badge might explain it," he told her. "The torch with wings—it could have been sewn on a pathfinder's jump jacket—the jacket of an American paratrooper."

"You mean a guy who jumped out of an airplane? That would be incredible. An American?"

"Yep." Something occurred to him. He touched the screen and scrolled to the self-portrait of the young woman. "Look at this pin on the shoulder of her dress."

"I thought it was a brooch or something."

"Look closer." He zoomed in on the object.

"It's the pathfinder badge." She leaned back in her chair, her gaze moving from the badge to the picture of her grandmother.

"I think I'm in the middle of a family mystery."

"You are. It's cool, Camille."

"I wish you didn't have to go." She pressed her fingers to her mouth. "I mean—"

"Me neither." A pure, ungovernable impulse took over. He leaned over and gently cupped her cheek in his hand. Soft. Her skin was so silky, and her hair smelled like flowers. She didn't move or pull away, merely regarded him calmly. Then her gaze shifted from his eyes to his mouth, and he kissed her gently, his lips lightly touching hers, tasting. Her mouth was warm and soft. Delicious with the flavor of sweet tea. Still she didn't move, but her slight inhalation signaled surprise, and maybe, if he was reading her right, a small pleasure.

"After that," he whispered against her lips, "I don't need dessert."

"Listen," she whispered back, "it would be a bad idea to start something."

"Why's that?"

"Because you're leaving. And I'm . . ."

"Delicious," he said. "That's what you are."

"Knock it off." She shifted on the bench, moving away from him. "I've told you I'm not interested in dating."

The kiss had been light and fleeting, but at the same time, dangerously intimate. This was a bad idea, Finn told himself. He had no business getting tangled up with this woman. On went the armor around his heart, and he reverted to his default self. "Then we could just make out. I'll change my ticket and stick around for a while."

She gazed at him softly. Touched the tip of her tongue to her upper lip—just briefly. Just enough to mesmerize him. "You know," she said in a low, sexy voice, "I've been wondering about you, too, the way you did about me. I was wondering why you're single."

Aha. He was going to have her eating out of the palm of his hand any moment. "Yeah?"

She smiled. Moist lips, bedroom eyes. "I figured it out, though."

"Did you, now?"

"You're a player. Women are *so* not into players."

Damn, he thought. He was surprised to feel a sharp sting where her words darted into him. He covered his disappointment with a laconic grin. "Let's go on an un-date, then. You're gonna love not-dating me."

"Why?"

"Because I'll treat you right. I'll make sweet love to you and we won't have to get all serious and involved, but it'll still be awesome."

Her cheeks flushed pink. "Very funny. I'm going now. Thanks for lunch."

A week after her meeting with Finn, Camille still couldn't stop thinking about him—the brush of his hands and his slow, sexy smile that melted her thoughts into incoherence. The timbre of his voice when he leaned in close to say something. The light in his eyes when he got excited about the found photos. And then the kiss. That kiss.

She kept catching herself gazing out the window, daydreaming, touching her lips. Finn had kissed her. She hadn't wanted him to stop. It was the kind of kiss she wanted to deepen and explore, to see where it led, because it felt different from any other kiss. Too bad they'd been in a public place where they had to behave.

Actually, it was lucky they'd been in a public place because it saved her from doing something completely foolish. She had told him in no uncertain terms that it would be a bad idea to start something. Still, it didn't stop her from thinking about him constantly.

She did something she'd never done before—stalked him on the Internet. He wasn't much for social networking, but she found several articles he'd written and read them as if they contained the secret of life. One of the articles was particularly poignant. Working with a French crime lab, he had helped identify the remains of three American soldiers who had gone missing during World War II.

Sitting at her desk in the small office tucked in the back of Ooh-La-La, she could hear sounds from the adjacent coffee shop. Brew-La-La had been open since sunup, serving up their own signature

local roast for early risers, commuters, and fisher folk heading out
to the bay. The gurgle and hiss of the commercial espresso machine
from Italy reminded her that it needed servicing. There was a meeting
with a sales rep penciled in on her calendar.

Yet no matter how hard she tried to force herself to focus on work,
it was too tempting to open a new search-and-follow on Professor
Malcolm Finnemore around the World Wide Web. He was a bad influence, clearly. He'd already tempted her into Googling him. What
else would he entice her to do?

She felt something strong and new, but wasn't ready to admit it to
anyone, least of all herself. His parting words haunted her: *I'll make
sweet love to you and we won't have to get all serious and involved, but
it'll still be awesome.*

Just not as awesome as falling in love. Nothing is as awesome as
that, she reflected.

She felt betrayed by her own thoughts. Falling in love was the last
thing she wanted to do. Her failed dating track record was proof of
that. Sometimes, when she couldn't help herself, she thought about
the things that were holding her back. Unlike a lot of single women,
she hadn't been burned by a bad relationship. On the contrary, her
marriage had been wonderful. Maybe too wonderful. She never
wanted to get that close to a man again, because the pain of loss was
simply too high a price to pay.

When the phone rang, she jumped with a guilty start.

Bethany Bay High School appeared on the screen, and Camille
snatched it up.

"This is Helen Gibbons, secretary to Mr. Larson," said the voice
on the other line.

Camille tensed, bracing herself. "Is Julie all right?"

"Yes, it's not an emergency, Mrs. Adams. However, Mr. Larson
would like to meet with you at your earliest convenience."

Camille scanned her list of things to do, which was tacked on the
wall next to the computer. It was a long list, one that she would need
all day to accomplish. Rhonda had just opened the door and was set-

ting a few key pieces out on the sidewalk to entice weekend browsers, and Camille had promised to help.

"I can be there in fifteen minutes," she said.

Phone calls from Julie's school didn't use to cause concern. They would be happy messages from a teacher or coach, letting Camille know that Julie had earned honors student status, or had won a blue ribbon in a race, or was getting a good-helper award.

Lately, she'd been getting "What's going on with Julie?" calls. Julie was in trouble again. She had skipped class. Her grades were slipping.

Adding to the discomfort of the meeting was the fact that Drake Larson was the reason she'd sworn off dating. Because even with a great guy like him, her emotions were flat. Feelings could not be plucked from thin air or manufactured out of whole cloth. If they didn't develop from a slow burn, like a photo print in a chemical bath, or if they didn't strike her with the force of a tsunami, they simply weren't meant to be, and she couldn't force them.

Could be that was the reason she kept thinking about Finn. He was a tsunami, for sure. What she needed to remember was what remained after the tidal wave passed—wreckage and destruction, and irretrievable loss.

The school secretary ushered her into Drake's office. The space was as neat and organized as Drake himself. He was the opposite of a tsunami. His desk was a flawless landscape of order; there wasn't even a power cord to mar the scene. On the wall behind him were his diplomas as well as a trio of iconic scenes from high school life—a varsity letter jacket hanging in a locker, the vintage bell that still summoned kids to school every day, and the surf rescue team in action.

Standing behind the desk was Drake himself—clean-cut, his pants and shirt pressed, his expression somberly professional. "Thanks for coming on such short notice," he said.

"Of course. I'm glad you called. I've been so worried about Julie lately."

He gestured to a chair in front of his desk. After the very difficult breakup conversation, he had promised her no hard feelings, but
she knew she had hurt him, and she felt awful about it. The little
wounds we inflict on each other, even inadvertently, cannot be ignored, thought Camille.

"Julie and Mrs. Marshall will be in shortly."

Mrs. Marshall—the school counselor. "After that day in the ER,
I thought you were done scaring me," she said. "What's going on?"

"Ah, here they are," Drake said, aiming a look over her shoulder.
"We need to have a conversation. And then all of us need to work
together on a solution."

Camille stood up and moved aside as Mrs. Marshall came into the
office with Julie in tow. Camille's daughter wore her usual "uniform"
of baggy jeans and T-shirt, old sneakers, hair in a messy bun. Julie
used to love putting together cute outfits and fixing herself up. "It's
because I'm one-quarter French," she used to say, speaking nearly
perfect French. "I am so *dans le vent*."

So cool. But that had been over a year ago. Now it was as if Julie
had stopped caring about her appearance. She didn't look sullen or
defiant as she took a seat on a folding metal chair against the wall. Just
resigned. Camille scarcely recognized her.

Camille turned to her. "What's up? Talk to me, Jules."

"They say I did something to Jana Jacobs."

"What do you mean, you 'did something'?" Camille frowned. "I
need a better explanation than that."

"There was a pickup game of soccer this morning—you know, like
every morning. And I knocked her purse in the mud."

"On purpose, or by accident? And how was a purse involved in a
soccer game?"

"Jana and her parents have already been in to see me," Drake said.

Troy and Trudy Jacobs had never been Camille's favorites. Both
lawyers with a family law practice, they suffered from a superiority
complex and disliked anything they deemed different. Trudy once

told Camille that she couldn't shop at Ooh-La-La anymore because the boutique's small book section featured banned books. Camille didn't miss her business.

"I told Jana I was sorry," Julie said.

"The Jacobses agreed not to press charges so long as Julie keeps her distance from Jana."

"Press charges? For what?" Camille was dumbfounded.

"The bag is ruined."

"It's an actionable event," Mrs. Marshall explained.

"So is Julie nearly drowning in gym class," Camille pointed out, bristling, "but I'm not going to go to the police over it."

Drake's face reddened. "We're here to discuss today's incident."

"I'll see to it that she replaces the bag."

"That dumb purse costs like five hundred bucks," Julie said.

"Then you shouldn't have destroyed it."

"I didn't—"

"Let's focus on the bigger picture," Mrs. Marshall suggested. "Julie hasn't been getting along with other students. She's been missing class, and her grades are slipping. We've spent a lot of time trying to improve the situation, but it's only getting worse." The counselor turned to Julie. "Can you tell us why these incidents keep happening?"

Julie gazed back at her with a completely neutral expression. "No, ma'am, I can't tell you."

"Come on, Jules," Camille said, frustrated by her intractable daughter. "We're running out of options here."

"Regarding options," Drake said, "have you thought about alternative schools?"

"What alternative? There's one school in Bethany Bay—this one. If it doesn't work, then what do you suggest?"

Mrs. Marshall handed her a glossy brochure with a business card stapled to it. "We'd all like to find a way for you to thrive and find success in school. You could start looking at other options."

Camille frowned at the brochure, which showed a group of smiling girls in neat uniforms. "Boarding school? You mean she would live somewhere else? Away from home? Away from family?"

"Sounds awesome," Julie said. "Where do I sign up?"

"Boarding school?" Camille's father shook the dirt off the French breakfast radishes he'd just picked in his garden, getting ready for their usual Friday-night dinner. "Did you tell them that such a thing is out of the question?"

"I didn't tell them anything," she said. "I'm still trying to get my head around the idea that my daughter is failing in school."

"How did this foolish notion come about?"

"Let's have Julie explain," Camille suggested.

Julie arrived a few minutes later, practically crashing her bike on the walkway in front of her grandfather's house. "Papi," she called, then apparently read the expression on Camille's face. "So, she's telling you about my terrible day."

"In fact, I was suggesting that you tell Papi yourself. Because I certainly can't explain it."

Julie sighed. "It was during morning soccer. Jana Jacobs was being rude, so I drop-kicked her fancy purse. I didn't think it would get ruined. It probably isn't. She just wanted to get me in trouble."

"Do you know what it feels like to get a call from school saying my daughter is behaving like a vandal?" Camille asked in frustration.

"Actually, I don't," Julie said sullenly. "I'm sorry. I said I was sorry to Jana. I'm going to work at Grammy's shop until I earn enough to replace it. I don't know what else to do."

"*Mon dieu,* why would you do such a thing?" Henry demanded.

She hesitated. "You wouldn't understand."

"I challenge you. Make me understand."

"I'm a loser," Julie said, her eyes narrowing in anger. "A big fat loser with four eyes and headgear. That's all anybody sees when they look at me."

Henry regarded her with a steel-steady stare. "How long has this bullying been going on?"

Julie stared back at him. "I don't know that word—*rudoyer*."

Camille switched to speaking English. "It means 'bullying.' But who said anything about bullying?"

"No one," her father replied. "But I know what bullying is like, and I can see that this has happened to Julie."

"You mean Julie's a bully?"

"I mean she's being bullied."

"Is this true?" Camille demanded, turning to her daughter. Julie had never complained, had never mentioned being pushed around. If someone was harassing her, she would have spoken up. Wouldn't she? Camille felt a flicker of doubt. "How can this be true?"

"It's not true," Julie said, her gaze shifting away. "Papi, that's ridiculous." Her cheeks turned an angry red.

Camille felt a cold prickle of dread. It was the gut sense she sometimes felt when she knew her daughter wasn't telling her everything. "Julie—"

"Papi doesn't know what he's talking about. I don't want to discuss it, okay?" Julie lashed back.

Now Camille was worried. Why was Julie suddenly a pariah? She could no longer ignore the fact that Julie's year had not gone well, but she had attributed it to the normal bumpy ride of adolescence. In the past, Julie had had plenty of friends. She was invited places—to birthdays, playdates, bike rides. Lately, the invitations had dwindled. When Camille would suggest calling someone, having a sleepover, going up to Rehoboth for the rides and games at Funland, Julie would decline, swiftly and unequivocally. These were symptoms, Camille realized. Dear God, how had she missed them? Why hadn't she realized? She thought she knew everything about her daughter, but now it seemed she had a giant blind spot.

"Something's going on," Camille said. "Julie, I need for you to level with me."

"I told you, it was a dumb thing over a dumb pickup game of soccer."

"I don't mean just today. I mean in general. What's happening at school? You used to love school. You used to make good grades. You used to tell me everything."

"I told you everything."

Camille glanced at her father. He was watching Julie with the most peculiar expression—an expression she couldn't read. The two of them locked eyes, and then Julie burst into tears—angry, frustrated tears. "I didn't say anything because you were dating Drake Larson, and when it didn't work out, Vanessa turned everyone against me, including stupid Jana Jacobs."

"No." Camille was horrified.

"You think I'm making this up? You think I wanted that to happen?" Julie swiped at her eyes.

"I thought you were friends with Vanessa."

"She was only ever nice to me because her dad forced her to be."

Camille felt a welling of guilt. Vanessa was beautiful, smart, and popular. She was also highly influential at the high school. Camille should have been more clued in to what was happening. "So it's Vanessa and Jana? Jules, talk to me. I need to know what's really been going on."

"Forget it. If you make a big stink and start accusing people, everything will go even worse for me."

"I need full disclosure if I'm going to help you."

"Did I ask for help? There's no way to help. The whole school hates me, and I hate them back." Tears welled in her eyes again, and she pushed a hand under her glasses to swipe them away. "Can I go to boarding school, like Mrs. Marshall said?"

"You're not leaving. No way."

"Your answer to everything is no." She flung herself into one of the patio chairs. "Can we just drop it and talk about something else?"

"We absolutely cannot," Camille said, pulling out her phone.

Henry caught her hand and gently set the phone aside. "Julie is right. The more you try to intervene, the worse things will go for her. That is the way bullying works."

"How would you know how bullying works?" She shot him an angry glare.

He set down his garden basket and sat next to Julie, motioning for Camille to join them. He took Julie's hand in his and held it gently. She tried to take her hand back, but he gently laid it on his knee, exposing a set of stubby nails, bitten raw.

Camille felt ill. Julie never used to bite her nails. When had that started? And why hadn't Camille noticed?

"Do you see this hand?" her father asked gently.

Again, Julie tried to withdraw it, her face turning red. "Papi—"

"I had this same hand, probably when I was about your age."

Julie stopped resisting and stared at him.

"I, too, was the victim of bullies when I was young. In fact, this happened all through my childhood, but particularly when I was a teenager."

"You never told me that," Camille said.

"It's not a pleasant thing to revisit, but I'm telling you now because I want you and Julie to feel you can trust what I have to say."

"What were you bullied about?" Julie asked.

"A bully does not need a reason. There are things that will never change, and one of these things is the cruelty that can take over a group of teenagers."

Julie pulled her knees up to her chest and rested her chin on them. "I'm sorry that happened to you, Papi. I know you didn't deserve it."

"And I know the same about you." He gently brushed her cheek with the back of his hand. "You are so very beautiful, my sweet."

Camille smiled past the lump in her throat. Their love had always been so strong and pure. He'd taken care of Julie while Camille worked, teaching her French and his favorite cooking techniques. He was the one who had taught her to kick a soccer ball and sing his old favorite songs.

"Tell us, Papa," Camille said quietly.

He leaned forward, resting his elbows on his knees and studying the ground. After a few moments, he looked up and said, "I was bullied all through my youth, even when I was too young to understand what was happening."

"Why you, Papi?" asked Julie.

"Because of who I was," he told her. "Because of who my father was."

"The mayor of the town, isn't that what you said?" Julie asked. "Did he die fighting? Was he a war hero?"

Henry regarded her with an expression Camille had never seen on her father's face. "My father was no hero," he said, his voice low, nearly breaking. "At the end of the war, he was shot as a collaborator."

"Oh my God," Camille said, reeling. "You never told me that."

"It would not exactly be a source of pride, now, would it? Not a story I want to share, that I am the son of a Nazi collaborator. I grew up in a village where my father was regarded as a monster."

Camille's stomach clenched. "Papa—really?"

He nodded, his expression strained. "This is a secret I've held in all my life. There is this shame our family has been carrying around for decades. I never told you because I didn't want you or Julie to be tainted by it."

Camille tried to get her head around this revelation. "So your father was a collaborator. Meaning he threw in with the Nazis during the war."

"Yes. According to all who knew him, he was quite a tyrannical one at that. When the Nazis moved in, he ingratiated himself with them. He persecuted Jews and betrayed resistance fighters. He allowed the town to be turned into a slave state for the Germans. Nearly every family in Bellerive suffered—and many died—because of Didier Palomar. Upon liberation by the Allies, the *épuration sauvage* took place—a period of savage revenge. Palomar was tied to a stake and shot while his pregnant wife looked on."

"Shot? You mean executed?"

"No. He was not given a proper trial. It was vigilante justice, but I imagine the outcome would have been the same if he'd been tried."

"And Lisette witnessed the shooting," Camille said.

"Was she a collaborator, too?" Julie asked. "Was your aunt Rotrude?"

"That, I do not know. I like to think they opposed the Nazis the way any self-respecting French citizen would. As for me, I grew up bearing the shame and guilt of my father's deeds. And that is why the bullying happened. Kids at school hated me because they claimed my father was responsible for the hardship, torment, and death suffered by their families during the war."

Camille went to his side and took his hand. "I can't believe you never told me any of this."

"No one enjoys speaking of things they're ashamed of," he said quietly.

"It's not your shame," Camille objected. "It was his—Didier."

"Mom's right," Julie said. "You weren't even born when all that happened. You had nothing to do with the Nazi occupation, right?"

"I know it probably doesn't make sense to you, but you must understand what it was like in Bellerive. A tiny village where everyone knows everyone else. The war was fresh in memory, and there were reminders all over—buildings reduced to rubble, bullet holes in walls, craters from bombs. My name was Palomar, and I was the heir to my father's property. I was a reminder of the bitterness and tragedy caused by Didier Palomar. Imagine me in school, sitting next to a boy whose father had been hauled away and shot in the street on orders from my own father. I can't say I would have behaved differently."

"Seriously?" Julie's eyes were wide with fear. "Your father ordered people to be shot?"

"So I was told. Some of the stories were likely apocryphal, but there is no denying that when the Germans occupied this town, Didier Palomar was their puppet, informing on his neighbors in order to show his support for the Nazis. And even though he paid the ultimate price, villagers still demanded justice. I was his flesh and blood, a living reminder of the things he had done."

"This happened?" asked Camille, aghast. "Papa, that's unbelievable."

He steepled his fingers together and stared at the floor. "Palomar was regarded as a monster. It seemed half the families in town suffered from his many betrayals."

"But that doesn't make it right for kids to beat up on you," Julie said.

He put his hand on hers. "We have already established this well-known fact—a bully acts on the flimsiest of reasons. Now, my dear one. Go and take a look at the ducklings. They hatched this morning. Your maman and I will get dinner started. Go, and we'll talk of happier things over dinner."

For some reason, Camille's thoughts darted to Finn. She wanted to tell him about Didier Palomar and see if they could discover more details about the mayor of Bellerive. Finn had promised to visit the town to see if he could help her fill in the details of Lisette's pictures. Now she wanted him to learn more about Didier—her grandfather, she thought with a lurching revulsion.

"I hate that you suffered," she said, following her father inside. No wonder he had left Bellerive, anglicized his name, and started a new life. "I hate that it still hurts you, all these years later."

"I try never to think of it, but there is no escape from certain memories. The parcel from Madame Olivier brought up so many reminders."

"I wish you'd talked to me about this."

"It was very grim."

"But if you'd said something, maybe it would have eased your pain. Hiding things away can be toxic, Papa. Have you ever thought of talking to someone about it? I mean, like the counselor I saw after Jace—"

He caught his breath. "Listen, all the talk therapy you endured after losing Jace did not work either. You still haven't ventured out of our safe little world here."

Her cheeks felt hot, burning with the truth of what he said. "Because it's our world. Because it's safe."

"You can no longer say it's a safe place, not at this moment," he pointed out, his gaze flicking in the direction of the garden.

She felt a stab of worry. "You're right. What am I going to do about Julie? I feel so awful for her. I just want to go and rip somebody's head off."

"Which, of course, will not work, unless you want matters to escalate. When I was Julie's age, the village priest passed away, and a younger one took over. He observed what was happening, and tried to punish the kids who were tormenting me. You can imagine what that did, eh?"

"Made it worse," Camille said. "What do I do, then? Force her to tough it out? Send her to boarding school? No way."

"They're totally cute, Papi," Julie said, her eyes shining as she came into the house. "I love baby ducklings." She went over to the sink to wash her hands. "I'm sorry the kids in your town were mean to you."

He poured wine from a decanter, and gave Julie a glass of bubbly water. "It was a long time ago. Perhaps . . . long enough. *Santé*," he said.

Camille noticed a glint in his eye. Long enough for what? "Papa, what's going on?"

"Dr. Ackland has cleared me to travel."

"That's cool, Papi," said Julie. "Are you planning a trip?"

"You're not going on a trip," Camille broke in.

"I am, *choupette*," he told her. "I have decided to spend the summer in Bellerive."

No, thought Camille. Just no. She couldn't let him go gallivanting overseas. His health was fragile. It was too far away. "Why would you want to visit a place full of bad memories?"

"The house is in a terrible state, and I must go look after my property."

"You never did before," Camille objected. "You said the Oliviers took care of the upkeep."

"True, but it's high time I took responsibility for the place. The cave-in of a slate-tiled roof is no small disaster. Seeing the things sent by Madame Olivier . . . Now I'm compelled to visit Bellerive, perhaps confront those unhappy memories at long last."

"It's too far," Camille said. "You're not up to a trip like that. What if something happens?"

"I have responsibilities. And I must go now—this summer."

He didn't add "before I die," but it was implicit. His cancer was in remission, yet both Camille and her father knew the possibility of a recurrence was extremely high. His care team had warned them of that.

She tried not to panic. "You should do exactly what you want, of course. But are you sure the doctor gave you the green light? Did you tell her you mean to fly overseas and visit a tiny village in France? Is she okay with that?"

His gaze shifted.

"Papa."

"I bet you didn't tell her," Julie chimed in.

"It's too soon," Camille protested. "You can't go jetting off all by yourself."

"And that, my poppet, is the reason I want you and Julie to come to France with me for the summer."

"Cool," said Julie.

Camille's reaction was swift and visceral. "Out of the question."

"Why is it out of the question?" asked Julie.

"It's too far, and we can't stay away so long." Camille felt a twist of fear deep in her gut. She had not gone anywhere in ages. She knew it was irrational, but the very idea of getting on a plane made the blood freeze in her veins.

"Mom, we have to do it," Julie said.

"We've never missed a summer in Bethany Bay. It's the best time of the year."

Julie laughed. "You're kidding, right? I'd do anything to get out of here."

"Jules, the answer is no. Papa, I hope you can understand."

"If you don't come with me," he said, "then I shall have to go alone."

Great. If she didn't go, she would be sending her aging father off on some crazy quest to revisit the past. Daughter of the year, she thought. That's me. "Let's find someone else to go with you. Lamont would jump at the chance."

"No," he said. "Not Lamont. He's staying here to look after the house while I'm away."

"Mom," said Julie. "We *have* to go."

"Indeed we do," her grandfather agreed.

"When can we leave?" Julie asked, practically bouncing up and down in her chair.

"Papa," Camille objected. "You can't just declare we're going to France without consulting me."

"Consider this your consultation."

"Thank you. Unfortunately, we can't swing it, Papa. I've got work—"

"I already thought of that." He held up a hand, palm out. "Your mother agrees that you can take the summer off from the shop. She and the staff will cover your duties for the entire season this year."

"Wait, you talked to Mom?" Camille bristled.

"She agrees with me entirely. This is long past due. I've already spoken to Billy as well. He says he can take care of any projects that come your way. He's hired an intern."

"He told me about the intern, but he didn't say why. The rat fink. I thought he was kidding. He's crazy if he thinks an intern can simply step in and start processing film."

"Isn't that how you got started?"

She didn't answer.

"I've already booked our flights. It is all arranged."

"No, it's not all arranged. You can't just make arrangements without me. Papa. We can't go."

"Oh my God, Mom." Julie's voice sounded taut with exasperation. "That's your answer to everything: *No. We can't.* Every. Single. Time."

"It's risky and irresponsible." Camille got up and started clearing the table, her movements swift with irritation. The prospect of a trip, even one her father yearned for, was terrifying to her. "Listen. We can't just take off. Our passports are probably expired."

"No, they're not," Julie said. "Mine's still good. I've kept track."

"Then you already know mine is going to expire next month," Camille said. Shortly before Jace died, they'd gotten a new passport for Julie so they could take her to Jamaica for Christmas. That trip had never happened, and the passports had been retired to a junk drawer.

"We can get yours renewed," said Julie. "How hard can it be?"

Eight

❧

*C*amille went to the library and fetched an armload of books, placing the stack on a long wooden table. The town library had always felt like a home away from home to her, a place of safety, filled with a comforting, insulated quiet, and the strangely appealing scent of books. It was located near the town center in an old Federal-era brick building, proudly maintained by a generous community.

After her parents had divorced, she used to come here to lose herself among the pages of books that transported her far from the strange new world of two households. In the wake of Jace's death, there had been no comfort, but she came to the library looking for signs that there was some kind of life for her on the other side of grief. And after Papa's cancer diagnosis, she had found books here that had taught her the unexpected grace in helping a loved one through illness. Today she needed something else—a way to navigate the rocky shoals of adolescence.

She was trying to decide which book to dive into first when a gaggle of high schoolers pushed and shoved their way through the door, earning a shush from the librarian in charge. For the most part, they settled down, slinging backpacks into study carrels or at computer stations. Camille spotted Vanessa Larson and Jana Jacobs among the kids—Julie's two chief tormentors. Great. She tried to ignore their presence, but a few moments later, she heard the hiss of a scathing whisper and saw movement out of the corner of her eye. The girls were settling themselves at a table on the other side of the floor-to-ceiling shelves.

"They are *so* checking us out," Vanessa whispered.

"Who?"

"Travis Mundy and Dylan Olsen. No, don't look now! Be cool."

"They're seniors. They aren't checking us out," Jana whispered back.

"Are, too. Keep watching. Just don't let them catch you. I bet I could get them to give us a ride to the Shake Shack."

Some things in high school never changed, Camille thought. The two of them were the pretty, popular girls, slender and stylish, young women just growing into their beauty. And perhaps getting their first taste of power.

"My parents would *kill* if I got into a car with a boy," Jana said.

"Then let's make sure they don't find out."

"We're supposed to be studying, remember? Coming to the library for last-period study hall is a privilege that can be taken away if we screw up."

Vanessa sighed. "Okay, whatever. I don't know what I'm going to do if I fail algebra."

"You're going to be forced to go to summer school, that's what," Jana told her.

"It's going to suck so bad, I can't even."

"Then just make sure you don't fail."

"How am I going to do that? Mr. Bristow is a total Nazi. He gives out four versions of each test so we can't copy each other. Oh my God, why am I so dumb in math?"

The most beautiful girls were often the most insecure, thought Camille.

"Doesn't he give tutorials after school?" Jana asked.

"Yeah, but nobody goes to those. They're so lame. But I'm going to have to do something. I refuse to give up one single second of summer because of algebra. My mom's organizing a clambake on the beach to celebrate the end of school."

Camille's temper did a slow burn. Vanessa was looking forward to a magical Bethany Bay summer, while all Julie wanted was to escape. She hated the thought that Vanessa had turned everyone against her daughter—and that Camille herself had been oblivious to it.

While dating Drake, she'd gotten to know Vanessa a little bit. The girl could be manipulative. When she wanted something from Drake, she played upon his sympathies, reminding him of her sadness over his divorce. And a divorce *was* sad, but Camille suspected Vanessa knew when to play the broken-family card.

She pulled her attention away from the girls and focused on the books—*The Secret Life of Teenagers. Late Bloomers. Bullying and Beyond.* Browsing through the tomes, she realized Julie had been showing classic symptoms of a victim of bullying—falling grades, behavior problems, isolating herself from her usual group of friends.

How could I have missed it? Camille wondered, sinking deeper into guilt with every page she read. There was a lot of information to take in. She narrowed her selections down to four books—plus one on villages of the Var, because her father refused to let go of his idea of spending the summer at his ancestral home.

On the way to the desk, she stopped by the table where Vanessa and Jana were whispering behind propped-up math books. "Hello, Vanessa," she said in a quiet voice. "Jana."

"Oh, hey, Camille." Vanessa sat up straight, eyes narrowed in a challenging stare.

Jana shifted in her chair. "Uh, hi, Mrs. Adams."

"I wanted to let you know that I'm sorry about what happened with your bag the other day," Camille said. "I assume Julie gave you a check to cover the cost of a new one."

"She did." Jana's gaze flicked to a new-looking purple handbag on the table.

"It was one of a kind," Vanessa piped up. "A Tonya Hawkes original."

Camille kept her expression neutral. "The new one looks really nice, Jana."

"But it's not the same," Vanessa pointed out.

"No, it's not." Camille set down her stack of books, pressed her palms on the table, and leaned forward, speaking more quietly than ever. "Julie didn't want me to say anything to you, because she thinks you'll make things even worse for her, but I'm sure you would never do such a thing. I want you to know that your campaign against her is going to stop."

"I don't know what she told you, but there's no campaign." Vanessa's cheeks turned an angry shade of red.

Right, thought Camille. "Good to know," she said. "In that case, I don't have to worry about any backlash against Julie, do I?" Without waiting for an answer, she picked up her books and carried them to the front desk. As she fished out her library card, she realized the volunteer at the desk was Trudy Jacobs.

Could this day get any better?

"Hey, Trudy."

"Hello, Camille." Trudy always seemed to look like a mom on a TV show—the outfit, the makeup, the manicure, the hair.

"I just saw Jana, and I let her know Julie and I both feel awful about her bag."

Trudy swiped her card and handed it back to her. "Jana was really upset about it. She's not used to being picked on."

Picked on? Oh, sure. "Julie has apologized," Camille said. "I'm sure they'll both feel better once they put this behind them."

Trudy pursed her lips as she scanned each of Camille's books. Camille could tell the moment Trudy perused the titles, because her lips pursed even tighter. Don't you dare say anything, Camille thought.

Trudy didn't say anything. Library volunteers were trained not to comment on a patron's selections. But her expression was ice cold as she handed the stack of books to Camille. "Good luck with all that," she said.

❧

"So what did I do?" Camille asked her mother and sister at their next Monday meeting. They were having their flat whites and lemon scones at an outside table to enjoy the brilliant summer morning. "I did exactly what Julie asked me not to do—I told those girls to back the hell off."

"Well, of course you did." Cherisse broke a scone in half. "You're doing your job as a mother."

"What if it backfires? What if they're even meaner to Julie because I stepped in?"

"I'll kick their asses," Britt said simply. "Sometimes that's the only thing a bully understands."

"I wish it were that simple." Camille sipped her coffee. She had no appetite for the scones. "The last thing I ever thought about when it came to Julie was that she'd be the victim of bullies. I wish I knew how to help. Why didn't I notice what was going on until now?"

"Because your kid's in high school," Cherisse pointed out. "It's her job to keep things from you."

"Really? Did we do that?"

"Oh, let me count the ways."

"But if a pack of girls was coming after me, I would have told you."

"Don't be so sure about that."

Camille twisted her watch around and around her wrist. "I just want to fix this for her."

Her mother covered her hand, stopping the nervous gesture. "You might need to step back and let Julie figure things out for herself."

"That's not fair. It's like throwing her to the wolves. God, teen girls can be so awful."

"And so strong. Look at the three of us. We've all weathered storms in our lives."

"If you asked Julie what she wants to do about this, what would she say?" asked Britt.

That we should all go to France for the summer. The answer popped uninvited into Camille's head. Ever since her father had brought up the idea, it was all Julie talked about. As for Camille, she vacillated, lying awake at night and asking herself: Should I stay or should I go? Should she accompany her father on a journey to his boyhood home, or cling to the life she had built so carefully for herself?

On the one hand, it was just for the summer. On the other hand, it was half a world away. For someone who never traveled, it might as well be on another planet.

"She's into this crazy notion Papa has about visiting the village where he grew up," she told them. "Which I know you're aware of, since he already talked to you about it."

"He did," her mother said. "It's a wonderful idea."

"It's absurd. I'm not dragging him and Julie to France for the summer."

"If anyone's being dragged," Britt said, "it's you. Also, 'dragging' and 'France' do not belong in the same sentence."

Cherisse touched Camille's hand. "Your father should do whatever he wants."

Camille felt a sudden burn of tears, and her stomach clenched. She knew exactly what her mother was thinking. "I'm afraid something will happen to him."

"And if it does, he'll deal with it," her mother said. "He'll have you and Julie to help him."

"I can't help him if he's in France."

"Then go, for God's sake," Britt said. "Just go. If she's being bullied, then taking her away for the summer might not be the worst idea," said Britt. "Honestly, Cam, this sounds like a dream come true. Just so you know, if somebody tells me I should spend a summer in France, I'm not going to fight them."

Because you wake up every day to a great guy and two kids, Camille thought. No nightmares of falling husbands.

"You can hang out with Professor Dreamboat while you're there," Britt added.

"Not dating, remember?" Camille scowled at her.

"Then just shag him. He's gorgeous," Britt burst out.

"Mom, do you hear the way she's talking to me?" Camille asked their mother.

"She's only doing her job as a sister. Listen, it's taken you a long time to get to the point where you're even open to dating. Don't shut down now. You've finally met someone who makes you blush when we tease you about him."

"I'm not blushing." Camille's burning cheeks made a liar of her. "I don't even think of him like that. I don't think of him at all."

"Sure you do, and you should. He lives in Aix-en-Provence. Isn't that pretty close to Bellerive?"

"I have no idea," Camille said. Forty-seven kilometers, to be precise. She'd looked at the map several times. Several dozen times. "If there's any hanging out to do," she said, "it would be with Papa. And I still haven't made up my mind about going."

Her mother dabbed at her lips with a napkin. "Your father just finished cancer treatment. This is what he wants. I don't believe you have a choice."

"Are you sure these are the right forms?" Julie asked Tarek, sitting next to him on the curb outside the post office.

"Yes." He turned the blank form so she could see it. "All you have to do is fill it out completely, get your mom to sign it, pay the fee for expedited service, and you'll have her renewed passport within two weeks."

She scanned the official-looking forms. "Really? Then we'd better get started right away." The *we* just seemed to slip out. Since the previous soccer fiasco, she and Tarek had been hanging out, sort of, like shipwreck survivors hanging on to a raft.

She still cringed when she thought about the soccer match that had incited the stupid purse incident. The trouble had started with the morning pickup game. It was pretty common for kids to kick a soccer ball around on the front school lawn. Soccer was huge at their school, and everybody played.

But not everybody played like Tarek. He was amazing. He had incredible moves and speed, and he was good at every position he played. You'd think a kid like that would be popular with everyone else, but no. Tarek looked different. He was from a foreign country. He was so good at soccer that you almost couldn't take your eyes off him. That morning, when he'd drilled a goal past Jana Jacobs's stupid boyfriend, Rolfe, Jana called Tarek a terrorist and told him to go back to where he came from.

From her midfielder position, Julie had heard the remark. She'd seen the look on Tarek's face as he'd left the field. And she'd seen Jana's couture purse on a bench next to a big, juicy mud puddle. She'd wanted to push Jana herself into the puddle, but she'd settled for the purse instead, not realizing Jana was going to make a federal case out of it.

"You need a passport photo and your mom's old passport. Do you have that?"

"I haven't even told her I'm doing this."

"Will she be mad?"

"She keeps saying we can't go, but I think she might be coming around. And I do have a photo we can use. My mom and Billy used to have a passport photo service. I found one on her computer."

"It has to be in the proper format. A two-inch square with the head in the middle."

"I'm pretty sure it is," she said. "How'd you get so smart about this?"

A shadow passed over his face. "We left everything behind. Everything we owned, and all our important documents as well. Fortunately, my parents had made digital copies and stored them online."

Julie tried to imagine what that had been like for him—walking away from his home, his neighborhood, his town . . . his father. "I'm sorry that happened to you and your family. It must have been awful."

"The worst part is that my father is still detained. My mother and our host family have been trying to secure his release."

"What's he like, your father?"

Tarek's large, dark eyes turned soft and beautiful. "He is my best friend. And the best soccer player I know. I learned all the moves from him."

"Oh, look, it's Jumbo Julie and Lawrence of Arabia," called a harsh-sounding voice.

Julie's head snapped up. Vanessa Larson, along with Jana and three others in their clique, were bearing down on them. As usual, they traveled in a pack, all skinny jeans and silky hair and nasty attitude.

"Ignore them," Tarek said.

"Sure," she muttered.

"You two make such a cute couple," Vanessa said, sidling closer.

Julie wanted to disappear without a trace, but there was no escaping the gaggle of girls. Humiliation felt like fire, the kind of fire built for human sacrifice.

"Lawrence of Arabia was an Englishman," Tarek said easily. "I am not an Englishman."

"No, you're a terrorist, that's what I heard." Vanessa did a lame imitation of his accent. Then she whipped out her phone and took their picture. "I'm going to post this online so everyone can see what a cute couple you are."

Julie still had a knot on her head where Vanessa had "accidentally" bonked her during surf rescue. The knot seemed to throb as her temper rose. "Why would you do that?" she asked, dismayed to hear a tremor in her voice. "Can't you just mind your own business?"

"Oh, look who's talking," Vanessa snapped. "You're the one who told your mom a bunch of lies about us. She saw us at the library and said you gave her some bullshit story that we're picking on you. As *if*."

Julie's insides turned to ice. Really? Had her mom really said something to Vanessa? After Julie had begged her not to? Everything was going to get worse. Way worse.

Mortified, she stood and gathered up the passport forms.

"Whatcha got there?" Jana asked, snatching up one of the pages.

"Hey—"

"Ooh, a passport application. Does this mean you're going away?"

"God, I hope so," Vanessa said. She grabbed the form and ripped

it in half, and then in half again, all the while holding Julie's gaze with
hers. "Unfortunately, they don't give passports to people who hang
out with terrorists. Oh, and your mom probably can't get one either,
because they don't give passports to murderers."

"What did you say?" Julie was incredulous. Scandalized gasps
erupted from the other girls.

Vanessa turned to them. "Oh, didn't you know? Haven't you ever
wondered where Julie's dad is? Her mom killed him when they went on
vacation. That's probably why she could never find another husband."

From the corner of her eye, Julie saw Tarek stand up. "Let's go," he
said in a low voice.

Too late. Julie dropped the rest of the forms. They wafted to the
ground, settling on the asphalt. Everything seemed to fall away, everything except the flawless, taunting face of the girl in front of her. Julie
surged forward, and shoved Vanessa as hard as she could.

Camille heard the ding of an incoming text message from Julie: *Catching up on homework at the library. Gonna be late to P's for dinner.*

Homework on the last day of school? That seemed surprising.
Maybe, Camille thought, Julie was doing some extra-credit assign-
ments to bring up her grades. In just a few months, she'd gone from
making straight As to low Bs and Cs. Camille hoped it wasn't too late
to bring those grades up. She was tempted to call Julie but didn't let
herself. She was trying not to hover so much.

She'd been busy with work all day, and she was eager to get to her
personal e-mail. Yes, she and Finn had been e-mailing each other. She
rationalized that they were collaborating on research for her father,
finding out more about the photos they had found in Lisette's trunk.
The truth, which she would barely admit to herself, was that she liked
corresponding with him. He was funny and entertaining, and quite
good at flirting. The fact that he was so far away worked well for her.
She didn't have to worry about actually having a relationship. Flirting
was nothing but harmless fun.

The current note in her in-box was a good example. *Subject: you're in my 3AM thoughts.*

The idea of him thinking of her at three A.M. was ridiculously enticing. She kept reminding herself that all she wanted was to find out more about Lisette and her world during the war years. Maybe that way, her father would drop the idea of rushing off to Bellerive, and instead content himself with a video call to the caretakers of his property there. Maybe he—and she and Julie—would stay safely in Bethany Bay, same as every summer.

Except that in Julie's case, Bethany Bay didn't feel safe anymore.

Worries kept Camille awake at night. She hoped Julie was just going through a phase, that she could make a fresh start now that summer was here. Camille had already set the fresh start in motion. Julie's braces were going to be removed and substituted with a nighttime-only appliance. She was also switching to contact lenses. Camille knew better than to believe it was a cure-all, but it might give Julie's confidence a boost.

She poured herself a glass of wine and sat down with her laptop.

TO: cadams@oohlala.com
FROM: mfinnemore@usna.mil.gov
SUBJECT: you're in my 3AM thoughts

Hey Camille,
Turns out Bellerive was definitely in the drop zone for Operation Dragoon. I drove over there yesterday to have a look. Found the property your father owns and took some photos. It's quite a place, wedged between the mountains and the sea. I'll send the pics later. You should see it. Rustic charm, drenched in sunshine. All that's missing is a glass of wine . . . and thee. Or is it thou? Whatever. You know what I'm saying.

Cheers,
Finn
[This email is UNCLASSIFIED.]

"You went to Bellerive," she said to her screen. "Wow, you went to Papa's village." It made her absurdly happy that he'd taken the time to go there. The other thing that made her happy was that line about her. "You're a flirt, Professor Finnemore, that's what you are," she told the computer screen.

TO: mfinnemore@usna.mil.gov
FROM: cadams@oohlala.com
SUBJECT: RE: you're in my 3AM thoughts

Finn,
Thanks for the field report. You've gone above and beyond. I feel guilty not paying you for your services. Looking forward to the pics.

Best,
Camille

She hesitated before hitting send. She wanted to make sure this sounded like a casual exchange, nothing more. She went back and changed *services* to *time* and then sent the note.

A moment later, a window popped up at the bottom of her screen.

IMAKEPESTO: Hi.

She frowned. Who was that? Since she didn't know, she clicked the *X* to close the window. There was a message from Billy Church about work—the Tidewater Film Society was collecting images from found film for an exhibit that would debut early next year. Did she want to get together with him to decide what to submit?

Of course, she said. She loved working with found images, and getting them out into the world might uncover the mystery behind some of them.

IMAKEPESTO: Hey Camille.

Another pop-up window. She scowled at it.

IMAKEPESTO: It's Finn.

Her heart sped up. She took a quick sip of wine. Then she clicked the reply box and started typing.

STEWARDESS: Oh. Hi there. I didn't recognize your screen name.
Imakepesto?
IMAKEPESTO: Yep.
STEWARDESS: Because . . .
IMAKEPESTO: Because "Bazillionaire" was already taken.
STEWARDESS: But . . . pesto?
IMAKEPESTO: Actually, I DO make pesto. You should try it sometime,
it's awesome. Stewardess?
STEWARDESS: I can type it with one hand. Leaving the other hand free
to hold the wineglass.
IMAKEPESTO: Ah. So practical.
STEWARDESS: Is it really 3am there?
IMAKEPESTO: Not anymore. You got my note?
STEWARDESS: I did. That was really cool of you to go to Bellerive.
IMAKEPESTO: Trust me, not a hardship. Fantastic little town, straight
out of a storybook. We found a great restaurant in the center of the
village.
STEWARDESS: We?

Camille cringed. Did that look as if she was fishing for details about his personal life?

IMAKEPESTO: Me and my research assistant, Roz.

She wondered what Roz was like. Then she chided herself for wondering.

STEWARDESS: Cool you have an assistant.

IMAKEPESTO: Had an amazing salade niçoise for lunch—Bandol tuna, fresh off the boat—and for dessert, honey ice cream served in this insane cone made from a sugared croissant.

STEWARDESS: Sounds lethal.

IMAKEPESTO: You're missing out. You need to see this place.

STEWARDESS: You sound like my father.

IMAKEPESTO: That's a bad sign. I don't want to sound like your father.

Oops, thought Camille. That came out wrong.

STEWARDESS: I mean he keeps saying he wants to go back for a visit.

IMAKEPESTO: He should. What's stopping him?

Me, she thought, but she didn't want to share that with him.

STEWARDESS: He just finished cancer treatment. The doc cleared him to travel, but I worry . . .

IMAKEPESTO: Then come with him. Bring your daughter.

STEWARDESS: Now you REALLY sound like him. He's been saying we should go with him.

IMAKEPESTO: You should. I bet he'd love to show you this part of the world. I know I would.

Quick, change the subject, Camille.

STEWARDESS: Hey, did you send those pictures you took?

IMAKEPESTO: Yep, just now.

She heard the rocket blast of an incoming e-mail. *Swoosh.*

STEWARDESS: Excited! I'm going to have a look right away . . . I shouldn't be keeping you up.

IMAKEPESTO: I like staying up late with you. It'd be even better if we were having this conversation in person.

STEWARDESS: I'm looking at the pictures now . . .

He was right. The town was utterly charming—old stone buildings, narrow streets, a grand Gothic church. The weather looked gorgeous—crystal-clear blue sky, everything drenched in sunshine. Grapevines and hollyhocks everywhere.

There was a young woman in a few of the pictures. She had silky-straight hair, oversized sunglasses, and was effortlessly dressed in a flowy top and capri pants. She looked like a high-end fashion model. The assistant?

Camille was not surprised that he had an assistant who looked like a model. "Move on, Camille," she muttered. "Look at the pictures."

IMAKEPESTO: When you get here, remind me to take you to this museum in the Vaucluse. It has an extensive collection from the war years.

"When I get there?" Camille asked the empty room. "You mean, never? And why would you assume I'm coming to France?"

She drew her attention back to the pictures he'd sent. The most arresting image was a hand-colored, vintage portrait of a man with pale blond hair and steely blue eyes.

IMAKEPESTO: Recognize this guy?

STEWARDESS: No. Should I?

IMAKEPESTO: Found it in the town records. Didier Palomar, mayor from 1937 to 1945. The label says "Maire de Bellerive."

STEWARDESS: Wait. What?

IMAKEPESTO: Pretty sure it's Lisette's husband. Which would make him your grandfather, right?

STEWARDESS: I've never seen a picture of him.

IMAKEPESTO: Say hi to *grand-père*.

She felt a chill as she gazed at the picture. Every hair was in place. His eyes, thin lips, bony face, chin held at a haughty angle.

STEWARDESS: Ick. According to my father, he was a collaborator. The most hated man in the village. Did you find out if he was really shot in '45?
IMAKEPESTO: No. We can look into that when we go back to Bellerive.

We. Did he mean him and the supermodel?

She set the print of Lisette next to the screen and studied the images side by side. Her grandparents gazed back at her across the decades—two strangers to whom she was inextricably tied. Lisette was a beauty, clearly much younger than Didier, her sleek hair and delicate features almost mesmerizing. Didier, not so much. Even in a portrait meant to flatter, he had close-set, pale blue eyes and wispy blond hair, and—

Camille caught her breath. She stared some more, looking back and forth at the photos. Lisette and Didier. She couldn't be certain from the Lisette photo, since it was in black and white, but the tones of the picture suggested that her father's mother had light blond hair and pale eyes. Lisette and Didier Palomar were both as blond as Vikings.

Then Camille grabbed a picture of her father—a shot taken soon after his arrival in America. In the photo, he was just eighteen or nineteen, close to Lisette's age. Camille compared their features. Like his mother, he had full lips, prominent cheekbones, wide-set eyes, and a strong chin. Unlike her, he had curly black hair, deep brown eyes, and olive-toned skin.

Between Didier and Henry, she could see no resemblance at all.

More unsettling was the fact that Henry's coloring—and hers, and Julie's, for that matter—was wildly different from his parents'.

The question nagged at her. How could these two Aryan-featured people have had a son with Henry's coloring? Was there some other branch of the family tree?

She set down her glass of wine and picked up the old camera, feeling its heft in her hands. Then she looked at Lisette. "Who were you?" Camille asked in French. "What were you thinking in that moment? Why do you look so sad?"

Camille tried to imagine the stories going through Lisette's head as she pressed the shutter, capturing a haunted moment. Camille had spent a long time studying every detail of the photograph. Based on the state of Lisette's pregnancy, the pictures on the film roll might have been the last photos she ever took.

IMAKEPESTO: Hello? Did I lose you?

Transfixed by the photos, Camille didn't reply to the message. She lifted the old camera to her eye and peered into the viewfinder, wondering what had gone through Lisette's mind when she took a photo. Still speaking French, she said, "I wish I'd known you. What could you have told me? What secrets are you hiding?"

PART 2

The Var

What makes photography a strange invention is that its primary raw materials are light and time.

—JOHN BERGER, ENGLISH ART CRITIC

Nine

❧

Bellerive, the Var, France
1941

Lisette Galli held Dr. Toselli's wonderful camera in her hands. "You're giving this to me? Surely you cannot part with it."

The elderly Dr. Cyprian Toselli, her employer, held up his hand. "Consider it a special gift for your sixteenth birthday."

She smiled. "I turned sixteen three months ago."

"You know how forgetful I am. It's my favorite camera, and it would be a shame to think of it sitting unused in its box. Sadly, I can no longer use it." Dr. Toselli, an expert photographer with many years of experience, was slowly going blind. A veterinarian by profession, he had planned to spend his retirement taking photos and printing the images in his darkroom. Now, sadly, he would spend it in the dark.

"It is too fine," she said. "I can't accept it." Ah, but she yearned to. For the past two years, she had been keeping house and tending the garden for a small wage. When he'd noticed her interest in photography, he'd given her lessons, which she had absorbed like one of the sea sponges sold at the Bandol docks.

"Lisette, it would please me so much to know my favorite camera is in your talented hands, capturing images the way I taught you. The moments of life are ephemeral and unpredictable. We must capture the best ones and keep them safe in our hearts. If you have learned nothing else from me, you must learn this."

His words brought a burn of tears to her eyes. Lisette's two older brothers had both been killed early on in the Battle of France. Étienne had served as a *chasseur alpin,* attached to a mountain regiment of foot soldiers. He had been shot while defending a strategic position along the Maginot Line in the northeast. Roland, perhaps even more tragically, died after a fistfight with fellow soldiers in his unit who had accused him of a shameful vice she scarcely understood. She had made a few portraits of them before they'd gone off to join the fighting, and now she cherished these images with all her heart.

She bit her lip. "You're far too kind."

"On the contrary, I am a selfish old man. I am greedy for the pleasure it gives me to help you learn to do something I have loved all my life. And also, I do not trust the Italian soldiers. Ever since they took over our little village, certain things have been disappearing. I know you will keep my camera safe."

She shuddered, remembering how the Italians had rampaged through the streets, claiming revenge for their comrades who had been killed during the invasion. The soldiers had raided the summer villas of rich English and Parisian aristocrats, but they were not above robbing the common folk as well. A tenuous order had been recently restored, thanks to a truce struck between the Italian Armistice Commission and local officials. But no one in Bellerive trusted the soldiers.

The Italian invasion was a horrible blow to France, which had already fought for—and lost—its northern region to Germany. Last June, Paris had been bombed in broad daylight and then declared *"ville ouverte"* to the Germans, and the new leader, Maréchal Pétain, had signed an armistice. While reading the news to Dr. Toselli, she'd discovered that all the world condemned the action. The president of America, Monsieur Roosevelt, declared that "the hand that held the dagger has plunged it into the back of its neighbor." France had been cut in two—the occupied zone to the north, and the so-called free zone here in the south. But there was no freedom here, merely a different foreign authority to answer to.

She set the camera in its box and latched it shut, gazing down at the initials *CT,* letter-pressed in the lid. "In that case, I will do exactly as you say. I will take marvelous pictures with your camera, and keep it safe, always."

He reached out to pat her hand, but missed the first pat. She discreetly moved her hand so that he could touch it. The gentle gesture brought tears to her eyes. Over the past several years, he had been gradually losing his vision to a condition known as macular degeneration. He told her the blindness closed in like the aperture of a camera lens, narrowing the field of vision until he felt as though he was peering through an ever-shrinking tunnel.

"Your pictures are excellent, with your keen eye for the details of daily life. Promise you will keep practicing your craft. The darkroom is for your use, as always." The darkroom in the pantry was a perfect laboratory, complete with photographic enlarger, special paper and chemicals, and fresh water pumped from outside.

He was a dear man, and Lisette would have helped him for no charge. But he insisted on paying her a wage. He understood the hardships of her family all too well, and he understood the dignity of work. "I don't know how to thank you, monsieur. You're very generous."

"Very good, then," he said. "That is settled, and I am content. What time is it?"

She looked out the window at the large clock face over the railway station. "Half past five."

"Perfect. I should like an aperitif, then, and perhaps a chapter of our book before you leave."

"Of course. I'll just be a minute." She tucked the camera box into her woven-straw market basket. Then she went and poured precisely two fingers of Ricard into a slender drinking glass, adding one chunk of ice from the precious supply in the icebox. Due to the deprivations of war, refrigeration was hard to come by, but Toselli had a special need for it. He was secretly making a wonder drug—penicillin—for the war effort. With his medical and scientific background, and the equipment from his veterinary practice, he knew just what to do, and Lisette was eager to help him titrate the medicine and keep it hidden.

If the invading forces found out, his supply would be seized and he'd probably be arrested. Lisette thought it was marvelous that this elderly man could contribute to the French cause. From the very start, she had guarded his secret. The occupying soldiers regarded him as a harmless old man, never realizing what was going on right under their noses.

"Let us go out to the garden terrace," he said. "I love to feel the sun on my face."

"Of course. I am right behind you."

He picked up the book she was reading to him and tucked it under his arm. Then he led the way across the small sitting room to the garden behind the house. He touched things as he passed—the back of a kitchen chair, the side of a cabinet, the hall tree with his hat, cane, and umbrella. Lisette was meticulous about keeping everything exactly in its place. She had made it her mission to help him organize his home so he could find what he needed.

She had always been a good student in school, yet under his tutelage, she'd learned things far beyond the topics offered by the nuns at the local school. Often he told her to curtail her cleaning and gardening duties in order to read more. They both loved reading of all sorts—novels and histories, classic tales of heroes and villains, poetry and current journals about the state of the world in the midst of the terrible things that were happening all around them. Although Bellerive had surrendered peacefully when the Italian army marched over the bridge and took up occupation in the *mairie* and the courthouse, these were worrisome times. The real news was found in the underground journals distributed mysteriously throughout the region, giving patriots the awful truth: the Nazis had overrun Paris. There were arrests, roundups, and deportations of Jews and foreigners, and according to Dr. Toselli, the only thing keeping the Nazis at bay in the Var was the presence of the Italians.

"It is a sad thing, choosing one conqueror over another," he told her. "Let's not read the news today. Everything is censored, anyway. I would prefer to check in with Mr. Holmes."

Toselli had a special project with Lisette, sharing with her his most favorite treat—a series of novels about Sherlock Holmes, a brilliant English detective who solved mysterious crimes. The books were in English. When they first started reading *A Study in Scarlet,* she'd struggled mightily with the foreign words and tortured pronunciation, but Toselli was incredibly patient and encouraging. He delighted in her swift improvement. They were now reading the third volume in the series, a story called *The Hound of the Baskervilles.*

She read a scene in which Sherlock Holmes stood in the hallway of a mansion, studying the ancestors of the Baskervilles, noting the family resemblance and wondering about a newly arrived cousin.

"Does the family resemblance truly exist," she asked, when she finished reading, "or do people see what they want to see?"

Monsieur smiled at her. "That is part of the puzzle, eh? It is no mystery where you came from. You are as fair and flaxen-haired as your dear mother. Who is probably getting your supper at home. You should go."

She placed the book on the table next to his magnifying glass. He was still able to see print with a powerful lamp and glass, and he might want to read on later. Then she bade him good-bye, gathered up her things, and stepped out into the sun-flooded street.

Before walking to her parents' tiny cottage at the south end of the town by the bridge, she had one more errand. It was Saturday, and she had to stop at the village church to make her weekly confession.

The church was dim and cool inside. The ancient stone floor and walls amplified the sound of her footfalls as she walked up a side aisle toward the wooden confessional booth with its carved gargoyles and griffin vultures. A few nuns and old people were present, some seated on prayer chairs, others kneeling in front of the main altar, heads bent in contemplation. She approached the confessional, leaning down to see if it was occupied.

It was empty, so she slipped behind the curtain and knelt down, making the sign of the cross. "Bless me, Father, for I have sinned . . ."

She waited for Father Rinaldo to respond, her mind wandering. It must be so tedious for the priest, listening to her petty offenses. She was simply not interesting enough to have anything of substance to confess. And although it was probably a sin in and of itself, she knew that if she ever did anything interesting enough to warrant a confession, she wouldn't admit it.

Maybe she should tell him how guilty she felt that she couldn't be more helpful to her parents. Her father, an expert stonecutter, had suffered a grievous accident a year before. Now he was confined to a wheelchair, and the family depended on the charity of neighbors and the Church to sustain them. Sometimes she heard anxious whispers in the night. They would soon be put out of their cottage because they couldn't pay their taxes. Her mother feared they would be reduced to begging—or worse. The threat of prison hung over their heads. There was talk of going to a charity house in Marseille, a horrifying prospect to her once-proud father.

Perhaps she should confess a crime of the heart. She had let Jean-Luc d'Estérel kiss her, several times, and she was probably going to fall in love with him. He was incredibly handsome, with large dark eyes fringed by thick lashes, a strong jaw, and a graceful aquiline nose. Jean-Luc was Jewish, which meant the Church would probably deem their romance sinful.

"Monseigneur?" she whispered after a few minutes had passed.

Still no response from the priest. A moment later, she heard a gentle snore.

Lisette sighed. "Very well, then. My sins are terribly boring." She whispered the Act of Contrition in Latin, then slipped out of the confessional. No penance today.

Carrying her basket, she left the church and wound down through the narrow alleyways of the village. She and her parents had a cottage by the bridge that spanned the river. Their next-door neighbor used to be in charge of the sluices that controlled the flow of water, but he had been evicted by the invading soldiers, because the bridge was a major strategic point. Now sandbags formed a makeshift embankment around the structure to protect it in the event of a bombing. Only a year ago, a bombing had been the last thing on her mind. The bridge was simply a way to get from one side of the river to the other. Now it was a target for bombs, a prize to be fought over by opposing forces.

She made the mistake of taking a shortcut past the Bar Zinc, a gathering place for soldiers. Not so long ago, her village had been a safe place, filled with friendly faces and abundant food and wine from the surrounding farms and vineyards. These days, Bellerive seethed with whispered rumors, black-market dealings, armed foreigners roaming the streets. A group of them was gathered at a sidewalk table, and inevitably, they spotted her. A babble of Italian catcalls erupted.

She pretended not to hear the harsh voices and kissing sounds, but one of them blocked her way. "Where are you going, pretty girl?" he asked in broken French. "What are you carrying in your basket?"

The camera. She clutched it closer to her body, hoping the leeks and greens from Dr. Toselli's garden concealed the precious box.

"Please," she said quietly. "It's just a few discarded vegetables for my parents."

"Very well, then, you must join us for a glass of wine." The soldier was swarthy and thick-limbed, his drab uniform reeking of sweat. He placed his hand on her arm.

She yanked it away as if burned, trying not to panic. "Do not touch me. Monsieur," she added.

"We are here for your protection. This is no way to show your gratitude." He took her arm again.

She cast a wild look around, hoping the barman or a passerby would help. "Leave me alone," she said loudly.

"What is this?" asked a smooth, French voice.

She whipped around to see Didier Palomar, the town mayor. Monsieur Palomar owned a fine *mas* called Sauveterre, his ancient familial manor surrounded by fields, vineyards, meadows, and creeks that flowed down to the sea. At Sunday Mass he was a haughty presence in fine clothes, his blond hair and steely gray eyes commanding attention. But he was French, and held a position of authority, a far more trustworthy ally than the hard-drinking foreign soldiers.

"*Monsieur le maire,* I am simply trying to make my way home to my parents. I have no wish to cause trouble."

"Very well, then, I shall accompany you myself." He said something to the soldiers in Italian. A couple of them made rude gestures, but they returned to their drinking.

"You are Albert Galli's girl, no?" Didier asked as they walked down a steeply winding street.

"Yes, sir." She was shaken by the encounter. Her voice sounded thin, and her wobbly legs barely supported her.

Monsieur Palomar placed his hand under her elbow. "Your name is Lisette."

She wondered how he knew. "Yes, sir," she said again.

"You've grown to be a lovely young lady. Best you steer clear of the soldiers."

"I will," she said, though she felt a deep resentment. What right had they to move into this peaceful village, which had committed no offense except to be in the path of Hitler and Mussolini's ambitions?

They reached the cottage, and she hesitated at the doorway, feeling a struggle between pride and manners. She was a Galli; manners won. "Would you like to come in for an aperitif?" she asked.

"How kind of you," he said, and held open the door.

"Maman, Papa, we have a guest," she said, seeing them in the tiny garden behind the house, an oasis her father had created with a stone enclosure and a small pond. "It is Monsieur Palomar."

The mayor strode out to the garden, taking her father's hand and then her mother's.

"Please, sit down," said her father.

"I'll bring something to drink," her mother said.

"You're very gracious, but I don't need anything," said Monsieur Palomar. "I simply wanted to see the young lady safely home."

Lisette stood in the dim interior of the house, taking the vegetables from her basket. She stashed the camera under the root bin. These days, there was no safe place. Every home was vulnerable, not just to soldiers being billeted there, but also to air raids.

"You must allow us to serve you an aperitif," her mother insisted. "I know it's been forbidden by the central authority, but I make my own *vin maison,* a lovely ratafia of peaches and herbs."

Monsieur Palomar paused, then gave a nod of the head. "Of course, then. I can see where your daughter gets her kind nature."

Maman scurried into the kitchen as the two men talked. "Take out the good pitcher, Lisette," said Maman. "Make sure there's not a spot on it."

While Lisette inspected the pitcher, Maman took the herb-infused wine from the icebox. Her brow knit in a frown, and Lisette knew she was yearning to set a better table for the mayor. But the taste of butter, milk, cheese, and meat was but a distant memory to the Galli family. Maman cut a few slices from the baguette and scooped a ladle of olives from their precious, dwindling supply. Olives were Papa's favorite. Maman must have caught Lisette's expression. "He is a very important man, Palomar is. He knows how to deal with the Italians. I've heard his farm still has its dairy cows and pigs."

Local farms were ordered to billet and feed soldiers. Strict rationing rules were in place, and shortages were rampant. Military activity had destroyed the usual transport modes by sea, river barge, and railroads. Most of the labor force had gone to war or into hiding, so there were not enough workers to tend the crops, nor was there fuel to power the farm equipment. Even here in the countryside, supplementing food supplies by game hunting, foraging, and growing local produce was regulated, which actually meant the whole yield had to be handed over and redistributed by the authorities. Even the hour of aperitif had been forbidden, although in private homes, the rules were hard to enforce.

Lisette took down the thick, stubby aperitif glasses. On the inside of the cupboard door were the photos she had taken of her brothers before they went off to fight. The pictures stayed hidden, as villagers had been cautioned against overt displays of patriotism. The soldiers were paranoid, suspecting everyone of being maquisards, bush fighters of the Maquis, whose guerrilla tactics and secret communication network made them a fearsome enemy.

She cut a glance at Monsieur Palomar. Framed by the open cottage window, he looked relaxed and confident, leaning forward with his elbows on his knees to talk to Papa.

"Palomar is very handsome, eh?" Maman remarked.

Lisette flushed. "If you say so. For an older man."

"He's not so very old, perhaps thirty," Maman said. "And a widower, so young."

"His wife died?"

"She did, just last year. Madame Picoche said she drowned in the Calanques. The swimming is so hazardous there. Let us be especially kind to Monsieur Palomar."

Picking up the serving tray, Lisette followed her mother out to the garden.

"Voilà," said her father with a genial smile. "A glass to welcome the evening."

Maman poured, and they touched each other's glasses in *salut*. Lisette had always thought there was something magical about those rare, sun-gilt in-between moments just as day slipped into twilight. Before her father's accident, it marked his transition from a day of labor to the relaxation of evening. He would shuck his *ouvrier*'s trousers and wash up at the outdoor basin, singing "Dis-moi, Janette" or some other old song. When she and her brothers were small, Maman gave them lemonade, and the family would sit together, enjoying the special time as they reconnected with Papa.

She was proud to see her father now, keeping his dignity despite all he had lost—his sons, his work, the use of his legs—as he conversed with the mayor of the town. They talked of the things that weighed on everyone's minds these days—the invasion of the Italians, the war with Germany in the north, the shortages, the air raids.

Lisette sipped her *vin maison* slowly, savoring the herbal taste. She didn't eat any of the olives, not wanting to hasten the dwindling of the supply. Monsieur Palomar seemed cordial enough, but there was something about him. She couldn't put her finger on it. Then he caught her staring, offered a genial smile and a tip of his glass, and she chided herself. This was the man who had shielded her from the foreign soldiers, after all.

"How is it," her father asked, "that you've managed so well through all this?"

"Albert," said Maman. "He is a guest. Don't be rude."

"No rudeness is meant," Papa clarified.

"And none taken," said Monsieur Palomar. "I am committed to protecting our village. Sometimes, this means facing terrible choices. Capitulate and avoid bloodshed, or resist and invite blood-shed. I have no taste for capitulation, but what choice do we have? Our national pride might be wounded, but it does not bleed like our citizens do."

"We are lucky to have a mayor who understands this," said Maman.

The light deepened, and the curfew bells sounded. "I must be go-ing. My sister Rotrude will scold me if I'm late to supper." He stood, and his face seemed haunted by sadness. "Her husband died in the fighting only a month after I lost my wife, and so she and her little daughter have come back to Sauveterre. It would be a quiet, lonely place but for the Italians billeted there."

"There are soldiers under your roof?"

He nodded. "I had no choice. Rotrude complains of their manners, and they drink our wine as if it's water. All my late wife's grenache is gone. I used to take comfort in drinking the wine she made."

"We're very sorry for your loss," said Papa.

"And I for yours. Alas, my wife never gave me children, so I can only imagine the pain of losing your sons." He squared his shoulders and looked at Lisette, his gaze scanning her from head to toe. "And there, I've made us all thoroughly maudlin. Let us look ahead to better times, eh?"

"More butter from Monsieur Palomar?" Lisette asked, taking her place at the supper table. For the past year, he'd been supplying them with rare treats of butter, cheese, bacon, coffee, and wine, supplementing the meager portions allowed by the rationing system. The mayor and Papa had become friends, and Palomar often said he would help the family if they ever needed anything.

"He's been very generous," Maman said, serving each of them a dish of soup and a cut of bread topped with the fresh butter.

Papa said a quick *bénédicité,* and then they raised their glasses. There was only water to drink, as the rationed wine was both scarce and foul. The shortages grew worse by the week. People were eating the workhorses they couldn't afford to feed. Soups and stews made of foraged foods failed to fill bellies. If a fisherman had a good catch, the bounty was requisitioned and fed to the soldiers rather than distributed to the populace.

Lisette forced herself to eat slowly, even though hunger gnawed at her belly. It was frightening to see her parents' sunken cheeks and thinning hair. Dr. Toselli, so jovial and robust when she had first started working for him, was sickly, his vision worse than ever. She had stopped accepting payment for her services, though she still visited him every day to keep house, to sit and talk, to read with him. She insisted that the English lessons were payment enough.

In addition to the lessons, he continued to school her in the art of the darkroom, and her obsession with photography grew. She helped Toselli with his penicillin production as well, even though he cautioned her about what would happen if she got caught. She didn't care. If her efforts supported the war against Germany and Italy, she would take the risk. She had even persuaded her mother to cultivate cantaloupes in the garden, though she didn't say why—they were the best for growing the mold that would yield the antibiotic.

"Delicious," Papa pronounced. He tipped the bread crumbs from his napkin into his soup plate and took one last bite so as not to waste anything.

"We have dessert tonight. Another gift from *monsieur le maire*." Maman lifted the pottery dome of the butter dish to reveal not butter, but—

"Chocolate!" Lisette said. "Maman, is that chocolate?"

Her mother nodded.

Papa cut the dark, glossy piece into three portions. "Bon appétit, my loves," he said.

Lisette bit into hers, closing her eyes to savor the delicious rush. Chocolate! Such a thing was unheard of in these times. She felt almost dizzy with the flavor of it.

"He wants to court you," said Papa. "He asked my permission."

Lisette's eyes flew open. "What? Who?"

"Monsieur Palomar would like to court you," Papa repeated. "Your mother and I have given our approval."

The chocolate taste turned to thick bitterness in her mouth. "This is absurd," she said. "Palomar is far too old for me. I don't know him at all, nor do I wish to."

"He has been exceedingly good to our family," Maman said.

"And I do appreciate that. But I already have a boyfriend—Jean-Luc d'Estérel."

"That's a girlhood flirtation," said Maman. "You're a young woman now. And besides, he's Jewish."

"So is Mussolini's mistress."

"How did you hear that?"

"I hear things. I know things."

"Then you should hear that the Germans are coming. They'll oust the Italians and round up the Jews. If Jean-Luc knows what's good for him, he'll make himself scarce."

"His mother is ill," Lisette said. "He can't leave her. And Marshal Graziani has ordered Jean-Luc to work for him, because he's the only one in Bellerive who has the expertise to operate the railroad switches and river locks." She knew Jean-Luc hated having to provide a service for the occupying military force. "I want nothing to do with Didier Palomar," she concluded, feeling ill as she eyed the remaining pieces of chocolate on the plate.

Maman took hold of both her hands. "There is no more money for rent. We have to leave the house by the end of the month."

"What? When did you learn this?" Lisette looked from one parent to the other. Her father sat in stoic silence, his expression stony.

"There was a notice a few weeks ago."

"Then I shall find a way to get some money," Lisette said, her heart thumping with desperation. "I can speak, read, and write English. I can cook and clean and sew. Surely I could find a position in Aix or Marseille."

"Don't even think of it. Horrible things happen to young girls who go to the city."

"More horrible than being courted by a man I don't know?" Lisette bolted from the table and charged out the door, ignoring the sound of the curfew bells. She ran until a sharp pain pinched her side. She had to tell Jean-Luc what was planned. Together, they would figure out what to do.

Breathless and clutching her side, she reached his tiny apartment above a cobbler shop and burst in on him. He was alone, bent over something on the table. He nearly fell off his stool in surprise. "Lisette," he said, jumping to his feet. "I wasn't expecting you."

"I had to see you," she said. "My parents want me to marry Didier Palomar."

"The mayor?"

"He's been supplying us with food. I assumed it was a gesture of kindness, but all he really wanted was to win my father's approval. Now we're being put out of our home because there's no money. If I refuse Palomar, we'll be begging in the street."

"Slow down," Jean-Luc said, clutching her upper arms and staring into her face. "Lisette, don't panic."

"I can't help it. We have only until the end of the month." She took a deep breath, reminding herself that hysterics would solve nothing. "I'm sorry," she added, looking around the tiny apartment. "How is your mother?"

"She's resting." He indicated the next room with a nod. Then he lowered his voice. "The doctor said there's nothing more to be done except to keep her comfortable."

Suddenly this made her troubles slink away into a back corner of her mind. "Jean-Luc, I'm so sorry. How can I help?"

"By being you. By being here." He touched her cheek. He had a very gentle touch.

Jean-Luc was the first boy—the only boy—she had ever kissed. Someday, she might even fall in love with him, the way people fell in love in the movies, with a blinding éclat of passion.

She heard a faint crackling sound, like a fire. Then she looked at the table where he'd been sitting, and for the first time noticed a large case filled with a jumble of tubes, knobs, and switches. It was a home-made radio.

She looked up at Jean-Luc, feeling all the color drain from her face. "My God. You're working for the partisans."

Lisette heard the *churr* of a nightjar, and then the sound she'd been straining to hear—a low whistle. She slipped out of bed and dressed quickly in a plain blouse and smock, then padded barefoot to the door. She paused, listening for her parents—the soft whistle of Papa's almost-snore, a light sigh from Maman.

Then she stepped outside. The street was dark, the quiet stirred by the nightjar and the burble of the river flowing under the old stone bridge. The scent of magnolia, cypress, and plane trees rode the breeze. Blackout regulations prohibited even the slightest leak of light from a streetlamp or window, so she stood for a moment, letting her eyes adjust to the darkness. She could make out the bulky shadow of the church at the top of the village, and the craggy profile of the bridge close by. Picking up her market basket and boots, she crossed the bridge.

"Over here," came a whisper. Jean-Luc d'Estérel waited with his bicycle next to the bridge tower. "Did anyone see you?"

"I don't think so."

He reached for her, planting a firm kiss on her lips. Her heart sped up as she savored the taste and smell of him.

"Are you sure you want to do this?" he asked.

"I'm sure. I only wish you had let me help long ago." She put on her boots.

"This work is dangerous, Lisette, make no mistake. A partisan was taken last week in Marseille, and Louis said he was tortured in ways I don't even want to describe to you. By the *French*."

Jean-Luc's friend Louis Picoche seemed to know everything. He relied on a small, tight-knit group who knew how to keep a secret.

"Those who side with the Vichy government and Pétain are not French," she hissed, feeling the heat of contempt. "We won't get caught. We're in the middle of nowhere, far from the big city."

They walked to the edge of town, speaking in whispers while Jean-Luc wheeled the bicycle, taking care not to let it rattle over the cobblestones. Once they reached the roadway leading to the coast, they got on, Lisette taking the seat while Jean-Luc pedaled. Clutching him around the waist, she felt utterly exhilarated by the rush of air in her face and the feel of his muscular body beneath her hands. The darkness only added to the excitement. Finally, after simmering with resentment against the occupying soldiers, she had a chance to do something.

They met Louis in a broad, empty field on the high ground a few hundred meters from massive granite calanques jutting out into the sea. When she was small, Lisette and her brothers would come here after chores on hot summer days to enjoy the sandy beaches tucked between the towering cliffs. Papa had taught her to swim in the azure water.

After the accident, Lisette had become the teacher. Her father had plunged into a terrible melancholy, alternately furious and despairing over what he called his useless body. She had organized Papa's friends to help. They had loaded him into a cart, brought him to the beach, and carried him into the water. Lisette had held his hands while he floated, encouraging him to swim. Seeing him rediscover the pleasure of weightlessness in the water had filled her with joy, and their outings to the beach became a regular occurrence. Maman would bring a baguette and something from the garden for a picnic, and sometimes for a few hours, they forgot what had happened to the boys, they forgot Papa's accident, and they forgot that foreign troops occupied their town. Lisette had taken some pictures of her parents at the beach as mementos.

Tonight, there was no forgetting. Louis had not told them what to expect. Jean-Luc had explained that the less each partisan knew, the better. There would be nothing to confess under torture if someone got caught.

"What I wouldn't give for a smoke right now," said Louis, pacing back and forth. "Can't risk it, though, not even a match strike." He tipped his head back and gazed at the empty black sky.

"Where would you even get a proper cigarette?" asked Jean-Luc. "Don't tell me you're dealing with the black market."

"I don't have one," Louis admitted. "I was just wishing for one. You know I'd never line the pockets of the collaborators. The war profiteers are as bad as the Nazis." He stopped speaking and tilted his head to one side. "Listen."

Lisette could hear the sound of the waves, but then she noticed something else. "It's a motor."

"An airplane," Jean-Luc said. "Are they making a parachute drop?"

"Yes. Supplies. Help me move these stones." Louis dropped to his knees and started removing some large rocks from a pile. Jean-Luc and Lisette pitched in. Under the stones was a square of canvas. Louis moved it aside and took out a box or case of some sort.

"What is this?" she asked.

"It's a transponder," Louis said. "This tells them where the drop zone is." He opened the hinged lid of the box and flipped some switches, and the equipment emitted a crackling sound. "I think it's working. Now we wait."

They lay back in the grass and looked up at the sky. The night was clear and filled with stars. Time moved slowly. Jean-Luc reached for her hand and gave it a squeeze. She smiled into the darkness, but a ripple of sadness coursed through her. When she had first begun walking out with him, everything had seemed so simple. Now, instead of outings to town festivals and to the beach, they found themselves committing acts of subterfuge together.

"There," Louis whispered. "I see something."

They watched a shadow in the sky. It grew larger, drifting, and they rushed to meet it as it fell to the earth. There was a large parcel bound with straps. Louis opened it while Lisette and Jean-Luc gathered up the chute. Her heart was pounding as they loaded everything into the cart.

"We need to hurry," Louis said, concealing the radio. They moved the rocks back into place and wheeled the cart to a stone-built *borie*. There, they unpacked the cache of small arms, guns, and Mills bombs, which Louis said were hand grenades. Other partisans, unknown to Lisette, would arm themselves with the fallen weapons to use against the enemy.

"Good work. We'll soon have the Italians heading for the hills," Louis murmured.

"And then what?" Jean-Luc asked. "Then the Germans will move in."

"That's why we're stockpiling weapons," Louis said. "Let's go. We need to get back before dawn." He slipped away, going off somewhere while Jean-Luc and Lisette rode the bicycle back to town. The darkness felt heavy now, the silence split by the rattle of the bike. Lisette held fast to Jean-Luc, and then dismounted as they approached the village.

A dog barked somewhere, and she recoiled. They made their way up the street toward the bridge. "I'll wait here until I know you're home safe," Jean-Luc said.

The sound of footfalls froze them where they stood. Two soldiers seemed to appear out of nowhere. "What are you two doing out at this hour?" one of them demanded. "Curfew hasn't been lifted."

Lisette's mouth went dry. She felt awash with guilt. "We . . . sir . . ."

"She's my girlfriend," Jean-Luc said. "We just wanted to be together."

"She's a beauty," said the soldier. "Perhaps you will share."

Jean-Luc planted himself in front of her. "Never. We don't want any trouble."

"You're already in trouble, my friend." One of the soldiers grabbed Jean-Luc by the arm. "What's your name? I'm bringing you in for questioning."

"He's done nothing wrong," Lisette said.

"Then he has nothing to worry about, eh? Go home, girl. Don't break curfew again." The two soldiers flanked Jean-Luc and took him across the bridge toward the *mairie*. Jean-Luc threw her a look, wordlessly cautioning her to cooperate. She was terrified for him, but what could she do?

Lisette stood frozen in place. Her chest was about to explode with panic. What would become of Jean-Luc? And his poor mother, bedridden in their meager apartment? She pictured Jean-Luc being tortured. The central administration made certain all citizens knew what was in store for partisans—beatings, starvation, sleep deprivation, threats to the family, deportation.

She jumped on the bicycle, riding as fast as she could to Sauveterre, the *mas* of Didier Palomar.

Ten

———————

L isette stepped carefully around a puddle of whitewash in the courtyard of the local primary school. Her husband, Didier, had ordered the roof to be painted white with a red cross as a signal to aerial bombers to avoid the target. The international symbol was supposed to be employed strictly for hospitals, but no one objected. Lisette wished every building in the village could be marked with the red cross.

Loaded with a bushel of apples from the orchards of Sauveterre, she went inside. Helping the schoolchildren gave her a sense of mission. The murmurs of children reciting from their primers filled the air. Sister Marie-Noelle welcomed her with a smile, motioning her into the refectory. The school was now coed due to a shortage of teachers. A portrait of Maréchal Pétain was hung on the wall, and each day the children had to sing a song that began with *"Maréchal, nous voilà."* Everyone had to pretend loyalty to the Vichy government.

"Thank you so much, Madame Palomar," she said. "The children are grateful for your generosity."

"I wish I could do more," Lisette admitted.

"Even the smallest gesture helps. Were you seen?"

Lisette shook her head. Every gram of food was supposed to be reported to the occupying authorities, but most of the townspeople refused to comply. Thanks to her status as the mayor's wife, she could be confident that the soldiers would look the other way. She set the basket on a table in the refectory where a group of little ones were lining up for lunch. The looks on their faces made her almost glad she'd agreed to marry Didier.

Almost.

She couldn't allow herself to look back over the past year, since she'd married Palomar. Without Didier's help, Jean-Luc would have been tortured and put to death, and her parents would have been evicted from their home. All Didier had required was her hand in marriage. Even the parish priest had approved of the plan, telling her it was a blessed thing to protect those she loved, though it might mean sacrificing her own dreams.

These days, the world was not made for such things as love and romance. One must be practical. Jean-Luc had been released to tend to his mother and to his job with the railroad. Lisette and her parents now lived in safety at the big, rambling ancestral *mas,* where there would always be enough to eat. As for Lisette, she learned to keep her own counsel and to steer clear of scrutiny.

Her wedding had been a brief, civil affair. A lavish celebration would not have been appropriate, given the tenor of the times. The marriage bed was only tolerable, an awkward exercise in body mechanics. The breathless passion she read about in forbidden novels never occurred. Perhaps it was never meant to. Yet sometimes, in the deep quiet of the night, she lay with her back to Palomar and stared out the arched window at the stars, and she dreamed.

"Take these, too," Lisette said to the nun, handing her a sheet of ration coupons. "It was a good harvest year, even without the usual laborers." She stuffed her hands into her apron pockets, self-conscious about her cracked and calloused skin and rough-edged nails. Didier was too proud to work in the fields; he deemed it beneath the station of the town mayor, but Lisette was far too practical to let the yield rot away, untended. She and her mother, Didier's sister, Rotrude, and even Didier's little niece, Petra, had all pitched in throughout the harvest.

"Bless you, Madame," said Sister Marie-Noelle.

"I'll come back tomorrow," Lisette promised.

As she carried her empty bushel basket outside, a small boy ran up to her and briefly put his skinny arms around her waist. "Thank you for the apples," he said, looking up at her with shining eyes. "They're my favorite."

She smiled down at him, gently brushing the hair from his face. His touch melted her heart, reminding her that there was one issue on which she and Palomar agreed—they wanted to have a baby. Sometimes she thought it was foolish to want to bring a new life into a world so filled with danger and uncertainty, but to give up the dream of a family would be to give up hope.

Her heart felt lighter as she rode home on her bicycle. At the edge of town, there was a rise in the road, and then an unpaved dirt track leading to the *mas*—the home she now shared with her parents, Didier, Rotrude, and little Petra, and a small household staff. A half dozen soldiers were billeted in a far wing of the house, but for the most part, they kept to themselves as they went about their duties.

Sauveterre was a beautiful, ancient farm, particularly in the autumn. The ocher-colored walls held a golden glow from the late-afternoon light, and shadows lay long across the fields. No wonder painters like Cézanne and Van Gogh, Chagall and Deyrolle spent so much time in the region, capturing the brilliant, changing colors and rugged landscape.

At several spots along the way, Lisette stopped and dismounted, leaning her bike against the hedgerow and removing her camera from the wicker basket on the front of her bike. Taking pictures with Toselli's marvelous camera fulfilled her in ways she couldn't describe. It was a refuge of sorts, when she forgot everything except the images she saw through the viewfinder or brought to life under the enlarger in the darkroom. She lost herself in her pictures of lavender fields, dry stone ruins, close-ups of wild thyme, action shots such as an eruption of butterflies or children at play. At first, Didier had frowned on her pastime, but when she made a flattering portrait of him and hand-colored it for inclusion in the town archives, he relented. Lisette was grateful for this, because her darkroom yielded something other than photographs of local folk and landscapes. She was adept at producing pictures for counterfeit identity cards used by the partisans.

She never worried that Didier would find out. Her husband was not a complicated man. He was made up of greed and vanity, and a certain surface charm that passed for kindness. He spent his days strutting about town, looking after municipal affairs. Since the occupation, those affairs were in the hands of the marshal, but Palomar enjoyed the illusion of control, flaunting his family money and political influence, and taking credit for keeping the peace.

She took two pictures—one of the wind-sculpted oak tree that seemed to point the way along the road to Sauveterre and another of the just-bundled sheaves of grain lined up in neat rows, ready to be stored in the barn or *bories*.

Working carefully, she put the camera away and rode home, giving Rotrude a wave of the hand as she wheeled the bike into the shed. Rotrude eyed the empty bushel basket roped behind the bike, but she didn't say anything. Like Lisette, she was in favor of preserving as much of the harvest as possible without attracting attention.

A twist of smoke and the sound of pounding metal indicated that Papa was working at the forge today. He did whatever he was able to do from his wheelchair, helping around the farm, from sharpening knives and scissors to stemming grapes to repairing tools. He seemed grateful to have a purpose.

Lisette washed up at the outdoor well, savoring the sweet, cold water, clean from the pump. In the kitchen, her mother was chatting with Muriel, the housemaid, and grinding grain in the mill for tomorrow's bread. Maman loved the big sunny kitchen with its shiny copper pots, floors and surfaces of Provençal tile. Seeing her mother safe and content made Lisette happy. Even now, a year after leaving the humble cottage in town, it felt like a small miracle to get up in the morning and serve her parents milk, still warm from the cow, or to make them an omelet of fresh eggs.

"How can I help?" she asked, tying on an apron.

"Muriel caught two fish today," Petra said, coming into the kitchen. "I don't like fish."

"There's rabbit, too," Rotrude said. "Muriel's a good shot." Although it was strictly forbidden to possess a firearm, the authorities tacitly permitted hunting pieces.

Petra climbed up to the table and set down a handful of wildflowers. "Lisette, will you help me make a crown?"

Lisette smiled. "Sure. Watch: you make a loop with the stem, and then put the next stem through the loop, like so." The spicy scent of lavender filled the air.

"We shouldn't waste the wild lavender," Rotrude scolded. "It's needed to make medicine for the soldiers."

Petra stared at the flowers on the table. "The medicine didn't help my papa, did it?" Like Lisette's brother, Petra's father had been killed in the first wave of fighting.

Rotrude's breath caught. "No, but he would want us to be resourceful, eh?"

"Well. These flowers are already picked, so we mustn't let them go to waste," Lisette said brightly, garnering a sweet smile from her niece.

That night at supper, Didier made a grave announcement. "A message came in over the wire at the *mairie*. The Allies have invaded French North Africa."

"The Germans will respond," Papa said.

"Yes." Didier's expression was somber. "For us, it means the Italians are out. The Germans will take over the occupation. That is a certainty."

As bad as it was to be under the thumb of the Italians, everyone knew the Germans would be a hundred times worse.

"Germans killed my father," Petra said quietly, touching her crown of wilting flowers.

"When, Didier?" asked Rotrude, her eyes large and round.

"Soon. We must find a way to make the best of it," said Didier.

Lisette nudged Dr. Toselli with her arm so he could take hold as they walked away from the town meeting. It was a miserable February day, the mistral wind skirling across the landscape with a vengeance. The whole village and the manor houses surrounding it had been oriented to shield them from the ubiquitous north wind, but on some days, even the south-facing stone walls were not protection enough.

During the town meeting, the German authorities had been formally installed as overlords of Bellerive. Now the occupied village simmered with rumors. They would round up the Jews and punish anyone who tried to resist them. They would seize property and crops for no reason and with no legitimate authority. In some towns, the Nazis turned synagogues into brothels to serve the troops. Bellerive had no synagogue, but it was whispered that the soldiers were on the prowl for women.

Any person who offended the German occupiers paid a horrific price. The mere ownership of a firearm—even an ancient, rusty shotgun in a shed—brought a death penalty. The Germans had slaughtered entire villages as reprisals for guerrilla actions.

"You should go back to Sauveterre with your family," the old man said. "I can find my way on my own."

"I told Palomar I was going to walk you to your house," Lisette told her friend.

"I have d'Artagnan to guide me." He held the leash of his beautiful guide dog loosely in his free hand. A friend who had used Toselli's veterinary services years before had generously donated the trained dog.

"D'Artagnan doesn't mind me," Lisette said. "Besides, I want to stop and see Jean-Luc to offer my condolences. He was so very devoted to his mother."

Toselli nodded. "Then we should go together, if that's all right."

"Of course. Are you sure you're warm enough?"

"I am tougher than I look, Madame," he said with grave formality, coaxing a rare smile from her as they made their way to Jean-Luc's house.

Jean-Luc greeted them with brief kisses. "I'm going to be conscripted," he said.

"What does that mean?"

"I've been called by the STO—the Service du Travail Obligatoire. Forced labor for Germany." He spat on the ground. "They'll never take me."

"Can you avoid it?"

"Not if I stay here."

"And now that your maman is gone . . ." Toselli said.

Jean-Luc nodded.

Lisette felt a lump in her throat. "We'll miss you. But we understand."

"Do you think Palomar will keep the peace around here, the way he did with the Italians?" he asked.

"He said he would find a way to get along with the Germans," Lisette said. Sometimes her husband's compliance with the invaders bothered her, but she never said anything. She didn't want him watching her too closely, because she didn't want him to figure out the truth about her photography work for the partisans and her laboratory work with Toselli, making penicillin.

Perhaps Didier, too, was engaged in secret work. Perhaps while appearing to cooperate with the invaders, her husband was actually helping the resistance. He had once said he believed in keeping his friends close, and keeping his enemies closer. That might be the reason he had been so agreeable when the new German marshal billeted an officer and three lieutenants at Sauveterre.

She returned home that evening to find a commotion in the courtyard. To her horror, the garden was filled with German soldiers, laughing and drinking Sauveterre wine as if it were water. A couple of brown-shirted soldiers were juggling hand grenades.

She rushed into their midst. "Stop this right now. You are guests in our home. I forbid you to behave this way."

"Easy now," said Colonel von Drumpf, swirling his wine in a goblet. "We are having a little celebration in honor of your good husband's promotion."

The group of Germans parted and there stood Didier, dressed from head to toe in a smart black beret, a black-and-red shirt, and matching trousers—the distinctive livery of the Milice—the despised Vichy police—Frenchmen preying on Frenchmen in order to save their own skin.

"I don't understand." Lisette feared that she *did* understand. She felt sick to her stomach. "What sort of promotion?"

"You heard the colonel. We're celebrating," said Didier, slipping his arm around her, a gesture more of possession than affection.

"He is the captain of the Milice," said von Drumpf. "He is sworn to protect and uphold the law. And what a handsome couple the two of you make," he added. "Both with that lovely fair coloring. I hope you are blessed with many beautiful children."

It was shocking to hear the Nazis talk of the blond-haired, blue-eyed ideal. They seemed to be obsessed with their notion of a pure Aryan race, regarding humans like livestock, selected for physical traits.

She felt Palomar's grip on her tighten, though his expression never wavered. Thus far they had failed to conceive a baby, and it was not for lack of trying on his part. He came to her almost nightly, but each month there was disappointment. There was no soul or grace in their coupling, only a grim sense of purpose.

"Go and fetch your camera, *chérie,*" said Didier. His lips and teeth were stained with wine. "You can photograph this moment for posterity."

She backed away in horror, somehow managing to keep her expression neutral. "I'll only be a moment," she said, and hurried into the house. She rushed to the washroom just in time to throw up.

"I don't feel well," Lisette said to Didier that Sunday. "I won't be going to church."

"Again?" He glared at her in annoyance. "People are going to think you're walking around unshriven."

"Perhaps they're going to think worse than that," she snapped, unable to hold her tongue. She had been feigning illness in order to avoid encountering the people of Bellerive. At church, she cringed under the fury-filled glares of the villagers.

"What's that supposed to mean?" He checked his ridiculous uniform in the mirror.

She didn't answer. The truth was, her husband had become the most hated and feared man in town these days. Now that he had openly sided with the Nazis, she could no longer pretend he was loyal to the French. He was the worst sort of collaborator, trading information about resistance workers in exchange for political and financial favors. She yearned to tell her neighbors that Didier's choice to join the Milice had nothing to do with her. But she was his wife, and everyone assumed she shared his views.

The next day, she went to the primary school for her regular delivery, bringing a bushel of grapes she'd scavenged from one of the vineyards that was no longer cultivated due to lack of labor. Sister Marie-Noelle met her at the entrance to the school. "Thank you, Madame, for your generosity." The nun's face looked taut, and she didn't meet Lisette's eyes. "I'm afraid I cannot invite you in."

"What's the matter?" Lisette asked. "Is everything all right?"

Sister Marie-Noelle stared at the floor. "Father Rinaldo was accused of being involved with the Maquis, and he's been taken away. We fear for his life."

Lisette caught her breath. "What? Where? Is he all right?"

"No one knows."

"How can I help?" Lisette asked, her mind already racing.

"It is best you keep your distance," said the nun, her voice barely above a whisper. "They were acting on orders from the Milice." She made the sign of the cross. "Father Rinaldo was accused by your husband, the mayor."

Lisette felt as though she'd been punched in the gut. "I didn't know," she whispered. "I am so sorry . . ."

"It's best you just go," said the nun.

Lisette left the grapes and rode as fast as she could to the *mairie*. No wonder she'd garnered such hateful glares when she'd ridden her bicycle into the village earlier. She dropped the bike in the courtyard of the municipal offices and went in search of Didier, finding him in his office, surrounded by envelopes and files stuffed with Nazi records and papers.

"Is this what you do all day, then?" she demanded, clearing his desk with an angry sweep of her arm. "Spy on our friends and neighbors, people we've known all our lives?"

He shot up from his desk. "Watch your mouth."

"I have been doing just that for far too long. I tried to believe you were doing the right thing for Bellerive, but now I know that's not true. You're as bad as the Nazis. Worse, because these are your people."

"You have no idea what it's like for me, trying to protect all of this, and the entire town, too." He stood and straightened his posture, looking falsely righteous as he came around the desk to face her.

"Then protect the town," she said. "Father Rinaldo is gone because you betrayed him. Madame Fortin fainted from hunger in church yesterday while you guzzled wine with Colonel von Drumpf."

His arm flashed out. At first, Lisette didn't even realize what hit her, or indeed that she had even been struck. She simply found herself on the floor, seeing stars and holding her hand to her cheek. No one had ever hit her before. It was like her first plunge off the cliffs of the Calanques into the sea—singular, frightening. She climbed to her feet and found her breath. "Monster! You have no right—"

"I'll do what I like."

"I shall report you," she retorted, her anger burning hotter than her cheek.

"To whom?" he demanded. "The authorities? Of course, that would be me."

Her mind raced. Where was safety now?

Didier must have guessed her thoughts. "You have no protection. Your crippled father can't help. You could tell him, but that would only drive him insane because he can do nothing for you."

Pressing a hand to her burning cheek, she backed away in horror. "I used to think you were a man who possessed a few good qualities. Now . . ."

"Now what?" he demanded. "By now you should know that anyone can be taken away. Anyone. Even your own father."

"What?" A chill swept over her. "My father has nothing to do with the partisans. You wouldn't—"

"He is lifelong friends with Raoul Canale, a known element of the FTP."

The Francs-Tireurs et Partisans were greatly feared by the Nazis, because they knew the terrain and were experts at sabotage and assassination. Even a breath of suspicion meant a partisan could be taken and shot.

"Papa and Monsieur Canale were partners at *pétanque,* playing their games in the park, nothing more," she said, trying to hide her panic.

"You had best hope no new information about your father comes to light," Didier said coldly. He caught her chin in his hand, his fingers biting into her. "If you don't conceive a child soon, you'll be as useless to me as your father. As useless as my first wife was, and look how she ended up."

Lisette did not allow herself to flinch. "Are you threatening me?"

"Do I need to?"

In the silent cave of Toselli's darkroom, Lisette lifted a strand of film from its chemical bath. These were the pictures she had taken of Didier's induction into the Milice. Studying the grinning, smartly uniformed men posing in the garden of Sauveterre, she finally understood. She was hopelessly and inexorably tied to Palomar. He had absolute power over her.

She maintained her sanity by keeping a secret photo diary, taking pictures and making prints, captioning them and keeping them in wooden tobacco boxes carefully labeled with the date. She trimmed the prints with sewing scissors and carefully penned the captions with a pen dipped in turquoise ink. Her solitary marches through the vineyards and meadows, along the beaches and rivers, became a kind of solace.

Jean-Luc was gone. She did not know where. He was probably dead, but she didn't want to think about that. Louis Picoche had gone underground. She heard he was a key figure in the Maquis de Var—a band of guerrilla warriors dedicated to winning the liberation of France by any means necessary.

It gave her a certain satisfaction to organize the prints. She savored the sense of order and control, false though it was, and it gave her something to do during her many sleepless nights. She carefully dated her latest print—17 May 1944—and placed it in a box. The pictures were a record of her days, good and bad. If she were blessed with a child, it would be a way to show him or her what the world was like during these frightening times. She refused to consider the idea that the child could turn out anything like Didier.

When she received a secret directive a few days later, she instantly incinerated the coded note and went about her business. The request was for a series of photographs of the coastline from the perspective of the church steeple.

Something was about to happen. That was all she knew.

"Where are you off to?" Didier demanded as she secured her market basket to her bicycle.

"Confession," she said.

"What for? You stopped going to church."

"Because everyone hates us for being collaborators. But I still need to be shriven, now more than ever." She spoke in a low voice so only he could hear. His reaction was one of silent, stone-faced rage. She knew he wouldn't hit her in view of the soldiers.

From the church tower, the landscape looked deceptively peaceful. She took the requested photographs and wound the roll of exposed film, leaving it in the designated spot. She was in no hurry to get home and took the long way to Sauveterre, past a beautiful forest that bordered the river. The light was too low for a good picture.

When she heard the sound of a plane overhead, she scarcely looked up. The sound was common these days—the Germans patrolling the region, the Allies looking to bomb key targets such as bridges and munitions warehouses. Something caught her eye, a scrap of fabric on the ground, half covered by dead leaves and underbrush. She picked it up, discovering a canvas packet with trailing, shredded strings. Her heart pounded as she recognized the stenciled words in English— FIRST AID. Inside was a small carton labeled *U.S. Army Carlisle Model*. There were bandages and a syrette inside marked *morphine*.

Leaving the bicycle leaning against a tree, she did a slow turn around the area. A few other items littered the area—more scraps of canvas, a buckle, a metal pin of some sort. The underbrush had been trampled in places. She stood still, listening. The cold wind whistled through the trees and stirred the dry leaves and grasses. She noticed a dark smear on the trunk of a tree—blood?

Goose bumps prickled over her arms. Her breath came in quick, nervous puffs. She made out a vague trail that wound deeper into the woods and led toward a stream. Following this, she came to a sunken spot near the water, concealed by broken branches and leaves.

More blood. Now she was shaking all over. She moved a dead branch aside—and froze.

A man lay in the hollow. He was covered in dust and wore the uniform of a paratrooper, a battered helmet on his head. He was shivering so hard she could hear his teeth chatter. He held a sidearm steady on one drawn-up knee, pointed straight at her. "Don't move," he said. "Don't make a sound. Don't make me shoot you."

PART 3

Bethany Bay

*In photography there is a reality so subtle that it becomes
more real than reality.*

—ALFRED STIEGLITZ

Eleven

❧

I'm confused about something," Camille said to her father.

"Welcome to reality," he said, puttering in the kitchen. Their regular Friday-night dinner would be a special one tonight. It was the end of the school year, and they were making Julie's favorite—rustic pizza baked on the outdoor grill. The dough was resting on a tray, ready to spin into homemade crust, expertly blistered and crisped under her father's watchful eye.

Camille had brought her tablet with the images and research she'd been collecting about Bellerive and Sauveterre.

"Do you recognize this?" She showed him the colorized portrait Finn had sent her. "It's from the town archives, and apparently it's a picture of Didier Palomar."

Her father dusted the flour from his hands and put on his reading glasses. He flinched visibly as he focused on the picture. "I've never seen that photograph."

"It's the reason I'm confused. If the colorizing is accurate, then he was blond and blue-eyed."

"He might well have been. His sister, Rotrude, was also fair and had pale eyes, as I recall."

"Your mother, Lisette, was fair, too. I mean, that's how it looks in the self-portrait she made." Camille studied her father's face, then looked at Didier again. "If he and his wife were both blond, how did you end up with curly black hair and brown eyes?"

He frowned. "I know nothing of my grandparents on either side. Perhaps the darker coloring is from them."

"Well, I don't know much about genetics, but I do know brown eyes are a dominant trait. Two blue-eyed people can't make a baby with brown eyes, can they?"

"Meaning?"

"Meaning . . . Suppose Didier was not your father?"

"Ah, but he was. That is the reason I inherited Sauveterre. I was his only heir."

"Could it be possible that your biological father was someone else?"

"Certainly. It all happened before my time, *chérie*. With foreign soldiers overrunning the village, taking whatever they wanted, women got pregnant and had their babies."

"Don't you want to be sure?"

A distant yearning softened his gaze. "If I found out for sure . . . *mon dieu,* it would change everything. But how would one determine that?"

"We could do a DNA test. It's a simple procedure these days. I mean, it's probably an unlikely possibility, but if there was something from Didier—a lock of hair, maybe?"

"He is seventy-three years gone, and after he was executed, he was buried in an unmarked grave."

"But . . . just suppose there was something . . . a personal item, maybe a hairbrush or an article of clothing . . ."

He shook his head. "It sounds quite impossible. How would we find a thing like that? And how would we know the material came from Didier? We could go to Sauveterre and find something," he suggested, sending her a sly look.

That again. He was still determined to make the trip to France.

"Let's call Madame Olivier and ask her to look in the storeroom where she found the trunk," Camille suggested.

"It is the middle of the night there."

She heard the rattle of Julie's bike outside and went to greet her. "Hey there," she said brightly. "Did you pass? Are you a tenth grader now—oh my God." She opened the door wider and Julie walked in. "What happened? Did you fall off your bike?"

"Nothing happened." Julie kept her eyes down as she walked into the house.

"This is not nothing." Camille grabbed her daughter by the shoulders. "Sit down. Tell us what's going on."

Julie sat on the edge of the sofa. Her backpack was in shreds. Her shirt was torn on one side, her jeans stained with grass and dirt.

Papa came over and sat next to her. "Tell us," he said.

For a few moments, Julie sat unmoving.

"Your face . . ." Horrified, Camille tipped up Julie's chin. "How did you get that bruise on your cheek?"

"I—it was an accident," Julie mumbled. "I'm okay."

"You're not," Camille said, anger flaring. "Who did this to you?"

"Nobody. Forget it, Mom. Please."

"I am not going to forget it, and you are going to start talking." Camille looked at her father. His face was soft with regret. "Sweetheart, tell us. We can't help you if you don't tell us."

"There's nothing to tell, okay?" Julie snapped. "You want to know who did this? Everybody, that's who. Everybody hates me. And if you want to help, you'll send me a million miles away from here."

"Was it Vanessa?" Camille demanded. "Jana? I'm calling the police."

"Oh, that's a great idea," Julie said. "Let's turn me into a federal case. Mom, you're only making things worse. You already made it worse when you yelled at Vanessa at the library."

Papa got a gel pack from the freezer. "Hold this on your cheek, *choupette*."

Nauseated by panic, Camille reached for her phone. Julie grabbed her hand. "Okay, really want to know? People are spreading rumors, and I got pissed and picked a fight."

"What kind of rumors?" Camille demanded. "And why?"

"You know why. Everybody thinks you made a fool of Mr. Larson, so the rumor started about . . ." Julie stopped.

"About what?"

"About you, okay? I didn't want to say anything, because it's bull-shit and you don't need to hear it."

"Hear what?" Camille was alarmed now. A rumor about her?

"People say you killed my father!" Julie blurted out.

Utter silence dropped over them. Camille felt as if she'd been punched in the gut and couldn't take the next breath of air.

"What an incredibly stupid thing for anyone to say," her father commented. "Who would come up with such a stupid thing?"

"It doesn't matter who. And I know it's bullshit, but that's what people are saying, and that's why I got in trouble."

Incensed, Camille grabbed her phone again. "This has gone far enough. I'm going to report everything to the police."

"Mom, I'm begging you." Julie plucked the phone from Camille's hand. "Maybe if you didn't act like the way my father died was such a huge secret, people wouldn't gossip and make stuff up."

"It's not a secret. I just don't like talking about it, because it's painful."

Julie glowered at her, and then at Henry. "You're just alike, you know that?"

"I don't know what you mean," said Camille.

"Both of you had horrible things happen to you, and you refuse to talk about it."

"That is a very good point. How did you get so wise?" asked Henry.

"I'm fourteen. I know everything." Julie sniffed.

Camille looked at them both, seeing their pain and frustration. "I thought I was protecting you—and yes, myself as well—by keeping the past in the past."

"I'm not blaming you, Mom. Or you either, Papi."

"We know that," he said. "Opening up is a risky process. But then, staying closed up creates its own kind of pain." He patted Julie's knee. "Perhaps this wise little one will do better than we have, eh? Perhaps she will learn to have more balance."

Camille took her phone back. "Julie, I totally respect what you're saying, and I absolutely don't want to make things worse. But you need to understand that I'm not going to ignore this. I can't."

Now it was her father who took the phone away, setting it aside. "We will talk about this more, and decide what to do. Not tonight, though. Let's have a nice dinner and talk about something else."

Julie slumped into his shoulder. "Thank you, Papi. Yes, let's do that. Please."

He caught Camille's eye over her head. She was on fire with fury over what had been done to her daughter, but there was no point in going on a rampage tonight.

While Julie went and washed up, Camille set out a plate of crudités and some drinks. A few minutes later, she could hear her father and daughter talking together, their murmured conversation soothing her own nerves. Papa had always had a calming effect on Julie. Now that Camille knew that her father had been bullied, she understood why he was so sensitive to Julie's situation.

Camille had been lying awake night after night, wondering why she hadn't seen it before. The symptoms had all been present, yet she'd been blind to them. The self-isolation, the weight gain, the dropping grades. How could she not have seen? Was she that oblivious to her own daughter?

She felt a familiar pinch of regret, one that had haunted her all of Julie's life. How different everything would have been if Jace had survived. Would he have been calm and compassionate, like Papa? Fierce and protective? Loving and affectionate? Camille didn't know how he might have dealt with a teenager, though in her mind, he did a spectacular job.

Could he have protected Julie from falling victim to bullies? Was there something Camille could have done? She felt horrible, knowing her precious daughter left the house each day to enter a lion's den at school. The thing about being a parent was that there were a million ways to go wrong. Camille sometimes felt as if she were driving in the dark, only able to see as far as the beam of the headlights. She never knew what lay ahead until it was staring her in the face.

At six o'clock the next morning, she met Drake at the portside park in town, wanting to catch him before he went on his daily run. The portside featured running and bike paths, playgrounds, shade trees, water views, and a decent chance of a private conversation. In a town the size of Bethany Bay, that could be tricky. He arrived with two coffees on a tray from Brew-La-La, and a smile on his face.

She hadn't told him the reason she wanted to meet.

"Hey," he said.

"Hey."

"I can't believe another school year is over. Man, the days just fly by." They took a seat on a bench overlooking the marina. He handed her a coffee—vanilla flat white, just the way she liked it.

She wondered if the year had flown by for Julie. More likely, the days had seemed endless.

"Thanks," she said.

"Best coffee in town."

She nodded, savoring the first lovely sip and wishing she felt the same spark of attraction he claimed to feel. One reason she had tried so hard to make things work with Drake was that he seemed like a great dad—high school principal, basketball coach, dog owner. She'd even fantasized, when they first got together, that their girls would be best friends.

"Thanks for meeting me," she said.

He turned to her and looked intently into her eyes. "I miss you."

"Drake—"

"I know, Camille. I just wanted to get that out of the way."

The statement made her unbelievably sad. She didn't miss him. Maybe she missed the sense of hope and possibility she had when they'd first started dating. "Drake, I'd give anything to not be having this conversation. Julie's been bullied at school, and the school failed to protect her. And Vanessa seems to be the ringleader." The words came out in a rush, she was so eager to get this over with.

"Whoa," he said, scooting back on the bench. "Hang on a second. Where are you getting your information?"

"You should have seen the way Julie looked when she came home from school yesterday."

He was quiet for a moment. Then he took out his phone and brought up a picture. "Was it anything like this?"

The picture on the phone screen showed Vanessa, her hair a mess, her face smudged, the neck of her shirt ripped and misshapen, as if someone had tugged on it.

"Drake, is that—"

"From yesterday. And believe me, I got the same story from Vanessa."

"Wait—she told you she'd been bullied?"

He nodded. "And I had the added bonus of her mother screaming at me, too."

Camille slumped back on the bench. "It was so much simpler when there was only one side to the story."

"Welcome to my world."

"Now what?"

"Now we get together—us, the girls, and a mediator. The school counselor wants to help. Then we try to figure out the real story, the real problem, and what will settle it."

She sat quietly, drinking her coffee. "I'd rather be waterboarded."

"I'm open to other ideas."

"It's just so nuts, our girls brawling like thugs for no reason. It's . . . embarrassing. I'm embarrassed for them."

"Freshman year is a rough time of life, and when you throw in an extra challenge, like a divorce or absent father, it makes things rougher."

She bristled at *absent father*. That made it sound as if she had a choice. But she did understand what he was saying. "Let's say we have that fun-sounding meeting with the girls. What would the goal of such a meeting be?"

"Obviously, we'd love for them to apologize to each other and become friends for life."

"Obviously."

"Realistically, we can tell them to give each other some respect, and most of all, some space. Out of sight, out of mind—it tends to be true for kids their age. I know it's hard to find space in a small town like this, though. They're bound to run into each other at the beach, or the movies, or downtown. We can set some rules . . ."

"And they're so good with rules," Camille commented. Was her daughter a victim? Or was she somehow part of the problem? Neither scenario was acceptable. She was irritated at Julie for not giving her the full scoop. At the same time she was skeptical of Vanessa's story, too. "All right. Let's get together sooner rather than later." Camille hated confrontation. She just wanted to get this over with.

"What's Julie doing later this morning?"

Julie stared at her boobs in the mirror. According to the girls in the locker room who teased her every time they caught her in the middle of changing clothes, she didn't have boobs at all. Just fat.

She stuck out her tongue at the mirror, then put on a sports bra. Mom had bought her a regular bra with a bit of padding, but it was uncomfortable and made her even more self-conscious than usual. The sports bra just kind of held everything squished into place. She glared at herself again, then put on her old jeans and T-shirt. To her surprise, the jeans were a bit loose, and the shirt was a bit tight. Mom kept saying her body had been changing ever since Christmas, when she finally had her first period. That was a relief, at least. Up until then, she was the only ninth grader on the planet who hadn't started her period.

With a sigh, she hitched up her jeans, shoved her feet into flip-flops, and went downstairs to check her phone. She'd heard a text message come in while she was getting dressed for the day. She'd slept too late, and it made her feel muzzy-headed. But it was the first day of summer freedom, and kids were supposed to sleep late, weren't they? Freedom felt more like prison to Julie. She had no friends. She couldn't go to the beach or take a walk around town, because she didn't want to run into Vanessa or Jana or their minions, a squad that included pretty much everyone else in her grade.

She found her phone and saw a message from her mom: *Meet me at the Surf Shack, 10:30 sharp.*

Could be Mom was coming around. Could be she realized swimming and surfing were not the end of the world. Julie jumped on her bike and pedaled as fast as she could to the beach. One of the coolest things about the town was its network of paved hike and bike routes in a roller-coaster-like network along the dunes. When she was younger, and not yet the hated fat kid, Julie and her friends used to ride for hours, ending their adventures at the Surf Shack.

It was the best hangout in Bethany Bay, located at the entrance to the beach. They served cones of curly fries and hot dogs, big icy drinks, coffee, and beer around an open-air bar that had swings in place of barstools. There was an annex with picnic tables, and a surf shop for board rentals and lessons.

When she walked into the annex and saw Mom, Mrs. Marshall, Vanessa, and Drake Larson, Julie realized she'd been played.

"Let's all have a seat," said Drake, gesturing at a table.

Vanessa wore skinny jeans and a crop top, her hair freshly shiny, as if she'd just been to the salon. An overabundance of Band-Aids covered her forearm, which she cradled as if it were tender. She had a gift for doing makeup, Julie had to admit. But no amount of cherry lip gloss could sweeten the smirk on her face as she sent Julie a private dagger glare. Julie tried to glare right back, hiding her fear of Vanessa—the master manipulator.

"I guess the reason for this meeting is obvious," said Mrs. Marshall.

"We didn't raise you to fight," Mom said. "You're better than that."

"I agree," said Drake. "You won't be acting like thugs anymore. We won't allow fighting, or insults, or harassing each other online. We won't let you gossip or spread rumors."

Julie kept her mouth shut and detached herself from the droning conversation. She reflected on the altercation that had happened on surf rescue day. All she'd wanted was to fit in, and Vanessa had ruined everything. She couldn't say for sure that Vanessa had been the one who had bonked her on the head with a stray board, but Vanessa's angry face was the last thing she remembered before getting swept into the riptide. Then there was the purse thing, which never would have happened if Jana Jacobs had kept her big mouth shut. And then the Tarek incident . . . okay, maybe Julie could have handled herself better, but when they called her only friend in the world a terrorist, she'd kind of lost it.

". . . not here to debate who started it or how or when. It ends here and now," Mom was saying.

"It's not just me," Vanessa burst out. "I can't be responsible for the way other kids act."

"If other kids are involved, we'll deal with them, too," Drake said, stone-faced.

"I have a question for you," Camille said to Vanessa. "What gave you the idea that I killed my husband?"

Go, Mom, thought Julie. This was more like it.

Vanessa blanched. "What . . . why would you ask me that?"

"Because you started a rumor that my mom killed my dad," Julie said. "Don't deny it."

"I don't have to deny it, because it didn't happen." Vanessa's face melted into innocent confusion. "Julie, why would you make up something like that? It's so mean."

"I didn't make it up. Why would I say that about my own mother?"

"I'm wondering the same thing," Vanessa shot back.

"Then you won't mind if we check your phone, just to make sure," Julie said.

Vanessa flattened her lips together, and for a moment, Julie thought she had her cornered. Then the lips curved upward into a perfect emoji smile. "Whatever. If you need to snoop on my phone, go ahead."

Vanessa really was the master. She had covered her tracks. Fine, thought Julie, narrowing her eyes to slits and refusing to look away. She would let Vanessa win this round. She would accept responsibility for the brawl.

"Vanessa," said Mom, "when I ran into you and Jana at the library the other day, I asked you to reassure me that there wouldn't be any retaliation against Julie. This wouldn't fall into that category, would it?"

"Oh my gosh, no. I don't want you to think I started something just because Julie destroyed Jana's purse."

"I wouldn't have destroyed it if you and she had kept your mouths shut about Tarek."

"Nobody said anything about Tarek," Vanessa fired back. "You're making that up, too."

"Who's Tarek?" asked Mom.

"Whoa." Drake held up a hand. "We're going to quit with the I-said-you-said and move on."

Julie was certain she was the only one who caught the smug gleam in Vanessa's eye.

Mrs. Marshall cleared her throat. "All right. Rather than rehashing everything, let's choose a path for moving forward. Let's talk about this summer. Vanessa, weren't you saying you're going to be a volunteer at the Boys and Girls Club?"

"Yes, ma'am. I love working with kids."

Please, God, Julie thought. Do not make me work with Vanessa this summer.

"And Julie?" Mrs. Marshall turned to her.

"I'm going away for the whole summer," Julie said quickly, before her mom could speak up. "To France, with my mom and grandfather." She didn't look at her mother, but could feel the burn of the mom-glare.

"Oh, that's just great," Vanessa bit out. "She *attacked* me, and now she gets a trip to France as a *reward*?"

Now it was Julie's turn to telegraph a smug look across the table.

Mom made a huffy sound. "That's not—"

"That sounds splendid." Mrs. Marshall clasped her hands together. "I was just going to suggest that the girls need some time and space apart. Let's pledge right here and now that you're going to make this the best summer ever. And come September, we don't expect you to be friends, but to treat each other with respect—from a distance, if need be . . ."

Julie tuned out the blah-blah-blah lecture. She just wanted the meeting to be over. And finally, mercifully, it was.

Julie knew her mom was majorly ticked off at her for bringing up France, but she wasn't sorry she'd spoken up. "See you at home," she said brightly, and jumped on her bike before anyone could stop her. When she came up over the rise of the dunes, she saw her mom's car parked at the house. Great. Let the lectures begin.

Then she spotted her mother walking to the rack of mailboxes at the end of the road. She might not ever admit it, but she really hated disappointing her mom. Sometimes when she watched her, walking all alone the way she was now, Julie was swept by sadness. She knew her mom was lonely, that she wanted to have a husband and a family like everybody else. But nothing good ever happened with the guys she dated.

There had been a glimmer of new hope when Mom had met that guy—Finn. He'd lit something up in her, something Julie had never seen before. But then Finn went away, and Mom was alone again. It made Julie feel rotten, because Mom was awesome. She was really pretty, and it wasn't just Julie who thought that. Lots of people said so.

Sometimes they said it to her with surprise—"Your mom is such a beautiful woman"—and underneath the surprise was the part they were too polite to say. "Your mom is so beautiful—but what happened to you?"

Braces, she thought. Glasses. They might be cute on other girls, but not on Julie. On her, they just looked even more dorky. Mom said she could switch to a nighttime-only retainer this summer, and get contacts, too. Julie couldn't wait.

When Mom came back with the mail, she looked furious. She held a stack of envelopes, and brandished a big thick one covered in official stamps and seals that said *U.S. State Department*. She dropped it on the kitchen counter.

"What the hell is this?"

"Oh, good," said Billy Church, lounging on the patio at Henry's house. "You got your passport renewed."

Camille was still steaming about that. "I didn't get anything," she retorted, glaring at her best friend, her father, and her daughter. "You did this behind my back."

Julie kicked at the ground, keeping her eyes averted.

"Guilty as charged," said Papa with his trademark Gallic shrug.

"You did this without my permission. It's criminal. You sent in my paperwork and my picture without my knowledge. You forged my signature."

"Because you wouldn't have signed it, and time is of the essence," Papa said easily.

"You're getting way too good at forging my signature," Camille said to Julie. "First the surf rescue permission slip and now this. You are *so* grounded."

"I'm already grounded from everything," Julie said.

"Well, now you're even more grounded."

"Drink your wine, Camille," Papa intervened. "There is no harm in getting a passport."

"Without my knowledge? You crossed a line. This is my life, and Julie's my child."

"It's done," Billy said. "Now you have a fresh passport, and the world didn't come to an end."

"That's not the point."

"What is the point, Mom?" Julie asked, finally looking up. "Papi wants to go to France. I want to go. Mrs. Marshall even said we should go. The only thing stopping us is you."

"I have my reasons." She pushed her glass of wine away. Her father had made a nice dinner for them, but she wasn't hungry.

"None of those reasons make sense," Julie said. "Mom. Please. Don't make me spend the whole summer here. I hate this town. I hate everything about it."

"You do not. Bethany Bay is our home. It's where we belong."

Her father made his French sound—*pah*—and put his arm around Julie, planting a kiss on her head. The two of them went to the garden together, talking with the intimate familiarity they'd always shared.

"It's just for the summer," Billy said. "And for your dad. You said he's looking to settle some things over there. Doesn't he deserve to make peace with the past?"

"Of course, but why does that have to entail uprooting ourselves for the whole summer?"

"Because it's going to be awesome. Think how good it'll be for Julie to see the world. And to regroup. You know, after the bullying thing."

"What am I teaching her by taking her away at the first sign of trouble? Isn't that letting the bullies win?"

"If you were sending her to chore camp in the Badlands—maybe. But France. That's a win for Julie, not the mean girls." Billy took both her hands in his. "Listen. I know you, Camille, and I know the one thing more powerful than anything else in your life is Julie's well-being. Imagine how shitty it would be for her to stick around here this summer."

"I want her to love it here," Camille said, gazing out the window. "The way we did."

"Then take her away for a while. She'll come back with a new appreciation of where she's from."

Observing her father and daughter together, Camille felt herself running out of excuses. Papa seemed so fragile, yet so determined to make this journey. Her own neurotic fear of moving out of her comfort zone was starting to affect Julie. Intellectually, she knew they were right. Julie deserved to have the kind of childhood Camille had enjoyed, exploring and traveling and not being held back by a mother who had been irreparably damaged by tragedy.

Maybe Billy was right—a radical change was called for. Maybe the way to save her daughter would be to let her spread her wings and explore.

Twelve

꧁

STEWARDESS: I'm being shanghaied.

IMAKEPESTO: You say that like it's a bad thing. What's up?

*C*amille stared at her computer screen. She and Finn had fallen into a pattern of chatting online and e-mailing regularly. Daily, in fact. And although she was embarrassed even to think it, their digital conversations were the best part of her day. What did that say about her, that the most compelling relationship in her life right now was with a guy thousands of miles away?

STEWARDESS: My father and daughter are determined that we're going to spend the summer in Bellerive.

IMAKEPESTO: Trust me, there are worse places to spend the summer than the Var. I can't wait for you to see it. You're gonna love it. Why do you feel shanghaied?

STEWARDESS: Because I'm being forced to go somewhere against my will. I'm not big on travel anymore.

Lame, Camille, she thought. He's going to think you're so lame. He probably thinks so already.

IMAKEPESTO: You sound like my granny . . .

STEWARDESS: Ouch.

IMAKEPESTO: . . . but you look like a stewardess.

STEWARDESS: Double ouch. What decade are you from? The 1960s?

IMAKEPESTO: You're trying to change the topic. What's so bad about coming to see me?

STEWARDESS: I'm not coming to see you.

IMAKEPESTO: Ouch.

STEWARDESS: I'm coming to help my father deal with his property. And maybe some things from his past.

IMAKEPESTO: So how did they shanghai you? In case I need to do it myself one day.

STEWARDESS: They renewed my passport without my permission OR my signature. Total forgery. Federal offense.

IMAKEPESTO: How'd they get a passport photo?

STEWARDESS: Too easy. I have the whole setup at my house. My friend Billy and I had an instant passport-photo service when we were first starting our business. Julie found one in the right format on my computer.

IMAKEPESTO: Julie sounds clever. Like her mother.

STEWARDESS: Then my father got the tickets. First class on Air France. I'm sure it cost him the moon.

IMAKEPESTO: Oh, the torture. Tell your dad to PLEASE shanghai me.

STEWARDESS: Anyway . . . It's my long-winded way of telling you we're spending the summer in Bellerive.

IMAKEPESTO: You have no idea how happy that makes me.

STEWARDESS: Really? Why?

IMAKEPESTO: Because I kissed you, and it was cool, and I can't stop thinking about you.

STEWARDESS: I never know when you're being serious or kidding around.

IMAKEPESTO: Then you'll have to get to know me better and find out.

STEWARDESS: Or you could just tell me.

IMAKEPESTO: Where's the fun in that? Okay, let's tell each other one fact about ourselves. I'll start. I know how to ride a bicycle backward. Really well.

STEWARDESS: I'm impressed. My turn: I haven't been on an airplane in five years.

IMAKEPESTO: Whoa, why not? Fear of flying?

Fear of everything, she thought, already regretting the turn the conversation had taken.

STEWARDESS: Yep.

IMAKEPESTO: There are pills for that.

STEWARDESS: I already have a prescription. Julie's really excited. Now I feel guilty that I've never taken her on a big trip like this.

IMAKEPESTO: She's gonna love it here. How's her French?

STEWARDESS: Fluent. Or nearly. She had a rough year at school, so it'll be good for her to get away for a while.

IMAKEPESTO: Rough in what way?

STEWARDESS: Run-ins with other kids. I'm not clear on whether she's the bully or the bullied.

She hesitated. She was telling this man a lot about herself. She wondered why it was so easy to open up to him. The distance, she thought. The shield of her computer screen.

STEWARDESS: So here's something else—not about me. My father was bullied as a child in Bellerive. He was vilified because his father was a collaborator.

IMAKEPESTO: Yikes. The war was very personal in small towns like Bellerive.

STEWARDESS: I keep thinking about the pictures I've seen so far. My father has dark hair and dark eyes. Olive-colored skin. Both his parents seemed to be fair. I even thought about DNA testing.

IMAKEPESTO: Curiouser and curiouser. I've done plenty of DNA testing associated with my work.

STEWARDESS: Really? Why?

IMAKEPESTO: Identifying remains. Grim stuff. But it's helped with repatriation of lost soldiers. Hey, listen, I've got a class to teach. Talk online again later? Or better yet, in person?

Camille felt a little flip of excitement. Simmer down, she told herself. This was about Papa and Julie and putting things to rest. Not about flirting with Finn.

STEWARDESS: Okay, I'll let you know when we're en route. D.C. to Paris, then on to Marseille.

IMAKEPESTO: Can't wait to see you.

Armed with antianxiety drugs, relaxation sound tracks, and any other gimmick she could find to survive her own neuroses, Camille boarded the plane at Dulles Airport with her father and her daughter. Despite all the preparations and support, she couldn't escape the memories of the last time she flew, returning home from vacation a widow, having to tell her young daughter she'd never see her father again. Julie had begged to go on the trip with them, but Jace had declared that it was to be a romantic holiday, a second honeymoon. Though they hadn't told Julie, they were going to try getting pregnant again. Julie's first words on hearing the news were, "It wouldn't have happened if he'd let me come." Camille wondered if her daughter remembered saying that.

Julie and Henry were the opposite of anxious. They were bright-eyed with excitement, settling in for the long flight to Paris. Papa had indulged in seats that reclined into flat beds and came equipped with mini–movie screens and far too many offers of drinks and snacks. Though she appreciated the creature comforts, Camille worried that he was too freewheeling with his spending because he knew time was short. She didn't know how to talk to him about it, though.

Julie was fascinated by every detail of the flight. She seemed more like the Julie from before, a girl who faced the world with a sense of wonder. Despite her trepidation, Camille had to admit to herself that this adventure might be just what both her father and daughter needed. And maybe, she thought, feeling drowsy from the pill she had swallowed at takeoff, it might be what *she* needed—a change.

Can't wait to see you.

She'd spent far too long trying to figure out what Finn had meant by that. Was it because he was excited about digging into the mystery of her father's past? Excited to see her? Or was that just something he said?

She thought about Finn and she thought about their kiss, reliving the moment over and over again in her mind. It had been the kind of kiss that caused everything to stop—even time. Even fear.

But time marched on, worry kicked in, and after the kiss, they'd parted ways. Finn had moved on with his life, a life far removed from Bethany Bay. Now they were going to see each other again. And then what? More kissing? A fling? She didn't consider herself good with flings. She usually ended up being the one who got flung.

The slow, soft music playing on her noise-canceling headphones, combined with the sleeping pill and the bone-deep buzz of the jet, lulled her into a strange twilight zone—not quite sleep, but not wakefulness either. She felt every bump and jostle of the flight, alternately cringing and tensing every muscle. She was vaguely aware of her father and Julie watching a French comedy film on the in-seat monitors. She ignored the muffled announcements, and most of the time she ignored all the negative fantasies playing through her head—the possibility of a plane crash, the thought of landing in a huge, foreign city and heading into the unknown. But throughout the flight, her mind kept circling back to the one thing she never stopped thinking about—the "and then what?" with Finn.

In the midst of a dreamy repeat of that kiss, she came groggily awake as lights went on and window shades went up all through the cabin. She shifted in her seat and rubbed her eyes. Julie was looking right at her. "That was pretty fun, wasn't it, Mom?"

Camille straightened up, wondering guiltily if some remnant of the dream lingered in her face. "What?"

"The flight. Jeez."

Camille tried to shake off the groggy feeling. She remembered then that Julie had never flown in a plane. They had gone traveling by car and by train, but they'd never flown anywhere. Flying was one of those things that made her sick with anxiety. And so, every summer, she dutifully planned a tame, predictable, relaxing trip to places like the Smoky Mountains, or Gettysburg, or Atlantic City, or Savannah.

Now that they had arrived in France, she felt a twinge of guilt for letting her own fears place limits on Julie. "What did you think?" she asked. "Did you like it?"

"Totally, are you kidding? Best night of my life."

Papa smiled and patted Julie's arm. "You didn't sleep much."

"I know. I was too excited."

Camille breathed a sigh of relief when the plane touched down at Charles de Gaulle Airport.

"We're in Paris," Julie whispered, her eyes shining as she waited her turn at immigration.

Then she took out her phone. "Hey, I don't have service," she said.

"You don't need a phone while you're here," Camille told her.

Julie's eyes narrowed, and she opened her mouth to complain.

Camille held up a hand. "When you're spending the summer in France, you don't get to complain about your phone."

Julie scowled. "Well," she said. "When you put it that way . . ."

"I'm putting it that way."

The next leg of the journey, a one-hour flight to Marseille, passed in a blur. The airport was small and modern, and Papa hired a car, a little Renault Twingo the color of a ripe grape. Camille loved the sound of the language spoken here. It was her father's variation of French—Occitan. Compared to the rushing crowds at Charles de Gaulle, life moved at a leisurely pace in the south, even at the airport and car-rental kiosk.

Once they were on the road, she looked out the window in wonder

at the spectacular scenery and picturesque villages with their shady
squares and gurgling fountains, clinging to impossibly steep hill-
sides. The hour-long drive took them past dramatic gorges draped
in pines, evergreen oaks, olives and vines, cherry orchards, and walnut
groves.

Julie eagerly followed the route on a map, calling out the names
of the tiny villages and landmarks they passed along the way—a castle
here, an aqueduct there, churches and ancient coppices along the
waterways. The fields of sunflowers and flax and lavender were just
beginning to bloom, the vineyards were thriving with bright green
new growth, and the sky was a marvelous shade of blue. Papa called
Madame Olivier to give her their ETA.

"She's making a special aperitif for us," he said. "I have not seen
her since I left Bellerive. She was a young bride back then. Now she
has a granddaughter—Martine, who is a year older than you, Julie.
I'm sure she's eager to meet you."

For the first time, Julie looked apprehensive. "What? You didn't
tell me there was another kid. Why didn't you tell me?"

"I didn't know until Madame told me, just now. It's good news.
You won't be stuck with a bunch of boring adults."

"Maybe I like hanging out with boring adults."

"Now you're getting cranky," Camille said. "Jet lag is hard, but
when we get there, be polite. And remember, you're the one who
begged for this trip."

"What if this Martine kid doesn't like me?"

"Nonsense," Camille said. "Everyone likes you."

"Uh-huh. That's the reason they're kicking me out of school."

"No one's kicking you out of school."

"That's what Vanessa said."

"And her information is always so reliable. Listen, we're half a
world away from all that, so let's enjoy where we are."

They came to a roundabout, and Camille noticed a sign pointing
to Aix-en-Provence, where Finn lived. The sign alone caused a flutter
of nervousness. But they passed by and went in another direction.

Her father grew quiet, and when she scanned the landscape, she knew why. A road sign pointed toward a hilltop village, a cluster of buff-colored buildings topped by a church tower: BELLERIVE 3.5 KM.

"Are you all right?" she asked quietly.

"Yes. It's very strange to be coming back here after such a long time."

"Strange in a good way? Or . . . ?"

"I'm glad to be coming home."

He had been away for more than five decades, yet he still called it home. A sign welcomed them to ONE OF THE MOST BEAUTIFUL VILLAGES IN FRANCE.

And so it was. Camille's breath caught; Bellerive was even prettier than the pictures Finn had sent and the other images she'd found online. Surrounded by vineyards, olive groves, and almond orchards, the town was nestled beside a rushing river. As they crossed the bridge, Papa said, "This is the Pont Neuf. The original one was destroyed when the Allies came to liberate the town." The winding streets, spiraling up to the church square at the pinnacle, were almost too narrow for the car as he showed them the shady squares rimmed by charming cafés and shops. He pointed out the *école maternelle* and the lycée he'd attended as a boy.

Camille noticed his haunted look. How awful to think of him as a little boy, tormented by bullies for the things his father had done.

"You hated school, didn't you?" Julie asked quietly. When he didn't reply, she said, "I know what that's like. And maybe they were mean to you for no reason at all. Mom showed me the picture of Didier Palomar. You don't look anything like him. Didier. Sounds like Diddler," she added in English. She stared out the window at the ancient stone-built school. "Didn't you have any friends at all?"

"I . . . no. Well, perhaps one." A softness came over his face. "His name was Michel Cabret."

"I'm glad you had a friend," Julie said. "What was he like?"

The soft expression made Papa look years younger. "He was quite wonderful. Clever and kind, even though being my friend made him unpopular with all the other students. I was proud to call him my friend. And then . . . I left for America and never contacted him again."

"Why not?" Julie asked.

"We quarreled about something—I don't recall what. Isn't that pathetic? It's a great regret of mine that we parted ways on bad terms."

"Suppose you try getting in touch with him now?" Julie asked.

He looked up and smiled. "Camille, you must stop letting this child grow up. She is getting too smart for an old man like me."

"Quit saying you're old, Papi. What about your friend? Do you think you could find him?"

"Do I think?" He chuckled. "Of course I can find him. I already have. This is something I learned from my very gifted granddaughter. I found him on the social network. The Facebook."

"Cool," Julie said. "Did you contact him?"

"Certainly not. He's undoubtedly forgotten me."

"Does he still live here?" Julie asked, her eyes alight with curiosity.

"I believe so, yes." He stopped at a crossroads and thought for a moment, then turned down a sunny cobblestoned street. "That was Michel's house," he said, indicating a stone residence surrounded by shade trees, with a small garden in back and a tailor shop next door, marked with a metal sign in the shape of scissors. "He was apprenticed to a tailor, and he later took over the shop."

"You should pay him a visit," Camille suggested.

Her father shook his head. "It's an old and painful situation. He wouldn't welcome me."

"How do you know?"

He didn't answer. Camille wondered what memories were hiding inside her father. Later, when they were rested, she would try to talk to him about it. They drove through the winding alleyways of the village, passing colorfully painted old doors studded with iron rivets, windows rimmed by climbing roses, hollyhocks, and geraniums, people walking to and from the shops with their straw panniers. The atmosphere was utterly charming, and it was hard to imagine what this place had been like when it was overrun by Nazis and their war machines.

After passing through the town, they drove along a narrow lane bordered by plane trees and surrounded by vineyards and orchards. The fields were dotted by unmortared stone huts, many of them collapsed and overgrown. "That is Sauveterre," Papa said, indicating a large property in the distance, dominated by a stone manor house. Sun-gilded dry stone walls enclosed gardens exploding with growth. The ocher-washed manor house, terraced fields, and surrounding forest hinted at a warm and gentle lifestyle from a forgotten era. The building showed its age. At one end of the main house, a blue tarp covered the gray slate roof. That was probably where the cave-in had occurred, prompting Madame Olivier to send the box of Lisette's belongings.

They passed through the wide iron and stone entry gate. There was a row of beehives in a meadow along a tall hedge, numerous sheds and barns, a henhouse, and a pond. The manor house was surrounded by lavish gardens, walkways draped with wisteria and clematis, and a sunny garden with wrought-iron furniture and lounge chairs.

"It's very much the same," Papa said. "I remember it just as it is now—the house and pathways, the vast fields where I could run and hide, the barns. I used to sit for hours watching the *magnanerie*."

"What's that?" Julie asked. "I don't know that word."

"The silk barn. We raised silkworms."

"Ew. Are they really worms?"

"Larvae, the caterpillar before the moth. I spent most of my time outdoors, though. The gardens were magical to me, my special place, where I could find peace and quiet."

"It's incredible, Papa," Camille said. "So ancient and beautiful. I can't believe this property is yours."

Drenched in late afternoon sunshine, Sauveterre was a world unto itself, with its gardens and surrounding fields and vineyards. "It is not so grand as a *bastide*," he said. "That is a true manor, like a small castle. Still, I'm told Palomar was very proud of it, because it's the largest *mas* in Bellerive. See how everything is oriented to the south. That is to protect the house and gardens from the mistral wind. It's a cold wind that blows from the north in the winter months."

Julie nodded, not bothering to stifle a yawn.

"Somebody's fading," Camille said.

"Madame will have a nice bed ready for you soon." Papa parked in front of what had probably been a carriage house at one time. As they were getting out onto the cobbled pavement, a bright-faced woman came rushing out to meet them.

"Alors, alors, bienvenue, tout le monde," she sang out, opening her arms. She was as charming as the manor itself, wearing a gauzy skirt and top with a shawl, beaming as she firmly clasped Papa in a hug and planted an audible kiss on each cheek. "Can this be my darling Henri?" she asked, stepping back, seeming to devour him with her gaze. "Look at you, as old as stone, but handsome as ever."

"And you are old as well, Madame, but no less beautiful. How are you?"

"Call me Renée, please. You're not a callow boy anymore, as you were when last I saw you. Now." She turned to Camille. "This is your fabulous daughter, eh?"

Camille found herself clasped in that firm embrace. Renée smelled of lavender and onions. "Thank you for having us," Camille said. "What a lovely place this is."

"Lovely but decrepit, much like myself," she said. "We keep it up as well as we can, but the restoration work on such an old place is never-ending. And now, happily for us, the roof cave-in brought us together, eh? And this is Julie, the wonderful *fillette.*"

Julie looked chastened by travel, tired and pale, but she smiled and submitted to the hugs and kisses.

"Come in immediately and meet the family. My grandson Nico will bring in your luggage."

The old plank door creaked on its iron hinges. Camille felt as though she was breathing in the past. She could clearly sense the atmosphere of a farm a hundred years ago. The kitchen was a snapshot of the past with its colorful Provençal tile, hanging copper pots, cupboards crammed with pottery, and a gas stove that was probably older than Madame herself. Light flooded through the windows, illuminating potted herbs and trays laden with savory socca, olives, spicy fish in oil, and bowls of fresh berries.

"This way," said Madame. "We've been waiting. You don't have to learn all our names at once." She gave a gamine wink.

The introductions went by in a jet-lag-induced blur. Madame Olivier, the matriarch, had come to Sauveterre as a young bride. In the intervening years, she and her husband, Jacques, had raised six children, two of whom still lived and worked at the *mas*. Their daughter Anouk and her two little ones lived here while her husband was on a UN peacekeeping mission in Africa. Georges was an expert in viticulture, cultivating grapes for a local winemaker. He and his wife, Edithe, had four children, two at university in Aix and two still at home—Martine, who was fifteen, and her older brother, Nico.

Camille tracked Julie's reaction to the two teenagers. Her smile was tentative and her posture closed—arms folded defensively in front of her. Martine, who apparently had inherited her grandmother's effusive personality, was having none of it. She beamed at Julie. "It's awkward at first, eh? But I'm an excellent friend. I won't disappoint you. Nico might. But I won't."

Julie's cheeks turned red. "I'm not worried about being disappointed."

"The French think Americans are very demanding. I've fixed up our room especially for you."

"In that case, you might never get rid of me," Julie said.

"Let us make a quick tour of the house," Madame suggested. "So you will learn where everything is."

The furnishings looked to be a hundred years old or more—tall cabinets and rustic benches, grand framed art pieces and age-pocked mirrors. The formal dining room featured hunting trophies—wild boar and deer—a stuffed fox, and a family of stuffed sage hens, all slightly moth-eaten and threadbare. Julie shuddered visibly.

"I was always afraid of them when I was small," Papa said to Julie. He turned to Madame. "I hope you didn't feel obligated to keep them on my account."

She beamed. "Do you mean to say we could be rid of them?"

"By all means. I'll help you, once I'm rested up."

She clasped her hands in delight. "My daughter-in-law, Edithe, has always wanted to redecorate. She's very talented at things of that sort."

"This is the piano I learned to play," Papa said. "It still sits in the same corner of the music room."

"Do you play, still?" asked Martine.

"Poor Henri just arrived," said Renée. "Don't make him perform like a monkey."

Papa simply smiled and took a seat on the bench, then tapped out a familiar folk tune, one he sometimes played on his piano at home. "Do you know this one?" he asked Martine as his fingers bounced over the keys.

Within moments, everyone was singing "Dis-moi, Janette." Camille stood back, enjoying the extraordinary moment. She caught Julie's eye, and they shared a look—*We're not in Kansas anymore.* Julie shrugged and sang along, familiar with the song from a young age. At the end, Papa gave an exaggerated bow.

"We have loved having the piano," said Madame. "I hope you'll treat us to more once you're rested up." She pointed out a solarium and a library, inviting them to explore at will. Then she led the way to the grand central stairway and took them along the uneven, creaky corridor to the upper stories. The bedrooms—a dozen in all—had tall ceilings and windows of wavy glass. The plumbing and electricity showed their age, but that only made it easier to imagine what it had been like in the past. There was a dormitory-like nursery for the kids, and Julie and Martine would share a sunny room with a balcony. "A balcony?" Julie said. "Seriously?"

Martine nodded, looking remarkably like her grandmother. "We're very grand here, eh?"

"That settles it, then. I'm really never leaving."

Camille let out a secret sigh of relief. It was good to see Julie making a friend again. She already looked brighter and more eager than she had in a long time. She had shed her troubles as if they were a heavy winter coat.

"Which was your room when you were a boy, Papi?" asked Julie.

"At the north end of the hall," he said, gesturing.

Camille didn't understand the look of sadness in her father's eyes until Julie ran to the end and opened the door. The room was a cramped and windowless linen closet, with neatly folded sheets and towels on shelves and sachets of dried lavender hanging from the corners of the shelves.

"Sooo Harry Potter. Why did you have to sleep here?" Julie asked, peering inside.

"The other rooms were for my aunt and cousin, and the household help who worked the farm," he said.

Camille remembered what he'd said about Palomar's sister, Rotrude, who had raised him after Lisette died. Rotrude had always resented the fact that her nephew would inherit the family estate. She must have been a miserable person to treat a little boy so poorly.

"We have a south-facing room for you now," Madame said cheerfully, showing him a bright, clean suite with a comfy-looking bed, fresh flowers, and a grand fireplace. "I know you must be tired, but please join us for an aperitif."

Everyone trooped out to a lovely garden surrounded by bougainvillea and shade trees, the perfect gathering spot for their aperitif. Jacques made a gracious toast, and trays laden with olives, cheese, tapenade, and crostini were passed around. A little boy of about eight or nine went up to Papa, giving him a sideways glance. "You are the landlord of Sauveterre," he said.

"That's right, I am," Papa replied.

"Are you going to take it back?"

"Don't be rude, Thomas," warned his mother, Anouk.

"No, little one," Papa said easily. "This has been your family's home for many years, and it wouldn't be right to put you out after all this time. Besides, I am too old to keep a big farm like this running. I just wanted to come for the summer. Is that all right with you?"

The little boy gave this a moment of solemn thought. "Do you know how to play soccer?"

"I do. When I was a boy, I was always the tallest on the team, and I made a good goalie. I might like to try it again while I'm here. Do *you* know how to play?"

Thomas nodded.

"Then I think you and I will be good friends," Papa said. He beamed at the little boy in a way that made Camille wish she'd given him more grandchildren. He loved being a grandpa and was so good with kids.

She looked over at Julie, and to her surprise—and delight—she saw Martine slip her arm through Julie's and say, "Timid and tired. Not a perfect combination."

"No," Julie admitted. "Is it that obvious that I'm timid?"

"Just a guess. I would be timid in this situation. Don't worry, though. You can get to bed early tonight. Your French is fantastic."

"Thank you. Papi taught me, ever since I was a baby."

"Come on," she said. "Let's go up to my room. Aspro, come." Martine patted her leg, and a small terrier dog scooted out from under the table, eagerly following the girls.

The lavish French aperitif, with everything freshly made from the farm, imparted a sense of timelessness. In this self-contained world, they still produced their own fruit and vegetables, wine, meat, and even silkworms and honey. After her second glass of *vin maison,* Camille started to feel . . . comfortable. Almost relaxed.

Until she sneaked a peek at her phone. Unlike Julie's, her phone worked fine here, as she had added an international usage plan.

The pop-up on the screen said *New Message from Malcolm Finnemore.*

Thirteen

As Camille watched Finn get out of his car—a disreputable old Citroën known as a *deux chevaux* thanks to its gutless horsepower—she felt ridiculously nervous. Jet lag had turned her first few days at Sauveterre into a dreamlike fantasy. Today, she had been wide-awake since four in the morning, and waiting for him to arrive had been an exercise in self-restraint. He was Christmas and school's-out and her birthday all rolled into one.

She felt like a girl Julie's age with her first crush, which was utterly silly, but she couldn't tamp down the confusing and undeniable flutters. She kept reminding herself that he was not for her, but her ridiculous self didn't listen.

"So this is the one who is going to look into your father's mysteries," said Anouk. She was about Camille's age, and like the rest of the family, seemed intrigued by the story of Lisette Palomar. When not tending her two little ones, Anouk was an avid reader. She read a different romantic novel every day, the paperback kind with attractive people on the cover, executing impossible, yoga-like embraces. "You chose well," she added. "He's gorgeous."

I know. Camille shrugged. "He's very knowledgeable about this region during the war years." She could feel a flush rising in her cheeks, and even though she tried not to smile, she couldn't help herself.

"Love looks good on you," said Anouk, studying Camille's face.

"I have no idea what you're talking about," Camille said.

At that moment, a squabble erupted in the back garden, the sort of sibling dispute that sounded the same in every language. Anouk went to investigate, and Camille hurried across the courtyard to welcome Finn.

Behind her, she heard Anouk's all-knowing sniff. *L'amour te va très bien.* What did she know? Camille thought defensively.

"Welcome to Sauveterre," she said to Finn.

And then there was that awkward moment when she didn't know what to do next. Hug him? Offer the French-style air kiss on each cheek? Jump his bones and worry about the consequences later?

He offered her the same devastating smile she'd been dreaming of since the day they'd parted ways. "Nice to see you in this part of the world." He didn't seem to feel awkward at all as he pulled her into a hug. He smelled amazing—fresh air and male sweat, something she'd never found sexy before, but which now inspired wildly inappropriate ideas. She wanted to press her cheek against his chambray shirt and stay like this for the next week or so.

"How was your trip?" he asked, letting go of her.

"It was fine. Julie loved it."

"That's good, but how was *your* trip? You said you didn't like flying." He grinned at her expression. "I know all your secrets, re-member? We've been e-mailing and chatting online, and I've been studying our conversations like it's my job."

"Why would you do that?"

He looked at her for a long moment, and a shiver of awareness passed through her. "You know why," he said.

She decided to make light of the comment. "Come and meet my father. And no, that's not as scary as it sounds."

"Good. Because fathers usually scare me."

"You're funny."

"It's true. No man wants some strange guy hitting on his daughter, even when the strange guy is me, and I'm awesome."

"Is that what you're doing? Hitting on me?"

"Is that what you want?"

Yes. *No.* "Do we need ground rules?"

"Never been fond of rules."

"Let's go find Papa. I think he's in the vineyard with the Oliviers, being all lord of the manor."

"I like the manor." He looked around at the abundant gardens. "What a fantastic place."

"I think so, too, but we've only begun to explore it. The foundation dates back to Roman times, and the main house was built in the eighteenth century. It's definitely showing its age." She indicated the blue tarp over the damaged section of the roof. "No one has cleaned out the attic in a hundred years or so. I swear they found a species of bat that's now extinct. It's like being in a time warp."

The vineyard was on a trapezoid-shaped slope outside the stone wall. The end of each perfectly straight row was marked by a blooming rosebush, like a bright exclamation point. Workers in straw sun hats were tucking the new growth of the vines into the guide wires of the trellising, and Camille's father seemed happy to pitch right in.

Henry and Madame came to greet them. "It is as if I'd never left," her father said, wiping his hands on a red handkerchief. "They are making me work like a rented mule."

"Go on with you," said Madame. "You insisted." She beamed at Camille. "Your father has won me over with his skills in the garden and the kitchen."

Papa extended a hand to Finn. "Now, remember your manners, and introduce me to your young man."

"He's not—"

"All right. I do not want to start sounding like your mother."

"Papa, this is Professor Finnemore. Finn, my father, Henry Palmer."

Finn smiled and shook Papa's hand. "Camille shared the photos from your mother's camera," he said. His French was smooth and charming, more formal than the local dialect. "With your permission, I'd like to find out more about her."

"Of course. I would like the same thing."

"It all started with a leaky roof," Madame explained. "When we went to the attic, we came across things that haven't been touched since the war. Since both wars, in fact. Come, I'll show you."

She led the way into the house and upstairs. Camille glanced at her father. "How are you feeling?" she asked quietly.

"I used to do the same chores when I was a boy. Although Aunt Rotrude never made me clean the attic."

The three of them went to the house, where Madame Olivier was waiting. "I had to take a break from the historical excavation," Papa said. "It's nicer out in the sunshine."

"So you're feeling all right?" Camille murmured, well aware that he hadn't answered her question, and equally aware that she was hovering.

"Today is a good day," he said. "Worrying about tomorrow will make it less so."

The four of them made their way upstairs. Camille could see Finn taking in every detail of the old house. The final stairway to the attic was narrow, winding up to a small arched door. When Madame opened the door to reveal the attic, sun-heated air wafted over them, carrying the scent of dust and age. "It is quite a stockpile of old things," she said. "Sadly, nothing has been sorted. Rotrude was not the best of housekeepers, nor were her parents, it seems, and perhaps the others before that. It appears Rotrude simply stuffed things away up here and never bothered with them again."

"Didier Palomar's sister—Papa's aunt," Camille told Finn. "She lived here as his guardian until he turned eighteen and moved away to the States."

"If I'd known what a mess she left behind, I would have helped," Henry said. "My aunt always resented the fact that she would have to vacate the *mas* in order to make way for the tenants. She went to live with her daughter—my cousin Petra—who was married by that time."

"I do apologize for the mess."

"It's not a mess," said Finn, his eyes shining. "It's El Dorado." Bars of light falling through the rafters illuminated slowly wafting dust motes. Camille tried not to stare.

"I'm glad you think so," said Madame. "Jacques and I always expected her to send for her things at some point, but she never did. After a time, we forgot about everything."

"It's understandable," Camille said. "Your life got very busy around here, what with six kids coming along."

She nodded, smiling broadly. "These days, when I look back, I don't quite know how we managed."

"And now you are reaping the rewards," said Camille's father. "You're surrounded by such a beautiful family. I always wanted more children, but . . ." His voice trailed off.

"You never told me that," said Camille.

He took out a white handkerchief and dabbed at his forehead. "You were such a joy," he said. "I wish I'd had ten of you."

Finn was too tall to stand up in the attic without bumping his head. "Would it bother you if we moved some of this stuff elsewhere?" he asked Madame.

"Bother me? It would be a big help to get it cleared out for the renovation work. It can all be taken downstairs for sorting." She dusted off her hands. "You can also get the children to help. Nico and Martine are excellent workers, and I imagine Julie is, too."

"How about we have a look around," Finn said, "and then we'll make a plan."

Camille surveyed the attic from gable end to gable end of the house. "There's just so much. We'll never get through it all."

"Sure we will," Finn said. "This is like a box of fine chocolates to me. It's what I came here for."

Of course it was. Camille moved away from him, chiding herself for assuming otherwise. "I don't even know where to start."

"We just start."

She picked up an old galvanized bucket, crusty with age and clogged with cobwebs. "Right."

"And then we call Vivi."

"Vivi?"

"Vivienne. My archivist."

"You have an archivist?"

"I do. She's like a research assistant, only smarter. Don't tell my research assistant I said that." He grinned.

"You have a research assistant also." She remembered that from his e-mails.

"Roz. She's fine, but does better in front of a computer screen."

Henry had already started rummaging through the old crates and cartons, his brow knit in a frown. He lifted a canvas cloth from a framed painting, sneezing as the dust flew. It was a formal portrait of a man in uniform—upright and blond-haired, with piercing blue or gray eyes. A small brass plaque read DIDIER PALOMAR. MILICE FRANCAISE. 1943.

"Look at this," Henry said. "Didier Palomar was vain as a peacock, eh?"

"Whoa. He was in the Milice?" Finn's eyes widened.

"I don't know what that is," Camille said.

Madame shuddered. "They were Frenchmen who supported and defended the Vichy regime and the Nazis. Many people believe they were even more offensive than the Germans because they betrayed their own countrymen."

"And Didier Palomar was one of them." Camille shivered despite the heat. "Papa, I truly don't think he could be your natural father."

He kept looking at the portrait. "Much as I would like for that to be true, I fear it is just wishful thinking, my pet." He dabbed at his face again. "It would change everything."

Camille wondered what he meant by that. *Everything?* "A DNA test would solve it, but we need to find a sample." She scanned the clutter. "What are the chances of finding something here?"

"You don't need to find a sample," Finn said. "Didn't you just say there's a cousin . . . Petra?"

"Your boyfriend is a good listener," said Madame.

"He's not my boyfriend," said Camille.

"Not yet, anyway, but let's focus," Finn said.

Henry nodded. "My cousin Petra was about ten years older than I, and quite happy to torment me when I was a boy. I assume she is gone now."

"And her children?" asked Finn.

"Your cousin never had children," said Madame. "But she is still living. I thought you knew."

"I had no idea," said Henry. He replaced the canvas over the portrait and turned to her.

"She lives in Marseille," said Madame.

"Your cousin is alive, Papa. This is huge," Camille said. "We don't need to worry about finding a sample of Didier's DNA."

"Camille's right," said Finn. "You get half of your DNA from your mother and half from your father. And since your parents got their DNA from *their* parents, you also have some DNA from your grandparents."

"Petra and I share a set of grandparents . . ." her father said, understanding dawning in his eyes.

"Then you will have about twelve percent of the exact same DNA," Finn supplied.

"You're very smart," Camille said.

"I'm a professor, remember?"

"Of genetics?"

"Okay, maybe I'm just a genius."

"And so humble. Can we contact her?" Camille asked her father.

"I imagine we can, but I've no idea if she would welcome a visit, much less cooperate with a DNA test, of all things." He paused, looking around the attic. "Petra and I were never close. She was quite beautiful, and she married a man with a grand house in the city. A solicitor, I believe. Neither of them had anything to do with me when I was growing up."

"It was all so long ago. I'm sure your cousin would like to hear from you." Madame glanced over at Finn. He was sweating as he stacked boxes by the door. "It is getting far too warm in here," she added.

"I agree," said Henry. "If you don't mind, I'm going downstairs to have a cold drink and a little rest in the garden, to recover from our work detail."

"And I'm coming with you. Let's call your cousin Petra on the telephone."

After they left, Camille and Finn were silent for a few moments. "It's strange and interesting, learning all these things about people long gone from us." Then she realized how that must sound to him. "Finn, I'm sorry."

"Don't be. You're right. When I think about my father, I wonder if the man I've seen in pictures, the man my mom and sisters and grandparents knew, is anywhere close to the man I imagine." He looked around the attic, standing there in a swirl of dust motes shot through by sunlight, looking curiously vulnerable. "And then I wonder how much it matters."

Julie winced as the rooster crowed, sounding as if he was right in her ear. "How does he know I was in the middle of an excellent dream?" she muttered.

"Dream . . . *un rêve,*" said Martine, jumping out of bed. "Is that right?"

"It's six in the morning," Julie said. "Nothing is right at six in the morning."

"You're funny. Come on. We have *des tâches ménagères*—what is the English word for that?"

"Chores, I think. Or maybe torture. When Papi said we were coming to Sauveterre, he didn't tell me it was chore camp."

"Get dressed," Martine said heartlessly. "Work will go faster if we get an early start. I'll meet you downstairs."

Julie flopped back onto the bed and tried to bury herself in the duvet. It was just her luck to share a room with a morning person. Martine's dog, Aspro, leaped on top of her and started digging furiously at the sheets. Martine refused to call him off, so Julie finally gave up.

Martine was already dressed in cutoffs and a cropped shirt, her hair held back with a crinkly scarf. A thin leather band around her wrist looked just right against her suntanned skin. Julie wondered if she had studied the art of being effortlessly stylish, or if French girls were just born that way.

"I'll be down in five," Julie said. She made her bed and got dressed, then went out on the balcony. Okay, so this didn't suck. The sunrise over the vineyards and the orchards bathed everything in gold, and sent Julie inside to grab her phone. The phone was only useful as a camera here. She had no cell signal, and there was no Wi-Fi in the house. For Wi-Fi, they had to ride their bikes into town and log in at the library or one of the cafés. She had been trading e-mails with Tarek, comparing notes on their summer adventures.

The stone balcony was pitted by age and covered with a thick vine, which Martine claimed was useful for sneaking in and out of the house. They hadn't sneaked anywhere yet, but Julie was looking forward to it.

She went downstairs and found Martine in the kitchen with Thomas and his little sister, Célie. Martine had fixed them a mug of milky tea sweetened with honey, and they were sharing a bowl of melon and berries with a bit of fresh mint crumbled on top.

God, did everyone around here get up at the crack of dawn? Whatever happened to summertime sleeping in?

"Good morning," Thomas said in English.

"Good morning to you. You're sounding very smart this morning." Julie poured herself some tea and opened a little glass jar of yogurt. "Your cousin is making me do chores—*des missions de routine*. Want to help?"

"No. But Martine says we have to if we want to go to the beach with you later."

"We're going to the beach?" asked Julie.

"You're going to love it," said Martine. "It's beautiful, and the water is crystal clear. We know the best places to go to avoid the crowds."

"Sounds fantastic. Let's get going on those chores."

The younger kids were assigned to gather eggs and scatter feed for the chickens. "I'm scared of the hens," Célie complained. "They're mean."

"You're meaner," Thomas said. "Just push them out of the way."

Julie and Martine went to work in the garden. "Two hours here, and then we are free for the day," Martine explained. "And look, there is a bonus." She gestured at the three boys who were already at work.

Now Julie understood why Martine didn't mind getting up early. Their names were Yves, Robert, and André. The three brothers were so good-looking Julie imagined a theme song playing when Martine introduced them. As it turned out, music actually was their thing. They were spending the summer working to save up money for their band.

"We're just starting out," said Yves. "No one pays us to play."

"But they're really good," Martine said.

"When can we hear you play?" Julie asked.

"We're doing the Saturday market in Cassis, down at the harbor. You should come," said André. He was the youngest of the three, and the cutest, Julie thought. He was totally cool, in slouchy shorts and a T-shirt with nonsense English—COMPTON SKATE TEAM 1982 CLASSIC—and shaggy, light brown hair.

The tomatoes needed to be trellised, a job she didn't mind, securing the plants to a frame made of old grapevines. André hovered nearby, and a couple of times she caught him watching her.

"You're a good worker," he said.

"This is not my first rodeo," she replied in English. Then she explained its meaning in French.

"This is not my first rodeo," he repeated, his tortured accent making them both laugh.

"I help Papi in his garden at home," she said.

"That's so cool, you're from America."

"Is it? I never thought so."

"Everyone here thinks America is the coolest."

"Ha. And in America, everyone thinks it's cool to be from France."

Julie was amazed that he—or anybody—thought she was cool. "Do you live nearby?"

He nodded. "In the village. My parents have a clothing boutique, and we live in an apartment above my granduncle's tailor shop."

She remembered passing the shop. "Is your uncle named Michel Cabret?"

"Yes." He looked surprised. "How did you know?"

"He was Papi's friend when they were boys."

Martine and Robert were at the far end of the row, grinning at each other as they worked on opposite sides of the trellis. "I think they're . . ." Julie paused. "I don't know the word for 'flirting' in French. Like this." She batted her eyes at him and sighed romantically.

He laughed aloud. "You're funny. The word is 'flirter,' same as English."

"It sounds better in French. Everything sounds better in French." She went back to work, but kept talking to him through the trellis. "Martine and I are taking the little ones to the beach later," she said. "What's that like?"

"Fantastic. I hope you don't mind hiking over the Calanques."

"Calanques?"

"Um . . . Very steep rocks that tower over the sea. You have to hike and climb to the best beaches. Clean water and sand, no crowds because they're hard to get to. Are you a good swimmer?"

"Sure. Everyone from my town is. Our beach doesn't have cliffs. It's low and sandy, perfect for surfing."

"You know how to surf?"

"I do okay." After her dad died, her mom wouldn't allow it. Too dangerous. But Julie and her friends—back when she had friends— had gone surfing anyway, practicing on borrowed surfboards, sitting out at the break and waiting for the right wave. She missed those days with her friends. She missed having friends.

She peeked through the trellis at André. "Maybe I'll see you at the beach later," she said.

"For sure. And at the Saturday market?"

"In Cassis," she said. "Is it far?"

"There's a regional bus you can take. Martine will show you."

By the end of the morning, Martine and the boys really did feel like friends. Julie didn't care that she had to come all the way to France to find kids to hang out with. Even doing gardening chores seemed like more fun than she'd had in months. They made a plan to meet at the bus stop in the village and go to the beach together. Anouk drove them to town with a basket of snacks, towels, and sunscreen, along with dire warnings to keep the little ones safe. The three boys showed up, and the bus lumbered down to a little coastal village with a busy harbor, tourist shops, and signs pointing toward the hiking trails that led to the beach.

Granite cliffs soared above the Mediterranean, and the water was so blue it hurt Julie's eyes. As promised, it was a rough hike to get to the most remote and dramatic peaks and inlets filled with crystal-clear water. A rocky descent brought them to a beach of fine sand, with only a few groups of tourists and locals lying out on towels or having lunch in the shade. Julie was too excited to eat. She and Martine took the little ones into the surf, and they squealed as they played in the waves. The guys climbed up the rocky outcroppings to jump in, yelling and splashing in the cool water.

"Let's give it a try," Julie said to Martine.

"It's too high," Martine said, shading her eyes.

"That's what makes it fun," Julie said.

"I'll stay here with my cousins," said Martine. "We're building a sand castle."

Julie climbed up the rocky path and stopped at a ledge that jutted out like a natural diving platform. Her mom would have a cow if she knew her daughter was about to jump off a cliff.

"Want to take the plunge?" asked André.

Julie was totally exhilarated. "Sure." Then she looked over the edge. "Yikes," she said. "I don't know how to say that in French."

"Yikes," André repeated, grinning.

"It's really far."

"About ten meters," said Yves. "The landing is plenty deep, so you don't have to worry."

"Yikes," Julie said again. But she was loving everything about this day, and she knew she'd love this, too. "I'll go first."

Taking a deep breath, she walked to the edge of the platform. The straight-down perspective was dizzying, but the water looked beautiful, its variegated shades of turquoise and deep blue flickering in the sunlight. Her stomach tensed, but she pushed aside the fear. After dealing with Vanessa Larson all year, a thirty-foot drop would be like a walk in the park.

She turned and looked back at the boys. André offered a nod of approval. Her mom was always warning her about not letting other kids talk her into doing dangerous stuff.

What Mom didn't realize was that no one had to talk her into anything at all.

fourteen

The Bond girls are here," Camille said, looking out at the court-
yard as Finn and two supermodels got out of the *deux chevaux*.
"Bond girls?" asked Anouk, leaning toward the window.
"Ah, you mean like the ones in a James Bond movie."

"Yes. The gorgeous ones who sleep with him and then try to kill
him."

"That sounds like my first marriage."

"I didn't know you were married before."

"I wasn't. I'm still on my first marriage." Anouk grinned. "Come
on. Let's go out and meet your competition."

"They're not my comp—" Her heart sank as she suddenly felt
dowdy and plain in her white cotton sundress. She flushed, knowing
she'd put it on just for Finn. It hardly mattered now, she thought,
following Anouk outside. There was no competing with Vivi, a
willowy Somalian who offered a brilliant smile as Finn made the
introductions. Roz was British, with long red hair, a toned athletic
body, and at least a dozen sharpened pencils sticking out of her
shirt pocket. The three of them were speaking English together
as they unloaded archival boxes, laptops, and camera gear from
the car.

Camille stuck out her hand. "The name's Adams. Camille Adams."
It was silly, but she couldn't help herself.

Finn sent her a confused look. Anouk snickered, then offered them
something to drink. "Mineral water would be lovely," said Vivi.

"I'd like one, too," said Roz.

"Shaken, not stirred," Anouk murmured as she went off to the kitchen.

"The two of you have some kind of inside joke going on?" Finn asked.

"We would never," Camille told him. Then she turned to her visitors. "All right, then. Should we get started?"

Vivi tackled the project with a fierce passion. There was site preparation work to be done before they delved into the artifacts. Within a short while, it was clear that they'd stumbled upon a major trove of information, not just about daily life around the farm and village, but about a compelling mystery buried deep in the past. They marked off the attic space in a grid pattern in order to keep track of the location of each object as they removed it.

The white dress was an epic fail, Camille realized, five minutes into the chore. She had pictured herself sitting in the shade with Finn, leisurely studying keepsakes and artifacts as they sipped sparkling lemonade and gazed into each other's eyes. Instead, she soon found her dress soiled by dust, cobwebs, and rubble.

Despite the wardrobe challenge, Camille enjoyed working alongside Finn's associates. Both women were so interesting. Vivi was the daughter of a cultural minister from Somalia, and a gifted marathon runner. Roz came from an industrial town in the west of England and had learned her research techniques by helping her grandfather, a notorious bookie.

"How did you both wind up in Aix?" Camille asked.

"One doesn't 'wind up' in Aix," Roz said with a laugh. "One focuses on it like a laser, and doesn't let up until one finds a way to live there."

"You've been to Aix-en-Provence, haven't you?" Vivi asked.

"Not yet, no."

"Once you see it, you'll understand," Roz said. "It's beautiful, it has the perfect climate, amazing food and wine, fantastic music, and plenty of men." Both she and Vivi glanced over at Finn. He had peeled off his shirt and was taking a water break over by the well pump. His physique gleamed with bright trickles of water streaming over him.

"Oh my God," Camille said, recognizing their very similar expressions as they watched him. "You've both slept with Finn." In a way, it was a relief. Camille had long been uncomfortable with her attraction to him. This was the perfect excuse to get over him. She was not about to become his next conquest.

"Unfortunately, no," said Vivi.

"Everyone *wants* to shag Finn," Roz added, still checking him out. "I mean, come on. But he has this unfortunate trait."

"He does?" Camille leaned in. Maybe he was an even worse player than she suspected.

"Yes. A very inconvenient sense of decency. He tries to keep it a secret so we'll think he's all that, but you'll see. He's ridiculously decent."

Vivi nodded. "He's terribly professional, keeps his distance from colleagues and students. Even the young and shameless ones."

"Professional?" Camille was skeptical. "He's an outrageous flirt."

"Ah, that is just a front," Vivi said. "He has a wall."

Roz nodded. "No one can ever find a way into his heart, and that sort of thing gets boring after a while, no matter how he looks when he takes off his shirt."

"And just so you know, he's actually interested in you," Vivi pointed out.

"What?" Camille's cheeks caught fire. "Why would you say that?"

"Because he told us on the way over here," she said.

"He . . . what? What did he say?"

"That he's super attracted to you, and he wants to shag you."

"He said that?" Oh my God, thought Camille. What a tool.

"No, he didn't say that," Roz explained. "But I'm sure he wants to. Just remember, he refuses to give his heart."

They worked for a while in companionable silence. Finally, Camille couldn't keep herself from wanting to know more. "Why does he refuse to give his heart?"

Roz shrugged her shoulders and made some notes on a clipboard. "Good luck getting an answer out of him."

"I think it's all to do with his first wife," Vivi said.

"Emily Cutler," Camille said. "He's never mentioned her to me, but it was on his Wikipedia page. I don't know why they split up."

"Ooh, you two will have plenty to talk about in between rolls in the hay," said Roz.

"I don't want to get that personal with him," Camille objected. "And I'm absolutely not going to roll in the hay. It's not . . . we're not like that."

"That's a shame, then," Vivi said. Her expression turned thoughtful. "We've never seen him smitten over a woman before."

"He's not—"

"Trust me, he's smitten."

"Come to the table, everyone. Henri has made the most wonderful salade lyonnaise," Madame declared, bringing a tray to the long outdoor table. "Camille, go and get Finn. He's over at the shed."

The Olivier family, it seemed, was conspiring to throw her together with him. She found him sorting through the things they'd brought down from the attic. "All these artifacts from a past no one can remember," she said.

"We're going to piece it together," he said. "The university in Aix has an archive of personal narratives of the war, and I have a classroom full of eager students. We can get them to identify and interview local survivors."

"My father's a bit startled by all the fuss."

"It's an opportunity for historical inquiry," Finn said. "I'd rather have my students working in the field than sitting at their computers." He studied Camille's face in a way that made her blush, wondering if he knew he'd been the topic of her conversation with Roz and Vivi. "Everything all right?" he asked.

She nodded.

"Julie? She's having a good time so far?"

She nodded again. "It's wonderful to see her hanging out with friends again. I worry sometimes about her doing something dangerous, but the kids seem great. She says they just take the bus to the beach and to markets, or they go walking around the village."

"I used to tell my mom I was going to the library."

"And you went where, instead?"

"Not the library."

She picked up the wedding portrait they had found of Lisette and Didier. It was a dead-eyed pose typical of the era, the bride and groom holding themselves stiffly as they stared into the lens of the camera. It was impossible to imagine what was going through Lisette's head at that moment. Had she been in love with Didier? He certainly looked handsome enough, and proud. Did she share his politics, approve of his decision to throw in his lot with the Germans?

"Do they seem like a fun couple to you?" asked Finn.

She shook her head. "So hard to tell. I always check out the hands—they can tell you a lot, because the subject doesn't usually think about what the hands are doing. In this shot, hers are holding the bouquet and his are behind his back."

"Maybe they both had something to hide."

"I wouldn't call that a maybe. I'd call it a certainty."

They were quiet for a few moments. She thought about her conversations with Vivi and Roz. "You were married," she said.

"So were you."

"Do you want to talk about it?"

"About as much as you want to talk about your first marriage," he said.

"Which is not at all."

"Right. But you have questions about mine."

"Yes," she said. "I have questions."

He spread his arms. "I'm an open book."

Sure, she thought. "How long were you married?"

"Ten years."

That laid waste to the theory that he was a commitment-phobe. "And it didn't work out."

"I suppose your next question would be why."

"Listen, if this is too personal, we can change the subject."

"I like getting personal with you, Camille."

She couldn't tell if he was being serious or sarcastic. "Right."

"Okay, here's the deal. Ready to get out your tiny violin of pity? My marriage, the condensed version. It was our ten-year anniversary, and I planned a surprise evening—champagne, flowers, a gourmet meal. Friggin' chocolate that cost a hundred bucks an ounce. Candles that magically didn't drip. When Emily got home from work and saw the spread, she burst into tears and told me she was pregnant."

"Oh my gosh, you mean you didn't want to have kids, so you dumped her?"

"Nice, Camille. Mind if I finish?"

"Sorry. Go ahead."

"Hell, yes, I wanted a family. It was all part of the dream. But I wanted kids of my own, not kids fathered by some other guy."

"Oh no, Finn. Really?"

"You think I'd make this shit up? There's an old-fashioned word for it—a cuckold. I think we should revive the word, because that's exactly what I felt like. I filed for divorce the next day."

"The next day? Did you ever think there was a chance of fixing it, maybe trying to stay together?"

"Here's the thing about infidelity," he said. "It doesn't happen in a vacuum. Even though she did the cheating, I suppose I played my part by not seeing the cracks in our foundation. Things hadn't been right for a while, and I ignored them. I finished my stint as a naval officer and became a teacher. The opportunity to teach in Aix came up, but she didn't want to go, and I did. So no, I didn't think there was any point in trying to stay together. Emily moved in with Voldemort and they had a kid together. They've since split up, and now Emily's a single mom."

"I'm sorry you went through that, Finn. And I'm sorry I made you talk about it." She knew he wouldn't welcome her pity, but the sense of betrayal and ruined pride must have been devastating.

"Okay, now it's your turn," he said.

Camille felt cornered. But this was Finn, and she was fast discovering that she could tell him anything. It was strange and kind of wonderful, knowing he wouldn't judge her. He'd just listen. "I was married for ten years, too. I just wanted a normal life."

"Define normal," Finn challenged her. "Does such a thing exist? For anyone?"

"It did for me," she insisted. "I had a normal life until I lost Jace. I assumed everything would always be good. Is that wrong of me?"

"No. It's romantic of you."

She felt a chill, the one that was deeply embedded in her heart. "We need to join the others for lunch."

He gave her a look that let her know he was onto her. "They can start without us."

She sighed. Finn had been totally honest with her about his first marriage. He deserved no less from her. "After Jace, nothing felt normal to me. If not for Julie, I probably would have drifted off into nothingness. About two years ago, I was finally coming out of the fog, and then my father was diagnosed with cancer."

"Ah, Camille. I'm sorry."

"Thanks. He's done with his treatment. There are still two tumors, but he's stable and says he feels all right. So . . . we'll see. There's a high likelihood of recurrence with this type of cancer. His advice from the doctor is to stay well and enjoy life."

"That's good advice for anybody."

"And it's time for lunch. My father made a salad. Don't worry, it's a man salad, with bacon and a poached egg on top."

"I wasn't worried. The bacon makes me extra happy, though."

She surveyed the collection of memorabilia, and her gaze kept going back to the wedding portrait. "We'll have to talk more later."

"Why, Madame Adams, is that your way of asking me on a date?"

"My . . . what? No."

"It is, too, and I accept. Where would you like to go?" He grinned. "Don't give me that look. You're in Provence, Camille. Things are going to get romantic whether you like it or not."

What could be the harm? she asked herself. She was here just for the summer, and he was helping her find out vital information for her father. It seemed silly to be a Sabine about it. "Okay. Surprise me."

Filled with nervous energy, she hurried through lunch, then went right back to work, digging into a carton labeled *linge*. True to the label, it was a collection of bed linens, faintly redolent of dried cedar and lavender. Most of the items were brittle and yellowed with age. She set each piece aside, labeling things the way Vivi had instructed.

She came across an old tapestry pillow depicting a tree of life. She held it up for Finn to see. "Antique or knockoff?"

He checked it out. "It's a beauty. Probably recent, though. Is there a tag inside?"

As she turned the pillow over, it struck her that it didn't feel like a pillow. The stuffing wasn't soft enough. And if it had been a proper pillow, wouldn't the mice have raided the stuffing for their nests, the way they had the other pillows she'd found in the attic?

One side had been loosely sewn up. She carefully unraveled the stitching to reveal a piece of heavy, stiff fabric inside. "I don't see a tag, but check this out." Reaching in, she pulled out a folded canvas sack the color of faded wheat. It seemed out of place, somehow. She unfolded the canvas and held it up. There were letters and numbers stenciled in black on the fabric, along with the words SEPT. 1943 (24 FT DIA). AN 6513—1A PARACHUTE. A worn pamphlet fell out of a tuck in the fabric. It was stamped with official markings and the title PARACHUTE LOG RECORD.

"Oh boy," she said, looking at Finn. The expression on his face was probably a mirror of her own.

"I think we're onto something," he said.

PART 4

Bellerive

A photograph is a secret about a secret.
The more it tells you the less you know.

—DIANE ARBUS, AMERICAN PHOTOGRAPHER

fifteen

❦

May 1944

Ne tirez pas." Please don't shoot.

Hank Watkins heard the woman's words through a haze of pain. Using all his strength to hold his sidearm steady, he sighted down the short barrel of the Colt semiautomatic and aimed for her chest. It was nearly dark, so he would have to take the shot quickly or risk letting her flee. Her short breaths came in audible puffs, like a cornered animal. His finger tensed on the trigger. The gun had a silencer, and with a single pull, he could be alone in the woods again.

His pulse felt light and quick, as though he had a small bird trapped in his chest, beating its wings to get out. The lush-leafed trees and the twilight sky circled above him. The woods were so different from the sugar-bush groves back home in northern Vermont. Everything was different.

"Je vous supplie, monsieur." I beg you.

The soft plea snapped his attention back to the present. Silhouetted against the darkening sky, the woman was indistinct. He couldn't tell whether she was old or young, pretty or plain. He couldn't tell anything about her. Better that way. Better not to know whose life he was about to destroy.

"Please," the woman said, her voice a whisper on the wind. *"Je ne suis pas armée."* She held her hands up, palms out. "Not . . . armed."

She sounded very young and scared. Hank couldn't remember the last time he'd heard the sound of a girl's voice. Maybe last winter, when he'd said good-bye to Mildred at the station in Burlington. The shoulder of his uniform had stayed damp from her tears all the way to New York City.

"I beg you. My friend. Not armed." With a sweater or shawl hanging from her shoulders, she looked poised to take flight.

Hank had never heard a voice quite like this one. Her English sounded so peculiar—a French accent blended with a British accent, near as he could tell. Her speech was so thick the English words still sounded French to Hank's ears. Would she betray him in French, then? Or in English?

His leg—his entire lower body—was on fire. If she decided to flee, he wouldn't stand a chance of catching her. She might be a Nazi sympathizer or spy. He needed to take his shot, or risk being captured.

And then it struck him that he was lying here contemplating murder. Of an unarmed woman.

This was not what he had come here for.

He thought about what the training courses had drummed into him: a pathfinder would jump out of a plane and into enemy territory without hesitation. He would risk everything, commit any act, sacrifice his own life for the sake of his mission. And yet in this moment, Hank could not bring himself to shoot a woman.

Still, if he let down his guard and lowered his weapon, she might alert the German occupying force. But that would still be more acceptable to him than killing an unarmed woman.

Who was she? Friend or foe? Some of the Frenchies had thrown in their lot with the Krauts, others had organized themselves into guerrilla fighting groups, and most simply wanted the damned war to be over. At any rate, he did have the ultimate escape hatch buttoned into a hidden shirt pocket—a cyanide pill.

But the mission. Shit. Shit. Shit and damn it all to hell.

"Don't move," he said, his voice low and broken. "Stay where you are."

This was his most important jump to date. He had volunteered to go in, scouting the territory in advance of a top secret operation. It was top secret, all right, but everybody knew the goal was to liberate the south of France. The Americans and the French were gung ho for the mission, but Churchill was a big holdout. Hank didn't pretend to understand the politics of it all, but he understood that his work on this scouting expedition was crucial. In order to persuade Churchill, they had to come back with a solid plan. That was why the intel provided by Hank and his unit was so crucial.

He had trained tirelessly for this, gone over and over the operation in his mind. When the red light in the Douglas C-47 cabin had blinked on, he had double-checked his parachute harness and gear. He'd made eye contact with the other pathfinders in his stick. It was a go.

Right then they had all counted themselves lucky, because as pathfinders and airborne scouts, they wouldn't have to make a combat jump. Their job was to scout out the area and set up vital signaling equipment for the Allied operation.

And yet here he was. Wounded, maybe dying, in some remote part of the French countryside, cornered by a girl who seemed to be as scared as he was. After dragging himself into hiding, he'd opened the sulfanilamide powder in the kit on his combat belt and sprinkled it on the leg wound, nearly screaming with pain. Maybe it staved off infection, maybe not. It hardly mattered now.

Very slowly, he lowered his weapon. "You can put your hands down. Do you understand? I'm not going to shoot you. Not now, anyway."

Her arms slowly descended. "Yes. I understand."

She sounded like a girl. She sounded like an angel.

Lisette dropped to her knees and moved closer to the stranger. She could tell he was either sick or badly wounded—or both. Still, she had seen something in his face—grit, determination—that made her cautious. "I can help you, but you must put away your gun."

It felt awkward and unnatural to be speaking English. She only ever spoke it aloud when she was with Dr. Toselli, reading Sherlock Holmes to him. She wasn't sure she was saying the words correctly.

"Okay," the man said. "I'm putting it down." His voice sounded gravelly and soft.

"Where are you . . ." What was the word for *blessé*? "Wounded. Can you move?"

"It's my leg. Ribs, too."

"You are American." She remembered the words on the kit she'd found in the woods.

No response. He was probably worried that she would reveal his position to the Germans. She took a deep breath, and then a leap of faith. "My name is Lisette. I can help you."

Luckily for her, Didier had no time at all for a wife who could not conceive a baby. If Lisette came home late, she wouldn't be missed. He spent his time hobnobbing with the German officials who strutted about town, helping themselves to wine and homegrown food, even romancing some of the young women and war widows. Lisette had learned to stay out of the way. By all appearances, she was a mousy little farm wife, keeping to herself and helping Rotrude take care of little Petra at Sauveterre. In secret, Lisette had become a skilled maquisard, helping the bands of fighters that worked undercover, committing sabotage, theft, even assassination—anything to disrupt the German war effort.

"Call me Hank," said the stranger.

"Hank." She tried to imitate his pronunciation. "You cannot stay here."

"You're right, ma'am. I can't move, though. This leg . . ."

"Let me see."

"It's too dark. We can't light a match or a fire. It'd give away my position."

"Your parachute and other gear—that is what will give away your position. It is your good fortune that it wasn't seen by someone else, someone who would report you. I must see to that right away."

"Okay."

She touched the back of her hand to his forehead. The intimacy of the gesture made her heart skip a beat. "You have a fever."

"Yes."

"Do you have water?"

"I did have. My canteen is empty now."

She did not know the word *canteen* until he handed her his flask. "I will fill it for you. I'll only be a moment." She took his *bidon* to the stream and filled it with fresh water, then brought it back.

He drank in long, thirsty gulps. "Thank you, ma'am."

"How long have you been here?"

"Since last night. I had a bad jump. A bad landing. There was a problem with the equipment, and the wind came up."

"Is someone looking for you? Comrades?"

"I can't say, ma'am."

He would divulge as little information as possible. She didn't blame him. "I'm going to fetch your parachute and bring it here, so there is no trace of you in the forest."

"Thank you. I'm very grateful to you, ma'am."

Lisette frowned. "I don't know this word, 'ma'am.'"

"It's a polite way of saying madam, I reckon."

"Call me Lisette," she said, then went to pick up the chute. The silk fabric snagged on the underbrush, so she tried to make sure she had gathered up every scrap. This was not the first time she had helped with a parachute. Ever since the Germans had taken over the region, the Allies had been dropping supplies and information all over the countryside. Small arms, heavy weapons, and explosives from the British SOE kept the maquisards armed. But never before had she been confronted with the prospect of a live paratrooper. She brought the bunched-up chute to him, along with the medical kit that must have fallen from his bag.

She handed him the first-aid kit and tucked the fabric around him. The temperature was sometimes cool at night, particularly for someone who was feverish and wounded. "I will come very early tomorrow morning," she promised.

"I'll be here," he said.

"Don't die, Hank," she told him.

"I'm not planning on it."

Hank was awakened by a creaking sound. His head was on fire. He grabbed his sidearm and waited, tense and watchful. From his hideout under the fallen tree, he could see only a patch of blue sky fringed by leafy branches. The fever caused him to see double, so it appeared that two huge, long-haired dogs charged into his hiding place and put their faces in his. It was really just one dog, giving him the once-over with its nose, its feathery tail swishing back and forth.

"I wanted Dulcinea to meet you," she explained, "so she doesn't bark later and give you away."

"That's good," he said. His voice was croaky. "I didn't die."

"No, you didn't die," said Lisette. She held the canteen to his mouth and he drank. The double vision fused into one. In the morning light, she looked so beautiful that the sight of her brought a lump to his throat. She had blond hair done up in two braids pinned over her head like a halo. Her eyes were sky blue, her skin like cream. She *was* an angel, thought Hank. A living angel.

"You have to move to a safer place," she said. "I've brought Rocinante to help."

He eyed the cart. A tired-looking mule was hitched to it. Even the thought of moving was excruciating. She was right, though. He couldn't stay here.

"Eat something first." She gave him a piece of bread with a chunk of ham and a boiled egg, and a handful of ripe plums. There was a flask of warm milk—from the cow this morning, she said.

The food was so good it almost made him dizzy again. He worried he might upchuck, because he wasn't used to food, especially fresh delicious food. Then the moment passed, and he looked at her, his heart filling up with gratitude.

"Ma'am. Lisette. That was the tastiest meal I've ever had," he said.

"You are in France. All the food here is tasty, even in wartime. I've heard the shortages in the cities are terrible, but I live on a farm. We grow everything we need, and if the Germans don't take everything, we manage."

Good, then. She didn't seem to be in cahoots with the Krauts. "I'm mighty grateful."

Without warning, she took hold of his dog tags, two of them on the beaded chain around his neck. "Henry Lee Watkins," she read. "And this is your serial number?"

"Yes. It's Hank for short. A nickname."

"And the *O*—that is your blood type?"

"Yes."

"And the final line . . . Switchback, Vermont."

Her funny pronunciation—*Sweetchbeck, Vere-moh*—coaxed a smile through his pain. "My hometown." Hank felt dizzy. He couldn't even remember what season it was. He'd left home in February, when the woods were blanketed in deep drifts of snow. Deep within the sugar maples, an awakening would begin, but the sap didn't usually start to run until March. Once that process started, the sugar season would commence and it was all hands on deck as they boiled the sap day and night, rendering it into maple syrup.

She carefully tucked the tags inside his shirt. "You must get into this . . . *hotte en bois*. I don't know the word in English. It's a special box the pickers use at harvesttime. The harvest will not be under way until October, so this *équipe* will not be missed."

The hod was mounted on a narrow wheeled cart that fit perfectly between the rows of the vineyard. She showed him how the side of the wooden box slid up so he could climb in. The thought of moving even a fraction of an inch made him nauseous. During the fall into the forest, something had gouged deeply into this thigh. He'd broken or bruised his ribs as well, and every breath he took was torture. He thought his ankle was broken or strained, too. It was swelling hard against his combat boot.

"Can't . . . move," he muttered.

She pressed her lips together, saying nothing as she unbuttoned his shirt and lifted his jersey. Black-and-purple bruises covered his rib cage on one side. Then she inspected the gouged leg. Though her face remained expressionless, something flickered in her eyes. Pity, maybe.

"I have to take you to a safe place," she said. She placed all the gear she could find in the cart. Then she spread the chute next to him and tucked an edge under him. Finally, she unhitched the donkey.

Shit. Was she going to use the donkey to drag him into the cart?

Yes. She was. And it was going to be excruciating. Inch by inch, she fitted the silk under him while he gritted his teeth against the pain.

She smelled of flowers and fresh breezes. It felt like a dream, being this close to a beautiful woman, though the pain coursing through him reminded him that he was wide-awake, in enemy territory, at the mercy of a lovely farm girl. He braced one hand behind him and tried to help, but any movement caused the agony in his ribs to explode. A sound he'd never heard before escaped from between his gritted teeth.

She spoke in French, which he didn't understand, but her soothing tone was full of sympathy. All the sympathy on God's green earth didn't spare him from what came next. She used the silk to form a sling, attached it to the donkey's harness, and laid two planks to make a ramp. "Jesus Christ and all the saints," Hank said, sucking air through his teeth. When he realized how she planned to get him into the grape hod, some other words slipped out, the kind of words that would get his mouth washed out with soap back home.

She said something else in French, then gave a sharp command to the donkey. At that moment, Hank *did* explode. He flew into a million tiny pieces of pain. Was this what dying felt like? A damned explosion? Maybe this was it for him, being dragged behind an ass by an angel.

At least he'd go out laughing.

"You lost consciousness," said a soft, thickly accented voice.

Hank blinked. Shadows and pain. Confusion. He blinked some more, trying to catch his breath. He was in a hut or shed of some sort, built of dry stone and twined with thick vines. A rough opening framed a landscape covered by vineyards, and in the distance there was a wooded area and a rushing stream.

Lisette had used the chute to make a pallet on the bare earth floor. There were supplies—an earthenware jug of fresh water, a basket of food, some bandages, and a jar of yellow powder. His M1A1 carbine was stowed behind his reserve chute, which had been unstrapped from him. Folded under the reserve was his aviator's kit bag.

She used a pair of scissors to cut away the leg of his trousers. The gouge was deep, the flesh ragged and inflamed around the opening, but the bleeding had stopped. She paused, catching his eye. Then her gaze flicked to his harness belt. Somehow he understood what she meant, and it made him wish he'd stayed unconscious. His hand shook a little as he unbuckled and tugged the belt free. He placed the thick leather between his teeth and clamped down hard. A sharp smell wafted in the air.

"Antiseptique," she said. "In English, it is the same, no?"

He nodded. Oh, sweet Jesus, he thought.

In training, they had told him to expect pain—from extreme missions, from wounds, or worse—under torture. Like all the fresh-faced boys eagerly signing up for adventure, Hank had dismissed the advice, too busy dreaming of falling from the sky like a leaf on the wind. He was going to see places and meet people so far from Vermont that they might as well be on a different planet.

He told everyone he was enlisting—with special permission to sign up at age seventeen—for the sake of God, country, and freedom. Deep down, he admitted only to himself that his real reason for going to war had been to escape Mildred Deacon.

Oh, she was pretty enough, and sweet as all get-out. Too sweet for Hank. She wanted to settle down and have babies and keep house while he went off to work at the quarry every day. Now, there was no shame in the family business—they were stonecutters for monuments of all sorts—but Hank wanted more. He wanted to see the world. And he was cocky. He volunteered for the trickiest missions, possible or impossible.

Clearly he had overreached, and this was his punishment.

He nearly bit through the leather, and tears squeezed from his eyes, but he managed to hold still while Lisette used tweezers to pull splinters and ripped fabric from the wound. It was a kind of pain he'd never experienced before. It felt as if the top of his head was coming off. He tried to go away somewhere, to travel deep in his mind to another place. Back home. Moonlight Quarry, where they dug glorious marble from the earth to create pillars for libraries, headstones for the departed, statues to honor heroes.

He had been at war less than a year, and he already knew that the real heroes were not the generals and battle commanders, but the everyday soldiers and common folk who endured the war, day in and day out, often fighting just to stay alive, and burying their dead along the way. When he'd first signed up, he thought it sounded heroic to be a specialized soldier dropped behind enemy lines for reconnaissance work.

Hank had never been much for school, but in special training, he became the scholar his parents never thought he would be. He learned to operate aids to navigation, to read a map and compass in the dark, to sense the wind and weather with the lick of a finger. He knew how to use compass beacons, colored panels, Eureka radar sets, even colored smoke. His stick, which consisted of a dozen pathfinders and the bodyguards tasked with defending them on the ground, had performed successful missions in Sicily and along the coast of Italy. Their job was to land in the DZ in advance of the main body, setting up visual and radio signals for the incoming troopers, finding pickup zones and landing sites, creating a clear field of action for the ground ops to come. Some fellows didn't think the work was as important as combat runs, but Hank had eagerly volunteered for the advance mission. When it came down to it, he didn't really want to kill anybody.

He felt lousy about his failed mission. He had no idea where the guys in his stick were, or what they thought happened to him. Even if he could get his communications equipment to work, he couldn't chance using it.

Maybe he would end up dying right here in this hut. The gangrene would get him, or a patrol would find him and shoot him on sight. Made him wonder why the devil he was letting this girl torture him.

Her ministrations caused a pain so deep that he foamed at the mouth like an animal, the spit bubbling past his clenched teeth and soaking the leather belt. His breath came in shallow gasps, each one causing the broken ribs to stab like daggers. At one point, he saw stars. He knew it was impossible, because he was hiding out in a shelter of stone, but there were explosions in front of his eyes. Even when he closed them tight, he saw the diamond pinpricks, stabbing into his head.

A faint voice penetrated the fog of agony. "I'm sorry," said a soft whisper. "I'm so sorry. I don't want to hurt you. I want you to get better."

He dragged his eyes open and the sparkling stars faded. He blinked and more tears fell, and then she came into focus. Lisette. His blond angel. To his astonishment, she was weeping as she worked, the tears creating silvery tracks down her smooth, creamy cheeks.

She was so damned beautiful. If this was the last thing he saw before he died, he was a lucky son of a gun.

Lisette told no one about the man who had fallen from the sky. She didn't want to burden anyone with dangerous information. And even more urgently, she didn't want to bring harm to the stranger. Yet if she didn't treat his fever and wounds properly, *she* might be the one to harm him.

On the pretext of taking photographs, she walked out to the countryside each morning and evening. Didier and their "guests" approved of her passion for photography, since they liked having their pictures taken while strutting around in their smart uniforms. To maintain her cover, she pretended to enjoy this aspect of her work, because it meant a steady supply of darkroom materials, and so she cooperated.

She took a different route on her walks so as not to rouse suspicion. Each time she approached the remote *borie,* she did so with breath held and heart pounding. Had he survived the night? The day? Would he be better or worse?

On the third day at sunrise, she arrived with supplies hidden in the bottom of her straw market basket. She stepped into the stone hut to find his carbine propped on its tripod and aimed at the opening. Having a gun pointed at her was such a strange, vulnerable feeling, yet she wasn't afraid of him. He was vulnerable, too, and he knew it. She was aware of the cyanide capsule he kept in a small metal tube in the bottom of his shirt pocket. Perhaps he had others hidden elsewhere. It must be terrible for Hank to hold that decision in his hands. The village priest warned that suicide was a mortal sin, but if it kept a man from giving up information to the Nazis that would lead to more death, was it still?

"Are you awake?" she whispered, keeping to one side of the carbine. She didn't want him to startle awake and shoot before he recognized her.

"Yeah," he said, the word coming on a wheezy breath.

"Did you sleep?"

"On and off."

She knew he was embarrassed by the old metal basin he used for a bathroom, and so she simply took it to the creek, emptied and washed it, and returned. She handed him a clean linen towel dampened with fresh water. The sun slanted in through the opening of the hut, and she saw that his face appeared swollen and red.

"You're still feverish," she said, trying not to seem alarmed.

He had been trying to repair his communications equipment. She could see the small parts spread on the ground beside him. She had a fleeting thought of Jean-Luc, so clever with radios, but she hadn't seen him in weeks.

She took out some bread and boiled eggs. At the bottom of the basket were more wound dressings and disinfectant powder. In a small wooden box was a glass tube in a syringe. "This is penicillin," she said. "It will cure the infection."

"Where the devil did you get that?" he asked, blinking at it. "Christ on a crutch, did you tell somebody?"

"Of course not. I have a friend who was a . . . *vétérinaire*. You understand?"

"Veterinarian."

Lisette hadn't said anything to Dr. Toselli about the soldier, but had simply, in the course of conversation, asked him "hypothetical" questions about how he might treat a certain type of wound. And Toselli—bless him—did not wonder why she was asking. He had told her that, given the gravity of the wounds she described and the persistence of the fever, a shot of penicillin was in order. He had even shown her how to administer the shot subcutaneously, having her practice on an unripe pear from his garden.

"This is made *en maison,* you know? From a fermentation and a medium of . . ." She searched her brain for the word. "Corn flour." After she had read him Arthur Conan Doyle's "The Adventure of the Dying Detective," Toselli had explained how infections and antidotes worked.

"And that makes penicillin?" asked Hank.

"It is the best way to treat the infection," she said.

"I reckon it can't leave me any worse off than I already am."

"Don't move." She carefully cleaned his thigh where she'd cut away the fabric, plunged the needle into the muscle, and injected the solution.

He made a hissing sound, but held perfectly still. "I've never been hurt so much by a girl before," he said.

"I'm sorry."

"Don't be. It's dangerous for you to help me."

"I'm not afraid of danger," she said. Then she checked his ankle. She couldn't tell if it was broken. She propped it on a bed of soft linens and placed a compress over it.

"You should eat," she stated. "You need your strength."

"Thank you," he said, unwrapping the bread and taking a bite, washing it down with a sip of water.

She felt a wave of tenderness for this man. He was so far from his home in America, where there was no fighting at all, yet he'd come across the ocean to fight for France. "I have never heard of Vermont," she said. "Tell me about it."

A smile flickered across his face. "It's in the northeast, near Canada. Real different from here. We have long, cold winters and short, beautiful summers. I'm not homesick for it, though. I wanted to see the world. But I didn't plan on this." He gestured at his ruined leg. "So far, you're the best thing I've seen in the world."

It was the fever talking, Lisette thought. Yet his words touched a hidden place in her heart. "Hank—"

"It's the truth. You saved my life. You're my angel, Lisette."

She tried to move on from the romantic words he'd spoken. She was a married woman. "Tell me more about Vermont."

"We're stonecutters—a family business. You know what that is?"

She shook her head.

He picked up a chunk of stone from the floor. "There's a quarry where we take the stone—Vermont marble, finest in the world."

"Ah. *Marbre*. That was my father's trade as well."

"We make pillars and monuments. Markers for cemeteries. Right before I signed up for the army, I worked on a monolith statue for a town that lost half its menfolk in the Great War."

"And you still wanted to join the military."

"I did. Lots of us fellows did. I wish I could say it was for honor and patriotism."

"But it was not?" She frowned.

"Nah. I was looking for adventure. When I heard about paratrooper training, I thought that was for me."

"And here you are."

"Just a dumb guy looking for adventure. You make me wish I was noble. You make me wish I was a hero."

She smiled at him, and it was the kind of smile that started in her heart and wouldn't stop. "You are."

In the midst of her terrible situation at Sauveterre, Hank was the one thing that gave Lisette a purpose each day when she woke up. She had a powerful need to help him, and she embraced her mission with a passion she had not felt in a very long time. Tirelessly and in secret, she tended to his wounds, brought him food and water, kept him as clean as she was able, and gave him a book to read—a collection of her favorite Sherlock Holmes stories. She took a risk and stole one of Didier's old razors so Hank could shave if he wanted to. In the toolshed, she found a small rock hammer and stonecutting chisel, and she brought those as well so he would have something to do to pass the long hours alone.

Soon after the first dose of Toselli's penicillin, Hank's fever spiked, and she feared she might lose him. She gave him a second dose, refusing to give up on him. She sat by his side for as long as she dared. Even when he was delirious, she spoke to him in French, just so he could hear the sound of her voice. She reminisced about her life in Bellerive. It was good to remember the carefree days of her childhood, when Papa was well and her brothers were home safe, and she could run free in the town and outlying fields with her friends, and her greatest fear was having Sister Ignatius find a tear in her school uniform.

Then she talked about the recent times—the wrenching loss of both brothers. Her father's accident, the poverty and shortages, the threat of eviction, listening to her parents' tormented whispers in the night as they wondered what would become of them. She spoke of the night Jean-Luc had been taken away, and her desperation to help him.

"Didier came to the rescue," she said. "That is what I thought. He convinced the authorities to spare Jean-Luc." She was surprised to feel the tears on her own cheeks. She had worked so hard to numb herself to emotion that she'd nearly forgotten what true sentiment felt like.

He grew restless, thrashing so hard that he overturned the carbine that was always by his side. She couldn't understand his vague mutterings, but she stayed beside him, trying to hold him still. After what felt like an eternity, his thrashing stopped.

Now his stillness disturbed her. She lowered her cheek to his nose and mouth to make sure he was breathing. As she did, she noticed something—his skin was cool, and damp with sweat.

"Oh, thank God," she whispered. "Your fever's broken."

He shivered, and she covered him up, gently patting his shoulder. He groaned and opened his eyes to slits, looking around the cave-like interior of the *borie*. She shifted her position so he could see her.

"Lisette," he said, his voice rough and quiet.

She smiled, liking the sound of her name on his lips. "Welcome back."

"That shot of penicillin did the trick, then."

"It was no trick."

He smiled briefly. "It's a turn of phrase. I mean, the medicine worked."

"Oh. Yes." She gave him water and something to eat. His gaze darted around the hut. "What is this place?"

"We're a kilometer away from the farm, and even farther from the village. There's a stream nearby and a forest. The vineyard has been abandoned, and no one comes here. Since the fighting started, there hasn't been anyone to work the vines, so they've gone wild."

"I need to get out of here," he said. "Find my stick—my team."

"It must be frightening to be here all alone."

He gazed at her steadily. "When you're here, I don't feel alone at all." His eyes were the richest color of brown. And despite the dirt and beard stubble, it was the best face she'd ever seen.

In the midst of war and mayhem, Lisette discovered something beautiful. She could tell no one, and could scarcely describe it to herself, but it was a feeling she had yearned for all her life. She was utterly seduced by Hank Watkins—his engaging smile, his ink-black hair, and dark brown eyes.

He was everything Didier was not. He was warm sincerity where Didier was cold, gentle where Didier was cruel, sweet where Didier was bitter. There was nothing she couldn't tell Hank. Nothing she couldn't trust him with. And that was extraordinary, because although he was a complete stranger, a foreigner, someone whose life had unfolded a million miles from hers, he knew her. And she knew him.

He knew everything about her, everything that was important. And it all seemed to happen overnight. It felt like a small miracle that she could feel anything at all, given the state of her marriage.

Didier no longer pretended to be kind. He strutted about, ordering searches and arrests of people suspected of aiding the resistance, taking a strange pride in his status with the Germans. When his boyhood best friend was shot in the street for possessing contraband explosives, Didier didn't even bat an eye. At home, he was a bully, and in the bedroom, cruel. He claimed it was Lisette's fault that they had not conceived a baby, and he taunted her for being barren. For the sake of her parents, she hid her pain and tried to stay out of his way.

She loved sitting and talking with Hank. He told her about distant Vermont, which sounded to her like a magical kingdom—thick forests of maple trees that gave up their sap at the end of winter, to be boiled into delicious maple syrup, which she longed to taste. He spoke lovingly of his family—two sisters, grandparents, and even great-grandparents. Two of them had passed the venerable age of one hundred.

She came to him one day to find him sitting up in the hut. Not only that, he was clean and shaven, and wearing an old linen shirt and dungarees she'd given him.

"What did you do?" she whispered, her gaze devouring his handsome face.

"I couldn't stand myself any longer. I had to get cleaned up."

"You went to the stream." She examined his bad leg. Yesterday's wound dressing was still in place, and his ankle was still bound. "My God, did you walk?"

"Crawled like a baby," he said. "Don't worry, it was in the dead of night, and I covered my tracks. When there's enough light to see, I've been reading," he said. "Thanks for the book. I don't have anything to give you, but . . . here . . ." He handed her a Mass card with the head of Christ and a prayer on the back. "The USO gives these out to all the soldiers. It's not much." He wrote *You're my angel* on the back. "A keepsake."

She slipped it into her pocket without taking her eyes off his clean-shaven face.

"Is it bad?" he asked, rubbing a hand over his jaw. "I reckon I missed some spots."

"It's not bad," she said. "You look so much younger now. How old are you, Hank?"

He hesitated, then said, "Almost eighteen."

"So young!" She was not much older, but being married to Didier made her feel ancient.

"I had to get special permission to enlist," he said, "but it wasn't a problem. They needed every man they could get for the big push to end the war."

She nodded. "We are not allowed to have radios, but we hear rumors and reports." She didn't mention Toselli's radio, which he kept hidden from the Nazis. "But no one has heard how this will end."

He hesitated, and in that hesitation, she read what he would not say. He had been sent here to scout the terrain. Surely it must mean something was in the works.

"Hank?"

"I was only given enough information to carry out my mission. One thing I know, because it's no secret, is the mobilization is huge. A million Allied troops is what I heard. Everybody knows Germany's been planning to invade England and now they have to fight the war on two fronts. They're outmanned and outgunned."

"Not in Bellerive. Not anywhere in this region. The Germans are in complete control. They have taken over everything, and they are aided by French traitors." She felt a wave of contempt for her husband. "That is why you're here," she said, knowing it was true even before he answered. "There is going to be an invasion in the south." The idea touched her with fire. "How can I help?"

"What? Lisette, this is dangerous business."

"Do you think I don't know that? My God, I have lived in the shadow of danger for years." She bit her lip to avoid saying more about her situation at home. "I am not afraid of danger." She hesitated. "I have been helping, in my way."

She had accustomed herself to trusting no one, but Hank was different. Now she opened her straw basket and took out the film rolls she had been shooting. "The highest point in the village is the church tower," she said. "From the very top, one can see for many kilometers in every direction. On a clear day, it's possible to see the mountains to the east. I was taking photographs from the church the day I found you."

"Holy moly," he said.

"I will never know what became of my pictures. It's safer that way. If . . . when you rejoin your group, you can take the film with you."

Comprehension dawned, along with a smile, on his face. "You're incredible, Lisette."

"I cannot fight for France like a soldier, but I can fight for France," she said.

Sixteen

※

*H*ank thought about Lisette all the time. He could be found out and taken prisoner, tortured or killed, yet he only thought about her. He lived for her visits. She was like a sprite from the woods, elusive and secretive, coming and going at random. He tried to imagine her life beyond the woods and the stream and the overgrown vineyard.

He asked her what she did with the rest of her day, but her answers were vague. She told him that she lived on a working farm, which she called a *mas,* a self-sustaining property where they produced everything they needed. With the Germans in charge, they were required to surrender all their produce, but they managed better than those who suffered from the punishing rations endured by city dwellers. The place was called Sauveterre, which she told him meant "Safe Haven." She said this with a twist of irony, because nothing was safe anymore.

When she wasn't with him, he went over and over their conversations in his head and practiced the French phrases she taught him. He was charmed by her quirky English, which she had learned from the novels of Arthur Conan Doyle. It made her sound slightly old-fashioned and extra smart.

Every once in a while, he managed to shift his thoughts from Lisette to the mission. Had the Brits finally agreed to the plan? Had his unit provided good intel? Were they still looking for him? Had they given him up for dead? Lost? Deserted? Captured? He could not think of a way to contact his unit without putting Lisette in harm's way. He knew she would do anything he asked, especially since she had all but confessed that she was helping the resistance by taking strategic photographs, but he didn't want to ask. He'd heard rumors about what the Vichy government officials did with resistance workers.

Bivouacked in this hiding place with a bum leg, he could only imagine what was going on outside. He wished he could be mapping the terrain, setting up radar sets and Krypton lights to signal the drop zone. Now that he'd met Lisette, he wanted that more than ever—to be part of the force that would liberate her village along with the rest of southern France.

He took out his frustration by fashioning a pair of makeshift crutches, gouging the wood with savage strength. Despite the searing pain, he knew he was getting stronger. His ribs were healing. It was now possible to take a breath without wanting to scream. The leg was another matter. But still, he was determined to get back on his feet, and soon.

And then what?

The question haunted him. He stared at the opening of the hut, which framed a view of the sky. He'd memorized what the sky looked like at every hour of the day. He could tell it was around nine at night, judging by the deep orange hues cast by the dying sun.

He heard the sound of someone approaching. Footfalls on uneven ground. As always, he held his breath, because even though Lisette swore no one would come near, he had to be vigilant. Then he heard her signal—the soft whistle of a bird.

And just like that, his heart was filled with happiness. She was magic that way.

"Bonsoir, mon beau monsieur," she said.

He heard a special note in her voice. A trill, almost. "You're in a good mood tonight."

"I am," she said, setting down a basket that emitted the most delicious aroma. "I've brought you a strawberry tart. And something special." She took a bottle from her basket. "Champagne."

"Wow, I've never tasted champagne. Are you celebrating something?"

"We all are. All of France. All the world." She tipped back her head and laughed, looking as fresh as a rose, and so beautiful his heart skipped a beat.

"There's news?" He sat forward, eager to hear.

She nodded. "There was a report on a contraband radio. The Allies have landed in Normandy and are in the process of taking back all of France."

"Really? When? How?" He couldn't get his questions out fast enough. Everyone knew a huge invasion was in the works to keep the Germans out of England, but the actual time and place were top secret. Now the news was out that there had been a massive invasion on the beaches of Normandy at the beginning of the month. The fighting had been brutal, but they had the Germans on the run, and were liberating villages one by one, making their way to Paris.

"I found a few bottles of champagne hidden away at the farmhouse. Let us drink to the liberation of France."

The cork was held on by a wire cage to keep it from popping out. When she removed the cage, it still didn't pop. "Let me show you something. It's a trick my father used to do, back when he . . . in happier times."

She drew out an odd-looking short saber. Hank didn't bat an eye. How quickly he had come to trust her, more deeply than he had ever trusted anyone.

She held the bottle in one hand with the cork facing away. "Each bottle has a very subtle seam," she said. "Can you see it?"

"Not really. It's getting pretty dark."

"Give me your hand," she said.

"Gladly." He loved the feel of her dainty hand covering his. She guided his finger over the smooth glass surface until he felt a slight ridge.

"The seam must be facing up. Then you take the saber and . . . just watch." In a quick, decisive movement, she slid the blade up the neck of the bottle. With a loud crack, the cork flew free, and a froth spewed onto the floor. *"Et voilà,"* she said.

Hank was both startled and delighted. "Well, how about that. Never seen anything like it."

"I have only one cup."

"I'll gladly share with you, Lisette."

She poured, and lifted the glass. "To France—and to the Allies who will make us free again." Then she took a drink and handed him the cup.

He was amazed by the taste of the champagne. "Holy moly," he said. "That is probably the most delicious thing I've ever tasted."

"Like drinking the stars," said Lisette. "That is how Dom Pérignon described it."

An impulse took hold of him and he leaned forward, took her face in his cupped hands, and kissed her.

She looked as stunned as he felt when he pulled away.

"I lied," he whispered, still holding her face between his hands.

"About what?"

"When I said the champagne was the most delicious thing I've ever tasted. Because it's not. You are. You are the most delicious thing I've ever tasted." He kissed her again, more briefly, entranced by the sweetness of her. "Like kissing the stars."

He was so crazy about this girl. What if he persuaded her to come back to the States with him after the war? What if he brought her home to Vermont as his war bride? What if they settled down and made a life together?

She finished the cup of champagne and poured another. When half of that was gone, he kissed her again. So sweet. He wanted to hold her in his arms forever.

Then she pulled back, regarding him with tears in her eyes. "Hank, this is not possible."

It was as if she had read his mind. "Don't say that." He touched a finger to her soft lips, still damp from champagne. "I love you. I'm completely in love with you."

She began to cry. "Hank, don't. You cannot. I . . . There is something I must explain."

"Oh, sweetheart, I could listen to you talk all day." Even a small amount of champagne made him giddy, probably because it felt so good to tell her what was in his heart.

"I am married. I have a husband."

He instantly pulled back. Jesus. His heart sank, weighted by shock and disappointment. A husband? How could this young, beautiful girl already have a husband? "I'm real sorry, Lisette. If I'd known, I would never be so disrespectful. Not in a million years."

That only made her cry harder. Her tears hurt him a hundred times worse than his bum leg. "What can I do to make it up to you? I wish I could take back the words. I'm so stupid . . ."

She gently placed her hand over his, and even that small gesture made his head spin. The tears shone like silver on her face. "Ah, Hank. Your words are beautiful, and I will cherish them always. Never think that telling me you love me is the wrong thing to say."

"But . . . you're married."

"I did not marry for love, and once it was done, I never dreamed anything would change for me. You brought this change, Hank. A wonderful, terrible thing is happening to us. I love you, too."

For a moment, he thought he'd heard wrong. "What? Did you just say—"

"Yes. I love you with all my heart. I know I shouldn't, but my heart doesn't listen." She used a corner of her apron to dab at her tears while a bittersweet smile curved her lips. She drank more champagne, then handed him the cup. "It's so impossible. At the same time, when I'm with you, I can believe anything is possible."

"But you're married," he repeated. He couldn't picture it. He couldn't imagine her in some other life, with some other fellow.

She nodded. "It is . . . not like this." Again, she took his hand, studying their linked fingers. "Not like you and me."

Slowly, reluctantly, he took his hand away from hers. "Tell me. I want to understand."

Her expression turned grim. "Marrying Didier was not my choice."

"That's his name? Didier?" Hank tried to conjure up an image of the sort of man she would marry, even though she didn't love him.

"Didier Palomar. He is a rich man, older than me, the mayor of Bellerive. His first wife died young, and he wanted another to give him an heir. My family was in great trouble when I first met him. Both of my brothers were dead, and my father had suffered an accident. He will never walk again."

Hank had never known such a loss. He could only imagine what it felt like for the families here, struggling through the losses and shortages of war. "I'm so sorry, Lisette."

"Didier was generous and kind at first. He seemed like a decent man. He promised that if I married him, he would keep my parents safe at Sauveterre." She paused, twisting her hands in her lap. "I never loved him, but I believed marrying Didier was a small sacrifice to make in order to save my parents from having to beg. Marrying him seemed . . . I thought it was the right thing to do. I thought . . . Ah, none of that matters now, does it? It's done. My mother told me that love would come when the babies came. There have been no babies." She drank more champagne. "Didier blames me. And that is not even the worst thing about him. The worst is that he is a collaborator, a member of the Milice, doing the Nazis' dirty work. I feel such horror and shame when he terrorizes my friends and neighbors, ransacking their homes, betraying them to the Germans, having them dragged away in front of their families. And there is nothing I can do to stop it."

"I wish I could put my arms around you and hold you close," Hank said.

"Then you should do just that." Without hesitation, she set down the cup and moved into his embrace, fitting herself into the curve of his shoulder. "Does this hurt your ribs?"

"No," he whispered. "Not at all."

She framed his face between her hands. "I cannot stop this. I cannot stop what I'm feeling for you, Hank. It is supposed to be a sin, but all I feel is love, every moment since I met you. And that in itself is a miracle, because I never thought I would know what it feels like to truly love a man with all my heart, and to have a man truly love me."

And with that, she straddled him so that he could feel the sweet warmth of her, and they kissed again, and this time, the kiss was different—deeper, more lingering. It was the kind of kiss that led to an intimacy that touched him like fire. He groaned in the back of his throat and lifted his mouth from hers, and it felt like the hardest thing he'd ever had to do.

"Your leg," she whispered against his mouth.

"It's fine. You're not hurting my leg. Or my ribs, or anything else. But, Lisette—"

"Shh. I want this, Hank. I need this. I need to know that I can feel again, that love is not just an illusion I read about in Toselli's books."

"It's real, Lisette. I love you, and I'm sorry your family's having such hard times. I wish I could make things better for you. I swear, I'd do anything to help."

"This is helping," she said, holding his gaze with hers while she unbuttoned her blouse.

In the midst of war, in the face of her husband's cruelty, Lisette found a love so pure and beautiful that sometimes she could scarcely breathe from the sheer wonder of it. She refused to feel regret or guilt for loving Hank Watkins. She had never felt such pleasure and delight in a man's company, in his touch, in the intimacy they shared.

She tried to seem normal as she went about her day, but it was hard to keep the smile from her face, the light from her eyes, the color from her cheeks. Her mother kept asking her if she had a fever, or if she had been drinking. Lisette said it was because of the secret news no one was supposed to know about—that the Allies had invaded France in the north, and it was only a matter of time before they came to the south.

She continued to visit Hank as often as she dared, only now her visits were deeply satisfying assignations. She took pictures, because she never wanted to forget him, but she hid the film in order to keep their secret. She promised it would not be developed until the war was over.

Didier seemed preoccupied with his German friends and took no notice of her at all. She was surprised one day in August when he and his sister, Rotrude, approached her in the kitchen garden, their faces grim.

"When did you plan to tell me about the baby?" he demanded without preamble.

The shock of his question took her breath away. She felt as if every drop of blood had drained into the floor. "I don't know what you're talking about."

"Don't be coy," said Rotrude with a mean twist of a smile. "Why wouldn't you share this joyous news with everyone?"

"Because it's not . . . I'm not . . ." But she was. She had known for the past week. Her menses had always been as regular as the phases of the moon, and only a few days after a missed period, she knew.

"You've thrown up your breakfast every morning for a week," Rotrude said.

Didier pinched Lisette's breast so hard that she cried out in pain. "My sister tells me the breasts are tender during pregnancy."

She turned away, hugging herself, her heart pounding in panic. Then, deep within her core, a steely spike of courage formed. "Then instead of bullying the mother of your child," she said, "you should take pride, because finally there will be an heir for Sauveterre, just as you've always wanted."

Rotrude stepped in. "Will you let her lie to you like that?" she demanded. "Your first wife never conceived. You've fucked every housemaid and fieldworker in the place, and have never managed to make a baby. What makes you think this one is yours?"

"Because he is the lord of Sauveterre and the mayor of Bellerive," Lisette said, praying his pride would supersede suspicion. The lie made her sick, but to do otherwise would doom not only her, but her parents. And without her, Hank would likely die in the wilderness.

"Lisette is right," Didier said, yanking her into a rough embrace. "We must have a special dinner tonight and share the news. Isn't there still a bottle of champagne in the *cave*?"

She swallowed hard, remembering the bottle she had stolen to drink with Hank. "I wouldn't know. The Nazis help themselves to everything."

"Everything?" Rotrude demanded with a sneer. "Even your wife, Didier?" She hated Lisette, because Lisette had supplanted her at Sauveterre. And if an heir was born, then Rotrude and her daughter, Petra, would be relegated to mere guests in the household.

"Will you let your sister speak to you with such disrespect?" Lisette quietly asked Didier.

He let go of her and turned to Rotrude. "Make sure there's a feast tonight," he ordered. "And don't forget the champagne."

After the encounter, Lisette couldn't even look at herself in a mirror. Pretending the tiny, fragile life inside her belonged to Didier was the worst sort of lie, but she had to hide the truth in order to protect Hank.

"Let us take Papa to the market," she said to her mother later that morning. She had to get out of the house. "Didier is demanding a big supper tonight. We can take the scooter. I have an extra petrol coupon from last month."

She loved taking her father out in the cart attached to the scooter. It made him forget, just for a while, that he could no longer walk. Going to town allowed him to reconnect with friends, the way he used to do. The Monday market was not the same as it had been before the war. With so few men to work the fields, and the Germans taking the lion's share, the yield was less bountiful. But this was the Var, and it was high summer, and there was fish from the harbor, big tubs of olives, and lovely spice blends. The gardens of Sauveterre were bursting with tomatoes and peppers, aubergines and courgettes, so they would have everything they needed for Didier's feast.

She left her parents at the Café de la Rive by the bridge, one of the few still open in the village. It was a foggy morning, cool for August. Papa's friends, the Cabrets, helped him to sit at a table. The ersatz coffee was vile stuff, just an excuse for enjoying a few moments of companionship. The setting by the river beside the mossy old fountain with the spitting fish, under a shade trellis twined with grapevines, reminded her of the old days. Seeing her mother and father with their friends filled Lisette's heart with warmth.

She had not yet told them about the baby. She didn't know what to say. For their own protection, she had never complained to them about Didier. Perhaps they would be thrilled to know they were going to become grandparents.

"Why do you look at us so?" asked her mother with a smile.

"You all look so content, four friends having coffee together. In that soft light . . ." She took out her camera and composed the shot, capturing the play of fog and shadow, and the expressions on their faces.

"Would you like me to come help you at the market?"

"No, Maman. It's fine. Once the fog lifts, it's going to be a beautiful day. I'll come back for you later." She disengaged the sidecar and drove away on the scooter. When she was well away from the bridge, she took a detour. Leaving the scooter concealed amid the old vines shrouded in fog, she ran to the *borie* to see Hank.

He grinned and opened his arms when she burst in. "Hi there, sweetheart," he said. "I didn't expect to see you until later."

"I'm supposed to be at the market," she said, "and I saw a chance to slip away." She covered his face with kisses, and when they made love, her ardor was so intense that it brought tears to her eyes. Yet in the aftermath, there was a kind of peace she had never felt before. To be held in the arms of a man who loved her, to know they'd created a new life together, was the sweetest blessing she'd ever felt.

Although she longed to tell him, she didn't dare. Not yet, anyway, with the future so uncertain. And there was a very small, dark place in her mind where she had to allow that the baby could in fact be Didier's.

"What is this?" he asked softly, gently touching the dark bruise on her breast. "How did you hurt yourself?"

"It's nothing," she said, the lie spilling easily from her lips. If Hank found out about Didier's cruelty, he would hunt her husband down and get himself killed in the process. "I must have bumped myself while getting Rocinante into his harness."

He leaned over and kissed the bruise. "Be careful. I can't stand the idea of you getting hurt." He rolled a largish, rounded stone toward her. "I made you something."

She sat up, pulling her shawl around her. He had carefully chiseled a phrase in the stone—*Journey Without End.*

"It's beautiful, Hank," she said, tracing a finger over the letters.

"It means I'll never stop loving you, no matter what," he said.

"I have to leave it here," she said, placing it near the opening of the hut.

"We can bring it back to Vermont after the war."

She pressed her cheek against his bare chest. "Vermont, eh? You are taking me to Vermont?"

"I am. And your dear parents, too, and if your Nazi-loving husband tries to stop me, he'll be damned sorry."

They lay in each other's arms, not speaking, only dreaming, and she knew it was the same dream. She hovered on the verge of tears, because she wanted to tell him about the baby. Instead, she slowly extricated herself from his arms and got dressed. "I must go back to the village now."

He put on his trousers and showed her his moves on the crutches. "I've been practicing. I'll be dancing the fox-trot with you one of these days real soon."

She was about to burst with her news. Throwing caution to the wind, she said, "Hank, *mon amour,* I have something to tell you."

"You can tell me anything, sweetheart. Anything at—"

His next words were drowned by the whine of aircraft and a series of muffled booms.

"Air raid," Lisette said. "My God—"

He hobbled outside and looked around. "There's too much ground fog. That's bad. They won't be able to see the landing zone."

"Hank, what is happening?"

"You need to run for cover. The Allied invasion is starting."

PART 5

Aix-en-Provence

Photography takes an instant out of time,
altering life by holding it still.

—DOROTHEA LANGE, AMERICAN PHOTOGRAPHER

Seventeen

❦

"W hat happened that day?" Camille stepped back from the long table scattered with documents, laptops, and an old-school microfiche reader. She, Finn, and Roz were at the university in Aix-en-Provence going through some barely readable printouts on microfiche, containing news reports about the liberation of the town of Bellerive.

"Depends on who you ask," Finn said, referring to a narrative accompanied by a photo of an American soldier washing the face of a distraught little boy. "Everybody has a story."

"It would help if we knew what we were looking for," Roz muttered.

Camille refilled their glasses of *citron pressé*. The iced fresh lemon was their only defense against the heat of the day. The archives were housed in a cavernous eighteenth-century building filled with meticulously cataloged files. Many had been rendered in microfiche, and a good number of those were now in digital form. But there was so much raw data, still uncategorized.

"This is Bellerive," Finn said a few minutes later, showing them a creased photograph. The picture showed a bridge reduced to rubble next to a river. There were no markings anywhere on the photo.

Camille felt a chill despite the heat. "It looks like so many of the others," she said. "Every town in the district has a stone bridge."

"This is part of a sign. And here, a piece of a garden fountain." He turned the photo and indicated a fragment of twisted metal with some print on it, and a broken piece of concrete in the shape of a fish. Then

he showed her a picture of a riverside café, dated a few years before
the arrival of the Allies. In that shot, the bridge was intact. There were
café tables arranged around the fountain under a grape arbor.

"The Café de la Rive," she said, and the chill intensified. "It just
feels so personal. Do you think this photo is from the day of the invasion?"

"Likely," he said. "Hey, do you want to take a break?"

She looked up at him, startled that he could read her mood. Startled that he cared. She wasn't used to this. She wasn't used to anything
about this—the feelings he stirred in her, the way she was drawn to
him. "What did you have in mind?"

A short time later, they were in his car with the windows rolled down.
Fields and fields of sunflowers flanked the highway, the intense yellow
creating a glorious contrast with the bluer-than-blue sky. It occurred
to Camille to ask where they were going, but she had decided, just this
once, to experiment with surrender. For the past five years, she had
been so preoccupied with being in control that she'd nearly forgotten
what it felt like.

He switched on the radio, and they listened to French pop songs
along the way. It was a singular feeling, letting go so completely, the
breeze snatching her hair through the window as the *deux chevaux*
trundled through the countryside and with "J'ai besoin de la lune"
wailing from the radio. She wondered if he realized how new this was
to her, exhilarating and risky, like teetering on a narrow precipice.

After a while, Finn said, "Back in the States, you said you weren't
a photographer."

"No, I said I didn't take pictures anymore."

"Grab that bag from the backseat," he said.

She turned and picked up a heavy canvas bag. "A camera?"

"Yep. I borrowed this from the photography department. It's one
of the best on the market today."

She unzipped the bag and took it out, a glorious high-performance Nikon. "It is," she agreed.

"Thought you'd like to check it out."

"Oh. Well . . . thanks." She looked through the viewfinder at the scenery outside and explored some of the camera's functions.

He glanced over at her. "I like watching you handle it. Like a pro."

"Really?"

"It's kind of sexy."

"Shut up." She could never quite tell if he was teasing. When she glanced over at him, she caught him in an unguarded moment, his face somber as he watched the road ahead.

"Was your dad a pro?" she asked.

He didn't answer right away. Then he said, "Yeah. Yeah, he was."

She'd guessed right, then. She was getting better at reading him. "I'd like to see some of his pictures."

"Sure. I'll show you one of these days. But today I want to show you something else." He turned off the main road, following signs to Gordes. There was a monument indicating that the entire village had been awarded a medal for its actions in August 1944. "Ever hear of Willy Ronis?"

"Are you kidding? Yes. He's one of my photography heroes. He and Cartier-Bresson. I've been obsessed with them for years. What made you think of him?"

"Want to go to his house?"

"What?"

The *deux chevaux*'s gutless engine whined in protest as he drove up a series of steep, ancient streets. They got out and walked up to the top of Gordes, passing ancient stone cottages decked with vines and flowers. He stopped at a neat, unassuming cottage with two weathered wooden doors. One was marked PRIVÉ and the other SALON RONIS.

"No way," Camille said softly. "Willy Ronis lived here?"

"He did." Finn slipped a donation into the honor box beside the door and held it open. Light streamed through the open window, settling on Ronis's most famous and remarkable picture. It was a shot of his wife in the nude, turned away from the camera's eye as she bathed in front of a rustic sink. The interplay of light and shadow gave it a painterly quality. Camille was inspired by the perfect timing and unabashed tenderness of the shot.

"It's quite a picture," she said. There were several others on display, shots of everyday life in the Luberon—a fieldworker resting against his panniers, a little boy running past a window, holding a toy airplane aloft, a cat climbing a curtain. "I like his joie de vivre."

"He lived to be ninety-nine," Finn said. "That's a lot of joie."

She smiled and stepped outside the stone cottage, surveying the winding streets, with their ancient doors and arcades. It was late afternoon, a time photographers called the golden hour, when the light was drenched in deep color, carving out shapes with razor-edged clarity. An elderly couple walked past an arch in the stone that was decked in twining hollyhocks. At that moment, a butterfly flitted past. The old man gestured at it with his finger just as the light touched it. And without even thinking about it, Camille lifted the camera to her eye and took the shot.

Back at the university, they met up with Vivi and Roz, who were cataloging more items from Sauveterre. "Sometimes you find out things you'd rather not know," Roz said, holding up a picture of a woman whose head had been shaved to punish her for being a Nazi's mistress. "We can stop if you like."

"No," Camille said, wincing at the woman's shamed expression. "Let's keep going. I want to know everything about that day."

"It's still in living memory for a few locals. One of my students prepared a list of them, with their contact information," Finn said.

She nodded. "I hope my father's cousin Petra is willing to share. Where was Lisette that day? Who was she with?"

"You might find some answers here," Vivi said, coming into the room and setting an old tin tobacco box on the table. "I found this on a high shelf in the attic at Sauveterre."

"I thought we cleared the attic out," said Roz.

"There was a high shelf in a corner, and I remembered something my father used to say—if you want to hide something, put it up high."

"Because when people are searching, they tend to look down," Camille said. "That makes sense."

"What's in the box?" asked Finn.

With a flourish, Vivi removed the lid to reveal the contents.

"Film rolls! Oh my gosh, I can't believe you found these." Camille's heart skipped a beat.

"Of course I found them," Vivi said. "I can find anything. And look. They're labeled and dated. Your mysterious grandmother was wonderfully organized."

"It's a shame about the film, though," Roz said. "Likely ruined, wouldn't you say?"

"Not if I can help it," Camille said.

"She's the world's leading expert at rescuing old film," Finn said.

"Slight overstatement, especially coming from you." She still felt terrible about ruining his father's last roll. "But if we can find a lab . . ."

"How about we try finding one at the largest university in France?" said Finn.

The darkroom at the university in Aix was old but well equipped and stocked with fresh, good-quality chemicals. There were no detectable light leaks. Camille took a deep breath, like a swimmer about to dive from a high place, and stepped inside.

Finn followed, brushing up against her in the small space.

"There's not much room in here," she said. Awareness shot through him, and she felt a surge of desire.

"I want to watch."

She liked working with him. She liked being near him. She liked *him.* It was exciting to develop the film and study the digitized results, and the edge of intensity she felt only made the work more interesting. Jace had never taken much interest in her work, yet Finn seemed to share her passion and curiosity. The pictures that emerged from the distant past showed her a portrait of courage—a wounded soldier and the woman who took care of him. It made Camille's fear seem petty by comparison.

There was a photo of a tall, dark-haired man with a bandaged leg. They thought it could be the American soldier who had left the parachute pack behind. There were several portraits of him. They were thoughtful, tender studies, beautifully composed, taking advantage of natural light. "More of Lisette's work," said Camille. She studied the face for a long time. "The soldier was someone important to her. How can we find out who he was?"

"How do you find out who anyone is?" asked Finn, bending close so she could feel the brush of his breath on her cheek. "You figure out what drives him, what he loves. And what he doesn't even realize he wants."

The darkroom revealed more about Finn than he realized. She watched him in the red glow of a safelight as he studied a candid shot of a group of children on the beach. "What are you seeing?" she asked him. It was a lovely composition—balanced, and clearly framed by someone with a practiced eye. She was sure Lisette had taken the photo. It had what Camille had come to recognize as her trademark timing, and an understanding of the subject.

"Something about this picture makes me think of my family," he said. "Between my mom and Rudy, and all the aunts and uncles and cousins, we're a loud, friendly, demanding clan."

Working together, they began cleaning up the darkroom. "Sounds fun."

"It is. I always thought I'd have something like that," he admitted. "A big family, I mean. Or even a small one."

"Small works for Julie and me."

"Camille, are you saying you want—"

"No," was her swift, fearful reply. "That came out wrong."

He studied her intently, then held the door for her to step out ahead of him. He was always doing things like holding doors, chairs, waiting his turn, listening with full attention. She loved his manners, the unstudied, thoughtful gestures that were second nature to him. "You're lucky to have her. She seems great."

"If you'd seen her a month ago, you might not say that. It's so hard to see your kid going through a tough time."

"I bet she'd say the same about you."

"She was my lifeline after her dad died." Camille shuddered as a shadow of the past flickered like a faulty lamp. "I remember thinking that after Jace, I would never know happiness again. And then, just a couple of months after he was gone, Julie crawled into my lap and smiled at me. Watching my daughter smile was better for me than months of grief counseling."

"I want one," Finn said.

"What, grief counseling?"

"No. A kid, smiling at me."

She made light of it. What else could she do? "You're barking up the wrong tree."

He studied her. Sexy. Smoldering. "Am I?"

"I have to go," she told Finn. "I can't . . . I have to go."

"Why?"

"Because . . ." She forgot what she was going to say. When he looked at her, she forgot everything in the world.

"That," he said, turning to her and giving her a lingering kiss, "is not a valid excuse. Let's discuss it later. At my place."

"Your place, eh?" She was intrigued.

"We're going to have a nice dinner at my favorite bistro, and then we'll bring a good bottle of rosé home."

"I should get back to Bellerive. Check on Julie . . ."

"She's fine. She has a whole houseful of people looking after her. Let me borrow your phone."

She handed it over without thinking. He tapped in a message and hit send.

"Hey."

"I let everyone know you're staying in Aix tonight." And with that, he turned off both their phones and stuck them in his pocket.

"Hey."

"You bossed me around all afternoon in the darkroom. Now I'm in charge." He ushered her out of the institute, and she followed, weirdly and reluctantly turned on by his attitude. He took her through the old town, where the evening was just getting under way. Aix was true to its Roman origins—Aquae Sextiae—with fountains in every square, bursting from walls or ornate stone basins, where the locals placed their wine to chill.

"There's a saying by Cocteau," Finn said. "'In Aix, a blind man thinks it's raining. If he could see with his cane, he would see a hundred blue fountains singing the glory of Cézanne.'" He shrugged. "Probably sounds better in French."

The Cours Mirabeau was lined with plane trees and cafés with scalloped awnings. It was open to pedestrians only, with colorful booths lining both sides of the street. Kids and nannies played around a mossy fountain in the center. The sounds and smells were overwhelming—fish fresh from the ocean, bouquets of flowers, incense, food being fried up in huge iron pans over gas burners. Street musicians played for tips, and to Camille's delight, Finn was a generous tipper. She felt utterly seduced by the joie de vivre here.

He brought her to a small square with yet another fountain, which was surrounded by café tables. The waiter served them from one of the bottles left to chill in the babbling water. They savored a slow, delicious dinner, finishing it with small cups of lemon ice. Camille felt his gaze unabashedly studying her eyes, her lips, the way she sipped from her wineglass.

"Let's go," he said, signaling for the check.

She was too relaxed to object. She wanted to explore this thing that was happening between them. It felt so new. Every look, every touch, even just the brush of his hand, ignited her senses. A feeling of wonder held her captive as they strolled to his house, a walk-up apartment in an elegant old converted mansion in the pedestrian quarter where the only traffic consisted of wandering tourists and the occasional scooter. Lime-washed walls and exposed beams gave the whole place a timeless air. It was like being detached from the world here, a hideaway set apart from everything else in her life.

She stood at an arched window whose shutters were open to the starry sky, and sounds drifted up from the street—laughter and music, a warm breeze rustling through the broad leaves of the sycamore trees. He came up behind her and slid his arms around her waist, bending toward her neck to inhale deeply.

"I love the way your hair smells," he said.

"Like darkroom chemicals?"

"Like flowers." He carefully lifted her hair to bare her neck and nuzzled her there. "I like the way you taste, too."

"Is that so?" She turned in his arms and stood on tiptoe to kiss him. This was a pivotal moment for her; she could feel herself poised on the fine edge of . . . something. She'd held all other men at arm's length, but Finn . . . She liked the way he tasted, too, of rosé wine and lemon ice, his mouth and tongue gently enticing her to yield. "You have no idea how much I've been thinking about this," she said.

"Yeah? That's cool, Camille. Because I think about it all the time." He took her hand and led her to the bedroom, another airy space, dimly lit and sparsely furnished with a big, low bed made up with fresh linens.

"I like your place," she said.

"I spent the whole morning getting it ready."

"Ready for what?"

"For this." He took off his shirt with one arm over his head. During the work at Sauveterre, she'd studied his chest and abs from afar. Now she put her hands on him, running her fingers over the contours, delighting in the soft, involuntary sound he made when she touched him.

He carefully unbuttoned her blouse, kissing each place he exposed. Then he slipped off her bra and skirt. Finally, he laid her back on the bed, and the fresh linens cushioned them with a lavender-scented sigh. Bracing himself on either side of her, he slowly, shockingly, removed her panties with his teeth.

Don't stop, she thought. Don't ever stop. She forgot everything except the sensations coursing over her as he caressed her, his touch less practiced than she would have expected it to be. The surprise and delight of this pleasure took her breath away. There were moments when she sensed genuine emotion from him—when he looked into her eyes and shuddered as he whispered her name, the syllables breaking with tenderness.

The night flowed on, following a course of its own, and Camille gave herself up to it, too replete with wine and lovemaking to think of anything at all. She didn't even feel herself drifting off to sleep.

He awakened her with kisses in places that hadn't been kissed in . . . maybe ever. Her pulse felt strong and heavy, her body softly aching with a desire she didn't bother to resist. Later, she thought, and then she stopped thinking at all. Afterward, they lay quietly against a bank of pillows, watching the sky turn pink with the dawn.

"That was . . ." She had trouble forming a coherent sentence. "Last night was . . ."

"I thought so, too."

"Not sure how I feel about you doing my thinking for me."

"Then we'll have to do a lot more of this so you can figure it out."

"Mmm." She felt so different with him. "I suppose we could do that."

"I'll find out all your deep, dark secrets."

She felt a small part of herself recoiling. "You don't want to go there."

"Let me be the judge of that."

"Can't we just . . . enjoy this?"

"We did, all night long." He made a sexy, wordless sound as he stretched again.

"You know what I mean. Last night *was* amazing. Let's not spoil it by . . ."

"By what? Falling in love?"

"Who said anything about falling in love?"

"I did. Surprised the crap out of myself, too."

"You're funny."

"You think?" He played with a lock of her hair, twisting it lazily around his finger. "What happened to you?" he asked. "Why hasn't some guy swept you off your feet?"

I think some guy is doing that now, she thought. She reminded herself that this was so very new. There was a big part of his life that was shrouded in mystery. Finn was haunted by a betrayal of the heart—she knew that. What she didn't know was . . . everything else.

She pulled back, still not trusting him. Not trusting herself. No one had ever made her feel this way.

Not even Jace.

The stark admission slipped past her wall of defenses. Her feelings for Jace, honed and perfected by time and remembrance and probably a big dose of self-delusion, had never felt this deep, this real. Her feelings for Finn were messy and intense and gloriously real.

Was it because she was older now? Because she knew her own heart better? Or because she was desperate?

She grabbed her phone from the pocket of his pants.

"Don't even think of getting out of this bed," he said with a luxurious stretch.

"I have to go," she said, looking at her phone. "My father has news."

"The DNA results are back." Camille's father patted the envelope in his pocket. They had met in the village for coffee. The café by the river bridge seemed to be a favorite of the locals.

"Wow. That was fast. Are you . . . did you open it?"

He nodded. "In fact, I received the results yesterday. I would have told you, but you were off with your new boyfriend."

A flush heated her cheeks. She still felt strange, almost light-headed from being with Finn. "So are you going to tell me now?" she asked.

"Didier Palomar was not my natural father."

"Seriously? I mean, I knew . . . I thought . . . based on physical traits alone, it seemed unlikely you were related to Palomar. But now we know."

"Yes. Now we know. But there is still much we don't know. Does this mean I'm a fraud? That Didier was tricked into believing I was his heir? What does it mean for Lisette? Was she unfaithful? A victim of rape?" He took out a handkerchief and dabbed at his forehead. "I want to feel relieved, but instead, it simply gives rise to more questions."

"I know, Papa. And I'm sorry there isn't more clarity. But I refuse to feel sorry that you were not fathered by Didier Palomar." She took out her phone and navigated to the pictures they'd developed in the darkroom, scrolling to the shot of the tall, dark-haired soldier. "This was from a roll of film we found. He appears to be an American paratrooper. Now I wonder if he could be the one."

Her father studied the small screen. "Lisette took this picture?"

"I think so, yes."

"Is there a way to find out more about this man?"

She nodded. "We're working on it. Finn has a whole historical inquiry class working on it." She pressed a hand on his shoulder. "If people had known this about you when you were a boy, things would have been much different. They would not have accused you of being a traitor and the son of a Nazi lover. They would have been kinder to you."

Her father's face changed then, his eyes taking on a distant glaze as the color drained from his cheeks. She touched his arm in consternation. "What is it?"

He gave himself a small shake. "Probably nothing. But . . . a flicker of memory, perhaps. When I was very small, a stranger came to Sauveterre. He was tall and walked with a cane, and he spoke to my aunt in a language I didn't understand."

She caught her breath. "English? Was he speaking English?"

"Honestly, I can't say. I was so very young, maybe four or five." He sighed. "The past is the past. It happened. There is no point in wondering how my life would have unfolded if I'd known."

"But . . ." She could tell there was something weighing on his mind. "Did you tell your cousin Petra about the results?"

"Of course. She was kind enough to agree to the test, and therefore I owe her the truth. She was the first one I called, even before I called you. At which point I am forced to tell you that you didn't take my call, so I had to send a text message." He wrinkled his nose. "You know how I feel about text messages. All those emotions and whatnot."

"Emojis. What did Petra say?"

"She was not surprised. She always wondered why I was so dark when the rest of the family were all fair. Of course, I asked her if she knew who might have been my father, but she has no idea. And since there is no Palomar blood in my veins, I offered to deed Sauveterre to her."

Camille gasped. "What do you mean, you offered her . . . ?"

"Sauveterre, the entire property, free and clear."

Camille realized then how deep her father's shame had run. He wanted nothing to do with Didier Palomar. "And?"

"And she laughed, and said she is eighty-two years old and has no use for a working farm with a falling-down house. She never had children, and her husband left her well off. I am going to pay her a monthly stipend, however, for the rest of her life."

"I'm glad the two of you got together," Camille said.

"I'm glad, too. People can change, after all. It makes me wonder . . ." His voice trailed off. "She wants to meet you and Julie."

"Of course. Just say when. Do you think she'd be willing to talk to us about her memories?"

"Something tells me she would like nothing better."

In Bellerive, the impossible happened to Julie. The kids thought she was cool and wanted to hang out with her. They wanted to hear about life in America. They even had a funny nickname for her—La 'Ricaine, short for *l'Américaine*. Each day after chores, the adventures started, usually with Martine taking the lead. So far, they'd ridden bikes along the Var, jumped into a waterfall in a deep river pool, climbed Cézanne's mountain—the one he'd painted on canvas fifty times—and played soccer late into the evening. Her favorite outing was a trip to the beach with André and his two brothers. Ever since she'd jumped off the cliff with them, they had declared her their favorite. André even sang an old-fashioned song about her, "Des filles il en pleut," which meant "It's Raining Girls."

"So it's good news," said Martine as they were in the garden, taking down the fresh laundry that had been hung out to dry. "There's a street dance in Cassis tonight, and our favorite boy band will be there. We should go. There is a market at the port with fun kiosks, street performers, and all the usual nice snacks."

"Absolutely," Julie agreed, feeling a little jump of excitement in her chest. The seaport village sounded like the perfect place to go on a warm summer night.

Julie knew her mom would say yes. Mom was really easy to deal with these days, because she was so busy with her history project. Also with Finn. Mom had gone out with guys before, but this was different. Instead of getting all cranky and nervous before a date, she just seemed excited. It was nice, seeing her mom like that, smiling about nothing and humming under her breath . . . and not worrying about every move Julie made.

"What are you going to wear?" she asked Martine, holding up one of her shirts, a plaid one she used to like but was sick of now.

Martine shrugged. "Something I can dance in. Do you need to borrow an outfit?"

"That's nice of you, but we're not the same size."

"Sure we are." Martine snatched a short denim skirt from the clothesline and tossed it to Julie. "Try this."

To Julie's surprise, the skirt fit when she pulled it up over her shorts. Snug, but not too snug. The expected muffin top didn't emerge. Apparently, all the swimming and chores and bike riding were doing some good.

"Cute," said Vivi, walking past with her arms loaded with more boxes from the history project.

By now, Finn's coworkers were practically family, showing up at Sauveterre every day, obsessed with finding out about Papi's real father. Julie was glad it wasn't Didier Palomar. Pretty much everybody was glad to not be related to a Nazi lover.

"We need something to wear to the dance in Cassis tonight."

"That," said Vivi, "is my favorite kind of problem. If you like, I can drive you down there, and you can get something new at the street fair."

"Really? That'd be awesome," Julie said.

That evening, the three of them drove to the coast in Vivi's mustard-colored Renault, a scenic ride along narrow country roads surrounded by fields and forests, vineyards, rock walls, and old farms. Castles, or remnants of castles, were as common here as rest stops were in the States. Julie loved it here. She loved it even more when Vivi helped her pick out a great dress and sandals for the evening. She and her friends danced and laughed, and when André took a break from playing, he put his arms around her and gave her a kiss. Her first actual kiss from a boy. Like everything else this summer, it was magic.

Camille's night with Finn was the start of something she wasn't ready to define—or maybe she was afraid to define it. And their assignations didn't just take place at night. They stole away together in the early morning after a swim at a secluded beach, or when others lingered over a lengthy Provençal lunch. One time, he cornered her in a shed on the property, and they went at it like a pair of teenagers rather than functioning adults. She could not deny that she was falling fast and hard for him, almost against her will. The feelings were too much too soon, she told herself. She tried to keep her heart out of the relationship, but her heart wouldn't listen.

She also tried to keep the burgeoning romance a secret, not wanting to have to explain it to her father or to Julie. Yet both her father and daughter seemed to be well aware of the situation. And Julie, never the soul of discretion, didn't hesitate to send the news to Camille's mother and sisters. They peppered her with instant messages and e-mails, wanting details. Camille could scarcely explain what was happening to herself, much less her family.

When she awakened alone at Sauveterre, she missed Finn, and then felt silly for missing him. She reminded herself that he would be here later today. He was driving Papa's cousin Petra from Marseille to Sauveterre so everyone would meet her.

Before that, Camille had an even more momentous meeting. Michel Cabret was coming to have lunch. Papa said that learning Palomar was not his father had given him the courage to make amends with his boyhood friend. Now he wanted to introduce Camille to him. Watching her father prepare for Cabret's visit, Camille had a strange notion. In some way, Papa's fluttery excitement reminded her of herself, anticipating the next encounter with Finn.

"Did your friend always make you nervous?" she asked, bringing a tray of fresh drinks to the garden, where they would have their lunch. In the shade of a pergola, the table looked inviting with colorful blue and yellow linens, Madame's bright cobalt pottery, and clear wineglasses embossed with a bee, the symbol of Sauveterre.

"Ah. Do I seem nervous?"

"Like a kid on his first—"

The garden gate opened with a rusty creak, and in walked a remarkable-looking man. The word that came to mind when Camille saw Michel Cabret for the first time was *impeccable*. A tailor by profession, he wore a lovely bespoke suit with a white shirt and silk tie, shoes gleaming with fresh polish, and a perfectly tilted hat.

They greeted each other in the French fashion—embrace, kiss, kiss—and then Cabret held out his arms to Camille. "You are even more beautiful than your father described. The only time he shuts up about you is when he's talking about Julie."

He even smelled impeccable, of subtle cologne and sunshine. She liked him instantly.

"Come to lunch, *mon vieux*," Papa said, glowing as he gestured at the nicely set table. "You'll see that I've developed some culinary skills over the years."

"So it appears." Cabret took off his hat and gallantly held Camille's chair. "Now. Henri tells me you have been exploring old Bellerive."

"We have. I developed Lisette's film rolls at the laboratory in Aix. Lisette was my grandmother. Would you like to see?"

"Certainly."

She set up her tablet so they could see the digitized prints. "We found several rolls of undeveloped film from the war years." She scrolled through the images, showing him the town and landscape through Lisette's eyes. "According to Papa's cousin, Lisette's parents were killed the day of the Allied invasion in August of 1944. Petra says they were here, at this café." She showed him two shots—before the bombing, and after. "It was hit by Allied bombs that were meant for the bridge over the river."

Michel studied the pictures. "I already knew this, because they were sitting with my own grandmother, drinking ersatz coffee, when the bomb hit. My grandfather was spared only because he had left the table to fetch something, but he was never the same afterward."

She stopped. "My God. That is incredibly sad. Even though it happened before either of you was born, it seems like such a terrible loss."

"One can only imagine," said her father.

"And this," said Camille, "is the most interesting and mysterious picture I found." It was the soldier photo. "We think he might have been an American paratrooper."

Michel studied the picture for a long time, a thoughtful expression on his face. "I've brought some old photos of my own," he said. "They are printed on paper, though, rather than digital ether." With a wink, he reached into his breast pocket and brought out two deckle-edged black-and-white pictures. "Here is a picture of Henri and me in 1959, our first year at the lycée."

Both boys wore school uniforms. Her father looked abashed in the ill-fitting dark blazer over a wrinkled white shirt. Michel, on the other hand, faced the camera with a proud grin. His blazer fit perfectly and his shirt was pressed to perfection.

"We were a mismatched pair, eh?" Papa said.

"In some ways." Michel held the next picture beside a shot of the soldier on Camille's tablet. "Here you are at sixteen or seventeen. The resemblance is striking, is it not?"

Camille reached for her father's hand and squeezed it while they studied the pictures side by side. Both the soldier and Henri had skinny necks and prominent Adam's apples, curly dark hair and dark slashing brows. Their faces were shaped the same. Even their ears stuck out at the same angle. "You could be brothers," Camille said. "Oh my gosh, we have to figure out who this guy was."

"To me, what is more significant is who he was *not*—Didier Palomar." Henry's eyes misted as he looked at the soldier, and then up at Michel. "And now let us speak of other things. There is something I must tell you. I was silent about my boyhood here, because I didn't want you to know about the shame of being Palomar's son. I learned to keep secrets, and it affected other parts of my life. Including my friendship with Michel."

"I'm so grateful you were Papa's friend," Camille said. "You were good to him when no one else was."

"I wanted to be his friend, and I wanted to be good to him," said Cabret. "There was no stopping my feelings."

"What a lovely way to put it," she said, beaming at them both.

"What we're trying to say, *chérie,* what *I'm* trying to say, is that we were friends of a certain kind. But at some point in my life, I decided my true heart would always be a secret. When I first knew I loved this other boy, it . . . I am not overstating things when I say it formed my personality. But at the same time, I tried to hide these feelings." He covered Michel's hand with his. "Until now. Now with certainty and no sense of shame I can tell you that I love him still, and he has been kind enough to keep his heart open to another chance."

She frowned in confusion. "Papa? I don't understand. Or maybe . . . Are you saying what I think you're saying?"

"*Chérie,* Michel and I . . ." He took a breath, reached over, and placed his hand on his friend's. "Michel was my first love, and I love him still. At long last, I want to come out, to let you know the truth."

She gave a short laugh. "What? But . . ." And then the laughter died as a piercing insight struck like a physical pain. "You're gay." She looked from her father to Michel. "You . . . the two of you . . . *Seriously?*"

"*Chérie,* I had these feelings from boyhood, but of course at that time . . . I didn't know how to handle myself. I simply had no context, no understanding of the situation. In those days, especially in a small country town, this situation simply did not exist. Or if it did, no one spoke of it. Camille, I'm so sorry. I never should have kept it from you for so long."

Her mind was whirling. "This is . . . my God." Papa . . . *gay?* How could that be? He was just Papa. Her father. He couldn't be—

He could. He *was.* When she looked at him and Cabret together, she could see it clearly, which was strange, because five minutes before, she couldn't see it at all. All her life, she hadn't seen it. But now missing puzzle pieces finally fell into place, seemingly all at once. After the divorce, Papa had never married or even had a serious girlfriend. He'd been social, but always single. Finally she knew why.

Rather than shock or surprise, she felt . . . something else. Tears— not of sadness, but of relief, perhaps. "Why didn't the thought ever cross my mind?" she wondered aloud.

"I was in denial myself."

"But why? I would have understood. I *do* understand."

"As I knew you would. I never worried about that, Camille. I should have spoken up long ago."

"You think?" she whispered. "Why did you keep it from me— from everyone—for so long?"

"It's something I've asked myself," he said. "I grew up a secret keeper. There was this terrible secret I was holding in about Palomar, and I'd trained myself to stay silent on all personal matters. I made a habit of taking on a shame that was not mine to own, and I nearly ruined my own life because of it." His voice broke, and he pulled in a shuddery breath. "The one relationship I wanted seemed impossible to me. I fell in love with a boy, but I didn't even let myself recognize what that was. I didn't even have a name for these feelings, yet I decided they must always be a secret. Finding out Palomar was not my father has liberated me. Letting go of my guilt over Didier's crimes finally opened my heart to a love I've never forgotten."

Michel dabbed at his eyes. "You were never far from my thoughts, *mon vieux*."

Camille was still reeling. "I wish I'd known. Oh, Papa, if only I'd realized what was going on . . ."

"You can be forgiven for not thinking of your parent in that way," Michel said gently. "Camille, thank you for letting me be part of this conversation. I know it must be difficult for you."

"I'm—it's not difficult. Just new. I think I need time to process this."

"Of course." He stood up. "And now I am going for a little walk in the garden, so the two of you can have a talk. My grandnephews have nothing but praise for Julie. With your permission, I would like to meet her."

"Certainly," Camille said. She held his gaze for a moment, unsure of how to feel. This man had once owned her father's heart, and it appeared they wanted to continue together. She took a deep breath. "I'm glad to meet you, Michel. Truly."

He offered a slight bow and left the table. She watched him go, a dapper man in his tailored suit, walking beneath a sunlit vine pergola. Her stomach felt twisted in knots. More tears flowed unchecked. "Papa, you've been alone all this time because you were hiding the truth. It must have been so lonely for you. Does Mom know?"

"We never spoke of it." He must have read Camille's expression. "I did love your mother as best I knew how, which was hardly adequate, but . . . I married her, because that was what people did—they got married and started a family. Cherisse and I threw ourselves into work—the house, the shop, our jobs. But no matter how busy we kept ourselves, there was no hiding the mistake I'd made. Your mother and I held each other in mutual respect and affection, but that is no substitute for deep, passionate love. I was resigned to the idea that the love I always wanted was forbidden, and happily for Cherisse, she found a love that was meant to be."

Camille nodded, picturing her mother and Bart together. "And maybe you have, too."

"We shall see. There is something I want you to understand," he said, using his handkerchief to dab at her eyes, the way he used to when she was a little girl. "I can have no regrets, because I have you. And you are my greatest achievement in life."

Her heart ached for him. She was still reeling, but also hopeful. "You should have told me. You're my father. You're the best father in the world. You deserve to know what love feels like." She paused. "The kind of love that made Jace sacrifice himself to save me."

"This is why Michel and I wanted to tell you. So that 'never' would change to 'now.'"

She looked at his handsome face, his tearstained cheeks, his smiling mouth. She still saw the father she had known all her life, but there was something new about him. Something different. A lightness. A clarity.

"I don't know what more to say," she said.

His mouth formed a tremulous smile. "You don't have to say anything. The way you're looking at me right this moment tells me everything."

Cousin Petra was a trip, thought Finn. She talked the whole way from Marseille, but it was all about her lawyer husband, her cranky mother who had lived with them until she passed away at the age of ninety-eight, the heat wave that was sweeping over the region, the unfortunate state of the Church these days, and the shifting political landscape of the EU. By the time he got her to Sauveterre, he was ready for a beer. He left the old lady with Camille and Julie and went to the kitchen to find a cold brew. When he turned around, there stood Camille's father.

"Is there another?" Henry asked.

"Here you go. Blanc de Belges—my favorite summer beverage."

"I'd like to have a word with you, and words always go better when paired with a cold beer."

Great, thought Finn. A word. After you'd been banging a guy's daughter, the guy usually wanted to have more than a word. Finn opened the bottles and lifted his. "Cheers. What's on your mind?"

"My daughter, Camille. She—"

"Sir, I know how this must look to you," Finn said, wishing he'd initiated the conversation sooner. But his feelings for Camille had exploded with such swiftness and intensity that he'd barely had time to draw breath, much less have a serious conversation with her dad. "Henry, I'm sorry I haven't said anything yet. I should have told you from the start how much I care for Camille. She's amazing, and I never expected to feel this way. It probably seems sudden to you, and it's early days, but I'm pretty sure I'm falling in love with her. I want to be part of her future. Hell, I want to be the best thing that ever happened to her. That's my hope, anyway." After that awkward stream of nervous talk, he downed half the beer in one go.

Henry took off his glasses and polished the lenses with his handkerchief. His expression was bemused. "Then we have even more to talk about than I realized."

"Oh, you mean this wasn't about—" Finn was in new territory. He had been since the day he'd met Camille. But it wasn't just Camille. She had a daughter. Finn had lain awake at night, mulling it over. Did he want to take this on? A widow with a teenager? "Look, if you're worried about Julie—"

"I intended to speak of something else," said Henry. "However, it's good to hear that you think so highly of Camille and Julie."

Finn felt a beat of concern. If this was something else . . . He knew how much she worried about her dad. Shit, maybe his illness had taken a turn for the worse. "Are you okay?"

"I'm gay," said Henry, putting his glasses back on. "I came out to her today."

There were speechless moments, and then there were *speechless* moments. Finn's brain stopped working as he tried to figure out how to react. Finally, he gave up trying to think and simply guzzled the rest of his beer. Setting the bottle on the counter, he said, "Okay, cool."

Henry burst out laughing. "Just so you know, you are not doing such a good job at acting cool."

Crap. Whatever. "Sorry. You caught me by surprise."

His laughter subsided. "No need to apologize. It's a relief to be able to laugh about it. I confess that for the first time in my life, I know what it feels like to be falling, the way you're falling for Camille."

"Okay, so . . . wow. Cool." Finn put his beer bottle in the recycle bin.

"Camille and I will tell Julie together," Henry said. "Ah, my two girls. Perhaps I waited longer than I should have to come out, but my life unfolded exactly as it should have. Camille and Julie have been everything to me. Every breath I take. Every beat of my heart."

"Sir, they're both special. I realized that the first time I met Camille." Then he remembered his anger about the ruined film. "Okay, maybe the second time."

Henry sipped his beer. "I wish I could stay with them longer."

Damn. "Are you all right? Listen, if you're not well, we need to get you to a doctor."

"No, you listen. There will be time enough for that conversation, and the time is not now. However, I am a realist. I know I won't always be here for her."

"I will." Finn blurted the words, yet they felt as true as any statement he'd ever made. "I won't mess her up. That's a promise."

Henry studied him briefly, then held out his hand to shake Finn's. "I choose to believe you. And I already suspect you've won her heart. Now you must win her trust."

"I assure you, this is perfectly safe," Finn said to Petra, helping her into the ATV for a tour of the estate.

Camille watched the old lady being hoisted into the open conveyance. Finn was being particularly gallant, and Petra was a surprise, to say the least. She seemed a good deal younger than eighty-two, healthy and reasonably spry, with milky-blue eyes and white hair in a pinned-up braid. Best of all, she had not hesitated to offer her recollections to Papa's story. Today, she wanted to take a ride to the far vineyards, because she remembered it was the site of Lisette's daily walks.

With Finn driving the four-wheeler and Petra in the front seat, Camille climbed into the back. Wearing a bonnet tied in place with a bright ribbon, the old lady scanned the sunlit landscape as they drove to the uplands, where the Clairette and Marsanne grapes grew. During the war years, those vineyards had been abandoned, yet according to Petra, Lisette seemed drawn to them.

"It is nice to be back," she said. "I'm glad for this chance to see little Henri again. That is what he was called—little Henri. He was a lovely child, and I feel terrible about the way he was treated, like a servant in his own household, ruled with an iron fist by my mother." She twisted her hands in her lap. "Not to mention the way the kids at school treated him. I wish I had been kinder. More protective. But when he was in school, I was a typical self-absorbed teenager, though that's no excuse."

"Do you remember Didier at all?" asked Camille.

"Certainly. Uncle Didier was very proud and quite vain. He used to stand at the mirror in the front hall and strike poses. Maman said he was loyal to his family and a good steward of Sauveterre. He did have a mean streak and I learned to keep my distance." Her expression softened, and she added, "I was fond of Tante Lisette and her parents, Monsieur and Madame Galli. Lisette was young and so pretty. She had a way of finding the fun in everyday things. She taught me to make a crown of flowers, for example, and to sing songs. Her favorite was 'Dis-moi, Janette.'"

"That's one of Papa's favorites, too. All these little details bring Lisette to life."

"She always seemed to be writing letters as well as taking pictures."

"Who was she writing to?" Finn asked. "Any ideas?"

"No, but since your discovery about Henri, I imagine the letters were to the man who fathered him. Is that terribly romantic of me? I would hate to think that she'd been forced by one of the soldiers. Some women were."

They stopped at a vineyard that was bordered by the woods and stream; Petra claimed this had been Lisette's favorite place for long, solitary walks. They walked amid the vines, which were vibrant and already heavy with grapes. Petra brought them to a pile of unmortared stone. "This was destroyed by a bomb the day the Allies came," she said. "It was the only thing Sauveterre lost in the war. My friends and I used to play among the rubble here. Come, I'll show you a mysterious thing we found, if it's still here."

With her walking cane, she poked at the grass growing up around the ruins. "Voilà," she said. "No one could ever explain this."

Finn bent down and parted the grass. There was a small cross forged of iron next to a carved stone chiseled with words in English: *H+L, Journey Without End.*

PART 6

The Var

I see my path, but I don't know where it leads.
Not knowing where I'm going is what inspires me to travel it.

—Rosalia de Castro

Eighteen

Bellerive, the Var, France
January 1945

The war ground to an inglorious end. Of course there were victory celebrations—homecoming parties for soldiers and fighters who'd been in hiding, dancing in the streets, toasts with the wine and champagne people had concealed from the Germans, feasts of food that was no longer scarce. But there were also more somber events—memorials and Masses for the fallen, marches of shame for collaborators and for women who had taken up with the Nazis.

Lisette struggled to find a sort of peace. After the Var had been liberated by the Allies, she acknowledged the joyous celebrations that erupted through the village, but her world had come apart.

When she and Hank heard the fighting on that August morning, he'd ordered her to run for her life. She'd rushed to find her parents. She had left them innocently having morning coffee, and had returned to find that they had been killed when the town bridge was hit. Survivors told her the first strike was sudden, and there was no time for her parents to panic or suffer, but she sometimes wondered if they said that just to soothe her. Cradling each of them in her arms for the last time, stroking their dusty, lifeless faces, she had felt as though the earth beneath her feet had fallen away.

Needing Hank more than ever, she'd returned to the stone hut, only to find it collapsed into a pile of rubble, circled by foxes and crows. There was no sign of him. She became obsessed with finding him. She spent hours, days, and weeks, working her hands bloody as she sorted through the collapsed pile, but he was gone. Had he escaped? Tried to join the fighting? Had the Allied invaders rescued him? She remembered something he'd once said to her: "The first person through the wall always gets hurt." Had he tried to be first through the wall?

She collected a few precious artifacts—his chute envelope and some gear, the Mass card, broken glass from their champagne bottle. The discoveries only raised more questions and lowered her hopes, and the loss felt like a kind of insanity.

When tanks manned by American soldiers in battle dress rumbled through the streets, the people of Bellerive went mad with the joy of liberation. Lisette asked every man she saw if he knew Henry Watkins, a paratrooper, but she received nothing in return except propositions. No one had heard of him and they looked at her as if she'd gone crazy. And every night, she prayed on her knees to a God who did not seem to be listening.

The men of the town—husbands, sons, brothers—came in from hiding or from forced labor in Germany, and the drinking and celebration took a dark turn. As they took stock of the death and devastation caused by the Germans and collaborators, and dealt with the trauma and shame of occupation, riots broke out.

Didier seemed to have no grasp of reality. As the Germans fled like a pack of scalded dogs, he carefully folded away the uniform he'd worn as an officer in the Milice. "I shall miss this," he said to Lisette, his voice slurred from an early morning bottle of wine. "It's very well made, is it not? Perhaps I'll take it to Cabret, the tailor, and have him remake it without the insignia."

Gérard Cabret was a hero of the resistance who had recently opened a tailor shop in the village. He now had a wife and a baby son, Michel. "Surely you're joking," Lisette said to Didier. "Cabret wouldn't touch that jacket with a barge pole."

"You think you know everything. I should expose you as the whore you are. I fucked you for years with no results, and now you're suddenly with child? Who is the father of that brat in your belly, eh?"

He is twice the man you will ever be, she wanted to say. "Your accusations will hurt you, not me," she calmly replied. "Your reputation is already in tatters. What will people say if you accuse me of infidelity?"

"Then maybe I'll beat it out of you," he said, rolling up his sleeves.

She stood, not even blinking as she faced him down. "Lay a hand on me, and I'll go straight to the village council," she said.

The threat froze him in his tracks. She knew he lived in fear of reprisals from the people he'd betrayed during his time in the Milice.

Ultimately, she didn't have to make good on her threat. One night without warning, Didier was taken while drinking his nightly bottle of wine, tied to a post, blindfolded, and shot. She watched this with a sense of dull shock and fully expected them to come for her next, but it turned out that her work for the resistance was well known. The returning maquisards honored her, and there was a marriage proposal from Jean-Luc d'Estérel, the boy she'd loved a lifetime ago.

She gave him a sad smile and a gentle no. There was no one for her but Hank. Even if she never saw him again, it would forever be Hank for her. Her one great love had come and gone.

She grieved with an intensity that cut like a knife. She kept her sanity by writing letters to Hank and sending them to Vermont in America, but they came back stamped *undeliverable*. The one thing that kept her moving through each moment was the baby. She talked to her unborn child about Hank as she erected a small iron cross at the remains of the hut, next to the stone he had carved for her. As her belly grew, she yearned to confess the truth about her baby's father—that he was an American hero who fell from the sky.

But if she revealed that, she and the baby would find themselves homeless and starving, like so many women and children in the aftermath of the war. Her only claim on Sauveterre was the fact that the child was assumed to be Didier's only heir. Despite his shameful actions, he was the ancestral lord of Sauveterre. The baby would inherit the *mas* one day. Perhaps in time, Sauveterre would be prosperous again, and old hurts would be forgotten.

She hid away her letters to Hank, knowing she had to let go of the dream that they might meet again. She couldn't bring herself to destroy the letters, for they contained her heart. As she was putting the box high on an attic shelf, she came across Toselli's camera and several rolls of undeveloped film. Her heart broke all over again, because she knew the pictures documented her time with Hank. She put the rolls away, because the hurt was too raw. One day in the future, she would develop the film. One day, she would show them to her child.

There was still a roll of film in the camera. She'd loaded it the morning of the Allied invasion and had taken a few pictures, never imagining the devastation that would take place that day. She had no heart for taking pictures, not anymore. For the sake of the baby, she tried to find that passion once again. She found Hank's cloth pathfinder badge—one of the few mementos she'd found in the rubble—and pinned it to the shoulder of her dress, hoping and praying the child was his. Then she studied herself in a mirror and focused her camera. A young woman with a pain as old as time in her eyes, her belly rounded like the cheek of a ripe pear.

The next time I take your picture, little one, she thought, you will be in my arms.

PART 7

Switchback

*I suddenly understood that photography can fix
eternity in a moment.*

—HENRI CARTIER-BRESSON, FRENCH PHOTOGRAPHER

Nineteen

—❦—

J ulie and her friends decided there was only one way to deal with the languid heat of August. They stuffed their totes with towels, sunscreen, and water bottles and headed to the beach. As always, she felt a little fluttery thrill when they met up with André and his brothers at their favorite spot, a white sand crescent bordered by cliffs and outcroppings, perfect for making daring plunges.

The guys had brought a rope to put up a new swing. They chose a flat area shaded by an overhanging tree that seemed to grow straight out of the rock.

"Somebody will have to climb out on the branch and secure the rope," Martine said.

"I'll do it," Julie volunteered.

"What if you fall?"

"Then I'll land in the water."

"You're a lot more brave than I am."

"I'm not brave," Julie said. "There's no point in being scared of something if you know you can do it." She draped the rope around her shoulder, and André gave her a boost. Shinnying out on the branch, she secured the rope. Okay, now what? She was turned the wrong way. Looking back over her shoulder, she saw the others watching her.

"How are you going to get down?" asked Martine.

"I should have figured that out before I climbed out here," Julie said.

"Can you move backward?" André asked.

She attempted to scoot back on the branch, but it was too awkward. Turning around seemed a little sketchy. She looked down at the perfectly clear turquoise water far below, glittering in the hot summer sun. Then she let out a sigh. She still wore shorts and a tank top over her swimsuit. Everything was about to get totally wet.

"Only one way I can think of," she said. Then she slung one leg over the branch and pushed off. The long, exhilarating drop was amazing. In those few moments, she felt as if she were flying. In those few moments, she could almost see her dad.

She plunged into the water feetfirst, letting the coolness engulf her, loving the deep silence of the sea. Hi, Dad, she thought, watching the sunlit blur of bubbles. I'm glad you're part of this adventure.

With a slow scissor of her legs, she drifted upward, arching her back to look at the liquid silver surface above. Her dad had been fearless; at least that was what she remembered about him. She liked to imagine he would applaud her for being so adventurous this summer, making new friends and getting so good at French that she even spoke it in her dreams. *I think you'd be proud of me.*

She was about to break the surface when someone grabbed her arm. "Hey," she said, twisting away from the phantom grip.

"Hey, yourself," said Finn, treading water nearby. "Didn't mean to startle you. I saw you go in, and I wanted to make sure you're all right."

"I'm fine." She paddled to the rocky edge of the inlet. "What are you doing here?"

"I came with your mom and Anouk's family."

"Mom's here?" Oh shit, Julie thought. She'd told her mother they were going to a museum in Aix today. Mom would freak if she saw her jumping off cliffs and out of trees.

"She's over there, on the beach," Finn said, clearly unaware of Mom's tendency to freak. "We took a break from all the research. It's too hot to think."

"Oh." As she climbed out of the water, she hoped he didn't start asking questions. Mom didn't know about all the cliff jumping and rope swings. That kind of thing made her head explode from worrying.

He glanced at her wet clothes. "So did you fall in, or jump?"

She indicated the rope, dangling from the thick branch high above them. "After I hung up the rope, it was the only way down."

"Seriously? Damn, Julie."

Great, she thought. Was he a worrywart like her mom?

"That's really cool," he said.

All right, so he wasn't a worrier. That was a good sign. She had liked Finn from the start, and she liked him even more now. And what she liked about him the most was how happy her mom was since they'd started going out.

She glanced at the beach in the distance. Her mom was busily digging in the sand with Anouk's kids. "Want to give it a try?" she asked.

Camille watched Anouk's husband, Daniel, playing in the surf with their kids. Home on leave from Africa, he reveled in family life. He was as handsome and serious as Anouk was romantic and bubbly, but when he was in the water with the kids, he cavorted like a little boy.

She took out Lisette's old Exakta and framed a shot. It felt just right to be taking pictures again after a long dry spell in the wake of Jace's death. That day in Gordes with Finn had been the turning point for her. Seeing the photos of one of her idols had reminded her of a truth she'd ignored for too long—life was beautiful and ephemeral, and a captured moment could last forever. Her long dry spell had ended. She remembered her passion for photography, leaping back into it with the kind of excitement she'd felt years ago.

If Finn had not pushed her, if he hadn't all but dragged her into remembering her old dreams and passions, would she have rediscovered it on her own? Maybe, she thought, just maybe, Finn was good for her. Maybe she would tell him that. And then . . . well, that was the problem. Then what?

She set aside the question and gave her full attention to the camera and the subject. "They're so excited," she said to Anouk, clicking the shutter to capture the ecstasy on the little ones' faces as their father chased them in the surf. "You have an adorable family."

Anouk smiled. "Thank you. It's wonderful to have him home. He will be back with us for good after one more six-month rotation. You know, there was a time when he couldn't imagine leaving his homeland. Then he spent a summer here with my family, as you have, and now he yearns only for Bellerive. Maybe it will cast its spell on you."

Camille did love the sun-drenched village. The pace of life, the golden light, the food and wine were only part of it. There was a spirit of creativity here that reached out to her—craftsmen honing their talents with single-minded focus—the forge of the knife maker, the ateliers where designers created jewelry and fashions, the artisans fabricating their wares for the markets, the antiques dealers rolling out artifacts from times gone by.

It was lovely. Camille couldn't deny that—but it wasn't home. Before long, she would be going back to Bethany Bay, and work, and real life. She'd bought some unique items for the shop—things as complex as sublimated fabric prints, or as simple as butter knives that stood on their own. Yes, there was a seductive spell that had woven itself around Camille. But as summer waned, her ties to home tugged at her.

With a sigh, she tucked away the camera and watched Daniel and the kids. "I always thought I'd have a bigger family. I'm not complaining," she quickly added.

"You'll have that with Finn," Anouk assured her. "He comes from a large family, no?"

"I'm not—we're not that serious." Finn was a distraction. A fantasy, like the landscape itself. Their attraction was like the sunlight here— brilliant, but also fleeting. It was true that he made her laugh, and that every day with him seemed like a new adventure. And yes, he got her talking in a way she'd never talked to anyone before. He made her feel sexy and alive, and thanks to him, she was the photographer she'd always wanted to be.

Still, she knew they were both holding back. His heart was out of reach, just as Roz and Vivi had told her. And truth be told, so was hers. She hadn't given her heart away since Jace, and she didn't know if she could ever do that again.

"That's not what I've seen happening this summer," Anouk observed, adjusting her sunglasses. "To me, this looks like a relationship, not a fling."

Camille glanced over at Anouk's beach novel, this one with a cover that was both lurid and enticing. The couple held each other in an embrace that was physically impossible, yet their total absorption in each other was strangely compelling. "How's the book?" she asked, trying to change the subject.

"Loving it," Anouk said dreamily. "Books like this, they take me places I'll probably never go. This one . . . ah, they're in Hong Kong. So glamorous. But she has a wall. She keeps a wall around her heart to protect herself from getting hurt."

"Smart girl."

"No, she's an idiot. And we're not talking about Rosalinda." Anouk set down the book.

"I don't have a wall," Camille said. "I have a *life*. A different life. It's in a town the size of Bellerive, an ocean away. Finn's life is here. We're having a . . . it's just for the summer. I have to go back. And he has to stay."

"Have you talked to him about it?"

"Of course not. There's really nothing to talk about." Shading her eyes, she picked him out on the beach, his long, lean body gleaming with water and sunlight, wet board shorts plastered to his muscular thighs. With an undeniable flutter of attraction, she followed him with her gaze.

"Go for a swim," Anouk suggested. "I'll join you in a bit."

Camille was about to do just that when Finn, in the distance, turned away from her. Instead of wading back into the surf, he climbed a rough path to a rocky ledge. A few swimmers were gathered on the sheer ledge, taking turns jumping into the clear, cool water.

The sight of Finn on the jagged stone outcropping made her shudder and draw a quick breath.

"You don't like heights?" asked Anouk.

"Understatement." Camille felt the blood surging in her ears as unbidden memories pulled her back to the worst day of her life. "When I was younger, I would have been the first one off the cliff, but I'm not that person anymore."

"Maybe you are, and you're holding yourself back," Anouk said. "Just a guess."

Camille forced herself to stop watching Finn. "Of course I am," she said. "I didn't come here this summer looking for a man. I came to help my father settle some things, and to get Julie away from a situation at home."

"And now you're taking her back to that situation."

"Yes." Camille had talked to Anouk at length about the bullying. "It was always understood that this was for the summer only. I hope she's better prepared to deal with the kids back home."

"Your daughter has changed a lot over the summer. She's turned from a girl into a young lady."

"I noticed." Camille felt a rush of pride. Julie had made friends; she seemed so confident in herself now.

"You're not the only one who noticed." Anouk gestured. "Isn't that Julie up there?"

"No, she said she was going to the Cézanne museum in Aix today." Camille turned and shaded her eyes. In the distance, atop the cliff, Finn held the end of a stout rope. As Camille watched in growing horror, he passed the rope to a couple of kids—a boy, and a girl who looked very much like Julie. She and the boy held the robe between them and ran to the edge of the cliff.

Then recognition dawned on Camille, as stark as her darkest memories, as her daughter took a free fall from the cliff.

Camille loaded the last of the luggage into the car, struggling to close the trunk. After a trip, she always seemed to bring home more baggage than she'd left with.

They didn't need to head to the airport until much later, but she wanted to make sure everything was ready.

Finn drove into the courtyard and parked. He regarded the packed car. "You're leaving," he said. Not a question.

Camille's heart skipped a beat. She had a brief, wild fantasy that he would beg her to stay—or vow to come to the States with her. And then what? "I'm taking Julie and my dad home," Camille said.

"You're supposed to be here another two weeks."

"I changed our tickets."

"Because of what happened yesterday?"

She winced, remembering the horrible, surreal moment of Julie's wild leap into the sea. "Because of a lot of things. Watching my kid plunging off a cliff is only part of it."

"She's safe," he said. "Nothing happened, except she had a great time. You ought to be proud of having a kid who's adventurous. I know I would be."

Finn didn't get it. He never would. The only way to protect her daughter was to keep her away from risks—like Finn. "My God, you were there, encouraging her!"

"She didn't need any encouragement. Camille, you can't keep her wrapped in cotton all her life. At some point, you have to trust your own kid."

"You don't get to say when that is," she lashed out.

"I didn't have to. She's brave and she's smart."

"Being brave and smart doesn't keep her safe. You have no idea what it's like to be a parent."

"True, I don't. But that's not what this is about. It's not about Julie either," he said, his eyes flashing with an anger she'd never seen in him before. "It's about her father."

The dart hit home, but Camille refused to flinch. "You don't know anything about him."

"Also true, because you refuse to talk about it."

"He was brave, too," she said. "And smart. And he got himself killed."

"And that sucks for you and Julie and for everyone who loved him," Finn said. "But what happened to him doesn't mean you have to shut down your life, hoping it won't happen to someone else."

"And it nearly did happen yesterday," she said, feeling a wave of icy fear. "So don't tell me—"

"How about you tell *me*. How did he die, Camille? Why don't you ever talk about it?"

She didn't think there was any way to make him understand. But he deserved some kind of explanation. She leaned against the car, folding her arms in front of her. "It was a climbing accident. And seeing Julie swinging off a cliff was like watching him die all over again."

His expression softened. "Ah, Camille. Damn, I . . . why didn't you tell me?"

"Because it was horrible, and I'm trying to keep it in the past and move on," she said, her voice breaking.

He touched her then, slowly and gently drawing her into his arms. "Oh, baby. I'm sorry. But keeping it buried isn't the same as moving on. Talk to me. I want to know."

She pulled away from the comfort he offered and walked over to a shaded bench in the courtyard, letting the cool shadows surround her. Finn sat beside her, silent and waiting.

Camille took a deep breath. She watched a butterfly making its way through the colorful stalks of hollyhocks along the ancient stone wall, first one bell-shaped blossom and then another, and then back again, as if it couldn't make up its mind.

"We were at Cathedral Gorge on vacation," she said. "Jace and I were roped together, and we were abseiling down to the riverbed from the top. The rope was secured to three safety points—the cliff edge, a boulder . . . and me. There was a sound I'll never forget, like a huge plucked string, and the rope around the boulder loosened. He lost his footing and fell." She paused, feeling the sensation of the rope tightening, biting into her, her gear and clothing scraping as she was dragged to the edge.

Finn covered her hand with his. She stared down at it, then carefully drew away, not wanting him to feel the icy memories. "I hung on as best I could," she continued, "but I started to go over. I screamed at Jace to catch a handhold. I screamed . . . and when I turned to look, I saw him . . ." She paused again, still haunted by the memory. "He cut the rope and fell."

Her screams had damaged her throat for weeks afterward. It had taken a full year for her fingernails to grow back. "There was an inquest. The ruling was that Jace had followed the only reasonable course open to him under the circumstances. He sacrificed himself to avoid taking me down with him."

Finn was silent for several moments. He took both her hands in his. "What a nightmare. I'm sorry, Camille. I'm sorry you went through that."

She forced herself to look at him—that face, those eyes and lips— and she wavered. Then she reminded herself that she didn't want anyone to love her that much again, so much that he would die for her. "So that's it. That's why I'm going home."

"It was a one-in-a-million freak accident."

"Yesterday was a horrible reminder that it could happen again. I'm done, Finn. You asked for an explanation, and that's it."

"Have you ever told this to Julie? I mean, the details . . ."

"No. She knows the rope failed and her dad fell."

"Guess what else she knows," Finn said. "She knows the world ended that day."

"What?"

"She told me that last night. After you freaked out and dragged her home from the beach, I talked to her about it. And like you pointed out, I don't know what it's like to have a kid, but it's probably not the best idea for her to think everything was over when you lost the guy."

Camille felt as if the wind had been knocked out of her. Somehow she found her voice. "She doesn't think that."

"Maybe not," he conceded. "Kids tend to exaggerate. But are you sure she understands that even after the nightmare you went through, life can be good again? Doesn't your kid deserve to know that?"

Camille opened her mouth to object. Then she closed it. His words made clear, devastating sense. What message had she been sending to Julie all these years? All of Julie's young life? Dear God, what if he was right? "So in your expert opinion, I've been so mired in my own grief that I missed out on the last five years."

"You tell me. I wasn't there for it."

She pictured her daughter growing and changing from a little girl in pigtails and a pink backpack, skipping off to school, to a high school freshman, filled with equal parts bravado and uncertainty. Did Camille savor life enough, or was she too frightened and sad to let Julie feel the joy of living? She got up from the bench and walked away, though she couldn't escape her own doubts.

"You know what drives me batshit crazy?" Finn asked. "You push me away when I get close."

"That's not—" Oh, but it was. He'd nailed it. This was never going to work. All she wanted was a quiet, stable life. Finn got in the way of that by igniting a whirlwind of emotion and reminding her of her own burning needs.

"You claim you already found the love of your life," he said, standing up, glaring at her. "And that you already lost him. What if—just what if you get another chance? What if you allow for that possibility? What if I'm your second chance?"

"We're too different," she shot back, feeling something like panic.

"What are you afraid of, Camille? That you'll never find a love like that again? Because I'm here to tell you, you're absolutely right."

"Then why—"

"You *will* never find a love like that again. That love is over. But if you'd give yourself half a chance, you might just find something brand-new with me. I'm asking you, why is that such a scary thing? What are you afraid of?"

"What am I afraid of?" she asked. *Maybe I'm afraid because I already have found something with you.* The thought filled her with wonder . . . and dread. "That it won't work, and we'll hurt each other, and Julie will get hurt, too."

"I'm not going to hurt you, Camille. I'd never do that."

"I appreciate your concern," she said, her throat thick with tears. "But it's time for us to go."

He stared at her for a moment, stone cold. She tried not to remember the moments in his arms, the dark, sweet pleasure of their lovemaking. He strode away and took a dossier from his car. "I've been working on the paratrooper angle for you. I narrowed the list down to three reconnaissance men who were lost while doing advance scouting for the August invasion. Three men were unaccounted for in the operation in the summer of 1944." He handed over the files. "You can take it from here."

Twenty

❧

*H*ome at last in Bethany Bay, Camille found that the world looked different. Having been gone, she appreciated her hometown in a new way. It was quite a privilege to live in a place where people came for vacation, to appreciate the sea breezes, the ocean and scenery. The shop was thriving, and the items she'd acquired in France over the summer were selling briskly. Her mother had curated a collection of art prints from the work of both Lisette and Camille herself, and customers seemed fascinated by the recovered images.

She sighed and opened a few windows, savoring the light breeze from the ocean. Home at last. The trip had passed in a blur of mixed emotions. She surprised herself by realizing she wasn't afraid of flying anymore. The fear came from something else—she was afraid of leaving. She might have left a new shot at happiness.

Fear was a relative thing. The fear of risking her heart was more powerful than her fear of flying.

To keep from missing Finn like crazy, she reminded herself of the good things that had happened over the summer. It had been transformative in many ways for Julie, not just physically but mentally and emotionally. Not so long ago, Julie had been angry and hurt, soothing herself by overeating and passing sedentary hours staring at her phone or tablet screen. Now she looked different, having thrived on a season outdoors, getting into athletics, honing her French—and her self-confidence.

"I have a bottle of prosecco, and I know how to use it." Billy

Church came into the kitchen without knocking. He set down the chilled bottle and enfolded Camille in a bear hug. "Welcome home," he said. "Long time no see. I want to hear everything."

She leaned into the familiar comfort he offered, and something inside her broke loose. "It was . . . ah, Billy. I don't even know where to start."

"With the bubbly," he suggested, and popped the cork.

She told him about all the history they had unearthed about her father, and how Julie had made friends, and Henry had finally found his true self in a reunion with a man he'd walked away from decades before. By the time they finished the bottle, she'd filled him in on all the high points.

"Julie said you fell in love with Finn," Billy said.

Camille gasped. "She didn't."

"She did. Clearly you've left a few things out."

"Well, she's wrong. I . . . we . . . It wasn't like that."

"Then what was it like?"

Magical. Camille couldn't stop thinking about Finn. She couldn't stop wishing things could have worked out differently. She wondered how long it would take him to move on to his next conquest. Maybe she should have stayed and fought for their relationship. Then she realized that the right guy would fight for *her*. Finn wasn't a fighter, though. He challenged her, made her question herself, made her wonder . . . "It was just a thing. And now it's over."

Billy knocked back the last of the prosecco. "Camille Adams, I have loved you ever since the day you shared your PB and J with me in third grade. But I've never been able to light you up the way he does. Just now, when I said his name, you nearly fainted."

"I did not. And for what it's worth, you're my best friend. I love you, too."

"Just not that way." He clutched at his heart.

"Stop it."

"Not until you admit I'm right. And Julie's right. You fell in love with that guy."

"Maybe I did, just a little. Or a lot."

"Then why are you standing here with me? You're going to let him walk away? You idiot. I love you enough to tell you to go after a guy who actually has a shot at making you happy. If you don't go for it, you'll break all three of our hearts."

"All four," Julie corrected, coming down from her room. "Hiya, Billy."

"Hey, gorgeous."

"Leave me be, both of you," Camille said.

Julie left her mom arguing with Billy about Finn. Mom didn't seem to realize that the more she pretended she didn't like him, the more obvious it was that she was totally in love with him. Julie wished her mom would admit that she'd finally found a guy who could actually make her happy.

Jumping on her bike, she sped into town. Another cool thing about Finn was that whatever it was he'd said to her mother on that last morning in France had caused her to unbend a little. Since they'd been back, Mom hadn't been so helicoptery. Only yesterday, Papi had bought them both new bikes—really good mountain bikes with compression brakes—and they made a pact that they'd go for a ride together every evening.

Julie was headed to the beach, because the surf report had just come up, and it was a good one. Tarek and his older sister were going to meet her at the Surf Shack. They were back in town, too, and they'd invited her to go surfing with them. Julie wasn't great at it, but she knew the basics, and today the waves were just right.

The beach was super crowded with little kids along the shore, and a line of surfers out at the break, waiting to catch a wave. She felt a little thrill of anticipation. There was nothing quite like the sensation of riding a wave, even for a few seconds.

The Surf Shack featured pictures of the youth rescue squad through the years, and she paused to look at the group shot from her mom's high school years. There was Mom, grinning and surrounded by her friends, proudly brandishing the under-fifteen trophy. She looked so happy there, so triumphant. She looked the way Julie felt when she'd gone off the rope swing in the Calanques.

She brought her board out from the shed. It was her dad's board, actually, and it hadn't seen much action since he'd died, but Julie was determined to change that. She remembered Dad telling her it was nine feet of fun, designed for learners, with a stable body and soft top. Tarek and his sister, Maya, were already there, waxing their rented boards. Tarek looked as if he'd grown a foot over the summer. His hair was longer, too, his grin just as friendly as ever. Maya was seventeen and gorgeous, with dark eyes and a flashing smile.

"The waves look perfect, just like they said on the radio," Julie said, borrowing the sticky wad of wax.

"We're beginners," Maya said. "Maybe you'll give us some tips."

Julie rubbed her wax over the ID mark on her board. *Property of J. Adams.* "I'll do my best."

"I'm going to get changed," said Maya. "Be right back."

Julie put away the wax, then straightened up and took off her T-shirt, tossing it into the basket of her bike.

Tarek stared. Yep, he was totally checking her out. She tried to picture herself through his eyes—no more braces, contacts in place of glasses so she could actually see while doing sports. None of her fat clothes fit anymore, and the stuff she'd found in France looked good on her, thanks to Vivi the supermodel, who had amazing taste.

"Well, look who's back," came a too-familiar voice in a sarcastic drawl, startling her out of her thoughts. "Julie and her boyfriend, Aladdin."

Julie felt weirdly calm as she turned to face Vanessa Larson. As usual, Vanessa was flanked by her squad of hangers-on, including Jana Jacobs. They all wore matching friendship bracelets made of colorful strands of leather and a blingy anchor charm.

"Yeah, go ahead and look your fill. Don't let me stop you," she said simply. She wasn't scared. Her voice didn't shake. She didn't let her gaze waver. "We were just going to hit the surf."

"That oughta make a big splash," Vanessa said. She gave Julie an obvious once-over. "So what did you do in France all summer? Fat camp?"

Julie didn't flinch. "Nice of you to notice," she said coolly. "Too bad for you there's no such thing as asshole camp, because you're stuck being one for life."

Behind her, she heard a very soft huff of laughter from Tarek. Vanessa's face turned bright red. "You think you're funny? Well, I think you're—"

"Who's this?" In all her exotic glory, Maya came back from the changing room. She looked like a goddess in an electric-blue bikini, her glossy hair spilling like a black river down her back. She offered a brilliant smile, and somehow, the smile managed to convey that she knew exactly what the situation was. "Friends of yours?"

"Yes," Julie said with a straight face. "Maya, that's Vanessa, Jana—"

"We were just leaving," Vanessa said, then turned to her squad. "Let's go for a swim. I'll race everybody to the outer buoy."

As they beat a hasty retreat, Julie caught Tarek's eye. "Some things don't change, do they?"

"Some things definitely do," he said. He couldn't seem to stop looking at her.

As they carried their boards out to the surf, she speculated on his meaning. And then she didn't think at all as they paddled away from shore, ducking under the incoming waves to get out to the break. It was one of those postcard-perfect afternoons everyone loved. There were families with little kids digging in the sand, running around and squealing. Tourists from everywhere were spread out on the sand under their rented umbrellas. Couples lazed in the shade, napping or slathering each other with sunscreen. As always, the local surfers owned the area beyond the break, seeming oblivious to the swimmers all around them. And then there were the kids like Vanessa and her gang, swimming and horsing around at the beach boundary, causing the lifeguard whistles to go off every few seconds.

Julie watched them for a moment, focusing on the buoy that marked the far boundary. It was the same buoy that had been the marker during drills the day she'd wound up in the ER. She didn't remember much after Vanessa had "accidentally" rammed her with her board. Julie had gone into the water, and for a moment she'd seen her dad's face, as clear as if he'd been right there with her. And then . . . nothing. Nothing, until she was gagging up seawater, surrounded by EMTs, anticipating a freak-out from Mom.

In France, Mom hadn't freaked out at all until that last day. But boy, her meltdown had been epic. And for once, Julie conceded that maybe, just maybe, it had been understandable. Seeing her daughter jumping from the rope swing had probably awakened an old nightmare. Julie had apologized up one side and down the other, but Mom had cut the trip short, and now here they were.

She led the way now with her friends in her wake. It felt good to count Tarek and Maya as friends. The Atlantic water was cool and dark beyond the shelf at the break, so different from the Mediterranean's bright blue clarity. They made it out and missed a few good waves. Finally, they got into the rhythm of the surf and she caught a pretty good ride. It felt great to be on the board—her dad's board. She paddled the way he'd taught her, matching the speed of the wave and then getting up in one smooth movement. "Don't try to outsmart the ocean," he used to say. "It's stronger than you, but it'll always bring you ashore."

Look at me, Dad, she said each time she got up on the board. Look at me.

Tarek and Maya got exhausted after a while, and switched to boogie boards in the shallow surf. Julie stayed out at the break. She was watching for the next wave when a shout caught her attention. There was lots of shouting, but there was something about this—a panicked edge. She straddled her board and looked around, but didn't see anything other than swimmers and surfers as usual. Then a wave lifted her high, and she spotted something out beyond the buoy. A slender arm waving, a blingy wrap bracelet flashing in the sun.

Something in Julie kicked in—impulse, instinct. A lecture from the first day of surf rescue: *Your gut doesn't lie.* And in this moment, her gut was telling her a swimmer was in trouble. She whipped a glance at the shore and saw one of the lifeguards jump down from his post and grab a rescue board. But Julie was closer. Her surfboard wasn't a rescue board, but she was a fast paddler, and it would do. She popped up on her knees and dug in, and within moments, she was riding parallel with the panicking swimmer.

She knew instantly the reason for the panic. Beyond the shelf where the water turned dark, a rip current was swirling. The undertow grabbed at her, turning her board into an out-of-control raft. She had to undo the ankle strap and let it go. Then she grabbed for Vanessa. Yes, the swimmer was Vanessa, but at the moment she was just a victim of the riptide that wanted to tow her far from shore.

"I've got you," Julie shouted, executing a rescue hold.

Vanessa gasped and choked, fighting madly. "Help me, oh God, I can't . . . I'm gonna drown."

"Quit fighting," Julie yelled directly into her ear. "I've got you. Remember what they taught us." The current felt like a powerful river, dragging them along. From the corner of her eye, Julie saw two guards paddling madly toward them on their boards, but the tide was faster. "It's going to be okay," she said. "Just don't fight me, okay?"

A wave lifted them, but Vanessa's head went under. She flailed, and Julie held on tight. When Vanessa came up again, she was choking and spewing seawater. "Okay," she gasped, her limbs going limp. "Okay, I won't fight anymore."

Keeping their heads above water, they moved parallel to the beach for a few moments that actually felt like forever, and then the tide began to circle back toward shore. By then, one of the lifeguards reached them. "Take her," Julie said. "She's okay, just scared." She made sure Vanessa was holding fast to the tow handles behind the rescue board, and the guard headed into shore, with Julie following until the other guard caught up with her.

At the lifeguard station, she and Vanessa were monitored. Vanessa was still gagging from the seawater. She shot Julie a glowering look. "I wasn't in trouble," she muttered. "Way to overreact, Julie."

"Whatever," Julie said, waving away the oxygen mask. "Did someone get my dad's board?"

The guards looked at each other, and her heart sank. "I need my dad's board," she said, moving toward the door.

"We have to write this up," said the older guard.

"I'm going to find my surfboard," Julie insisted.

"It's here." Jana Jacobs stood in the doorway to the station. The board was propped between her and Tarek. "It washed in down the beach." She offered a tenuous smile, and held out the friendship bracelet with the anchor charm. "Hey, that was cool what you did."

"That's okay," Julie said. "You keep it." She didn't need the bracelet. She knew where her anchor was. "Thanks for grabbing the board."

"Thanks for grabbing Vanessa," Jana said. "We were really scared."

"I'm fine," Vanessa said from behind the O_2 mask. She paused, then said, "I'm fine, Julie. Okay?"

Twenty-one

⚜

$\mathcal{C}$amille found her daughter sitting on the rocks at the base of the lighthouse, just outside the fence. It was sunset, and Julie sat very still, her hair damp from a shower, her legs stretched out in front of her. How beautiful she looked, strong and calm, like a new person, very different from the shrinking, tentative girl who had let herself be pulled out to sea in a riptide only a few months ago.

"Hey," Camille said, climbing over the rocks.

Julie turned to her. "Am I in trouble?"

"Should you be?"

"Should I have let Vanessa drown? If I'd had time to think about it, I might've been tempted."

"Very funny." Camille smoothed her hand over Julie's hair. "This new cut you got in Aix is great on you," she said.

"Thanks. Do you think Deep Cuts will figure out how to keep it?"

"Sure. You just have to tell them what you want, and don't let them lead you astray."

"I miss France," Julie said.

Me, too. Camille batted the thought away. "Papa used to remind me that sometimes the best journey of your life is the one that takes you home."

"And sometimes it isn't," Julie pointed out.

They sat in silence for a while, listening to the crying gulls and the surf surging against the breakwater rocks. Camille thought about

Finn's observation about Julie when they'd parted ways. Much as it stung, there was a grain of truth in what he'd said.

"Listen," she said. "I've been meaning to tell you something. It's always been true, but maybe I've never said this, Jules." She turned to her. "You are the best thing that ever happened to me. You are my greatest achievement and you've given me the proudest moments of my life—not just today, but every day. And I'm afraid I never made sure you understood that fully. I'm afraid I led you to believe that when your dad died, my life started to suck, irreversibly. The loss was horrible, and so was the grief. But you're here, and you're my miracle."

"Mom, okay. I get it." Julie's voice sounded thick. The expression on her face was soft with affection—and understanding. Camille realized this was exactly what Finn had been talking about. How had he known?

"Oh, sweetie, I'm not trying to make you sad. I just want to make sure you know you've been my whole world. It's not the world I imagined for us when your dad was still here. But we had a wonderful life and we still do; it's all because of you."

"Mom, that's nice. It's totally sweet. But . . . Okay, here's the thing." Julie turned to face her, drawing her knees up to her chest. "As much as you worry about me, I worry about you. In a few years, I'll be on my own."

The words turned Camille's blood cold. "Of course you will. It's not my favorite thing to think about, but that's the way it works, right?"

"I mean really on my own. You'll always be my home base, but I want to go far away, see the world, go back to Bellerive and visit Paris and Sydney and all the places I haven't seen yet in the world."

Great, thought Camille. That's what she got for taking Julie to France, giving her a taste of travel. She should never have—

She stopped herself from thinking like that. "I don't blame you, Jules. Everybody needs to see the world. I did the same thing at your age." She pulled Julie into a hug, inhaling her candy-sweet scent. "There are certain journeys you make in your lifetime that stick with you always. You remember the feel of the air on your skin, the quality of the light, the food you ate, the smells that wafted in the air. Most of all, you remember how you felt about the person you were with. And how you felt about yourself."

"That was this summer, for me," Julie murmured against her sleeve. "I'm glad you get it, Mom. You totally get it."

Camille drove a rental car from the Burlington airport to the town of Switchback, Vermont. In the passenger seat, her father gazed out the window, while in the back, Julie listened to French pop songs on her phone, occasionally coming out with a tuneless sing-along phrase that made Camille smile.

It was the final—and most important—trip they would make all summer. For Papa, it was the most important trip of his life. She glanced over at him. His jaw tightened and released, tightened and released. "How are you doing?" she asked softly.

"As you'd expect—excited. Nervous. Filled with an emotion I can't describe."

She reached over and patted his arm, then turned back to her daughter. "That makes three of us, eh, Jules?"

"Totally." Julie plucked out her earbuds. "Look, the sign says four more miles."

Camille flexed her hands on the steering wheel. Her search for each WWII veteran on Finn's list had led to this moment. The high school math teacher from Philadelphia was not a match. He'd passed away, but his daughter assured Camille he could not have fathered a child in France in 1944. Yes, he'd taken part in Operation Dragoon, and yes, he'd been in the Var, but not until August of that year, weeks past the date of conception. The second man—a retired farmer in North Carolina—was still living, and although he recalled the summer of '44 in detail and had done reconnaissance work in May of that year, he was never near Bellerive.

The final prospect on Finn's list was Corporal Henry "Hank" Watkins, ret. He had answered the phone himself, and when she'd explained the reason for her call, a long pause had ensued. Just when she thought the call had been dropped, he'd said, "How soon can you come?"

Two days later, they were here—a small town in Vermont. Julie navigated them through the pretty New England village and then out along a country road to a snug wooden house where Hank Watson, a widower, lived with his daughter and her husband.

When they drove up to the house, the ninety-year-old veteran came out on the porch and down the steps. He had a crooked leg and walked with a cane. When Papa got out of the car, the old man set down the cane and opened his arms. Under his breath, Papa said, "*Mon dieu,* it's him," and strode forward. Two strangers, and yet they connected instantly, the recognition palpable. The two embraced, and everyone within fifty feet of them burst into tears—Camille, Julie, Hank's daughter Wendy, and his son-in-law Nils.

"It's a miracle," Hank said in a rough, wavering voice. "Thank you," he said, looking at Papa with wonder in his eyes. "Thank you for finding me."

After further hugs and introductions, Wendy herded everyone to a deck overlooking a pretty garden surrounded by orchards and maple groves. The table was set for afternoon tea, with cloth napkins and good china, cookies and iced maple bars made, she explained, from their own maple syrup. There was a selection of sandwiches, and a bottle of Dom Pérignon in a bucket of ice.

"I can't stop looking at the two of you together," Camille said, unable to stop the tears of joy. "This is . . . oh my gosh." She embraced the two of them together.

"We can probably skip the DNA test," Wendy observed.

The family resemblance was obvious to them all. Both Hank and Henry were tall and slender, with dark brown eyes and strong jaws and faces and hands so similar they looked more like brothers than father and son.

"This is so, so cool," Julie said softly.

"I have something just for you," Hank said. He took something from his pocket and handed it to her.

She held it in her palm. "Is this a Purple Heart?"

He nodded. "Awarded to me after the war. I want you to have it."

"You're kidding." Julie gaped at him.

"Your grandfather told me you did a very brave thing," Hank said. "You rescued a friend from drowning. Perhaps saving lives runs in the family."

"But—"

"I don't need it, young lady, but you have many adventures ahead of you. Keep it for me."

She clasped her hand around it, stepped forward, and gave him a hug. "I don't know what to say. I'll take good care of it."

"That's all I ask. Now we'll always know where it is."

"Can I get a picture?" Camille asked, blinking away tears of happiness and pride. Julie and Wendy had captured everything on their phones, but Camille wanted a special photo. Very carefully, she took out Lisette's Exakta. *Bonjour, grand-mère,* she thought, feeling a peculiar kinship with a woman she'd never met, a woman whose hands had cradled this very camera just as Camille was doing now. A woman who had photographed the man standing before her, seventy-three years ago. When she lifted it to her eye and took a picture, capturing his expression, Hank gasped.

Camille lowered the camera. "I take it you remember this."

"Indeed I do. And thank you for e-mailing the photographs you found. It was overwhelming to see them, though less so than this moment." He didn't once let go of Papa, and kept staring into his face. "You are as handsome as she was beautiful," Hank said. "She was very beautiful."

Papa nodded. "I'm sorry you lost her."

Hank gave him another hug. "I've found you. I couldn't be happier."

"Let's have a toast," said Wendy. "We can all sit down together and Dad can tell his stories."

Hank took hold of the champagne bottle and picked up a short, slightly curved saber. "This is something I learned when I was in hiding in France, recovering from my injuries," he said.

"It's always been his favorite party trick," Wendy said.

"*Le saberage.*" Papa beamed.

Hank nodded, then expertly used the saber to open the champagne with a distinctive pop. "To an incredible reunion," he said after everyone lifted a glass. Then he picked up the saber again. "This is the only souvenir that survived from that time," he said. "When the bombs hit, I was lucky to escape with my life. I encountered some Germans on the run, and one of them challenged me. He was a boy like me, and I just had to threaten him with the saber, and he ran away."

As Wendy and Nils poured and served, Hank grew misty again. "To Lisette," he said simply, and everyone lifted their glasses.

Papa handed him the fading Mass card with the Sallman *Head of Christ*. "This was with Lisette's belongings. There's something written on the back, but we couldn't make out what it says."

"I wrote, 'You're my angel.' And she was. I would have died without her." In a voice that gradually grew stronger with memories, Hank began to talk, filling in the missing pieces of the story. He had been just seventeen when he was dropped behind enemy lines in advance of the raid in order to do reconnaissance. Healing from his wounds in a remote stone hut, he fell in love with the girl who had saved his life. "Lisette had a hard time during the war. She married Palomar in order to save a partisan from being detained, and to protect her parents. When she discovered he was a collaborator, she was deeply ashamed to be his wife. It was always my aim to bring her home to the States after the war, but in the chaos of the August raids, we lost each other."

Camille quietly told everyone what they'd learned about that day— that Lisette's parents had been killed in the bombing, that the Allies liberated the town and had the Germans on the run.

"There was a lot of ground fog that morning," Hank said. "My hideout was hit in the raid, but I was able to pull myself out of the rubble. I followed the river to the sea and found a Red Cross unit that took me to Marseille. I was delirious with infection by then, and eventually awakened aboard a hospital ship. The infection was nearly fatal, and it took me two years to recover."

"He almost died, more than once," Wendy told them.

"I later learned that the region was liberated in a matter of days," Hank continued. "I've always believed Lisette's photographs—the ones she took from the church tower at the top of the village—helped coordinate the invasion. Henri, your mother was truly remarkable. I've never forgotten her."

He took off his glasses and wiped his eyes. "I returned to the family business after two years at the veterans' hospital, but I never stopped thinking about Lisette. Finally, in 1950, I had saved up enough money to return to Bellerive. I was still a young man at the time, still unmarried, determined to find her again. I spent my life savings to get to France, and I actually paid a visit to the farm called Sauveterre."

"*What?* You went to Sauveterre?" Papa stared at him. "In 1950? I would have been four or five years old that year."

Hank nodded. "I had no idea. None, until Camille's call. When I found my way to Sauveterre, I was greeted—very brusquely—by a woman in charge. Madame Taro."

"Aunt Rotrude, Palomar's sister. She was my guardian when I was growing up," said Papa. "You needn't be polite. She was never a pleasant woman."

"She told me that Lisette had died in April of 1945. I verified this through public records at the town hall in Bellerive. There, she was listed as '*morte en couches.*'" He paused again. "My French is very limited. I knew this meant she died in childbirth, but I also assumed it meant the child died with her. I grieved for her, but in time, the pain faded. I came home and met Wendy's mother, and started a new chapter with her. Lisette was my first true love. But for most of us, life is long, and loving again didn't take away from the memories."

Camille had a swift, unbidden thought of Finn. She wished he could be here for this moment.

With stark yearning, Hank studied Papa's face. "Henri, it breaks my heart to realize I missed out on your life."

Papa didn't speak for a long time. "You walked with a cane," he said.

"I have, ever since the war," Hank replied.

"A cane with wings carved into the handle."

Hank and his daughter exchanged a look. "I still have that cane," said Hank, "but I don't use it anymore. I carved it myself—the wings were from the pathfinder insignia. How could you know, Henri?"

"I remember you." Papa's voice wavered. "I told Camille it's one of my earliest memories. A man came to the kitchen door one day, a tall stranger with wavy dark hair. The man had a crooked leg and a cane with wings carved into the handle, and he sounded funny when he spoke in a foreign language. Then Aunt Rotrude said something in the funny language, too—just a few words. I was very curious, but she shooed me away."

Hank took Papa's hands in his. The two of them locked eyes for a drawn-out moment. "Yes. *Yes.* I saw a small boy peeking from the hallway when I was inquiring after Lisette. Dear God, why didn't she tell me?"

Papa bowed his head, and no one spoke for a few moments. "I imagine my aunt was afraid to lose Sauveterre," he said. "I was presumed to be the son of Didier Palomar, rightful owner of the place, and Rotrude's role as my guardian gave her a roof over her head." Papa squeezed Hank's hands in his. "I wish I'd known, too. I wish I'd known that the visitor was my father, seeing me for the first time. But I never knew. Neither of us ever knew."

Camille and Julie only spent the day, although Papa planned to stay longer, to get to know the man who had fathered him. He walked with Camille to the car and hugged her close. "Thank you," he said. "None of this would have been possible without you."

"It's a privilege to be a part of this, Papa," she said. "I love you so much, and I'm so happy that you found your father. I'll develop the photos right away and make sure you and Hank get copies to share with everyone." She hugged him again. "Are you sure you're all right to come back on your own?"

"More than all right. I feel complete in a way I never have before. Perhaps it's just the high of discovering so much about the past, but I truly do feel different." He took a step back. "There's something else you should know," he continued. "This fall, I'm going back to Bellerive for a longer stay."

"Papa, no. You shouldn't go alone."

"I won't be alone, *chérie.*"

She caught the soft, contented look in his face. "Oh . . . Michel?"

He smiled. "At long last."

"Ah, Papa." She was feeling overwhelmed by emotion.

"I know, Camille. Look what has happened this summer. Life as it reveals itself is filled with riches. What will happen, will happen. Worrying will not affect the outcome."

"You're right, but how can I not worry?"

"By wishing me well. I waited so long to find happiness. I hope you aren't making the same mistake, turning away from Finn when he just might be your next great love."

She flushed, hoping he wouldn't see her pain. "Finn and I . . . we've gone our separate ways."

Then why, she kept asking herself, did she want to call him immediately, tell him about the extraordinary meeting with Hank Watkins? Why did she wish Finn had been here to see the joy of the reunion? Why did she lie awake at night, remembering every touch, every kiss, every whisper?

Boarding the plane for Dulles, Camille felt a familiar beat of panic. She slowed her steps, took a deep breath, and walked forward. Maybe she'd never lose her fear of flying, but she was going to do it anyway, because of the destination. Maybe next time, she'd be a little less afraid.

When she got back home, she tried to keep her focus on Julie and

work. Yet her wandering heart kept leading her back to Finn. She realized that one reason she kept pushing him away was that he was so
alive, so *present*. And why did she shy away from that? Why was she
afraid of the deep intensity of the feelings he stirred in her?

She pondered this as she organized the darkroom to develop the
film from the Exakta. Before turning out the lights, she went to the
shelf by the mantel and took out her old Leica. She hadn't touched it
in years, not since the last trip with Jace.

She'd paid too much for the Leica at an auction house. Despite
Jace's objections about the cost, she had to have it. After the accident,
she had not touched the camera again. There was still film in it—
her last pictures of Jace. She'd never developed the film because she
didn't want to expose her final memories of him.

Holding the camera flat on the palm of her hand, she weighed her
options. She could put it away again. She could open it right now and
destroy the pictures. Or she could expose the film and see what she'd
been afraid of seeing for so long.

Deep breath.

Then she turned out the lights and went to work.

Less than an hour later, Camille was looking at the digitized contact
sheets from both cameras on her laptop. The pictures from the trip
with Jace were good, but now she realized that back then, she was
still learning her craft. The photos she'd taken in Vermont showed
more confidence and maturity. There was one portrait of her father
and Hank that captured their surprise and delight so perfectly that it
brought fresh tears to her eyes.

There was one shot Jace had taken of her, a simple snapshot. It had
been the year of the unfortunate hairstyle, but her smile blazed across
the years—the smile of a young woman who had no idea how hard a
loss could hit. There was another shot of the two of them, which she'd
taken with the shutter set on a timer.

Irrational as it was, she'd held the notion that once she looked at the pictures, she would see their marriage as it truly was—not perfect. Just perfectly ordinary. An ordinary life. And she'd spent the past five years convinced that their marriage, their love, had been extraordinary, never to be equaled, and certainly not surpassed.

She stared for a long time at the pictures. The final shot was one she'd taken moments before their final climb. There was Jace, grinning and confident, draped in rope and carabiners, ready for adventure.

Her last image of him. "Hi, Jace," she said softly to the empty room. "It's good to see you again."

He had been canonized by gilded memories. She'd forgotten his flaws—and he did have them. He'd been annoyed at her that day, scolding her for taking pictures when she should have been focused on roping up for the climb. He'd never quite understood her passion for photography. Jace had thought the shop was fluff, filled with knickknacks for tourists. He was only human, after all. Yet the flaws were obliterated by the spectacular way he'd died.

Jace was a good man, a fine doctor, and he had loved her. In an act of indisputable heroism, he'd traded his life for hers. Yet sometimes, when he'd been alive, he didn't *see* her. Now she faced that truth with a clarity that cut like a knife. "We weren't perfect," she said aloud. "We didn't need to be. And getting over you is not going to take away what we had."

Deep down, she had the sense that Jace had never been as attentive as Finn, never as interested in her, never as understanding of the things that ignited her passion. But he'd given his life to save her, and nothing would trump that. Now she looked at it a different way. If she didn't finally move on with her life, what had he sacrificed himself for?

Camille poured herself a glass of wine, taking her camera and Lisette's out to the front porch. She sat on the top step and looked out at the quiet evening settling over the neighborhood. Julie was at an end-of-summer clambake with a group of friends—and those friends included Vanessa and Jana, surprisingly enough. Bringing home her great-grandfather's Purple Heart had been the grace note to a wonderful summer.

Camille loaded fresh film into the Leica. Holding it up and looking through the viewfinder was like meeting an old friend again.

You look like a pro, Finn had said to her.

It's kind of sexy.

Stop it, she thought. But the memory of that day hung on—the drive to Gordes. She still felt the wonder of walking into the house where Willy Ronis had lived, where he'd found his best moments as an artist in the ordinary, everyday life of his family. How well Finn seemed to realize that.

He understood what Jace never had. Photography wasn't a hobby. Not for Lisette. And not for Camille.

She drank the wine, not fighting the tears. "Ah, Jace. I love you with every inch of my heart," she said, speaking aloud into the evening air. "I always will. And I'll never, *ever* forget you."

She thought about what Hank Watkins had said. *Lisette was my first true love. But life is long, and loving again didn't take away from the memories.*

"I'm still here, Jace, and you're . . . not," she went on. "We will never grow old together. We'll never worry about Julie together. We won't have any more kids. We both wanted our future so much, but we'll never get to have one, and I can't spend my life regretting it. And so I have to say good-bye. For my sake and for Julie's, I have to. My happily-ever-after is never going to happen with you. But that doesn't mean it's never going to happen."

She finished her wine, then went and picked up the garden stone by the gate, the one with Jace's initials and the phrase "Always in my heart." She moved it to the fringe of woods at the end of the backyard, where no one ever went. Then she replaced it with the one from Sauveterre, the one chiseled by Hank in 1944: *H+L, Journey Without End.* Once again, her thoughts returned to Finn. She mentally relived the first time they'd met—right here on her front porch. He had met her on one of her worst days, and she'd dashed his hopes of finding the last pictures his father had shot.

She picked up Lisette's camera and focused on the lighthouse in the distance. A memory of their conversation drifted into her mind. His sister Margaret Ann had found the film roll in a box of their father's things that had been in storage.

The memory niggled at her. She wondered if the box had been anything like the box of things Madame Olivier had sent to her father. Things left behind by someone gone too soon.

A lone seagull flew past the lighthouse, and Camille took the shot, so grateful to have her grandmother's camera. She remembered the moment as if it were yesterday. Finding the camera. Realizing there was film inside. Knowing there was one person who could help her sort out the images: Professor Malcolm Finnemore. That was the moment that started it all.

The pictures in Lisette's camera had taken Camille on a journey she'd never expected. She had learned so much from the phantom woman. Lisette had been smart. Intuitive. Talented. And above all, fearless. The love of her life had literally fallen from the sky, and she'd given her whole self to him and damn the consequences. Had she lived, Lisette would have risked all and gone with Hank.

Camille felt ridiculous by comparison. Cowardly. She did love Finn, so much that her heart felt ready to burst. She should have stayed and fought for him. She should go back and fight for him.

Lisette's last images had opened the door to her heart as surely as— And then it hit her. Hard.

"Oh my God." She scrambled to her feet and rushed into the house. Rummaging through her desk, she found the courier's slip that had been delivered to her with Finn's film. The copy was dull and smudged, but she could make out the sender's address and phone number.

Margaret Ann picked up. Camille hastily explained who she was, then asked, "Where is your father's camera? The one that was found with his effects from Cambodia."

"I have it here, with everything else," said Margaret Ann.

"Whatever you do, don't open it. Don't wind it or touch anything on it."

"Fine, I won't touch the camera. It's been in its case for forty years," said Margaret Ann. "Why?"

"I'll explain when I get there."

"There," Camille said, securing the parcel for the courier service. "It's done."

"What?" Julie was ironing. *Ironing.* She never ironed, but her new clamdiggers and white cotton shirt were getting special treatment for the first day of school. "Are those the pictures you found on that old camera?"

"That's right. I'm so glad I thought to look in Sergeant Major Finnemore's old camera. I blew it when I ruined the first roll Finn sent me. We'll never know what was on that, but at least we have this one. It's the best way I can think of to make it up to him. I already e-mailed the digital images, and now I'm sending the film and prints."

She had taken pains to make the pictures as perfect as she could. The images were startling and mysterious, but Finn was an expert. He would read the photos, the way he had for her. Maybe he'd find answers to questions that had haunted his family for decades. Or maybe he'd find a new mystery to solve. "It brings everything full circle," she concluded.

"Well, that's just dumb." Julie put on the shirt and folded away the ironing board. She checked herself in the mirror of the hall tree. "You can't be done with Finn. He makes you happy. This summer was the happiest I've ever seen you."

"And summer is over. You've got school, and I've got work."

"Right. Work." Julie plucked a gauzy peasant blouse from the laundry basket. "Wear this one today," she said. "It looks great on you."

Camille remembered the last time she'd worn it—on a date with Finn, the day he'd taken her to Gordes. The day she'd started taking pictures again. The day had ended with a magical, golden evening half a world away. She remembered how he'd undone the tasseled tie at the neckline, sliding it down to bare her shoulder and kiss her there.

She pushed away the memory. "I'm not going anywhere, except to the darkroom."

"You can still look great." Julie took a breath and started to say more. Just then someone tapped a car horn outside. "There's my ride," she said, shouldering her book bag. "Gotta bounce."

Camille gave her a hug. "Today is going to be awesome. And you're amazing."

Julie's smile was a bit shy. "Yeah. Well, we'll see."

"I'm really proud of you, Jules."

"So far, all I've done today is iron a shirt."

Camille laughed and held open the door. She waved at Tarek and his sister. Her heart swelled as she watched Julie going down the walk with a decided spring in her step. She was inches taller, with the figure of a young woman now, not a little girl. Look what we made, Jace, she thought with a wave of affection. We did well. She's doing well.

Alone in the house, Camille slipped on the peasant blouse and a pair of skinny capris, and headed for the darkroom. Back to school for Julie, back to business as usual for Camille. She had some prints to make for a D.C. client. She was studying a contact sheet, trying to decide which print to bring to light, when she heard the crunch of tires on the driveway, and then a knock at the door. The courier, probably. Here to take away the last tenuous remnant of Finn.

She picked up the parcel and carried it to the door. But it wasn't the courier. On the other side of the threshold stood Finn. He wore a rumpled shirt and jeans, and was holding a thick manila envelope and a bouquet of flowers.

She stepped back in shock, then yanked open the screen door. "I just hit send an hour ago," she said.

"I saw your message come in on my phone as I was driving. Something about pictures?"

She almost forgot to breathe. "Your father's pictures. There was an exposed roll in his camera—"

"Cool, but I'm not here because of somebody's pictures," he said, stepping inside. He laid the flowers on the counter and handed her the envelope. "Lisette's letters to Hank," he said. "We found them among the stuff from the attic."

"Oh my gosh, that's amazing. She wrote letters to him?"

"So it seems. I didn't read them," he said.

"Then I won't either. I'll send them to Hank, and he can decide." She looked up at him, still reeling with surprise. "Thank you, Finn. But you didn't need to bring them in person."

"True. I'm not here because of the letters. I'm here for you."

"What?"

"I've been traveling all night to get to you."

"What?" she said again, gaping like an idiot. "Why?"

"Because you left, and we're not finished."

"What's that supposed to mean?" Her heart felt as if it might beat out of her chest.

"I love you. That's what's not finished. Don't write us off, Camille. We're not such a long shot. Besides, you once told me you specialize in long shots."

"I was talking about old film."

"I'm talking about us. And we're not a long shot. We're going to love each other forever."

She looked down, because she had to make sure her heart was still inside. "You can't just come in here and say . . . You . . . you said we were going to be together just for the summer."

"I lied in order to get you in bed."

"Hey—"

"The main reason I lied is that I didn't want to scare you off. I'm actually a lousy liar, but I would do anything, stoop to any level, to get you to keep me around." He took her by the shoulders and gazed down at her. He had beard stubble, and lines of fatigue bracketed his eyes, but there was such energy in his expression, such confidence.

"What are you doing here?" she asked, her voice shaking.

"To say what I should have said before you left. Listen. I'm sorry for what happened to you five years ago. I'm sorry your husband died and your heart broke. What happened, what he did, was tragic and heroic, and I get that you don't believe someone will ever love you like that again. Maybe you're right. I won't love you like he did. I'll love you the only way I know—my way. Your husband died for you—the ultimate sacrifice. I hope I'm the kind of man who would do the same. You make me want to be that kind of man, the kind who would die for you."

"Finn, my God . . ."

He pressed a finger to her lips, stopping her words. "But I'd much rather *live* for you. *With* you."

She laid the palm of her hand over his heart. Warm, alive, strong. Suddenly she wanted to tell him everything, but she scarcely knew where to begin. "I'm still afraid to fly."

"What?"

"Bear with me. Finn, I wasn't expecting this. I need a moment. But I want you to know I'm scared to fly. But I'm not letting it stop me anymore. When I went to Vermont to find Hank Watkins, I didn't hesitate. I just did it, even though I was scared." She moved her hand to his lips, the way he had to hers. "And I'm probably afraid to love you, Finn, but you know what's even scarier? I thought I'd missed my chance."

A smile lit his face like the rising sun. "Oh, baby. You'll never run out of chances with me."

She knew she was staring up at him with stars in her eyes. "This is not how this day was supposed to go."

"How was it supposed to go?"

"I . . . forgot."

The kiss that he gave her was soft and sweet, and beautifully emotional—his closeness, his warmth, his breath. She wanted to melt into his embrace and stay there for the rest of her life. After a moment she didn't want to end, she pulled back.

"You're jet-lagged."

"I'm jet-lagged."

"Swaying on your feet. I can feel it."

"Then we'd better lie down," he said.

"I thought you'd never ask."

"This is you, jet-lagged?" Camille asked, rolling over in bed and tucking her elbow under her cheek to look at him. She loved his chest—the muscular landscape of it, the whorls of hair, the cadence of his breathing.

"I was. I am. But I rallied."

Oh boy, did he ever. He'd rallied all over her.

"I'm going to need to spend the night, though. No way I can drive all the way back to . . ." He stopped. "I don't have anywhere to go. I left my teaching post. I'm homeless. Guess I'll just find a place right in Bethany Bay."

She felt a flutter of nervousness. "Finn, I'm not sure you've thought this through. How do you know you'll like it here?"

"Oh, let's see. There's a beach. Surfing."

"Not in the winter. It's nasty in the winter."

"A quaint town with a library, at least two bars, and a fisherman's pub. A hot girlfriend."

"I have a teenager."

"I know. She's awesome, like her mom. And when she's not being so awesome—"

"Which is a lot of the time, when it comes to teenagers."

"We'll deal. You'll have to trust me on this."

"My mother and sisters."

"Can't wait to meet them. They're going to love me."

"How do you know that?"

He brushed a lock of her hair from her neck and kissed her there. "Because I love you. I'll treat you right, Camille. Swear. I'll make you so happy they'll lay flowers at my feet. Beer in my fridge."

She still couldn't believe this was happening. "I have exes in town. Guys I used to date. You know, trying to move on."

"I have a theory about that. You were trying *not* to move on. That's why none of those others worked out. Until me. *I'm* your move-on guy."

She laughed softly, feeling ridiculously happy. "Still, you're going to bump into them. It might be awkward."

"I can do awkward. Hell, you've seen me do awkward." He propped himself up on one elbow and gazed down into her face. "Camille Adams, I love you more than anything else I've ever loved in this world. And when you left, I realized I almost missed out on something special because I hadn't figured out how to put us together." He brushed the sweetest of kisses over her brow, her lips. "There's good news."

"What's that?"

"I've figured it out."

Epilogue

※

Springtime swept over the landscape at Arlington Cemetery, a light breeze creating a storm of petals from the blossoming cherry and dogwood trees. The buzz of a military aircraft overhead mingled with the *clop-clop* of hooves. Four liveried horses drew the caisson, which bore the flag-draped coffin of Sergeant Major Richard Arthur Finnemore, bringing him to his final resting place. The white horses perfectly matched the alabaster markers spreading out in all directions. The solemn procession moved past the rows of headstones before stopping at the burial site on a grassy hill.

A remarkable number of people were gathered for the ceremony— Finn's mother, Tavia, and all his assorted siblings, nieces, and nephews. Camille reached over and took Finn's hand, giving it a squeeze. Julie sat beside her, and Michel arrived, pushing Papa in his wheelchair. Some of the survivors—men who had been saved by Richard's sacrifice—came to pay their respects.

Finn looked over at her, and the emotion in his face touched her heart. She offered a tremulous smile, hoping to convey all the love and grief aching inside her. "It's okay," she whispered, placing his hand on the bundle in her lap, the sweetly sleeping baby they'd named after Finn's lost father.

Two years after Camille had developed the film in Sergeant Major Finnemore's camera, he had been located. The very last image on the camera—the final image he'd shot—turned out to be the key that unlocked the mystery of his disappearance. Just before surrendering to the enemy, he'd snapped a photo, dropped the camera, and gave himself up, enabling the team to stay in hiding and leaving a clue to his whereabouts. Studying that final image, so painstakingly developed by Camille, they had focused on a tiny detail—a crate bearing a serial number. After months of work, they traced the supply box to Lomphat, Cambodia, a town that had been obliterated by bombs. A local survivor eventually led them to a crude burial site of remains known only to God.

Finn's own DNA had been used to identify his father's remains.

Strains of "Amazing Grace" wafted on the air. There was a flyover by military craft. Four men on either side of the flag-draped coffin marched in crisp tandem, sidestepping to the freshly dug cavity in the earth. Eight riflemen, handling their weapons with white-gloved care, shot a salute. The ensemble played taps as the flag was folded into a mournful triangle.

Tavia received the flag in her lap. She looked up at her children and then leaned over, seeming to collapse upon the thick triangle of fabric. Finn and his sisters surrounded her and helped her up. She handed the flag to Margaret Ann and turned to Camille. "I'll take the baby," she said.

"Of course." Camille gently placed the infant in her arms. "He had a remarkable grandfather. I hope you'll tell him all about it one day." She walked over to Finn's side, and they stood together at the grave site. "Are you all right?" she gently asked him.

He took her hand and brought it to his lips. "Yes. Never better. God, I love you so much." Then he slid his arms around her, and her heart filled with bittersweet emotion—grief and joy, gratitude and regret, pride and melancholy. But most of all, love.

Two years before, she had never imagined a moment like this. Yet here she was, with a man she loved more than the very air she breathed, with her father, who was finally living and loving the way he was meant to, and with her daughter, now poised to take flight on her own adventures.

She looked around at the faces of her extended family. What a beautiful journey they were on, the long, sweet journey that had brought them home.

Acknowledgments

*T*his book began with a journey, and the plot unfolded through sun-drenched rambles amid the hill towns and coastal villages where women like Lisette struggled to survive a war they scarcely understood. When the imagination is lubricated by frequent vineyard luncheons in the company of a kindly husband, all the better.

But the real work of writing a novel isn't always so idyllic. Most of it involves unending solitary hours getting words on the page, a process fueled not by wine and socca but by Red Bull and microwave burritos, all while being haunted by the feeling of imminent failure.

Fortunately for me, the lonely hours end as publication begins. Thank you to the amazing creative team at William Morrow/ HarperCollins—Dan Mallory, Liate Stehlik, Lynn Grady, Pam Jaffee, Lauren Truskowski, Tavia Kowalchuk, and their many talented colleagues. Thanks also to the ever-wise Meg Ruley and Annelise Robey of the Jane Rotrosen Agency, who do it all with humor and panache.

Then there's the home team—Willa Cline and Cindy Peters, keeping me alive online; and Marilyn Rowe, mother-in-law and booklover with mad proofreading skills. And as ever, the brain trust—fellow writers who regularly confound patrons at the Silverdale Barnes & Noble with lengthy discussions about unlikely fictional topics. Thank you, Elsa Watson, Sheila Roberts, Lois Faye Dyer, Kate Breslin, and Anjali Banerjee. Your generosity knows no bounds.

As ever, thanks to my husband, Jerry, for remaining calm at all times.

'If you enjoyed *Map of the Heart*
then why not try Susan Wigg's
heartwarming novel *Family Tree*'